The Summers of Us

TAYLOR CROOKS

ISBN 978-1-5011-7321-9 (Paperback)
ISBN 979-8-9927626-1-7 (Hardcover)
ISBN 978-1-4767-4660-9 (eBook)

Cover art and sand dollar graphic by Rachel Sierra
Book design by Taylor Crooks

Printed by IngramSpark in the United States of America.

First printing edition 2025.

Published by Bookcomber Publishing
taylorcrooksauthor@gmail.com
@taylorcrooksauthor

*"Summer is falling, it's a distant dream.
If I turn around, you're runnin' back to me."*

—Lizzy McAlpine

Avery,

You deserve a rollercoaster.

Now

June 13

I USED TO LOVE THE BEACH.

Whenever real life grew to be too much, I would shut my eyes and dream of lying on the shore, sand crawling into my bikini, the sun's rays kissing my skin with burnt pink lip gloss.

I never envisioned the waves crashing too close. Never thought the sun was too hot. Never painted the ocean as a figure roaring across enemy lines.

It never gave me a reason to.

Summers at Piper Island weren't real life. At least, they didn't *feel* like it, but now, after last summer, I'm surprised I have the courage to drive back and pretend nothing ever happened.

When the ocean appears over the causeway—a blurry mirage in the distance—I force a smile at it, cracking the window to let the salt air make a mess of my blonde hair.

It's instinctual, how my fingers find the cold necklace resting on my clavicle. There, eight coquina clam shells dangle—one for each summer spent here.

A cluster of palm trees sprout across the road, their leaves swaying in the wind. People drive past me on Main Street with their hands surfing the air outside the windows. Last summer's tan has wilted from my own arms, leaving my skin the color of dried sand. It almost made it the year, but winter eventually kills everything still reeling from summer.

Aunt Blair's house is a shell of its former glory—like a coquina clam shell, I suppose, with the snail slurped right out of it. A hole left behind as evidence of the carnage.

The rocking chairs have lost their rock. Last year's flowers lie dead in their pots. Sky blue paint, once so welcoming, peels off the siding. It has faded into a bleak kind of gray that sneaks up on the summer sky and scares you off the beach.

I get out of the car and inhale; I can smell the ocean nearby: lurking, waiting, ready to pounce. I exhale the same air through my nose, readying myself to enter the house.

I walk up to the porch. It takes ten knocks for the door to swing open.

Eight Summers Ago

Age 10, June 13

I HUGGED MY SHIVERING KNEES TO MY CHEST, rested my chin on top. It was freezing in the car, just the way Mom liked it. I couldn't take it anymore, so I rolled the window down to invite a warm breeze in. The air smelled different out here where the ground flattened toward the sea; it was fresher, less polluted by lines of traffic exhaust and *city*.

Two months ago, I was in my aunt Blair's room in our apartment, holding my baby cousin Hadley out of the way while Blair packed all her things in boxes. She tried her hardest to stay strong in the face of her boyfriend Josh, but it was no use. Hadley's father had already chosen drinking over his family. I figured they'd been having problems, since Blair and Hadley moved in to our spare bedroom when school started last year, but Blair finally gave up.

Well, *Josh* gave up, so Blair had to as well.

That was why we were on the way to visit Blair and Hadley at their new house in Piper Island. For months, there was talk of inheritance from a great aunt I never knew. Chatter about savings accounts.

Whispers of something called "child support." A bunch of adult words I didn't care about. One day, conversation shifted to "beach house" and "fixer upper," words that stuck out like yellow dandelions in my front yard. Mom sold it to Blair, pocketed the commission, and sent her on her way.

I wished Mom would do something like that to help us start over too.

Mom was at least crazy enough to let me stay all summer, now that Blair was all settled in. She tried to talk me out of it with murmurs of "dangerous water" and "wet, sticky sand," but "a bike ride from the ocean" and "sandcastles" from late night calls with Blair won out.

As homesick as I could get sometimes, I knew Blair's house wouldn't feel far from home at all.

"We are almost there." Mom pointed to a *Piper Island Welcomes You!* sign surrounded by palm trees and other beach plants Raleigh soil wouldn't dare grow.

I smiled. I'd never felt welcome by anything in my life, but suddenly, a massive sign was greeting me, wispy clouds were waving, and salt air was whipping my hair around. It didn't make any sense, but it all felt like it was put there for me.

We drove over a bridge, the last stretch of road before we reached the island. I threw my hands in the air, fingernails grazing the top of the car, shouting like I was on a rollercoaster headed straight for open water. The deep blue horizon appeared in the distance, contrasting with the blue sky right above it. Miles of dark ocean pushed away from me. White ribbons sliced toward me, over and over, completing Quinn Kessler's welcome parade.

Between my squeals, I thought even Mom laughed, despite her blank stare and her white knuckles gripping the steering wheel.

From the downward slope of the bridge, the whole town looked like a chessboard, houses all lined up on a grid. Pine trees, water towers, and businesses peeked out like chess pieces.

As we drove into town, I saw gas stations, mini golf, gift shops, and everything in between, boasting silly names like Seas the Day and Beachy Keen. Most houses were lifted above the ground, with golf carts, grills, and hammocks sleeping beneath them. Families unloaded from long car rides. Bikes zipped across crosswalks. Teens walked in hordes, wearing nothing but bathing suits. Barefoot beachcombers rested on pastel chairs outside an ice cream shop called Sunset Scoop.

Maybe one day I could do the same. I could bike barefoot along the stretch of trees, burn my fair skin into a tan, and eat ice cream before *and* after dinner. Ice cream *for* dinner. I could be rule-less. *Free*, I supposed they called it. I pictured myself there, hoping the sand and salt water was enough to make a new version of me.

"Those kids are going to be so burnt!" Mom said as we turned onto a calmer street.

We pulled up to a small blue house. It could have fit inside a snow globe. The fresh navy paint contrasted with the blinding white railing. I'd never been to a beach town before, but this was exactly what I expected to see planted on that sandy soil.

Blair flailed her arms at us from the porch, Hadley perched on her hip.

Before Mom even stopped the car, I jumped out and ran up to the porch. It wasn't a long trip, since Blair lived inland enough that her house didn't have stilts.

"Blair! Hadley!" I wrapped my arms around my aunt's waist and tickled the bottom of Hadley's feet. I breathed in the smell of laundry detergent and beach all around us. It was salty and sweet and sour at the same time.

Blair pulled me in. "We're going to have so much fun this summer!

I made a list of cool things for us to do. You can add more if I missed anything. It's on the counter inside."

"As long as Mom lets me."

Blair leaned in closer, holding Hadley tighter, and whispered with a wink, "What she doesn't know won't hurt her."

I smiled in return, but I wasn't sure it was genuine. Mom would be upset if I did things without her permission. She saw the world with thorn-colored glasses and it was my job to keep from getting pricked. My friends at school told me to ask for forgiveness instead of permission, but forgiveness was never my strong suit. Lying gave my soul a slimy feeling.

"Hi, Jen!" Blair shouted to Mom.

Mom lugged my suitcase up the stairs. "Quinn, you need to start pulling your weight if you expect me to let you stay here. And don't you ever get out of a moving vehicle. I could have run you over."

"I'm sorry." I looked at my toes, which I'd painted purple last night.

"Can't you ever just let her be excited?" Blair grabbed the bridge of her nose, shaking her head. "Sorry. I'm very glad you're letting her stay."

Suddenly the air felt muggy from more than the June beach weather. I looked between them and the thick air. They looked at each other all weird but said nothing more about it. *Sisters*.

"I promise I'll take very good care of her." Blair stroked my hair and goosebumps whispered down my spine. She kept calm to show Mom she was capable of taking care of me. Being only twenty-four, twelve years younger than my mom, Blair always had to prove herself. She was never smart enough, never responsible enough, never good enough. *Older sisters*.

I looked over at Hadley's smile and chubby legs, which were evidence to me that she got enough food and sleep to be okay. That was all parenting was, anyway—keeping your kid alive—so both my mom and Blair had done a good job. I would never tell her that, though. Or about how excited I was to spend the summer with Blair.

Mom handed Blair a typed list of rules I wasn't sure I wanted to follow. I didn't want to be in bed by eight, or eat the whole food pyramid with every meal, or ride a bike with knee pads on. This was a *summer vacation.* It was meant for sleepless nights and ice cream for dinner. That's what I'd always read about summer.

When they finished talking, I hugged Mom goodbye. I promised I'd be safe. I promised to call her as much as I could. I promised not to walk around in just my bathing suit like those *silly kids.* I promised to look both ways, reapply my sunscreen, and wear a helmet when I rode a bike. That, at least, I could agree with.

I waved until Mom's car was out of sight. Blair held the screen door open with her hip, smiling. The cool air welcomed me inside. Finally summer could begin.

The house smelled of brand-new paint, Blair, bleach, and some fresh beach candle glowing atop the kitchen table. The furniture stood tall, despite being plucked from different time periods and planets altogether. In case I ever forgot I was at the beach, glossy seashells in a dish, coral bookends, and crisscrossed oars above the TV reminded me of my new home.

My room at the end of the hall shone a golden shade from the sunny side of the house. My bed took up most of the room, dressed in a white comforter with teal seahorses. My white wicker dresser matched the headboard. I couldn't believe this was for *me.*

Blair showed me the kitchen stocked with Fruity Pebbles, mandarin oranges, yogurt, Kraft macaroni boxes, orange juice, and all the supplies for peanut butter and jelly sandwiches. I could certainly work with this.

She took me over to the kitchen island where a pink pen and a single piece of paper—which she called an "itinerary"—waited for us. Blair had already written on it, using hearts as bullet points.

Ice cream at Sunset Scoop.

Watch the sunset.

Go to the candy store.

Read beach books.

Mini golf.

Stargaze.

Watch the sunrise.

Stay up all night.

Have the best summer ever.

"It's perfect," I said when she asked what I thought. I didn't have any of my own ideas to add, so I clicked the pen in and out to fill the silence.

"If you get an itch to add anything, it'll be up on the fridge for you." Blair rocked Hadley on her hip. "Now, what do you want to do first?"

Now

June 13

"Quinn!" Blair pulls me into a bear hug. "I had no idea you'd be here so early!"

When we pull back from the hug, I take her in: brown hair strewn about like a dandelion puff. Eye bags swollen. Everything red where it should be peach.

Inside the house, shoes gather in clumps around the front door. Half-empty cups leave condensation rings on all the tables. Blankets and pillows lie across the couch in silent battle. A dust bunny in the corner has grown into a rabbit. It smells mostly of mildew, greasy fast-food containers, and a bloated, leaky trash bag.

"Do you want lunch?" Blair leans against the kitchen island. Stacks of unopened mail have made a home that the itinerary must have run away from. No pink, sparkly words wait to be inevitably crossed out come August.

"I can heat up something, or we can go to Hammerhead's, or I can give you some money for groceries."

"I'm not hungry, but maybe we can go get ice cream later?" I write up an itinerary with my voice instead. It doesn't come out pink or sparkly. "Everyone's coming over later for a bonfire."

Blair smiles. "Sounds good. I'll leave you to it."

I walk down the hallway to my room, leaving Blair to retreat to her burrow in the middle of the blanket and pillow war.

I shove my clothes into my dresser, then crack open the window and throw myself onto my bed. I close my eyes to unwind to the sounds of the world outside the window. Distant seagulls whine, pine trees rustle, katydids click.

The sounds of my favorite season.

The sounds of my favorite place.

I just wish they still had the power to fix me.

Now

June 13

THIS TIME LAST YEAR, my five best friends and I kicked off summer on Mason's boat, *Kingfish*. He zipped us around the marsh grass while the water slipped into the color of sky. I watched Holden and Jorge fly off the tube while I wrestled the wind from my hair. Haven and I danced to steel drum music. We ate at the restaurant on the land side of the sound where people tolerated iffy popcorn shrimp and cold French fries for the view of distant trees and salt grass, everything pink and orange and red where the sun pulls down.

I looked at Everett, orange soda still fizzing on my tongue. The sun drew white sheets on the water and painted Everett's face golden.

I was free. Kelsie and Everett were broken up. That summer was my oyster, so to speak.

He looked at me at the same time I looked at him—warm, like the leather seats baking my skin.

They all must be doing something like that now, finishing up a perfect day inside the beginning of the sunset, toasting to our last summer before college. Smiling. Swimming. Cracking jokes.

This is what replays in my mind on Blair's kitchen floor, elbow-deep in a pail of suds, scrubbing the brown grout until it at least begins to resemble white. It's a real *Cinderella* story, except I'm Cinderella, the evil stepmother, *and* both stepsisters all at once. I told them to go without me today. I didn't think I'd be doing this instead, but things have a funny way of changing.

Sometimes, they change like the tides, slowly and gradually—a face aging with each new wrinkle. Sometimes, they change like a rush of water through a river, abruptly and suddenly. And sometimes, you don't even notice the change until you're wearing a dusty old pair of knee pads because it hurts to be on the ground like this.

Then you realize how quickly time passes when you're occupied with other things.

A knock at the door pulls me from my trance. I wipe fallen hair from my face with a sudsy hand and open the door.

Everett Bishop.

"Welcome back, Quinn," he says like he was in the middle of rehearsing it. He smiles with the right side of his face and brushes moppy black hair off his forehead.

The look on his face says what he couldn't last summer—what he still can't say now. There's sorrow behind the stars in his eyes, and maybe a little bit of those galaxies I found there last summer, too.

His voice isn't any different—it stopped deepening years ago—but it takes me a moment to remember how he speaks like he's already written the words, how my name dances from his mouth.

A laugh dances from mine. These things will never change.

"It's good to be back." My heart is a penny, flipping between what we could have been and what we are now. I'm not sure where it lands, but I pull him into a hug anyway.

The last time I hugged him like this was just before last summer's abrupt end. If I'd had a clearer head then, I would have known it was our last. Ironically, seventeen managed to be my most naïve summer, but that's what happens when you go so far beyond jaded that you loop back around and convince yourself things might actually be okay.

I'm back. It's time to start over.

"It's good to see you," I whisper into his chest.

He smells like coconut-tinged cologne; I forget I don't like coconuts.

I forget that *I* smell like sweat and bleach and the grime I've coaxed off the floor. *Shit*, and I'm wearing knee pads. I pull back and fix my hair. It falls right back into my face, wet and stringy. "Sorry, I've been cleaning up."

"Can I help?" Everett closes the front door. His white-toothed smile contrasts with his olive skin. "Also, I brought s'mores stuff for later."

My cheeks are hot coals. My heart leaps at the very fact that he's standing in the living room at all. Have I been plucked from this timeline and put back into seventeen? "You didn't go on the boat?"

"We'd never go out knowing you're stuck here."

I shrug. "I didn't want to burden you guys."

A look of shock strikes his face. "You're only burdening me if you don't have s'mores with me." He shakes his head and grabs the back of his neck. "I mean, you don't *have* to, I just wanted—"

"I'd love to have s'mores with you." I cut him off and take the bag from his hands, smiling. "And I'd love your help."

It doesn't feel like the first day of summer anymore. A gentle evening breeze brushes through my bangs. My goosebumps, confused about the June chill, are soothed by my hoodie. Dewy grass adds to the confusion. Mosquitoes kiss my ankles and leave itchy welts behind.

After scrubbing the rest of the floor and bleaching mold off the walls, Everett and I lie on beach chairs on the edge of Blair's backyard. My bones lie to rest, unwound and burning from within. Fireflies light up the trees, so we play a game from the past.

"I bet the next firefly is going to be on that branch sticking out past the rest." Everett stretches out to soak up the moonlight. He needs moonlight because he *is* moonlight, like how humans need water because we *are* water.

Our knees touch and I feel his leg bounce, or maybe it's mine.

I watch the silhouette of the tallest pine, waiting for a yellow light where the sky meets the trees. The sky turns one notch darker before my eyes. It feels like a forbidden glitch I wasn't meant to see.

The firefly flickers a few trees down.

"There it is!" I point in the darkness.

Everett points out another firefly on the edge of the yard. We wait in the darkness between their sparks. I expect it to reemerge closer to us, but it lights up above the back deck.

The game fizzles out once the fireflies stop flickering, once the day officially detaches from night. I lean the beach chair all the way back. My hair pools on the grass.

It's dark enough to see all the stars in the sky. Beyond the trees' looming silhouettes, Sagittarius is a rainbow umbrella among a shore of black ones. I swallow hard and close my eyes. The story of Sagittarius and Scorpio plays on my eyelids—Sagittarius the Archer taking a shot at Scorpio the Scorpion. This was how the universe intended it, written in the stars as an inevitable strike in the sky, like all the other ungranted wishes resting up there.

We sit like that for a little bit, listening to the symphony of cicadas and locusts in the trees starting then stopping then starting again like time is a conductor they're following. Then the katydids snarl in response. Everything around us sings a perfect tune Everett and I can't find our place in.

Until we do.

"How are you?" Everett's voice breaks the silence.

"Good," I say out of habit.

"But how are you *really*?"

I bite my lip. I'm not going to cry, not even in the face of such a lethal question. Those are words that always bring stifled pain to the surface—the final raindrop that splits open a dam—but no, not on my first summer night. Not in this moment with Everett.

I decide on the truth without the tears. "I miss last summer."

I feel it on my face, wide and unrelenting and real: a smile. I haven't smiled like this since the Ferris wheel. Visions of white moonlight and sugared air and Everett smiling next to me dance in my memory. That night taught me that joy is a prequel to everything after; pain waits at the bottom of the Ferris wheel.

My brain remembers this at random times, grants me a punishment for joy. It shoots my smile down, flicks my shoulders into a slump, curses my heart to the bottom of the ocean. The sinking feeling in my stomach isn't a welcome one, unlike the flutters of cotton candy and our first kiss.

"I can't really explain it, but there's this feeling I get when I think about our time last summer, you know…" I lower my voice to pretend I'm not acknowledging it. My throat feels raw despite my efforts to fight crying. "…before." The tickle inside my nose spreads to my eyes, and tears fall anyway. "I'm scared I will make it happen again."

Everett clears his throat. "Quinn, you're allowed to be happy."

"I know."

I *do*—but it feels like a bomb ticking out of time, like chanting "Bloody Mary" in Haven's mirror, like finding a sick, stray dog on the side of the road. Stop it at the last second, don't look it in the face, don't call it by its name:

Happiness.

If you acknowledge it, there will be no more to spare.

I toy with a stray pine needle—better the pine needle than the skin around my fingernails.

I fixate on a cluster of stars I don't actually know the name of. I've never wanted a shooting star more than right now. The night is perfect for one—a new moon, no light pollution from Blair's street. *Stars, please give me this. Let me wish for happiness.*

Everett makes a subject-changing *tsk* sound between his teeth. "What's made you happy lately?"

Happiness is so fleeting to me, such a noticeable rise from my usual lows, that I remember every positive moment vividly. High school graduation, me and my mom skipping niceties and attacking my cake with forks, a call with Haven while I packed for this summer. Today brought a spike in joy, so I brace more strongly for impact.

"The sailboat billboard on the highway before the causeway. You know, the one with the rich people eating hors d'oeuvres? It's always how I know I'm getting close. Then when I got on the causeway, I rolled the windows down. It's tradition."

"I still remember the first time I saw the ocean over the causeway. I think I might have cried."

I laugh. "Did you write a poem about it?"

"Of course," he jokes.

I recite old poetry off my lips, my tone sarcastically wistful. "Waves crashing on the shore, stealing shells and bringing more."

"Where'd *that* come from?"

"An actual poem I wrote when I was eleven." I giggle and hide my face in my hands despite the darkness. Happiness becomes me. I don't try to stop it or brace for impact.

"You've always been such a sap."

"So have you!"

"You have to show me the whole thing." He laughs. "Now I wish I'd actually written a poem, so I could be a bigger nerd than you."

"Shut up." I throw the haggard pine needle at him. "What's made *you* happy lately?"

"The look on Jorge's face when I officially beat him out for valedictorian."

"I bet he was happy for you." Then, because I *have* to, I add, "*Nerd.*"

"Being a nerd sucked when I had to give a speech at graduation."

"Please tell me you went up there and sang 'The Piña Colada Song.'"

"Every last word. They had to boo me off the stage. I can't figure out what they didn't like about it."

I laugh, ear-splitting and real. "I think I have an idea."

He laughs along with me, then lets the locusts fill the silence. "What else has made you happy?" he asks, serious again.

"The sound of locusts," I say with a mystical smirk. Ever since he taught me the difference between the sounds of different bugs, I would lie in my bed on lonely nights in Raleigh and listen to the locusts, thinking of the bike trail, his front porch, and other conflicting times. But I haven't heard the sounds as one again until now, this moment, where the cicadas, katydids, and locusts act as background noise to something bigger, but manage to symbolize the entire memory.

"Cicadas are my favorite."

"You know, we've never given the crickets enough attention."

"They get enough. What else?"

There's no need to light a fire when both of us are content in darkness, so I look at him even though I know he can't see me. The stars can, and Sagittarius probably twinkles in anticipation. "Seeing you. Thank you for helping me clean."

Thank you for being there.

Thank you for knowing I needed it.

Thank you for being you.

"You know I only came over for s'mores."

"Of course. I only let you in for the s'mores."

"Obviously."

We laugh, no fire, marshmallows, or chocolate in sight.

JORGE KILLS NINE MATCHES and an entire bottle of lighter fluid before the fire takes hold. It lights our faces orange. Embers fly around his face like a sparkler on July Fourth.

Fire crackles. Smoke douses the air. Stars blanket the skies above us. Jorge leans back in his chair, wearing pride on his face, now glowing in the firelight.

Haven rests her head on his shoulder, burrowing into his black hair chopped at his shoulders. She already told me they started dating in April, but seeing it in person brings a new perspective. Haven wouldn't have dated him when he first joined the friend group—she was too hung up on a guy who threw beer bottles on the dunes, and Jorge has always been more sensitive. He hasn't bought a new pair of shoes since his feet stopped growing and he picks up trash from the beach while he's looking for shark teeth.

Haven, like me, has changed like the sand around a coursing river. That change is a welcome one.

She smiles at me across the fire, her black hair glowing orange in the bonfire light. We already exchanged official hellos when she got here, falling to the grass when she burst from her family's golf cart and ran into my arms.

The six of us ease into the fire's calming warmth.

It invites Everett next to me, moving his beach chair closer than it was in the darkness. I fall into a trance on Everett glowing in the flames. His hair is the color of dying embers.

He notices my stares and meets my gaze, his brown eyes marshmallow soft. He pulls a leaf from my hair and tosses it into the fire.

I don't feel guilty about my smile. "Thanks."

"This thing is a beast!" Holden screams from the side yard. He wrestles the water hose from its winter hibernation in a game of schoolyard tug-of-war. He untangles it enough to reach the fire, then sits in his rocking chair with a huff. "You're welcome."

Haven performs a slow clap, earning a middle finger from Holden.

I play along. I missed him enough to please him just this once. "Thanks, Holden. You're so strong."

"I know." He flexes his biceps, flashing the smile three years of braces gave him. "It's all those marlins I've been reeling in."

"You *wish* you'd ever caught a marlin," Haven says, rolling her eyes.

"How dare you say that." He points to Haven, then to me. "And how dare *you* be gone so long."

"Guilty."

He takes his shirt off and throws it into the darkness behind us.

"God, Holden." Haven rolls her eyes and looks at Mason. "How do you handle him?"

Mason snickers. "I don't."

"What? I don't want to smell like fire later."

We're sure to smell like burnt wood by the end of the night—even Holden's tossed shirt—but that's one of my favorite scents to shower away, right next to sunscreen.

Mason's the first to dig in to the marshmallows. Holden lets his entire marshmallow burst into flames while everyone else spins their marshmallow gently at the top of the flames.

I let the flame burn my marshmallow a toasty brown shell, squish it between two graham crackers, and let it melt the chocolate before my mouth does the rest.

Over s'mores, Haven tells the story of how she and Jorge started dating. It started with a mutual agreement to go to prom together but ended with a midnight chat in the car over cherry slushies. They had their first date at Hammerhead's and Holden asked to wait tables that night. He filled their sodas every five minutes and brought out five baskets of hush puppies.

"Your first mistake was having your first date at our job," Holden says. "Your second mistake was going out with him." He throws a marshmallow at Jorge.

Jorge catches it and throws it in his mouth. "Love you too, man."

I point at Holden. "*Your* mistake was stalking Haven on her first date."

He throws his hands up. "I was keeping my baby sister safe."

"I was born two minutes *before you*," Haven says.

He shrugs. "The point still stands."

I imagine Holden peering around the doorframe during the date. He's a walking juxtaposition—a boxer holding a kitten, a secret riptide on a calm ocean. He can try to intimidate Jorge, but I'm sure all he did was look like a duck who thinks fluffing its feathers is scary.

We take turns telling stories from the past year apart. Everett talks about his valedictorian speech, how he smirked at Jorge before he started. Haven recounts winning prom queen and accepting her tiara and sash after she spilled barbecue sauce on her dress.

In the middle of my second s'more, the fire starts to feel too hot. My face loses its smile. A ringing in my ears replaces the sweet sound of catching up with my best friends. This is the empty feeling that sweeps over me sometimes. It's always uninvited, but I've gotten better at riding it out.

Empty used to be something I craved—schedules, thoughts, bags before beachcombing. Sometimes empty is the fullest a person can be. Now, I'm empty the way that empty things suck—promises, hearts, bags *after* beachcombing.

I lie back in the beach chair, lift my chin to cool my cheeks. I can't find the stars past the golden orb of flame, but soon enough, this feeling will pass. It *is* nice to be back in Piper Island. Even though the same moon spills everywhere, this is the sky I've spent the last eight summers with. Piper Island is where Everett is my second moon. Piper Island is where I grew up, in an ideal world where growing is only impacted by what happens in the summer, where life can only be shaped by summer.

Only now, I wish for the opposite.

Everyone else laughs with reckless abandon around the fire. I wish I could be like them instead of slowly nodding and forcing a fake smile. Green envy tugs at me, a monster I've gotten to know well.

"What are your plans this summer, Q?" Haven asks.

I shrug, a shallow smile on my face. "I don't know. Blair didn't have an itinerary for me today."

Summer was always a season of turning the mundane into something special, thanks to Blair. I still remember what she once wrote in a book she gifted me a few summers back: *This summer, keep doing that living you do. Maybe fall in love while you're at it? Love, Blair.*

But this is our last summer before college, so the six of us are on the precipice of greatness. We're dangling off a cliff's edge, jumping over the clock ticking at double speed. I want to stop time and fill it with life again. For me and Blair. Summer at Piper Island is the only way to fall in love with living again.

Holden's eyes widen. "Let's make our own. I mean, it's what we've always done."

"Yeah, go get something to write with," Haven says.

I run inside and fish Blair's pink gel pen from the junk drawer Everett and I organized earlier. I grab an old Sunset Scoop receipt that shouldn't have survived the culling.

Back in the dying heat of the flames, we brainstorm ideas until the early morning officially detaches from the night, speaking the summer's plans into the cloak of darkness, the stars as our witness.

"Sneak into the waterpark at night."

"Climb the lighthouse."

"Party all night."

"Or until we fall asleep."

"Eat the whole Hammerhead's menu."

"Ew, no."

"Try all the flavors at Sunset Scoop, but we can share each other's!"

"And it doesn't have to be all at one time."

"What is your obsession with eating everything?"

"Have a spa night."

"Eat sushi on the beach at night. Just because I've always wanted to."

"Have a kickass July Fourth."

"Kick Jorge's ass."

"Hey! I'll kick yours instead."

"Find a perfect lightning whelk."

"Sleep in."

"Finally catch a kingfish from the pier."

"And a blue marlin from the boat!"

"Sneak some beer at Mom's fiftieth!"

"Dream on."

I let the moment take me, this slice of living. Far from the golden decks of *Kingfish*, Everett and I still find each other when there's nowhere else to look. His knee finds mine again in the darkness. The touch is laced with noxious memories and sweet lullabies I've forgotten the notes to.

Even though he can't see it, the smile on my face doesn't falter.

Eight Summers Ago

Age 10, June 13

WHEN I SUGGESTED MINI GOLF after ice cream at Sunset Scoop, I hadn't thought Blair would actually agree, but thirty minutes later, we walked into Safari Adventure Mini Golf.

Blair paid the boy dressed as an explorer while I picked a putter and a light blue ball. I pushed Hadley into the elements, a hot Piper Island afternoon disguised as an African safari. The mini golf hut was painted with black and white zebra stripes. A plastic giraffe peeked through the fake trees.

At the first hole, my ball went everywhere on the green except the hole. I tried to blame the sun peering into my eyes, or the pine cones strewn about, or the lion growls from a speaker hidden in the bushes, but in truth, I was just bad.

Blair wasn't much better. She marked another five for herself on the scorecard with the cute miniature pencil.

A family played in front of us—a mom and dad and a girl and boy who looked close to me in age. The boy got a few hole-in-ones, causing the family to erupt into cheers. His cheeks turned red in embarrassment, but I could see the secret smile on his face. The girl laughed when her dad almost putted the ball into the artificial blue pond.

I smiled. It was nice to see joy; nice to see parents laughing alongside their kids.

At the next hole, too distracted by the hippopotamus peering at me from the water, I hit the ball straight into the pond. I cupped my hand over my mouth, relieved when all Blair did was laugh. I leaned over the thick, damp rope meant to protect people like me from falling in. The ball bobbed like an ice cube in a tall glass, but I couldn't quite reach it with my putter.

Someone behind me said, "Let me help."

The boy from the family in front of us smiled. He lay down on the green, which allowed him to swipe his putter far enough to fish the ball out. He plopped it into my hand, dripping in fake blue water.

"Thank you."

"You're welcome," he said, then walked back to his family.

"That was very nice of that boy," Blair said when he was farther away.

"Yeah," I said, wiping the icky feeling of the water on my shorts.

We finished the course around fake zebras, rhinoceroses grazing in tall grass, and an elephant standing between us and the final hole. We didn't even bother with the score, just put our putters away and headed to the car, happy to have played. I managed a couple steps in the parking lot until I froze with the reality of what I'd done. I couldn't go another step without righting my wrong.

Blair turned around when she heard my sandals scuff against the pavement. "You okay?"

"Yeah, I just forgot something. I'll be right back."

I ran back into the building and took a few deep breaths before I pulled the cute miniature pencil out of my pocket. I knew what I was doing when I'd put it there, knew I was stealing it, but I didn't have time to think about my actions. Reality only set in when the excitement died down, so I dropped it back into the cute cup with the rest.

"Forgot this. Sorry." I smiled innocently at the safari boy and turned around before he could identify me in a police lineup.

On the way back to the car, I walked past the family from earlier on the way to theirs. Somehow, I found enough courage in me to yell, "Thanks again for getting my ball!"

The boy and girl turned around. Their parents kept walking to their car, leaving the three of us in the middle of the parking lot just about where I caught myself red-handed.

"No problem," the boy said, then looked down at his flip-flops.

"I like your shirt." The girl smiled. "Yellow is my favorite color. I got a yellow ball. Is your favorite color blue?"

I looked at my yellow tank top, the beachiest shirt I could find for my first day of summer. She was observant enough to have remembered the color of my ball. "Cotton candy blue is my favorite color."

"Cotton candy blue is pretty good." She brushed black hair behind her ear. "I'm Haven Rivera-Sanchez. This is my twin brother, Holden."

Holden looked up from his flip-flops to say, "I'm Holden." He cut his eyes at Haven, dropping his smile. "My *twin sister* never lets me speak for myself."

Haven rolled her eyes. "*Nunca quieres hablar por ti mismo.*"

"*Lo haría si no lo hicieras.*" Holden shook his head, then looked at me. "What's your name?"

I didn't understand their conversation, but even if they hadn't told me they were twins, I would have figured it out by now. From their tone of voice, I could tell they were poking fun at each other like Mom and Blair did. Plus, they were leaves floating off the same branch: tan skin, thick eyebrows, and dark eyes mirroring each other as much as fraternal faces can.

"I'm Quinn Kessler," I said, laughing at their exchange.

"Do you live here?" Haven asked.

"I'm here for the summer." I pointed to Blair and Hadley waiting at the sidewalk. "That's my aunt Blair and my cousin Hadley."

Haven waved at them. "Hadley's so cute."

"Holden! Haven!" their mom called, leaning against their red van with a phone pressed to her ear. "*¡Es hora de irnos!*"

"We have to go but we should play sometime." I let out a sharp gasp when Haven pulled one of the pencils from her pocket. She took their scorecard from Holden and scribbled on the back. "Here's our mom's number."

They waved at me with big smiles and turned on their heels.

I waved to their backs, watched Haven slip the pencil back into her pocket. Haven Rivera-Sanchez *kept* the cute miniature pencil. The sign inside clearly said to return them and even said please, but she made it all the way to her car without regretting it.

The Rivera-Sanchezes were so cool.

Cool was exactly what I needed.

Eight Summers Ago

Age 10, June 18

I stared at the Rivera-Sanchezes' phone number on the fridge for the next few days. I sipped orange juice for breakfast and watched it taunt me next to a Hammerhead's menu.

What if I called and they hated me?

What if I called and they *didn't* hate me but then one day decided that they did?

Blair pushed me to call, insisting they'd be crazy not to love me. I pretended to believe her, chewing on a hangnail while she dialed.

Mrs. Rivera-Sanchez picked up after the first ring.

Haven got to the phone so fast you would have thought she'd been waiting for it.

That brought us here, on a dock on the sound side of the island. Holden unloaded fishing gear and three fishing rods from his wagon.

Blair promised me it was okay to walk there alone since we were only a few streets from the twins' house, but I asked her not to tell Mom anyway. Mom never let me play alone with the neighborhood kids back home. I was less than a week into my new life and already a liar, but what Mom didn't know wouldn't hurt her.

The air squeezed like a pair of tights after a warm shower. There was a pinch of fish guts in the air, but the wind pushed away the rotten part before it got too close. Haven and I stood on ballerina toes for a peek at the water below.

"Do you guys do this a lot?" I asked Haven's reflection in the dark water below.

Haven flashed a peace sign on the calm ripples. "Holden does and Mom makes me babysit."

Holden shook his head from the fishing line tangled in his hand. "Don't believe a word she says."

"I guess Quinn will be the tie breaker," Haven said.

I looked at the purple polish chipping off my toes. I didn't know which twin to believe, but if fishing was just like the movies, I'd rather watch nail polish dry. But Holden had dug through a can of worms for me, so I was willing to give it a shot.

Holden wrapped a wriggly worm around a hook, kissed the air around it, and bowed his head in salute. "I'm sorry, worm. Thank you, worm."

He launched the worm into the water, then showed me how to cast my own. I nodded my head with uncertainty like my mom did when she wanted people to stop talking to her. Finally, my bobber bounced with the tide.

AFTER TWO HOURS, all the worms had died for nothing. The fish made a meal of the worms but were too smart to bite. I sat next to Haven on the dock, our rods propped on our knees.

Haven reeled in another half-eaten worm. "I can't do this anymore. This was my fourth worm."

"Dad got us two cans," Holden said, leaning over the rail covered in sun-dried fish scales.

"I don't care. We're bored."

"You too, Quinn?" Holden looked at me with soft eyes.

His voice was so close to hurt that I didn't want to tell the truth, but my mom taught me that lying was worse than stealing. If you steal, at least tell the truth about it. "It's not that. It's just that we haven't caught anything."

"We've been hanging out," he said with a shrug.

He was right, and I felt bad for complaining. Maybe that was the point of fishing. We *had* been hanging out and learning about each other. I learned that they moved here from Mexico when they were four. Haven never went to bed without braiding her hair in an effort to train her wavy hair. Holden always gave his ice cream cherries to Haven. Haven's favorite shade of yellow was the center of a daisy. Holden liked rainy weather since it made the best fish hungry.

Holden taught me about fiddler crabs and the migration of blue herons and the time he swore he saw a mermaid tail off this very dock.

After Haven told me about the mermaid show at the local aquarium, she asked me to join them sometime. We talked about big dreams of opening mermaid museums, owning a mansion on the water, cooking s'mores for dinner, and eating cherry popsicles until we threw up.

The feeling in my gut left me breathless. I felt included and wanted, like I'd been best friends with them for my whole life. I wished I'd met them sooner. I wished they lived in Raleigh with me, or that I lived here with them and never had to hear my mom cry herself to sleep again.

I'd never met anyone who talked so much about things that didn't matter, never met anyone who made me care about every little nothing like it was everything.

Haven talked like she couldn't say enough.

Holden said even more with his mouth shut.

I never thought I had much to say, but Holden and Haven made me feel like they would listen to me talk about orange juice and mermaid scales and the best way to roast a s'more until their eyes got droopy.

"I promise it's worth it when you get a bite. Sometimes the fish are stubborn, but I'll let you reel mine in when I get one."

"Pinky promise?" I held my pinky out for him.

"Pinky promise." He took mine in his.

I watched him reel in another worm heart, wrap another, wipe the dirt on his shorts, and kiss it goodbye.

HAVEN RESIGNED TO THROWING corn kernels at Holden—a more economical bait that Holden said only sometimes worked. The only thing it caught was Holden's attention. He finally noticed, or finally decided to care, and stuck his tongue out at her.

Haven gave up and pulled out a sandwich with bread, peanut butter, and sticky marshmallow goo from the wagon. "You ever had a fluffernutter?"

I nodded and took the half she held out to me. A few years back, we were low on groceries and my dad made them for dinner. We ate them on the porch steps at dusk, our bare feet on the concrete. We used to watch fireflies mingle through the darkness when we knew Mom was on the way home from work. I was the best at guessing where they'd end up the next time they lit up. Dad credited my young eyes and the determination I'd inherited from Mom.

But that was before everything happened, back when Mom was different and Dad still loved us.

"Do your mom and dad still love each other?" I said with peanut butter bread stuck in my molars. The words escaped so casually you'd think I was asking her where she got her shirt.

Holden looked at Haven, willing her to answer.

Haven finished her bite. "Yes, but I know Mom doesn't like it when Dad doesn't finish fixing stuff around the house. One time he took the shutters off the house and took forever to paint them. They look good now, though." She shrugged and wiped marshmallow from the corner of her mouth.

"They were on the kitchen table for weeks," Holden said dramatically, like weeks were years.

"You're too much like *Mama*," Haven said.

"You're too much like *Papa*," Holden retorted.

I got a taste of the parents they'd watched and supposedly become. Did people think I was like my mom? Did they think I also triple-checked the locks on the door and looked both ways nine times before crossing the street? Did my mom resent the daydreaming I got from Dad?

"Do they ever fight?" I asked.

"One time last year we got off the bus and saw Dad getting in the car. Mom was crying on the couch. She didn't tell us what happened but she took us to Sunset Scoop."

"We think they had a fight, but then Dad was waiting for her at the table when we got home. We went to bed and everything was normal when we woke up." Holden shrugged.

They said it so coolly, like it was normal to talk to new friends about how close their parents got to living in different places.

It didn't sound like the Rivera-Sanchezes' world ever got close to breaking. It sounded like ice cream filled the small cracks in their foundation. Maybe real moms and dads were supposed to be happy together. Maybe that was the story people sat on a dock all day to catch but never did.

"Do *your* parents still love each other?" Haven's voice danced with the wind.

All I could do was shrug. "Not anymore."

"I'm sorry," she mumbled between chews.

I almost told her why. I almost told her about my dad, about all the nights I thought the ghastly sounds of the house settling was him breaking locks and sneaking back in to our lives. I almost told her about the night I unlocked the door after Mom fell asleep, like a little girl letting Santa Claus in. I locked it soon after having a nightmare about a strange man wandering in to kill us. At that point, though, my dad was a strange man too.

They wouldn't care. They'd just pretend to understand.

"It's fine," I said. It *wasn't*, but that was just what people said. My mom said it even when her eyes were all puffy and red.

It wasn't Haven's fault my parents couldn't just fight about unpainted shutters.

Piper Island sunsets were different than the ones back home. The lush trees in Raleigh hid the sunset too early in the day. Here, the sun peeked through the pines. Here, the sound made a clearing perfect for an orange and pink sky. Here, the clouds were marshmallows drenched in cotton candy and orange pulp. Here, cicadas cooed wildly from the pine trees and frogs sang from the marsh.

None of us caught any fish. Eventually even Holden sat down with us, still determined to catch one but unwilling to toy with them. I brushed bread crumbs off my knee.

"Holden, we should go. Mom's gonna get mad again." Haven loaded up the wagon. "You know Mom's rule about streetlights. And we have to take Quinn home."

"Fine, we'll just cast it one more time. They turn on too early anyway."

I stood up to help Haven, but before I could get to her, I felt a tug on my rod. A jolt ran down to my toes.

The pole stooped down. Another tug. The rod was so heavy I was afraid it would snap. I forgot everything Holden taught me.

"I feel something!" I screamed loudly enough to scare the frogs away.

"Reel it up all the way!" Holden said.

This was the bite Holden kept telling me about. The hours we sat here finally meant something. I flicked back my wrists like I watched Holden do a million times. The glassy water shattered. A fish caught the sunset on its scales.

The fish slammed against the dock on its way out of the water. Holden pulled it into his hands and held tight to keep the silver fish from flopping out. "It's a bluefish! I can't believe you didn't feel this on the line!"

I couldn't believe it either, even though it was only big enough to fit in his palm. He held the fish up and I trusted him enough to get a closer look. The fish looked back at me, its eyes bulging from its face, gray and silver skin glistening in the sun.

"It's so cool, isn't it?" Holden's smile competed with the sunset.

"Yeah." I watched its gills struggle against the evening air.

"That was pretty cool, Quinn," Haven said.

"Thanks, guys." I smiled with all my teeth.

Holden unhooked it, kissed it, and released it back home.

I missed it already, but I knew it was happier without me.

Eight Summers Ago
Age 10, August 10

THAT MORNING, I PUT ON the only clothes not packed in my suitcase: the yellow tank top Haven liked and some shorts I should have washed four beach trips ago.

With my suitcase in tow, I said goodbye to Blair and Hadley when Mrs. Rivera-Sanchez—who insisted I called her Saray—picked me up. I promised Mom I'd be ready for her to pick me up by four, so the twins and I woke up early so we could make the most of our last day. The best days of summer were the ones you needed to set an alarm for, anyways. Today, an alarm meant walking into an arcade with my new best friends for one last bite of summer.

The smell of cheesy food hit first, then bright, flashy neon lights. Machine *clinks*, *beeps*, and *pings* begged for our attention. Saray settled into a booth and sent us bouncing between all the hungry games.

WHEN WE FOUND OUR WAY back to Saray for lunch, we were red in the face and sweaty from laser tag after winning against a team of mean middle schoolers. A steaming pizza waited for us on the table next to ice waters and two cherry slushies.

"No fair, Quinn gets her own." Holden slunk into the booth, taking a huge gulp of the slushy.

"Holden, please." Saray looked up from a half-completed crossword. "Be grateful for what you get or it'll all be Haven's."

"Ha!" Haven grabbed it from Holden and took her own gulp.

"You too, Haven." Saray didn't even look up that time.

Haven stuck out her bottom lip, shoulders slinking next to me in the booth. I emptied my water before we even started on the pizza, then I thanked Saray for the slushy and started in on it.

"No problem. How's your last day treating you?"

"Good." I nodded and etched lines in the Styrofoam slushy cup. "I can't believe it's my last day. I remember mini golf like it was yesterday."

It didn't seem like there had been two months of long, summer days between then and now, but that was how things felt when you looked back on them. It was how fourth grade felt back in June when I'd just completed it. I hoped it was how fifth grade would feel instead of spending every day missing cherry slushy brain freezes and stale pizza.

Saray nodded. "That feeling will only get worse the older you get."

"Mom, you sound *so* old right now," Haven said, lips cherry red.

"Well, I *am* old. One day, you guys will be too and I just won't know what to do with myself." I almost thought she was serious, but she said it with an exaggerated accent like the dramatic TV shows she watched, which made Haven and Holden groan.

It was nice to be part of their family for a day, to groan alongside them over pizza and drinks like I also thought my mom was embarrassing.

When we finished our pizza, I decided the best use of our limited time was the games meant to win tickets. We killed the rest of our tokens and managed a sizable stack of tickets. We combined our tickets to buy handfuls of jelly bracelets, bouncy balls, and a pile of Blow Pops.

I was working on an orange Blow Pop when Saray led us outside just before four o'clock.

We sat on the curb with sucker sticks perched on our lips, watching Main Street for my mom's car. Haven and I stacked our wrists with bracelets. I was shocked they didn't melt into jelly clumps from the sun hanging so heavily in the sky. Holden bounced a ball against the uneven pavement, chasing it around parked cars when it ran amok.

I took special note of the way the air felt—heavy against my skin. The deep afternoon blue sky and the sun were a warm hug. I knew I had air and sun and sky back home, but it wouldn't feel this freeing for a while.

"What are you going to do when you get home?" Haven asked.

"I don't know. Maybe cry." I laughed, but I feared it might actually happen once I drove on the unfamiliar side of the causeway, left to watch the summer rewind in the rearview mirror.

The bookstore and beach.

Crickets that sang with the ocean as its audience.

Popsicles and peanut butter sandwiches.

Fishing and exploring the island.

Frogs that splatted against the driveway, pulled from their camouflage in the moonlit grass.

Fireflies that snuck out of the jar while you were hunting for more.

This summer, I learned that fireflies didn't glow if you trapped them in a jar. They needed to be free to be beautiful.

"*I* sure will." Haven smiled, but it looked wrong with such sad words.

"What's it like here when summer ends?"

"Pretty boring, actually. Once all the tourists leave and it gets cold, most of the fun stuff closes."

I nodded, but really I thought she was lying to make the leaving easier.

"I have something for you." Haven fished through her pockets and pulled out a silver necklace that glinted in the afternoon sun.

A small purple shell shaped like a butterfly wing dangled from the chain. She rested the shell on her sweaty palm.

"This is a coquina clam shell. They're my favorite because they're purple. Also, some of them have this hole already there. I always wanted to make a necklace out of them, so I made you this to remember us by."

Itching to put it on, I fumbled with the hook, snagging baby hairs. The shell fell just below my neck, cool against the summer air. "I love it."

Even without this necklace, there was no way I'd forget this summer. I vowed to wear the necklace every day until I died. I didn't care if Mom begged me to take it off for picture day, or if it felt scratchy when I was trying to sleep, or if I ever hated Piper Island.

"Give this to Hadley when she's old enough to wear it. It's what used to be on the chain." She dropped a glassy blue heart pendant in my hand. The rainbow flecks scattered throughout it reminded me of my ice cream order—cotton candy, always with rainbow sprinkles.

"I will." I smiled and shoved it in my pockets with the specks of sand I hoped would stay there forever. "Thank you."

"I'll miss you." Haven pulled me into a hug.

I hugged her back. Her hair smelled of cardboard pizza. I felt like crying, but this was a different cry. It meant I'd had enough fun to miss it already. It meant I didn't know how else to stretch the dwindling clock. It meant I wanted to.

"Please come back next summer."

"I will," I said. I felt a sting where my eyes usually were.

Haven held out a curved pinky to me. "Pinky promise?"

I smiled and intertwined mine with hers. "Pinky promise."

Now

June 23

"You're so fired," Holden says.

"It's midnight. Everyone's sleeping. There aren't even security cameras." Mason fumbles with the waterpark keys. The chain-link fence doors creak open loudly in the tension of nightfall. Mason is way too relaxed to be breaking into his place of work with a crew of adventure-hungry friends.

We follow him into Pirate's Bounty, relying only on the moon and the pool lights so we don't draw attention to ourselves.

My eyes adjust in the pale moonlight. The usually bustling waterpark bleeds an eerie midnight gray. The usually haphazard chaises are in perfect lines Mason must have straightened out at the end of his shift earlier. The royal blue umbrellas have been wound down and tied with neat bows. The water in the kiddie pool is so still, the moon is a complete circle in its reflection. The racer slides have no line. The lonely mats wait for their victims at the bottom of the stairs. The only thing the same as its daytime state is the chlorine smell.

"This is a bad idea, I know it. I can feel it in my wrists." Holden anxiously massages his wrist with his other hand.

"For the last time, fisherman wrists aren't a thing," Jorge says.

"Then why did I predict the hurricane wouldn't hit us? And why do I know we're all leaving here in a cop car tonight?"

"You *don't*," Haven says.

Mason slides open the concession stand and sits on the counter. "To be fair, he *did* predict he'd vomit up all those hot dogs last year."

"We all predicted that," Everett says, close enough to me that our shoulders battle for dominance.

"You whined about it enough," I joke.

"You people have no sympathy, do you? First, you drag me out here for some sordid midnight affairs. Then, you make fun of me for the result of *your* prank? What's next, you're going to make me walk the plank?" Holden points to the pirate ship structure in the kiddie pool.

Mason rolls his eyes and puts a chip bag in Holden's hand. He smirks and massages Holden's shoulders. "Sordid midnight affairs? You *wish*."

"We have sympathy. Just not for you." Haven taps her brother's nose.

Holden pops open the chips, his paranoia seemingly gone.

Haven doesn't seem worried either as she grabs a large cup and fills it to the brim with cherry slushy. Her face glows red from the neon sign on the machine that churns ice and syrup all summer long. She's pleased with herself, since this adventure was her idea.

I'm with Holden. I don't want the night to end with red and blue flashing lights, but Everett pinky promised me it would be fine. Plus, it's better to busy myself at night. The demons pull harder when night falls. They're strong enough when I'm alone, but unrelenting when it's dark. Night demons project *what-if*s on the ceiling like glow-in-the-dark stars, ringing shrill telephones in my head when I shut my eyes.

"This place is so cool at night," Everett says, eyeing the concessions.

There's a lot to choose from: potato chips and candy bars shelved on the wall, ice cream asleep behind a sliding glass door, lollipops on a never-ending carousel ride. The bags of cotton candy have lost their fluff, but the popcorn bags are about to burst at the seams.

Mason grabs a bag of cheese puffs. "You know what's even cooler? *Swimming* at night."

"I'll drink to that!" Haven runs over to the poolside.

We follow her to the perfect lines of chaises. I ruin it and slide one to the edge of the pool, scratching it against the gritty concrete.

"Hey, watch it!" Mason says, then winks so I know he's joking.

Jorge didn't wear a shirt, so he's the first to jump in. His splash refracts the pool lights into orange fireworks.

Mason and Holden jump in at the same time as Haven works out another slushy sip.

Everett unties his Converses. He looks at me and smiles meekly in the moonlight while he takes his shirt off. His chest cuts into a bed of muscle sculpted by the shadows. My eyes wander to places I know they shouldn't, just like they did last summer. It's different now, so I look to the constellations instead, pinching my bottom lip between my teeth.

He cannonballs into the pool. It splashes on my knees. I shiver. That's how water used to feel; it used to kiss the skin I wanted to crawl out of, making me want to stay instead and be kissed by the water forever. I don't let water kiss me anymore, but I sit by the side of the pool. I listen to my best friends swimming, laughing, and revenge-splashing each other. I throw the cheese puffs Mason brought over into Holden's mouth. We miss almost every one. Everett fishes them out with a grimace.

Haven swims to the edge where she left her slushy. She swallows a sip, light reflecting on her face from the water. "You having fun?"

"Of course." I smile.

I'm not *lying*, but it's just harder these days to be part of the world happening around me. There is a bit of truth to my words, though; doing something dumb and teenage like this is exactly what I need.

Haven scoops her hair into a bun. Her curly baby hairs pirouette onto her forehead—fitting, since she's the only person I know who dances through life with the careless whimsy of wispy hair. She searches for rainbows in storm clouds, calls warts "frog kisses," and can't go a day without eating a cherry popsicle. She sees the world in yellow.

"I'm glad." She gives me her cheese-puffiest smile and kisses the air with a loud smooch.

I pretend to catch it, popping it in my mouth like a big fat cherry. That always makes Haven laugh.

She swims back to play chicken. They let me be the judge and I fudge the results in Everett's favor. I don't think they notice. Holden's a cheater anyway. I finish the cheese puffs and muster a beat of courage. I slip out of my sandals, plant myself at the edge of the pool, and cross my legs just before the edge of the water.

Everett swims up. He crosses his arms on the concrete and leans his face on them. He smiles at me as if to ponder the vastness of the universe. I wonder a similar thing when I look into his eyes: *Just how far does infinity go?*

"I see you're making your way in," he says definitively.

"My way ends right here." My cheeks warm. The edges around my chest are malleable putty, and he could do whatever he wants with it just by existing.

"Let's go somewhere drier, then."

I nod. I'm trying to be better at trust.

He hoists himself from the pool. Water slides off his body and darkens the concrete in water droplet shapes. He dries off and wrestles his shirt back on.

His head pops out of his shirt collar. "Race you to the slides!"

Before I have a moment to process, he takes off running. By the time I untwist myself from the edge of the pool, he's already started up the stairs. I follow, the stairs creaking all the way to the top.

"You win." I hunch over, panting, my hands on my knees.

He smirks. "It wasn't a race."

I shove his shoulder. "Damn you."

Everett sits down on the wooden platform. I join him next to the dark, gaping mouth of one of the slides. It's eerily quiet up here with the water off. We lean back on the wooden railing. Down at the pool, we can see Holden and Mason playing Marco Polo. Jorge steals a sip of Haven's slushy and she tickles it out of his hands.

Before us stretches the navy-blue panorama of the Atlantic Ocean and Piper Island. Beach house windows, streetlights, and neon restaurant signs pepper the horizon. The pier itself has a beating heart, awake now with late night fishermen. Infinitesimal lives spill from tail lights, stoplights, and golden upstairs windows.

What would it be like to jump inside and live a different life?

The moonlight paints a white line from the horizon to the sand, breaking with the roaring waves in its path. Gray clouds muck up the constellations like a bruised banana, but I still find the Dippers, then Scorpio and Sagittarius. I find the unnamed cluster that resembles a pool of fish, then have to look away from the sky.

From here, the horizon looks like it did last summer on the Ferris wheel. Moonlight has always reminded me of Everett. Ferris wheel creaks, string lights, arcade *pings*, sparkling vignettes of the Boardwalk at night. It makes me want to do something stupid.

Something brave. Something like last summer.

I weave my fingers between Everett's and hold on tight.

He squeezes back.

My heart thrums in tune with the waves, from my thumb into his hand. Shame joins the symphony of emotions. I'm an idiot—too broken to fall in love, but pieced together just enough to send mixed signals. Regret takes center stage, but I don't want to let him go, so I brace against the mental image of my heart melting down the slide and into the pool.

We're more than two people hanging out on a closed water slide under the stars.

We're more than two people who ride Ferris wheels and sing karaoke.

Or, we *could have been*, if it weren't for me.

Everett shifts beside me. His eyebrows furrow when he looks from our hands to my face. "Are you happy right now?" he asks, so close that phantom goosebumps coast across my neck.

"Breaking into a waterpark at midnight is surprisingly fun."

"It almost makes ruining my college admission and any semblance of a career worth it."

I laugh. "Come on, you're supposed to be the adventurous one."

"I am." He pulls two lollipops from the concession stand out of his pocket. "That's why I grabbed these. Don't worry, I put enough cash on the counter for all of our snacks."

"So you're *not* the adventurous one," I joke.

"Guilty. We couldn't be trespassers *and* crooks."

"So, not *guilty* either."

"Shut up." He shakes his head with a chuckle and nudges my shoulder.

"Thank you for being cautiously adventurous. Some worker will be *very* confused tomorrow." I can't help another laugh from escaping as I unwrap my lollipop. "To cotton candy!" I say, then whisper, pointing at his lollipop, "And piña colada."

"Did you just say what I think you did?" Everett laughs.

"Piña colada," I say again like a bad word. "I give up, you finally win. I *guess* it can also be the taste of summer."

Our summers together have only ever tasted like indecision and disappointment, but right now, we sit under the moonlight, licking the sweet taste of summer off our lollipops, hypothesizing about the lives of the people tucked into the sleepy homes around us.

Our hands are unclasped. We sit only as close as friends do.

Because that's what we are. *Friends.* Even though we were once almost more, when summertime tasted like French fries and butterflies and the delusion that nothing bad could ever happen.

From behind a house I'm currently deciding a backstory for, sirens begin to rip across the night. Red and blue lights whiz past all the other lives on the island.

"Run!" I hop up to clamber down the stairs, shouting to the pool. "There's cops!"

Everett runs behind me, the creaks even louder than the sirens. Everyone else is still peeling themselves from the pool when Everett and I zoom by. We grab whatever we can and run, leaving shoes, clothes, wrappers, and other incriminating evidence behind.

"Run for your lives!" I shout.

I ignore the pain of running barefoot over fallen palms and seashell shards. I check behind my shoulder for glimpses of the flashing lights I don't want to find. The rush makes me stick my arms out and scream like I used to on the causeway, like I'm on a rollercoaster headed straight for open water, or maybe even the moon beyond that.

We run in and out of the white UFO beams of streetlights. I giggle to myself, watching our flickering shadows grow and shrink with each beam. I lead the pack, stealing glances at my friends' faces, both stunned and excited.

Everett watches his future flash before his eyes.

Haven tries not to spill her slushy.

Jorge battles with a pile of Haven's clothes.

Holden and Mason hold hands.

We're wild teens, howling at the moon in our bathing suits.

I feel it. I hear it. Screams of joy all around.

This is what this summer is all about.

We run past a few houses, across Ocean Drive, and through the pampas grass between the dunes. Our path opens up to the expanse of the beach, which isn't as stark in the thick of it. Still, this side of the dunes is an invisibility cloak. We trudge away from the public beach access and stop to recover where the sand flattens out.

"Holy shit," Holden says, panting. "What did I tell you guys?"

Haven gasps. "I left my new sandals!"

"I think I dropped your cover up," Jorge confesses.

Mason groans. "I'm so fired."

"I told you!" Holden exclaims.

Stricken with an attack of laughter, I double over with my hands on my knees. I laugh and pant into the sand, finally managing to say, "I can't believe that just happened."

Everett laughs beside me, then everyone joins in, including Mason, who is most definitely fired.

This is the first time I've been on the sand this summer, my first time hearing the waves grumble from so close to their bite. This reunion isn't like I imagined it on the drive here—the smell of hot piss and decaying fish, the waves foaming at the mouth to lure in a new victim.

No, it's not like that. The waves still whoosh. The sharp air still pinches my nose. The sand is still frustratingly sticky, but it welcomes me like an old friend.

Holden and Mason race to the water's edge in the darkness, Jorge not far behind them. All three of them blindly trust that only flat sand and shallow waves lie before them. They make contact with the water, exclaim about the cold, splash each other, and exclaim some more.

A deep yearning glows within me. What would the ocean feel like right now? I consider testing it out, breaking the rules for just a slice of the past, but I stay on this stretch of sand. I flick on my phone flashlight to hunt for ghost crabs, Everett and Haven following behind me. The ghost crabs are almost invisible, their shells camouflaged against the sand, but their movements give them away. Their bulbous, black eyes widen. They scurry from the flashlight like guilty teens running from the cops.

I giggle to myself, armed with a secret: The cop car veered away from the waterpark before I even made it down the stairs.

Sometimes it's not trouble you need to outrun.

Seven Summers Ago

Age 11, June 12

I KEPT LAST SUMMER'S PINKY PROMISE.

I didn't know what magic the Rivera-Sanchezes wielded, but somehow they knocked at the exact moment I sat down with my orange juice after running myself thirsty from unpacking. When I opened the door, Haven and Holden smiled in the shade of Blair's front porch. I jumped out of my skin to pull them into a hug. I headed out to spend the day with them, but I knew Blair would want me back before dark.

Saray was right; it did feel like only yesterday that I had hugged them both goodbye. Fifth grade was the blur I hoped it would be. The past year made the twins' features sharper, but it was the kind of growing only noticeable since we had done it apart. Haven's hair was longer and she stopped braiding it at night so it could curl how it wanted to. Holden had gone through some indecisive haircuts and his hair had settled on something akin to a seagull's nest. Their faces battled zits just like mine, but theirs were stronger fighters.

I biked next to Haven while Holden skateboarded. When I'd arrived that morning, Blair had surprised me with a sky-blue beach cruiser and brand new books in the basket. Along the sidewalk beside Main Street, we biked past a seafood restaurant named Hammerhead's, the shopping center, Beachy Keen, and Safari Adventure Mini Golf.

The water tower grew as we approached the park tucked between palm trees and pines. On top of a mound of sand in the distance was a wooden castle playground. It boasted swinging bridges, a never-ending wooden railing, and pointy towers fit to throw Rapunzel's hair down.

The sand was still wet from morning dew so it was easier to walk on. A swing set squeaked in the distant wind.

Holden had already bounded up the stairs for the highest tier of the castle. He was talking to two boys that looked our age.

"That's Mason and Jorge," Haven said, leading me up the stairs. "We grew up with Jorge but Mason just moved here during the school year. Jorge's the cute one. His parents own that restaurant we passed, Hammerhead's. Their hushpuppies are to *die* for. You like hushpuppies?"

"Never had them before."

"Okay, we *have* to take you there. And the candy store and Sunset Scoop and the bookstore. Oh, and mine and Holden's secret spot in the pines by the bike trail. And we can't forget to get another shell for your necklace." She pointed to the necklace still around my neck.

"I can't wait." I smiled at the thought of this summer. It sounded even better than the last. I loved the way Haven talked like she was too eager to finish one word before the next spilled out like melted honey.

I held tight to the shell, which felt like holding tighter to the memories. Part of last summer's pinky promise was wearing the coquina necklace to remember Piper Island. I kept that promise, especially when I needed a memory from this stretch of sky. I did have to take the necklace off in bed, but I never forgot to snap it back around my neck each morning.

"Mason's the blonde. He lives on the sound in this huge mansion. He and Jorge are best friends, but we're part of the group too."

I wondered if this meant one day I could be a part of this group.

When we got close enough for introductions, I waved and listened to Haven's summary of me: my annual visits to Piper Island from Raleigh, Blair's little blue house on Plover Street, and baby Hadley. She excitedly told them of my obsession with cotton candy ice cream and its shade of blue.

We smiled and waved at each other slowly. I learned that Jorge had been skateboarding since he was in diapers and that Mason's favorite ice cream flavor was pistachio, which the group loved to tease him about.

Once introductions were over, Holden started a game of hide and seek. While he counted down from thirty, I ran silently through the aisles, across bridges, down ramps to different levels. I scanned the shadows for a good enough clump to hide in. Holden was getting dangerously close to zero so I darted into a room on the sand. It was just big enough to crawl in, so I angled my head to fit. The sand was damp and cold away from the rising sun, sharp against my bare thighs.

Holden was searching, so I pulled my legs closer to my chest, gripping tightly and breathing short, hitched breath on my knees.

I thought maybe I was the only person who'd ever been in here, but there was writing on the walls. It was jagged over the existing wood grain, like it was written over the edge of another sheet of paper. The wooden slats told stories in bleeding marker and pencil scratches.

Some were bad words people at school said when the teachers weren't around. Some I heard Mom say to Dad when she thought I wasn't around. Most of them were written by couples, hearts drawn around their names, dates faded to match their age, even notes that felt too personal for a public hide and seek spot on an island.

Pedro + Kendall; D + L; Holly + Charlie; Mac loves Milana; T & A.

My mind wandered into a flurry of questions. How many of them grew up here together? How many of them vacationed here? How many were a fleeting blend of local and tourist? Did their relationships match how faded the writing was? Should I have done them a favor and retraced their names? How did it feel to be so sure of love that you marked its existence into wood? What did love even look like?

Footsteps thundered above me, and I felt them in my skull.

Holden sang, "Come out, come out, wherever you are!"

The steps above stopped shaking. I allowed another shallow breath.

"Found you!" Holden peeked his head under the opening and tagged my shin.

I was the last one found, so I became the seeker next. I scared Mason and Jorge when I found them holding themselves halfway down the tall slide. I heard echoes of them duetting a song from a mile away. When I was the hider again, I joined Mason and Jorge in the floorboards of a wooden car. Even though we couldn't really speak, hiding with them made me feel close to them, because we *were*—I could almost feel their hearts beat quicker when Haven stepped too close.

Hide and seek melted into swinging. We swung in a line, hitting the highest peaks at alternating times like ripples on the sound. Mason challenged us to see who could fling our shoes the farthest. We took turns launching our shoes into the sandy grass. Jorge's sneakers beat our measly sandals.

I was swinging barefoot, my hair a reckless mess from the wind's noisy, cold *whooshes*. I closed my eyes and pretended to be a cloud floating across the island. It felt real, like what I imagined a rollercoaster might.

SUMMER SKIES CHANGED FAST. All day, the clouds feasted on water until they got too plump to stay alive. I thought the sky would stay alive long enough for the sun to set, but I knew it wouldn't make it through these dark gray blankets.

Haven and I read more love stories written on the castle walls, then we joined Mason on the curb. We watched Holden and Jorge skate across the white lines of the parking lot, a hilarious divide between coordinated and almost too uncoordinated to watch. Their wheels made an angry growl against the asphalt.

We talked about every single topic that entered our minds. I defended rainbow sprinkles on ice cream, but assured Mason that pistachio wasn't too bad without bits of nuts. Mason and Haven wanted me to crush on this cute actor they both liked from one of Saray's telenovelas. I argued that orange soda was better than cola while Haven fought for cherry. We all agreed summer was the best season. Haven whined that Mason and Jorge were the only ones in the group who could find their name on all the beach souvenirs in Beachy Keen.

"Just once, I want to find something with my name. I'd even buy those dumb pirate bottle openers!" Haven said.

Mason was in the middle of a case against tourists when a drizzle fell from the sky. The cool droplets left soft, tiny kisses on my skin.

I looked at the sky getting less gray with each drop. "Raining must make the sky so happy."

"But isn't the sky crying?" Through the mist, Mason blinked his blue eyes like a surfer sifting for waves in a rainstorm. "That's what I've always thought."

"I think they're happy tears. How nice would it feel to finally shed all that weight? You can tell the sky is happier now. See how much brighter it is?" It had to be happy tears, otherwise the world wouldn't feel so brand new afterwards. As much as it sucked to cry, it always made me feel better.

"I never thought of it that way," Mason said.

"Quinn, you want to learn how to skate?" Jorge looked at me after another lap around the parking lot, his black hair gelled back from rain.

Mom never really made a rule against skateboards in particular, but the bandages on the boys' knees would have put skateboards high on her *Don't Touch* list. That, and wheels. But she wasn't here and this was summer and I thought it looked like fun, so I let Jorge teach me.

He and Holden held me steadily on the skateboard. All I could think about were bandages and wheels. And helmets—they didn't have helmets. I squeezed Holden's shoulder so tight I worried I'd break him. I thought about wet roads and slippery wheels. Bandages slipping off in the rain. I couldn't stop screaming.

"Just trust yourself," Jorge said. "You have to stay calm."

I didn't explain that trusting people was last on my list of talents. Pinky promises I was good at, but trust? Not so much. I managed a pinky promise to myself. *Stay calm enough to get a ride in.*

With a tiny push, the boys sent me reeling through the rain-soaked world. I grabbed at the raindrops like they were tangible enough to hold me there. I clenched my knees just right and leaned before I lost my balance. I was doing it. I was skateboarding. My mouth was like a cloud that couldn't contain its excitement.

Maybe rain was actually the sky's happiness, too heavy to hold back.

I made it a few parking spaces before I realized I didn't know how to stop myself. I screamed for Holden and he ran over to catch me before I could scuff myself red.

And then the clouds split in two. It was too heavy to skate or see or even breathe. Maybe rain was actually applause? It certainly roared against the world like it. Maybe the sky was as proud of me as I was. My new friends sure were; I looked over and saw them cheering for me through the rain falling in sheets.

Because this was Piper Island, we lay on the sidewalk and let the rain melt us into one unit of friends old and new. I couldn't make out the sky from the rest of the world, everything bright white. I opened my mouth for the rain droplets and attempted to keep my eyes open, but trying made me laugh, breathless from the cold air and rain. If it weren't for my new friends laughing and yelling sweet nothings into the void, I wouldn't have been so keen on being soaking wet. Instead, I would have thought about one of my mom's tales of snotty noses after cold rain. Could my friends change other parts of me, too?

Before we headed home, I ran to the castle one last time through thick ribbons of water. The sand there was dark brown and flattened from the rain.

I found relief in my first hide and seek room. I wiped the sky's happy tears from my eyes and found a rock in the sand. The drier sand in there stuck to my skin like bandages.

On a space mostly untouched by names, I carved my own name. I added a plus sign, then scratched out an empty line below it. I wrapped it all in a heart, jagged in a war against the wood grain.

I left it open for the name of a boy who would one day love me.

I hoped once he wrote it, it would never fade.

Six Summers Ago
Age 12, July 4

THE SMELL OF A POOL should be bottled up and sold on cold days.

The last two summers, I had an amazing July Fourth with my friends, so part of me wished I was with them today, but mostly I was excited to spend the day with Blair and Hadley. Hadley'd been asking for days when we'd finally go to the water park. On the drive to Pirate's Bounty, Hadley heard us talking about the kiddie pool and asked to swim in the *cat* pool instead. We laughed and Blair told her she could go with me if she kept her life jacket on.

The busy July Fourth crowd made it hard to find a spot around the pool. We weaved through parents with their eyes splitting time between phones, books, and their swimming children. We found three chaises farthest from the entrance and set our stuff down.

After Blair helped me put sunscreen wherever I couldn't reach, I sat crisscrossed at the edge of the pool. I wanted to wait the recommended fifteen minutes for my sunscreen to soak in, but Hadley jumped right in.

"It's so cold!" she screamed. Her life jacket pulled her to the surface.

"Does it feel good?" I tested the water with my toe.

"Come in!" Hadley held her arms out for me like I was the kid and she was the adult.

Blair insisted nothing bad would happen if I went in before time was up, and she would help me reapply when we dried off. So, I jumped in to join Hadley. Cold water shocked me with teasing pin pricks. I kicked for the air as soon as I went under. Hadley reached for me when I wiped my eyes. I was tall enough in the three feet to be the adult again. The water was like Jell-O with a four-year-old propped on my hip.

"Can we go on the cat slide?" Hadley asked. She looked at the kids walking their foam mats to the mouth of the racing slides. It was a forbidden journey only older pirates were allowed to embark on.

"You're too little, I'm sorry."

"Well, can *you* go on the cat slide?"

"Yes." Should I tell her that her almost teenaged cousin was afraid of a dumb water slide? Lying was worse, so I said, "But I'm too scared."

"Oh, okay." She shrugged. "That's okay. We still have our pool."

We found a mostly empty patch of water between the red, white, and blue blur of people. I waited for Blair to look up from her book before I sent Hadley paddling in front of me. She made it a couple feet out, flapping like a bumblebee fallen into water. When she swam back, I couldn't resist scooping her back in my arms. She wrapped tightly around me until we were a pretzel, soggy from pool water.

We played I Spy, looking around at the kaleidoscope of color before us. Green dinosaur swim trunks, the American flag above the concession stand, the blue umbrella shading Blair. I couldn't find her "something orange" because it was actually coral: the life raft hanging from the lifeguard stand. After that, Hadley kept assigning something-corals, mystified by this new color I taught her.

I spied the brown of her darkening freckles. She giggled and spied mine right back. We balanced on two pool noodles that floated our way. I stopped Hadley from taking a huge bite out of it, but then she pretended to because it amused her to see me freak out.

Blair made her way over with goggles and pool rings. I tightened goggles around Hadley's head and felt my own snag at my wet, sticky hair. Blair threw the rings and I kicked off the wall for a hot pink one. Even in the shallow end, the water pushed hard against my ears. My goggles filled up in that slow way that I didn't notice until I couldn't keep my eyes open. Tiny white bubbles stuck to my arm hairs. I wicked them off my skin, watched them disappear.

This was why I loved swimming so much. It was the only time I could truly be part of a world I didn't belong in, at least until my lungs forced me back into the real world. I held up the pink ring ceremoniously, then gave it to Hadley who was tired of being trapped in her life jacket and scraping for the rings with her toes.

WHEN WE FINISHED EATING LUNCH, I told Hadley we had to wait thirty minutes before we swam again. Blair told me that was an old wives' tale, which, sure, my mom was *old*, but she wasn't a wife anymore.

I was ready to get back in, but Hadley was curled up sleepily in her towel, so I settled in for my own nap. The wet towel sent shivers across my body. I nodded off to the sound of Blair flipping through a book with a shirtless man on the cover. I couldn't fall asleep, so I watched Blair read and relaxed in tune with the page flips and distant water splashes and palm tree shudders.

"How's your mom doing?" Blair said without looking up.

I picked at some loose threads on my towel. I knew it was just a formality to fill the silence. Maybe she felt me staring at the new aging freckles burned on her shoulders. Or maybe she was just curious about her sister. She knew I talked to her on the back porch last night while she gave Hadley a bath.

"The same." My voice was quiet, joining the lulling hum around us.

Blair knew what I meant. To say my mom was the same was to say she still cared too much about pointless things. She went on dates knowing nothing would come of them. She buried herself in her work so the silence didn't wipe her out.

She walked life afraid.

Untrusting.

Worried.

To say my mom was the same was to say she was exactly like me.

Technically, *I* was exactly like *her*. I knew it was apples that fell from trees. I just spent a perfect pool day worried about wet sunscreen and parental supervision and swimming cramps.

Blair nodded and finally looked at me. Her tongue pushed through her cheek. "You know, it's okay to live a little." If she wasn't looking at me, I would have thought she was reading some kid-friendly part of her book out loud.

"Yeah." I inhaled, exhaled, waited a million years, then said, "I do. With the twins. And Mason and Jorge. I mean it, it's been a busy summer so far, doing all this living with them."

"Talk to me. What adventures do you get up to after I drop you off?"

"You know." I shrugged. "The usual itinerary things."

Mom always let me get away with "fine" when she asked how school was, but Blair looked at me with one dark eyebrow raised until I gave her a proper answer.

My lips drew pink lines in the sky and made bullet points from hearts as I filled the air with all the summer's events so far.

"We go to Sunset Scoop and ride our bikes to the beach. We sit at the dock while Holden and Mason fish. Sometimes I join in but I haven't caught anything since my first time fishing. We eat a lot of Hammerhead's leftovers. Haven even caught a fish with the hushpuppies as bait. Oh, and Holden and Jorge have been trying to teach Mason how to skateboard. I've tried a little more too, but I'm still not very good. Haven and I would rather collect shells on the beach. We're in a competition to see who can find an unbroken sand dollar first."

I smiled, thinking about Mason almost face planting in the road until Holden caught him. Thankfully I'd loaned him my knee pads. I thought about how dry my throat got after too many hushpuppies and the unbeatable way orange soda made it all better. I thought about the jar of sand dollar shards that made a home of my bedroom windowsill, and how amazing it would feel to replace them with a perfect one. I thought about how my skin hardened when I licked melted ice cream dripping down my arm.

Sometimes I managed to do things like that without a care.

"Also, we actually go *inside* the twins' house some afternoons to play cards and watch movies. We try not to fall asleep on the couch but we end up doing it anyway since the A/C feels too good after a long day in the sun. Haven calls it 'sun tired' and, boy, does it feel like that."

After blabbering every thought as soon as it came to me, I finally came up for air. Blair looked at me with an expression that mirrored mine, like she was living the itinerary through me.

"That sounds like living to me. Completely-unaffected-by-all-that-shit-you-went-through kind of living." She slapped her hand over her mouth like she couldn't believe it had just betrayed her. "Sorry, I didn't mean to curse or say anything like that. I didn't mean that."

Whether she meant to or not, I knew what she was talking about.

For me to have gone through "all that shit I went through" was to say that I couldn't do any living without running from the shadow trailing right behind it. Good times were only a sign of bad ones to come. The world needed that kind of balance.

Blair meant to say that *I* walked life afraid.

Untrusting.

Worried.

"It's okay. I hear bad words all the time at school." I ignored all the other things inviting the shadows to encroach.

"You're a good kid, Q." Blair smiled, different this time. It matched the sorrow in her brown eyes. "You know, sometimes I worry about how growing up with divorced parents will affect Hadley, but then I think about how great you've turned out. I can only hope Hadley turns out half as great."

I didn't say anything, just smiled with my mouth closed and tried not to let the shadow find me under this umbrella. It wasn't Blair's fault I felt this way. Plus, she thought I was great, so maybe I was just a little bit great.

"I hope you keep doing all that living. It sounds pretty fun."

"Pinky promise," I said, then I decided I'd better force a nap to ward the shadows off.

WE SWAM UNTIL THE SKY CHANGED COLORS. We swam until those changes spilled into darkness. We were still swimming, cold water clinging to our skin, when the fireworks were about to emerge from the night sky.

It was almost time for the Piper Island Fishing Pier firework show. Although we weren't on the shore, Pirate's Bounty was a popular place to watch them without fighting the evening traffic. The last two years, my friends and I never made it in time and ended up watching them through some trees at a gas station pump, then we lit sparklers in the twins' driveway as consolation.

Hadley and I claimed a shallow spot in the kiddie pool as Blair walked back from the concession stand, a shadow against the colorful concessions lit up orange.

She offered each of us a Rocket Pop. "An homage to summers past."

"Thank you," I said between my first licks.

It tasted like the past two July Fourths, melted fast in my hand, the juice dripping into red, white, and blue droplets in the water.

The floodlights cut out, followed by a blip of silence. A whole different set of lights cut in. Our eyes traced a glimmer of light, lost sight of it, then found it again as a dandelion puff against the night sky. A chorus followed, booming, whistling, and crackling so loud I couldn't help but blink even when I knew it was coming. The air smelled like Haven's room when she tried to straighten her damp hair. The lights danced on Hadley's face, too many colors to spy before they fizzled out in curly smoke ribbons in the next blast.

Hadley watched the exploding sky in awe. She puffed her cheeks up and blew air out to extinguish the fireworks hundreds of feet away. To her, fireworks were just birthday candles ready for a wish, a simple obstacle before frosting and cake.

I wished I could see the world the way Hadley did, concerned there was a fire in the sky that needed blowing out, confident her breath was powerful enough to put it out.

Now

July 1

"Hurry!" Everett shouts behind him.

The ferry waits for no one. I pick up speed despite the fact that I'm wearing my spilled iced latte. We round the corner of the loading dock, waving our arms like the ferry would even care. We scan our tickets and stumble across the ramp. At the bottom level of the ferry mostly full of locals avoiding the wind, we find a booth.

"We need to skip breakfast next time. And coffee." I wipe coffee from my arm, cheeks, and neck.

"We need to leave four hours early next time."

"Or just pull an all-nighter." Everett laughs and slides two fingers down a strand of my hair. "You forgot some."

This is the one thing Everett wants from our grand final summer—to climb the lighthouse on Loggerhead Island. Only accessible by ferry, the island doesn't allow cars, so we have a golf cart rental waiting for us. Had we missed this ferry, it would have taken another hour for the next one and we might have missed our golf cart rental window. I thought waking up before the sun rose would give us enough time to make it, but my bacon came out too late at Landlubber's Cafe and we stopped for coffee at a different cafe up the road. Too many locals were in line for coffee on their way to work, so it took longer than we anticipated.

On the water, the ferry rocks enough to tell me that we've taken off. With my eyes closed, it feels like I'm on a swing. About to fall off the rails. About to jump off just because I shouldn't.

With my eyes open, the shrinking land teases me. The seagulls at the stern multiply by a pile of Cheez-Its. The waves juggle my life in their hands. I don't like my chances. The subtle rock of the boat reminds me too much of last August, of Hadley.

I avoid eye contact with the windows and the sprawling ocean behind them, my eyes deciding that the linoleum table is more interesting.

Everett puts a hand on my knee under the table. Until then, I didn't notice how vigorously I was bouncing my legs. His touch pulls my gaze up to him, pulls my heart like taffy.

His questioning eyes are beacons on a night sky. "You okay?"

I nod and swallow, then try to force a smile. His eyes ground me. "Yeah. You want to climb the lighthouse, so we're going to climb the lighthouse."

"Thanks for coming."

Everyone else is busy today, so even though the what-ifs kept me up last night, I agreed to join him. I deserve to fall in love with living again, and that starts with ignoring the tornado of catastrophic thoughts that enters my mind whenever I'm out to sea. *What if we capsize? What if a whale surfaces? What if I glance at the water wrong and hallucinate the ghost of her?*

Everett points to a spot on the patterned linoleum. "This looks like a blobfish."

The corner of my mouth turns toward the ceiling. There's no blue sky above, no clouds either, at least not on the floor level of a passenger ferry, but Everett has brought the clouds to us. We can touch them. Decode their squiggles. Tell stories from the beige and white mosaic.

I point to a spot next to my forgotten coffee cup. "This looks like a tree with an owl hole."

"Or the big red storm on Jupiter."

The clouds on the table show us Christmas stockings, a cricket playing a banjo, two children fighting over a kite string. We map a new world despite the real world just beyond the windows. That world isn't for us.

Until it is.

The ferry jostles into Loggerhead Island Marina. After we disembark, Everett slinks into the driver's side of the golf cart and takes off for the lighthouse. The roads are shrunken, only suitable for bikes and golf carts. Landscaped trees line each side, breaking only for long driveways and the Cape Cod style houses sprouted at the end. We drive through palm frond shadows. I stretch my arm out to catch the wind, knit something like magic with my fingers.

The lighthouse, which is a mere chess piece from the banks of Piper Island, towers over the palm trees and mighty oaks. You could unearth stories from the shapes in the worn paint. The color of the moon and its craters, it looks straight out of a vintage postcard. From the parking lot, it's as tall as the Boardwalk Ferris wheel, and since I conquered that one last year, I know I can do this. I didn't get on a boat for nothing.

This is for Everett.

I look at him in hopes that he can read the sentiment in my eyes as we enter the ground floor room. It's dark and musty in the bottom of the lighthouse. Curiosity takes over as we examine the black and white blueprints like historians.

Before we ascend the staircase, an actual historian teaches us about its dramatic construction, the Destruction of 1877, the ghosts that "haunt" the stairwells as a result. I don't believe in ghosts, but I still shiver from the thought despite the hot, humid, unventilated room. Visions of ghosts cross my mind, tattered souls wandering the beach in ruffled, white dresses, lost in one way or another.

I wish they were real, so I'd know Hadley was still here.

I'd know Hadley was being taken care of.

Is Hadley over there, on the banks of Piper Island? Does she wonder why everyone left her there? Is it cold when night falls? Does she stand over a perfect sand dollar, screaming at distant beachcombers to grab it before the ocean takes it?

Do they know she's really talking about herself?

I don't believe in ghosts, but would it make things better to know that she's there and I just can't see her?

This is for Everett, so it's not time to cry. I bite my lip and look toward the end of the spiral staircase to distract myself.

I have the entire climb to compose myself, pretend I'm only distraught from the endless steps and summer heat. Everett goes ahead of me, clambering up the first set of stairs. We pass a few windows, which must have been put there to revive the lighthouse keepers, remind them of their ascension, assure them they're not too far from sunlight. Dust motes come to life inside the golden rays. Distant footsteps echo as we approach the top.

The stairs spit us out at the top. Once our eyes adjust to the blinding sun, the view takes our breath away. A sea of lush green treetops, paper white rooftops winking in the sunlight, waterways carved through the marsh grass like fireworks, exposed and ruddy in the low tide.

The panoramic view showcases each shade of blue swirling in the sky. No longer *just* blue; the sky is *every* blue. The horizon is moon jelly blue from a blanket of clouds miles away. The swath directly above us is sapphire blue, unobstructed by the spider web clouds. Where the blues meet, the sky is the color of Neptune. I bet if I touched it, my fingers would freeze.

Water surrounds us on all sides, its own confident shade of blue, unique from the sky, but only blue because of it. Since the lighthouse is situated on the top of the island, half of the view is the churning sea.

"Wow," I exclaim once I catch my breath. I could stand here forever, watching the tides cover the marsh and reveal it again. "Is this everything you hoped it would be?"

"More." The wind makes a mess of the hair just above his forehead.

My hand springs into action, but it's a fruitless endeavor this high up. His hair has a mind of its own, as does mine. "I can't believe you've never done this. You've been here, what, five years now?"

"Almost six, but they're only open in the summer and we've just never gotten around to it."

"I wonder what this looks like in the winter."

"Black, white, and dead, like those pictures at the bottom of the stairs."

I giggle. I understand what he means. Winter might as well be colorless, a photograph of summer left to wilt in the sun before it boards itself up for the off-season. This winter sent me into hibernation, but instead of sleep, I became consumed with homework, exams, college preparation, therapy, and my weekend job at the tennis court. On the coldest, busiest days in Raleigh, I wished to be a Piper Island toad warming on a rock, but there was life to live and a mind to keep in line, so I couldn't.

The first day the warmth came back, sap rose in my soul.

I woke up hungry for more. At least that has never changed.

"Except the sunsets. They're more vibrant in the winter. Something about clean, dry air and a lower angle on the horizon," Everett says.

"You researched that?"

He smirks at me. "You weren't born knowing that?"

"Of course I was." I smirk. Heat creeps on my face from more than just the sun.

Somewhere out in the middle of the water, a dolphin comes up for air, its gray skin glistening in the sun.

I gasp. "Look! A dolphin!"

It's gone as quickly as it came, but it returns a few waves down. With it returns our gasps. We lean farther off the railing like a few inches will make it easier to see. Another one appears behind it, then another, until all three dance among the waves.

I raise an eyebrow and look at Everett. "You know you can make wishes on dolphins?"

"You researched that?" he asks.

"Yeah, something about extending your good luck on a rare sight." I let him believe it for a half second, then nudge his elbow with mine. "No, I made that one up."

"We should still wish. You can't be too careful."

Nodding, I close my eyes and wait for a wish to emerge from the dark waters of my mind. I need to stop trying to fix the past, but I can't help the first thing that comes to mind.

I wish Hadley didn't get in the water that day.

Staring at the water from the cosmos, of course it's my first thought. Ghosts must be real, after all, and the ones at the lighthouse have been speaking to me all day. That's what echoed up the staircase. That's why the dust motes were so thick in the sunlight.

Everything is a ghost. Every memory is haunted.

The wall in my hallway, the ice cream shops, the books about the stars: all footprints washed away with the tide.

"What'd you wish for?" Everett asks.

It doesn't matter whether I tell him—this wish cannot come true— but Everett doesn't deserve the sorrow of the truth. Not on his day. Not on top of the lighthouse. Not in the presence of dolphins.

"Happiness," I say with a smile.

Five Summers Ago

Age 13, June 17

HOLDEN AND HAVEN DIDN'T SEE DANGER LIKE I DID.

Of course Saray insisted on coming to Sapphire Beach Boardwalk with us. My mom would have done the same, and she would have been upset with me if she found out we'd walked around by ourselves in such a public place. Walking around alone only felt safe on the island; Piper Island had a bubble around it that would never burst.

I didn't mind that we had to walk so close to Saray. How could I be mad? She bought me cotton candy.

Haven was not as content. Her sandals snapped louder than usual on the wooden slats beneath us. I offered her a pinch of cotton candy. She smiled and took some.

Boardwalks were pretty, but they also reminded me of gas stations—something about the bright lights visible in broad daylight and the vague smell of car exhaust. Not to mention the sweaty people we slunk through and the smell of cigarettes and beer everywhere.

We made our way to Tsunami, and then it was just me dissolving cotton candy on my tongue next to all the parents waiting for their adventurous children to get off the ride. Making small talk with Saray beat dying on a rollercoaster thanks to flimsy harnesses, even if that meant I had to watch my best friends die instead.

Saray started in, asking me questions about school and how I was going to fill my summer and the off-season back home. I told her that I loved school but always counted down to the summer on my school planner. I told her I planned to spend the summer doing everything with the twins and Mason and Jorge just like last summer, with riding Tsunami as the only exception.

She laughed and said something in Spanish, then agreed.

I told her all about my mom. I didn't tell her about my dad.

I thought she might have a clue. She was a mom, after all. *Haven's* mom, no less.

When the twins' train car made it down the big drop, they put their hands to the sky, mouths open wide. I couldn't hear them over the wooden creaks, but I knew they were screaming for their lives. Even though it looked like a fun time, I couldn't shake the words Mom said when we drove past the bright, beckoning lights of the North Carolina State Fair years ago. *Promise me you'll never get on one of those death traps.*

Promises are sacred, especially when sealed with pinkies.

The twins ran back to us.

"Quinn, you have to ride it with us next time!" Holden sounded like he was still on the rollercoaster.

Haven nodded, her hair crazy from the big drop.

"I like watching," I said to my flip-flops.

"It was nice of Quinn to keep me company," Saray said. She put a hand on my shoulder, squeezing tightly like we were buddies bonded from waiting together.

It was a weird feeling—a motherly touch not meant to scold me or keep me nine steps from danger.

We started to feel the effect of the June afternoon sun and escaped under a shaded picnic table. We ordered steamy corndogs from a vendor for lunch. It was almost too hot to eat them, but Holden still challenged me to an eating contest. I objected, but Haven took him on. Holden won, but I told them both I was the real winner for still having my corndog.

"I missed you, Quinn." Saray laughed heartily, revealing the wrinkles around her eyes. Mom had those same wrinkles whenever I actually got a laugh out of her.

Saray's phone pinged. "It's Everett's mom. She wants us to meet them at the front."

"You're going to love Everett." Haven grabbed my wrists and said with a laugh, "He's just like us—can't find his name in the gift shops."

I laughed and bit the last crunchy part of my corndog on our way to the front. I didn't have the heart to say I'd recently found my name on a few items.

Haven had told me little bits about Everett Bishop, their new friend from school. His mom, Liezel, immigrated to the United States from the Philippines and met his dad, Hank, in Chicago. Everett grew up in Chicago and moved down here once Hank sold his construction empire and used the profits to build a beach house, have a simpler life with his wife and son. What an impossible dream.

"He's way too nice and mature to be one of us." Haven looked at Holden, smirking. "I know an immature teenager when I see one."

Holden rolled his eyes and flipped her off, just like an immature teenager would. Saray couldn't resist a laugh, despite the promise to ground him later.

At the mouth of the Boardwalk, I saw who I assumed were Everett and Liezel. He had black hair curled like the ocean waves crashing below us. He was taller than her already, standing with his hands in the pockets of his board shorts.

The moms did some secret parental exchange while Everett joined us past the ticket booth.

"Everett!" Haven said, grabbing his wrist. "Meet Quinn!"

"Hello to you, too," he said to Haven. He turned to me and waved. "Hi, Quinn. I'm Everett Bishop. I've heard a lot about you."

I made a point to look him in his brown eyes, trying to make mine look just as happy as his. "Same. I mean, I'm Quinn Kessler, not Everett Bishop. I've heard a lot about you, I mean."

What in the hell, Quinn?

Everett laughed. "So Haven was right, you are funny."

"The *funniest*," Haven said.

What other things had Haven told him about me? He was probably expecting my dirty blonde hair and freckles, but was her story similar to what she told Jorge and Mason two summers ago?

If she told him I was funny, did she also mention the not-so-funny things? It didn't seem that way, because he seemed interested in me. Or maybe he really was as nice and mature as Haven said. Or both.

"It's great to meet you." I smiled and stared at a beauty mark in the center of his cheek.

It had to have been put there on purpose by some universal force that kissed little brown dots on people's cheeks. It was the same force that gave me and Hadley our freckles, but it must have lingered with Everett, molding his with more purpose so he could still wear his kiss long after summer was gone.

"I'm bored. Can we go ride rides again?" Holden faked a yawn, earning another sharp look from Saray.

"I forgot the world revolves around Holden Rivera-Sanchez." Everett crossed his arms and smirked, which earned a few laughs from everyone but Holden, who seems surprised someone finally played along.

We said goodbye to Liezel and headed to the end of the Boardwalk where the rollercoasters were. It smelled like a weird mix of fried Oreos, onion rings, soft pretzels, and popcorn. We slunk past the arcade's midday neon and the rigged games for the people who liked to throw money away.

When a game attendant noticed us, I looked down and pretended my ears didn't work, just like Mom taught me to do whenever a stranger tried to talk to me.

Back at Tsunami, I was a speck, a mere whisper among the distant screams, squealing chains, and groaning wood. Holden and Haven headed for the line, their hair waving goodbye for them. My sandals were stuck, melted in the sun like a piece of gum. Haven and Holden shrank from our sight.

Everett looked at me. "You don't want to ride it?"

If I hadn't been frozen here in this blistering heat, wearing fear on my face like sunscreen, I would have thought this Everett was very perceptive. Or maybe Haven told him more than I initially thought.

I shook my head. He must have thought I was so lame. Saray looked between us, sorry but silent.

"We could do the Ferris wheel instead." Everett pointed to the other towering structure above us.

Looking at it was dizzying. It felt like there was a wheel going round and round in my head. The Ferris wheel was a spindly, shaky monster that stared straight at the parts of the ocean deep enough to drown in. From that high up, it turned wooden slats into concrete bricks, people into ants, me into a pancake.

I raced through the horrors and gulped. "I'm scared of that, too."

"I am too. I was just testing you. You passed." His smile melted off one side of his face.

The way his chest puffed out when he spoke made me think he only just decided he didn't like spindly, shaky monsters. Or he could just be like me, with a mom who painted darkness in her child's eyes. I couldn't tell. No matter the truth, that made at least two smart kids in this place. We could make our own fun. That was what smart kids did.

"Let's ride the carousel," I said because I was getting tired of being a jagged shard of my mom. I wasn't crazy enough to ride the monsters, but carousels had to count for something.

Everett let me lead the way, half a shadow behind me. The railing was cold and stuck to my sweaty arms.

"How old do you think that gum is?" Everett pointed to a clump of gum next to his Converses.

It boasted its soot-colored glory. It looked like bird poop, or a very unlucky penny. I thought really hard about it, my fingers wrapped around my chin, a scientist mulling over the possibilities of the unexplored ocean.

"I think it's fresh. This is a boardwalk in June. It could easily look that bad after one day." I pointed to everyone around us: parents pushing strollers, gaggles of scary teens, seedy guys stumbling all by themselves. "Our shoes are filthy."

"True, but look how smooth it is. People have been stepping on this baby for years. It almost makes you want to chew up a piece of gum, stick it there, and come back a few hours later."

"I can't promise I won't send the twins to destroy it, Dr. Bishop."

I had no idea why I added that last part, but before I sank into myself, Everett chuckled. "That would be cheating, Dr. Kessler." He tightened a fake tie around his neck, his voice uppity.

My face warmed. He was willing to be just as dorky as me.

Everett Bishop really was as nice as Haven said, but mature, I had my qualms about.

When it was our turn on the carousel, I darted for the white and orange horse I'd been eyeing in line. It was a chore to pull myself up. I figured out the seatbelt situation and rested my temple against the bar. Everett buckled into the gray and teal horse next to mine.

Hidden in the shade of the carousel, the light bulbs glowed brightly in the daytime. Golden trim, red curtains, and porcelain horses waited for their millionth trip around nothing. I saw myself in an oval mirror behind Everett's head. My reflection shone back, bulb-yellow, red-faced, and freckled.

Everett looked at me in the mirror. I looked back at his beauty mark, yellowed in the light.

He turned around to look at the real me. "Haven told me about your necklace," he said.

"Oh, this?" I grabbed the three coquinas.

"When will you put this summer's shell on?"

"When it feels right."

"I think it's really cool. Piper Island does seem like a place you'd never want to forget."

"It is." I smiled and let go of the memories trapped in each shell.

A bell went off and the carousel cranked up. The horses started their dance to an airy carnival jingle. I watched the Boardwalk go up and down with me. Even though we were barely moving, my stomach got confused.

I looked at Everett to steady myself. He was already looking at me.

He must have been dizzy, too.

"How do you like North Carolina so far?"

"It's different," he shouted over the music. "So much quieter and slower. And you guys talk really weird."

"You think I have an accent?" I gasped fake offense. I never thought I was one of those southerners with a thick accent, but if anyone could sniff out the southern twang in someone's voice, it was a northerner. The thought of him noticing things about me the same way I'd noticed things about him made me feel warm inside.

"Like a hillbilly," he said in an offensively drawn-out accent.

"Your impression is awful." I laughed with my entire mouth.

I caught myself in the mirror, careless next to a boy I'd just met, conversing over the carnival tunes like we'd known each other forever. It felt like we lived on this Boardwalk and the carousel was part of our daily routine. Our new introductions felt more like old talks and old laughs. Natural, like how the moon churned the tides.

If this was what being on a rollercoaster felt like, then maybe my mom was wrong. Still, I needed to be careful. I needed to listen to my stomach, mad at me for the cotton candy and corndogs, and maybe something else I wasn't ready to admit just yet.

When we stopped spinning, a couple of kids ran to their parents who were hiding under the palm tree shade. The parents greeted their kids with open arms and mouths. They spoke words I couldn't make out over all the Boardwalk whirs, but the sight alone made my stomach untwist and twist again.

I wanted to run back around and ride again, but I'd already broken too many pinky promises, so I peeled my sweaty thighs off the horse and followed Everett out of the shadowy wonderland. On the way back to Saray, we passed a trash can that smelled like vomit. It toyed with my stomach. The twins still weren't done; they were back in line to ride Tsunami yet again.

Tsunami was easier to keep an eye on from this far away. The drop snarled when a train car rounded the curve. The wood looked beaten down from exposure to the elements, and you were supposed to trust that suffocating wood with your life.

Behind me, the carousel sang a lullaby. It was a twinkling sweet music box, the quintessential sound of sugar stomach aches and perfect days.

The two rides competed, yanking me in their impossible game of tug-of-war.

I looked at Everett. "You should join them."

He chewed on his lip. "I'm okay. It looks pretty scary to me."

"I'm glad someone agrees with me."

Under the shade of an umbrella, we talked about everything. What made us tick, what ticked us off, what stories we told ourselves to fall asleep. His favorite movie genre was science fiction, but he watched Hallmark movies with his parents. I told him about home: Saturday morning tennis with my mom and ice cream for dinner when I got a good report card. I told him there was nothing more fun than summer at Piper Island. I challenged him to catch up on the Piper Island adventures he'd missed the past few summers, and he told me that *mathematically*, he would catch up by the middle of February. I giggled and asked him if he *also* earned ice cream for dinner when report cards rolled around. He assured me he did get a food reward, only it was a Filipino dish called *pinakbet*, cooked with his choice from the fresh seafood market. "King crab legs," he said.

Everett pointed to a cluster of clouds in the sky. He spoke its shape into existence as an alien riding a UFO. I said it looked like spaghetti boiling in a pot. Saray agreed with him after some convincing. The wind that high up changed the clouds frequently enough to keep playing. The sky sent us a starfish. A cactus. A monkey wearing a Santa hat. A garden gnome.

The twins walked back with their clothes clung to them all wrong. They apologized for taking too long, but I didn't mind.

I was enjoying my time.

THE SUN FINALLY SET, so now the Boardwalk made itself glow. Lights zigzagged all around us, lining food vendors, wrapping around palm trees, and canopying between lampposts. Everything untouched by light was a deep purple color that smoldered opposite the golden glow.

After dinner and a competitive frenzy in the arcade, the Rivera-Sanchezes got on the Ferris wheel for a better glimpse of that post-dinner Sapphire Beach sunset.

Everett and I sat across from each other on a picnic table. He toyed with a bouncy ball he won with his arcade tickets while I pulled away at a new bag of cotton candy I bought with the twenty Blair had given me. It felt right for such a sky, all pink and cotton candy-esque on the horizon. My stomach reeled from all the junk food.

And Everett, I was finally ready to admit.

"I can't watch you eat that stuff." Everett eyed the bag and grimaced.

"It's one of my favorite things ever. It's what summer would taste like if you could turn it into strings, spin it, and stuff it into a bag." I rubbed the pink sugar between my fingertips.

"When you put it like that, it makes me almost want to like it."

I raised my eyebrows. "Well, what does Dr. Bishop like?"

"Dr. Bishop's a piña colada kind of guy. You have to admit, coconut is pretty summery too. If you could beat summer with a hammer and shred its insides to pieces, that's what it would be."

"Piña colada?" I wrinkled my nose. "It makes my jaw clench. Come on, just have a taste." I held some cotton candy out for him, a fluffy cloud shaped like nothing but cotton candy. The sweat on my fingers melted it into a darker pink.

"That's disgusting," he said, but his voice sounded all light and dreamy like cotton candy.

Or piña colada, if you were weird like Everett Bishop.

Now

July 4

THE ENTIRE ISLAND HAS LITTERED THE SHORELINE for the Piper Island Fishing Pier fireworks show. The sand is nearly inhabitable at high tide, so people are squeezed together in the short stretch of sand. Distant laughter travels over the dunes.

Haven and I spent the day biking the island, then we dressed up in red, white, and blue and biked to the Bishops' July Fourth cookout. It was a small affair. Hank grilled hot dogs for us, our families, and a few of his and Liezel's friends. Blair was invited, but she decided to catch whatever backyard fireworks shows were visible from our front porch instead. She made me promise not to stay with her and promised *me* she'd watch at least one show.

When night fell, Liezel passed out sparklers and let us light up the world orange. Tiny fireworks crackled from our hands in anticipation for the real ones. Hot sparks burned pin pricks on our hands. I wrote "Quinn" in cursive and wrapped it in a heart in the air. I ran to the edge of Everett's driveway, leaving an orange streak behind me.

The memories of the day wash over me as I shiver in the breeze, standing with my elbows against the railing on the back deck. Mason and Holden dared to rub elbows with everyone on the sand, but Haven, Jorge, Everett, and I are on Everett's back deck, watching the horizon like lighthouse keepers.

The clock ticks closer to nine-thirty. Do the constellations know what's about to happen? Do they twinkle with bated breath for the dandelion puffs to erupt before them?

We listen to the ocean and the laughter from the sand until a whistle washes over the crowd. A glowing line smears the sky and bursts into a firework—bright, loud, and steady. A string of crackly ones stall, then the rest take shape. My eyes blur, half blinking every time a new set goes off. Booms and crackles and colors fill the sky and reflect the same picture on the band of ocean stretched before us. Neighboring beach shows erupt as small blips on the distant shoreline.

I can't help but smile. Guilt doesn't erupt beneath it.

Fireworks stain the world; I spy each flickering color. The dunes glow green. The pampas grass glows orange. My arms glow red. Everett's smile glows blue. He's already looking at me when I look at him, our stares lingering enough to turn every color.

"How many shows are happening in the world right now?" I ask.

He leans in so I can hear him over the blaring static. "Infinite."

His breath feels like a firework across my neck. Beautiful and romantic, but not at all trying to be.

More quickly than a firework shoots to the sky and turns to smoke, the finale begins. The fireworks sing over each other, too many to make out one color from the next. Before long, everything stills. The conductor has waved his final baton. Smoke hangs heavy over the ocean like early morning fog.

Applause from the beach fills the void. The Bishops' back deck and the neighboring ones roar in very drunken applause.

We head below the house, where the Bishops usually park their cars. String lights hang from the rafters and illuminate the patio furniture. We play a few rounds of cornhole in the driveway with the adults until it gets late enough for everyone but us to leave. Everett's parents head up to bed after Everett pinky promises them we won't stay up too late.

When we hear the front door close above us, Everett goes into the shed next to their outdoor shower and emerges with beer. "You guys wanted a kickass July Fourth?"

So much for pinky promises.

I HAVEN'T BEEN DRUNK since one night two summers ago. I kept good on my word not to drink again, thought I learned from my mistakes, but the glow of the string lights and haze of the late night prevailed. I'm barely drunk, at least not like I know I can be. I count the beer can tabs in my pocket as a reminder. Three.

I snap another off the next can, shove it into my pocket with the rest. We're on our third attempted game of the evening. We started off with Clue, but Holden swore he solved the murder two rounds in and ruined the game. Next was Rummikub, which Haven won since she was the only one who got her tiles out after the first drawing. We were at a loss for what to do next until Holden got the idea to play Truth or Dare.

Mason goes first, daring Holden to ask the neighbors for something from their cooler. He marches across the street to the neighbors' driveway where they're having their own party. We can't hear their exchange, but he returns victoriously with a soda can.

Jorge asks Everett to tell the truth about the most illegal thing he's done. Besides sneaking into Pirate's Bounty—and the beer in his hand right now—it was sneaking outside candy into the movie theatre, which earns a few exaggerated gasps from the rest of the group, but a secret nod of shared guilt from me.

Prompted by Holden, Haven tells of her scariest experience, the ghost that haunts her *abuela's* house in Mexico.

"Holden insists it isn't real, but *abuela* says it only haunts *chicas*," Haven mutters. "It probably just hates you."

"I think if it's not haunting Holden, it must like him." Mason swigs from his can. "Right?"

"Doesn't everyone just *love* Holden? Even the dead," Jorge says.

"Hey, don't be jealous that this is the only thing that likes you." Holden nudges Haven with his elbow.

Everett dares me to do the Macarena. I jump up from the patio furniture, giggling that this is his dare. Haven helps me and we fumble through the steps. I sit back down and finish my fourth beer, my brain doing its own Macarena. I'm a loose cannon, high tide, pampas grass swaying in the wind. I'm only a few pegs of drunkenness beneath that night two years ago when I made out with a guy whose name I barely remembered. I could get there. I don't know the conversion rate between beer and tequila, but the first sparks of fire burn within me. This is a dangerous place to be. This is an incredible place to be. This is exactly the place to be.

I don't know how many drinks Haven's had, but I dare her to chug the rest of the can she's holding. She leans her head back so hard that beer dribbles onto the airbrushed *Haven* shirt Jorge bought her so she'd finally have a souvenir with her name. She finishes with an exasperated exhale.

Haven dares Jorge to kiss her. So she's exactly as drunk as I am right now. Jorge looks at her like she's the only person under the house and kisses her in the same manner. When she comes up for air, she wipes fallen beer from her chest.

Holden fake gags, or maybe it's real. I laugh at the absurdity of it all. Is it even that absurd?

Everett feels warm next to me, or maybe it's me who's warm. My face is a hot sidewalk mirage. Likely red. Definitely pink. No matter who's to blame, it's unbearable being skin-to-skin with him, sweating where our thighs touch. My heart beats, bathing in the warm beer.

Jorge seeks revenge and dares Mason to kiss Holden. Mason doesn't make quite the show that Jorge did, but he grabs Holden by the cheeks and gives him a quick peck.

Haven cheers, then leans across the coffee table, brushing her hair behind her ear. She whispers as if nobody else can hear her, "Quinn, I dare you to kiss Everett."

Even the partygoers across the street must have heard her. Certainly the hibiscus bushes by the outdoor shower did. My heart clenches up and pulses in my temples. I should have seen this coming.

I glance at Everett, who might as well be a statue. Like always, I can't read his poker face, but it's worse now that my brain's gone to mush. It feels like I swallowed concrete, but isn't this what I wanted? In an ideal world, surrounded by the people who make me feel steady in an ever-churning world, with varying levels of beer mixing with my blood, this would be the greatest opportunity to kiss him again.

Unfortunately, thick vines hold me hostage. Those vines do not sway like pampas grass in the wind.

Everett can't kiss me without it meaning something.

Everett can't kiss me and then go back to nothing.

Everett can't take it.

I tell myself these things like I'm not just talking about myself.

I force a smile at Everett. Haven doesn't seem to think she's done anything abnormal. Holden, Mason, and Jorge are perched in silence like ospreys waiting for a fish to jump from the water.

"I have to go to the bathroom," I say.

When I stand up, my feet fail me, and I nearly fall back on the sofa. But I quickly recover and slink up the stairs. I'm walking on clouds, up an escalator, propelling without thoughts to the front door. Talk about an escape. Inside, the dull kitchen sink light leads the way to the hall bathroom. I catch myself on the corner of the island, thankful it's not sharp.

I do use the bathroom; I wasn't lying. Too much motion has made the world spin on its axis. I steady myself on the edge of the sink, stare at myself in the mirror. My face is on fire. My mascara and eyeshadow show signs of their wear. My teardrop earrings fall in the wrong direction. My hair is swept into this mess with me. I laugh abruptly at my reflection. *What is happening? Kiss Everett?*

And what if I did?

Should I have kissed Everett?

No.

Yes.

I don't know.

I reach for the soap. The dispenser clatters into the sink. *Shit.* I cup my hand over my mouth. Silence. Are Everett's parents stirring? Silence. Another laugh leaves me. Thank God their room is upstairs. Everett's room is downstairs. *What is happening?*

Everett's room is downstairs.

I float over to his room. It's like a magnet or something, not me. Plus, the door is cracked. It's not like I broke in or anything. I've passed his room a few times over the years, but this feels forbidden, dangerous. I flick the light on with a chuckle that might only exist in my head. His green comforter is disheveled. Everything else is spotless. A clean room is important, but beds don't need to be made. Sounds like someone else I know.

On the wall above his desk, he's tacked his collection of postcards. Most must be from his nomadic grandparents. *Greetings from London! Hello from Manila! Banff National Park wishes you were here!*

The Chihuahua, Mexico one is from Haven and Holden. They sent me a similar one.

The postcard of downtown Raleigh is from me. I sent it when I was fourteen from a class field trip to a museum. I turn it over to read my message: *Today I saw a cloud that looked like a katydid. I could almost hear it buzzing from way up there. I think I heard it say, I miss you, Everett! See you under the same sky in June! -Q*

I wasn't surprised to see that Everett saved all his postcards, but what nearly knocks me over is what's on the windowsill. Next to a turtle with a hat from the pier shop, next to the bouncy ball I already knew he'd kept from the Boardwalk arcade, sits his shark pressed penny from the aquarium four summers ago.

The memory feels blue. Moon jellies. Regret. Butterflies. Warm penny wishes. Even warmer cheeks.

Everett raps on the door. "You okay?"

I turn around and can't help but laugh. He acts like *he's* intruding on *me*, but I'm the one caught red-handed in his room. I'm the weird one. I run my red hands through my hair. It doesn't do what I thought it would. The tension still zaps between us. "Sorry, I don't know how I ended up here."

He laughs, his hands in his pockets. "It's cool."

I graze the penny with my finger. "You still have it."

"Of course I do." His eyebrows furrow. He enters his own room like he's not welcome. Leans against his dresser. Arms crossed—the only other place he likes to keep his hands. "You don't?"

"I do. Just didn't think you would too. Mine's in my jewelry box back home. Remember the sea turtle?"

"Yeah."

I'm babbling too much. A babbling brook. I laugh. I've never heard myself talk this much. Can't decide if I like the sound. He's too quiet. I know I don't like that sound. His silence.

The spinning comes back. It never left.

A few paces away, there's too much space between us.

Something within me shifts. My heart and my lungs beat in quick confusion. Words no longer come easily. The beer stops writing on my tongue. There's only Everett. Curly, charcoal hair. Tan skin. The muscles visible where his arms wrap within themselves. Broad shoulders. His cheek that's always been home to the most beautiful beauty mark I've ever seen.

We're not fourteen anymore. That couldn't be clearer.

Perhaps it's a deep dive into madness. Perhaps it's just the truth that's always existed. Perhaps I haven't gone anywhere not yet travelled.

I can't take it anymore.

I kill the space between us. My hand ends up on his chest. I smooth out a crinkle in his tee shirt. There aren't any crinkles on his face, but I smooth those out too with my thumb.

I want to kiss Everett. I always did. We're already in his room. All we'd have to do is shut the door.

A truth vinyl spins in my head. "I don't know what got into me down there. I wasn't thinking straight. I shouldn't have run away. I'm here now."

He swallows so hard I see it in his Adam's apple. I think I hear it, too. A tsunami of noise. Finally, he takes his eyes off the penny they've been glued to. Looks at me, his eyebrows still knitted together. Clears his throat. There's no mistaking the fire in his eyes, the unspoken words on his lips. Nobody has ever looked at me the way he's looking right now. He wants to kiss me, too. I know it.

I wrap one hand around his neck, still warm like a summer night. My heart is about to burst from my chest.

He grabs my wrist, pulls my hand from his neck. Swallows. Something like pain on his face, but shouldn't there be joy? "Quinn, you're drunk."

Doesn't he want me?

"You're not?" I ask like I've been struck by the sky. I can't remember if he's been drinking, but he doesn't smell like beer. Not like me.

His pupils are dark, apologetic, cavernous. He rubs his thumb on my wrist. Warm and cold all at once. "Not like this."

He lets me go.

I'm freezing cold.

I float alone in a cavernous ocean. It only knows how to take. Take. Take. Take until I'm nothing.

He smiles at me sullenly. "Come on, let's go back downstairs."

THE RAIN FALLS DRAMATICALLY on Everett's driveway later that night. I lie dramatically in Everett's hammock. Everyone else left when the rain started, but I stayed to listen to the world receive the rainfall. The rain bathes the world of its sins, leaving it glittery and new.

Some beer has drained from my head, but the world still feels a bit blurry. I still the swaying hammock, freeze my eyes on the street to steady my stomach. I'm still not sober enough to go home yet, but I'm not drunk enough to kiss Everett; it's in the past now, but does it still swirl in Everett's head?

The stairs groan like stones skipping on each rung—Everett is on his way down.

He hands me a water bottle and sits on a chair across from me. "You feeling okay?"

"Yeah." I yawn and temper my fatigue with ice cold water. "Thank you for the water."

He shrugs. "No problem."

What is he thinking right now?

The unknown of it all feels like standing waist-deep in the ocean, unsure what's lurking just outside my line of sight. A defensive stingray, a perfect lightning whelk, something more nefarious, or nothing. It's usually nothing at all.

These thoughts don't leave my mouth, but they sit on the soft breath leaving my nose, the ache strewn across my face watching wet hair shade his face from the dull string lights. My eyes play tricks on me. I've been watching the rain for so long that looking at him brings lingering purple and orange motes to my vision.

I make a spot next to me on the hammock, brush my hand across the worn-down knots.

Come sit next to me, my hand says.

He stands up, makes some dramatic noise of it, and shuffles to the space next to me.

The hammock sways awkwardly until we find our rhythm. I steady us with my foot on a wooden beam. I'm dizzy again, but it's from more than beer and swaying—his body pressed against mine. His wet hair drying in tame ringlets. The smell of Old Spice. His biceps once pearled in water droplets, now dried off with a towel. His room that got to watch. What would his arms look like if we ran to the end of the driveway and let the rain make a mess of us?

His skin is warm from the steam, even warmer in the rainy midnight air. He smells like petrichor on a full moon night, something equally as light as it is dark.

"I could fall asleep out here," I say. My head lands on Everett's shoulder. I'm too tired to move it. I don't want to move it. My head is full of concrete. This time is ours, a sneaky chasm of our days usually packed with other people, a cave of secret moments only the rain and insects have ever seen. The rain claps for us against palm tree leaves, car windshields, scallop-encrusted driveways.

"It's like sleeping on a cloud," Everett says.

"I used to watch the clouds out my car window and wish I could sleep on them."

"Me too. I didn't realize sleeping on clouds would mean falling from the sky."

"Were you drunk earlier?" The words escape my mouth without thought, without hesitation.

"Does it matter?" His voice cracks.

"Yes."

"Then I was."

"Tell me the truth."

He clears his throat in the silence. "I wasn't."

I nod. He knows how badly I want to kiss him. All my cards are on the table, both of us staring at them, neither of us picking them up. He was sober when he laid his own cards on the table. *"Not like this."* That can't mean anything but *"I want to kiss you when we will both remember it."*

We'd both remember this. It's hard to forget rain this heavy.

"Are you still drunk?"

"Not like I was."

"What are you thinking right now?" he asks. Unspoken words dance between the spoken ones. *Tell me how you feel about me.*

"Nothing." My unspoken words stay that way.

I want to kiss you, but I'm too scared.

I want to fall asleep out here with you by my side.

I want you.

"Tell me the truth."

I open my eyes to look at him, until it's too hard to look at his puzzled expression, so I make eye contact with the dark, wet street again. "Rain."

"No, what are you *really* thinking?"

"That sleep would be nice." I lean my head back, smiling so my teeth glow the color of string lights.

"Oh my god, you're killing me."

"You mean you're *not* thinking about sleep, *Dr. Bishop*? With the rain falling like it is?"

"Of course I am." He pokes the spot above my knee. With my eyes closed, I can pretend it's because he wanted to reach out and touch me. Not because there was a speck of ash left over from the sparklers. Not because there's a freckle on my thigh that looks like a button begging to be poked. "Quinn, I dare you to tell me a secret."

I want to kiss you, but I'm too scared.

I want to fall asleep out here with you by my side.

I want you.

"They found some new species of jellyfish where the sun doesn't shine," I whisper so it sounds like a secret.

He laughs. Like really, truly laughs. The sound buzzes through my skull like a jellyfish sting.

"No *really*. It's all see-through and glowy."

"Translucent and bioluminescent."

I glance at him with a smirk. "So you've heard."

He rolls his eyes, then drops the subject.

In his silence, the rain picks up. I close my eyes again. It's impossible not to. My eyelids are heavy. I can't make sense of the words that leave my mouth, drunk on lack of sleep. Drunk on what makes you drunk.

"You think we can make it out here all night?" I ask the red hibiscus bush basking in the darkness. I tell my secret without telling it. *We*. I touch the same spot on his thigh like if I don't acknowledge him, he'll float away. I might float away too. Is it possible to end up somewhere more wonderful than this?

"I tried it once. It's eerie out here past midnight. Too hot and still."

My sleepy head floats on his shoulder. Fatigue tapes my mouth shut. *Take me to dream land where everybody floats.* Where nothing is too hot. Where nothing is still. Where I don't have to be drunk to shake this fear from my bones.

"Quinn. You can't go home like this. Let's go to bed." He taps my cheek, making new constellations from my freckles. I'm back in the land below the clouds. Below Everett's house. Everett's house. *Everett. Bed.* "Inside. You can stay in the guest room. My parents won't mind."

"I want to stay out here forever," I mumble from the gap in my lips.

"The bugs will eat us alive." He stands up, leaving me to spin on my own. For once, the bugs aren't on our side.

I pry myself back to reality, follow Everett up the stairs. Our footfalls aren't as steady as skipping stones. The magic dies inside where the rain and heat don't live.

He guides me to the guest room, snaps on the lamp next to the bed, and peels back the covers for me.

"I'm sorry, Everett," I whisper as I crawl into bed. A million secrets go unsaid, but Everett knows what I'm sorry about.

I want to kiss you, but I'm scared.

Reality is too hot and too still.

I'm sorry.

Everett takes my earrings off and leaves them on the bedside table. He pulls the comforter to my chin and turns off the lamp. "Goodnight, Quinn."

Four Summers Ago
Age 14, June 20

"I CAN'T BELIEVE I'M DRIVING YOU to a boy's house right now!" Blair looked at me in the rearview mirror, her face bright as the sun reflecting off the ocean.

"It's just Everett," I said as if I was trying to believe it. As if I saw Everett as a boy with "just" before his name. As if he didn't matter that much and I actually got sleep last night.

"*Just* Everett? Come on, you talk about him all the time, and I think he's a very nice boy."

"That doesn't mean anything." Except it did. Not that boys couldn't be nice and be talked about without it meaning anything, but it was different with Everett. Blair didn't have to know that, so I rolled denial from my eyes and huffed dramatically.

"Whatever you say." She dotted a pinky over her eyelid to fix her eyeshadow in the mirror, the same way people checked their teeth for food or lipstick stains before a date. But she wasn't going on a date.

And neither was I.

It was just a day at the aquarium.

So what if I caught myself in the same mirror checking my teeth for lingering bits of breakfast? So what if I wiped the summer sheen off my cheeks and wished I'd snuck some mascara and lip gloss from Blair's bathroom? So what if I paired cutoffs with my fanciest linen tank?

The reason we were going to the aquarium at all was that Blair won four tickets in a SUNY 95.1 radio contest, and she begged me to bring a friend. My first thought was Haven, but the Rivera-Sanchezes were in Mexico for the first two weeks of summer. That left Everett. Sure, I could have invited Mason or Jorge, they were *fine*, but they weren't Everett. Everett just *got* me. Ever since we met, we'd taken what was strange about each other and found a way to fit in those curves.

Blair pulled into the driveway of his beautiful house. Everett was the only one of us that lived oceanfront. Even Mason, whose parents could have probably bought the whole island, didn't live close enough to sleepwalk to shore. Everett lived close enough to have to turn his lights off at night for the baby sea turtles.

Everett walked to the car with his fists shoved in his pockets and his head down, looking up just in time to open the door.

"Hi," I blurted from the back seat.

He fastened himself into the passenger seat and turned around. "Hi, Quinn." He smiled at me, then hung over the seat to tap Hadley's knee. "Hi, Hadley."

It was weird seeing him up front next to Blair at first, but I quickly got used to it. With me in the back looking out for Hadley, it was easier to keep my eyes on everything else too. Everett Bishop was in my car. Sitting next to my aunt. Teasing my cousin. It had been less than a minute and already he'd wedged himself into my family for the day. It was real now. I slunk my sweaty thighs down the polyester seat and hoped it made me invisible. I checked my face for redness. Wiped more sweat off my forehead and onto the seat. Wished I could do the same to Blair's eyeshadow.

"So, Everett. What's your story?" Blair asked protectively, filling the empty shoes of my father.

Isn't that what dads were supposed to do? Grill anyone that got too close until they looked like blackened shrimp on a barbecue skewer?

Oh my God, Blair. I slapped my hand on my forehead and pressed my head against the cool window. She was supposed to be the cool aunt. When had she become so lame? How did she expect him to tell her his life story on the way to an aquarium? Where would one even begin?

But Everett didn't *look* fazed; he hadn't a complaint on his breath. "I moved here from Chicago last March."

Everett decided his life story began in Piper Island, or maybe he thought that was all Blair cared about. Maybe that was all *he* cared about. He told her about transitioning mid-year into the local middle school, trying and hating sweet tea, how long it took him to get used to southern humidity and moody weather.

"There was a point when Quinn actually knew more about Piper than me." He turned around and smirked at me.

I scoffed playfully and wondered how much of my face he saw—if he saw the sheen the way I did.

"I'm sure you caught on fast, just like Quinn did, huh? It's pretty amazing here."

"Especially in the summer. Even with all the tourists." Everett looked at me again, his eyebrows raised in the beginning of a laugh.

I rolled my eyes. "I'm not a tourist. I'm *local adjacent*. It's different." I checked myself in the mirror. Resented the rosy cheeks staring back.

"All I'm saying is that tourists love the aquarium."

I stuck my tongue out at him. "Haven loves the aquarium."

"Haven is Haven," he said.

I couldn't argue with that.

When we got to the aquarium, we stammered into a heat that was like a desert mirage snarling off the sidewalk. Fish statues hung suspended above a wishing fountain. Everett walked next to me as Blair held Hadley's hand over asphalt so hot it could melt the shoes off our feet.

Once we got past the ticket booth, Blair told us to meet her and Hadley in three hours. We hadn't discussed this before, but Blair must have had her own idea of how today was going to go. The way she looked at me, eyes shiny like her abalone eyeshadow, told me she wanted me to be alone with Everett, playing Cupid in a world where Cupid should be shot.

I sharpened my eyes at her but softened them before Everett noticed. I smiled at both of them and hoped Blair could see through to the disdain. "See you in three hours." I surprised myself with how normal I sounded when I would have preferred to lie out on the sidewalk and cease to exist.

But instead we set off into the freshwater exhibit while Blair and Hadley stayed back to "use the bathroom first."

The air in the room was thick. If you breathed in too much, your lungs couldn't hold it all. It was so warm and damp that our clothes clung to our skin like wet bathing suits. It was thick and warm and damp—the perfect air for two people who didn't know how to act around each other.

I bet that was how Everett's hands would have felt if I held them right now. Not that I *wanted* to hold them. Neither did he. His hands were deep in his shorts pockets. And I was, well, me.

Everett walked to the first tank. I joined him, staring at an alligator floating idly in the water. It looked fake until it finally looked at us like *we* were the attraction. What was she thinking? Did she have some alligator friend in there that was so cute and cool that she didn't know what to do in all the thick, warm water? So she just thrummed there, her only movement a steady blink, trying to figure out what to do?

"Do you have something in your eye?" Everett asked.

"Yeah. Must be an eyelash." That was why people normally blinked their eyes, right? Not because they were pretending to be a love-stricken alligator in a tank or anything stupid like that.

"You might want to *gator* it out."

I looked at him. Seconds of silence passed before my mouth won the battle between smiling or not. Finally, we erupted into an ice-shattering laughter. It was a wonder it didn't break all the tanks around us and send us swimming through the glass ceiling.

I swept a ceremonious finger through my eyelashes. "I think that *gator* it." The pun sounded even dumber from my mouth.

Now with the proverbial ice all broken, Everett and I walked across its shiny shards to the next tank. He made another ridiculous joke. I did a disappointed-but-not-really head shake until it spilled into a giggle. We did this same push and pull at every exhibit. We teased a pond slider turtle for facing the wrong way. We named him Holden since his expression was stuck on annoyed and his defiance looked intentional.

Everett made a terrible joke about a school of rainbow trout swimming in a fake current, thus never going anywhere at all.

"If I could speak fish, I'd tell them it's a trap." My gaze was fixated on the way they moved in unison through the fabricated stream. "Do you think they know they aren't really moving?"

"I don't think they know what water is."

"Of course they know what water is." I said, half offended. "Maybe not while they're in it, but they sure do know how it feels to go without it." My mind wandered off some sad, deep end into my own woes.

"That's very poetic of you, Q. Now I feel bad for these trout. You've made me really *char* about them." Everett stopped my mind from careening, like a fake stream that kept me from veering too far at all.

"Ouch. That one was bad." My smile made it seem like it was his best. The best at being the worst. The best at pulling me out of the deep end.

"That's not very *char*ring of you." He winked.

When we'd exhausted our jokes in the freshwater room, we walked through the double doors into the Tidal Zone. Finally, I could breathe again, A/C peeling our clothes off our skin.

"What I like about this aquarium is it makes sense. It's like we're working our way from freshwater streams to the bottom of the ocean."

"You sound just like a tourist right now, Everett Bishop."

"I resent that, Quinn Kessler."

My name sounded a whole lot like he practiced it in the bathroom mirror the same way I'd practiced my facial expressions last night. It sounded a lot like the smile on his face—soft and confused about how much he truly resented being called a tourist.

When I smiled back, it was nothing like the ones I decided on last night. Instead, it felt soft and confused about why his dumb jokes didn't sound so dumb at all to my ears.

"You ever done a touch tank?" Everett led us to the touch tank.

"My mom says it's how you get diseases." I hid my hands in my pockets like he always did.

"Come on, you gotta try it. It's awesome."

"When my mom told me not to fall for peer pressure, I don't think this is what she meant."

"You're not falling for peer pressure; it's *pier* pressure." Everett pointed to the pier painted on the wall behind the touch tank, just in case I didn't hear the pun in his inflection. "Pier pressure is way more fun. And not dangerous like the peer pressure moms warn us about."

I let out a little snort. "You're so dumb. Why do your puns still surprise me?"

"Because you don't spend enough time with me." A look flashed across his eyes. He gulped and stammered, "Come on, touching a hermit crab isn't a gateway drug." Everett stuck his hand in the touch tank, gently inching back a hermit crab shell to force it out. The hermit crab dangled out, antennae dancing wildly in the water. "Hi, Quinn!"

I knew the crab was a crab, but a small part of me believed it really was waving at me, begging me to join in. It only sounded *vaguely* like Everett putting a voice on.

Part of my mind wanted to listen to Mom's voice in my head, but something about the dopey grin on Everett's face made me want to touch the hermit crab. And a sticky anemone, a stout horseshoe crab, a spiny sea urchin.

I touched the starfish at the same time as Everett, feeling an unrehearsed, dopey grin on my face with each touch.

When we finished, Everett didn't laugh when I was on my second hand-wash. Or when I checked my forearms for that salty smell and washed a third time. In fact, he joined me.

We made our way to the Reef, coming face to face with rainbows of corals and Nemos, Dorys, and Gills all around them. I was sure Hadley and Blair would think the same considering how many times we'd fallen asleep watching *Finding Nemo* together. I was about to make a joke about how they weaved in and out of the coral, but Everett was standing before the jellyfish tank.

It was dark over there. A large sheet of dark blue outlined his silhouette. Even in the shadows, I knew his hands were stuffed in his pockets.

I joined him in the quiet. These jellyfish demanded a special silence, the way they floated through the water like it wasn't even there. Their bodies were illuminated by the blacklight, a soft blue outline carving out what we otherwise might have missed.

How could something so beautiful be so dangerous?

I watched Everett watch the jellyfish. His face and that beauty mark on his cheek were lit the same ultraviolet blue. His mouth was open slightly, lost in awe. He was so beautiful, even with that expressionless expression, watching another beautiful creature pulse through the water.

He must have felt my stares, because he turned to look at me. This gave me two seconds to decide if I wanted to pretend I wasn't just staring longingly or pretend that my own expressionless expression was only from the jellyfish.

In a moment of courage, I kept my face on his, taking back some control with a soft smile. "Your face is a little blue."

"So's yours." He smiled. His teeth shone bright white in the blacklight. "I wish I had a pun for it, but it's just blue."

Just blue. If just blue were as beautiful as him, then I hoped for a lifetime of just blues. *Just blue* like the very deepest the summer sky gets. *Just blue* like the off-brand cotton candy ice cream colored the wrong shade. *Just blue* like a dark living room during an afternoon thunderstorm.

Just blue. The haze that kissed us from the moon jelly exhibit at Piper Island Aquarium.

My heart was thrumming too fast. My hands felt cold and clammy. My guard fell to the floor around *two* beautiful, dangerous things.

"Blue is kind of ugly," I said. I knew it would shatter the moment, but ruining nice moments was easier than letting them ruin you.

The look in Everett's face ruined me anyway. His face fell so subtly that I would have missed it if I hadn't been so mesmerized by him. My heart went with his face, both of them scorned and lifeless. I'd never seen him look like this, but I should have known I'd make him feel like this eventually. Better to show myself—the poison that hid beneath my guard—sooner and let him run away and save himself before it was too late.

"Come on, let's go to the Deep Ocean," I said in an attempt to revive the moment.

Everett followed me quietly downstairs to the next exhibit. It was just as blue, but I felt more comfortable away from the moon jellies. In the two-story showcase tank, small hammerhead sharks, stingrays, and a sea turtle swam around in circles. A school of skinny, silver fish like the ones in the fountain outside carved their own path.

Everett and I had carved our own path as well, swimming between discomfort and delight throughout the day. After what just happened, this tank brought us back to delight. Inside the tank was a spherical indentation meant to get you closer to the fish.

"I dare you to go inside," Everett said. "Real peer pressure this time."

I raised an eyebrow. "Meaning it's dangerous?"

"No." He smirked and rocked on his heels.

"Then you go first."

"Pinky promise you'll go in, too?" He held his pinky out.

I linked pinkies with him. "Pinky promise."

He crawled into the tank, an inviting smile on his face. If he could do it, then I could too. I pinky promised, after all. I shrugged and crawled my way into it. It was deeper than it looked. I turned around and rested my back against the clear tank, dizzy from the water's distortion, paranoid we were going to burst through it. The shape pushed us into the middle. We were pressed into each other on one whole side. My throat felt stuffed with cotton, but not the candy kind.

Everett pointed to the belly of a hammerhead, the gaping mouth of a stingray. A sea turtle swam over us. I gasped and laughed like I never thought I could. I pointed at it, smiling my cheeks into apples. We were wrapped up in another *just blue* haze, and Everett watched me instead of the sea turtle.

I wondered if his cheeks were apples, too.

OUR THREE HOURS WERE ALMOST UP, so we worked quickly through the rest of the tanks. Halfway across the floor, I stopped in my tracks. My pulse quickened so rapidly I felt it in my toes. A chill zapped through me. The cotton feeling came back.

Everett stopped. "What's wrong?"

"The whale," I said to our toes. "I'm afraid of whales."

I couldn't look up from the blue ocean lights dancing on the carpet. I was too afraid to even look at the beast responsible for the large, whale-shaped shadow we were standing in.

"Whales? *That's* your fear? Why not sharks?"

I didn't tell him about my real, deepest fears, the ones you shouldn't bring up in an aquarium with your friend. I didn't tell him I would have swam with the whales if it meant being able to trust people. If it meant I could stop calling someone my friend when I really wanted them to be more.

"It's something about the shape. And the size."

I pictured the horrid ridges carved down its bloated white belly. Barnacles stuck to its fins like mold to an abandoned beach house. I'd only ever seen them in Hadley's picture books and that scene in

Finding Nemo, but I turned my head when I knew it was coming. "Let's go look at the seahorses, then." He held his hand out.

A hand is different from a pinky, but my mind wasn't working right, so I took it. Let him lead us to shallower waters. I was holding his hand. Everett Bishop's hand, wrapped in mine like a seahorse's tail grips swaying sea grass. I couldn't figure out who let go first, but I still felt his touch buzzing in my hand as he cracked jokes about the baby seahorses and snow crabs and lobsters. I didn't catch the punchlines.

When we were done exploring, we killed the rest of our time waiting for Blair and Hadley in the gift shop. I squished a penny into a sea turtle and Everett squished his into a shark.

On the way out, it was hotter than earlier. The sidewalk melted our shoes on the way to the car. We followed slowly behind Blair and Hadley, our shoulders brushing each other's without a spherical tank needing to do the squishing. Everett stopped me at the fountain and pulled two unsquished pennies from his pocket.

My hand acted on autopilot, opening for the penny. At this point, Blair was nowhere in sight, probably watching us through rows of hazy car windows, giddy because we were staring at each other in front of a wishing fountain.

"You can't pass a fountain without making a wish," he said.

He closed his eyes. He mulled over a wish for a few seconds, then threw the penny behind his shoulder. The way his eyes shifted under his eyelids made it seem like he'd done this at a million other fountains. His confident smile indicated that every single wish had come true.

Before he could catch me staring, I closed my eyes. I whispered my wish into the penny warming in my palm, sent it soaring behind my shoulder, and listened to it splash the water. I pictured it floating down to make a permanent home next to someone's wish for money or fame.

It was the same wish I had whispered to every cheek eyelash, flickering birthday candle, dandelion puff to the wind. It was what I would wish on a shooting star if I were ever lucky enough to see one.

I wish my dad had never hurt my mom.

The wish didn't come true, of course. That was what happened when you wished for something that couldn't come true. Or when you assigned belief to things that didn't make logical sense. You couldn't rewind tape that was already spun out.

Maybe I should have wished that I'd see a shooting star one day—then I could ask the star for help and hope it had enough power to turn back time and fix the unfixable.

Life didn't work that way. Wishes were for fun. At least, they were supposed to be.

"What'd you wish for?" Everett asked.

I opened my eyes and blinked away the sudden brightness. My face managed a smile that I tried to hide between my lips. "I can't tell you. You know the rules."

"Well, I wished that you'd tell me your wish."

"That's a dumb wish. And you told me, so it can't come true."

"Huh, you got me. I guess you're right."

"Guess so." I raised my eyebrows with a smirk and turned on my heels toward the car.

THE DRIVE BACK TO EVERETT'S HOUSE was filled with talks of our favorite sea creatures. Everett recited his top puns for Blair. Blair rolled her eyes at them the same way I did. Hadley excitedly babbled about her favorite fish. Her cheeks rested on her new dolphin stuffed animal. The evening air streamed in from the cracked windows.

It helped me forget the jellyfish threatening my mind.

When we got there, Everett thanked us again and said his goodbyes. While Blair backed out of the driveway, I rolled my window down.

I waved and shouted out the window, "Hey, Everett! *Sea* you later!" I emphasized it so he could hear the pun.

He pivoted on his front porch, waving back. "You *shore* will!" He shouted his own pun through megaphone hands.

A laugh escaped me while I rolled the window up. I threw my head back onto the headrest with a smile, watching the houses blur by.

"You like him," Blair said with a laugh from the driver's seat.

"I do not," I said. I watched my face turn red in the rearview mirror.

Four Summers Ago
Age 14, June 22

"SLOW DOWN!" EVERETT SHOUTED FROM BEHIND ME. I barely heard him over the *whooshing* wind.

When I agreed to grab Sunset Scoop with Everett, I didn't think it would transform into a bike race to the beach, but winners couldn't complain. The wind was salty from the nearby ocean, humid from the summer evening, brisk from my growing speed on the bike. My muscles burned through every push, but I leaned forward and gripped the handlebars so tightly my knuckles lost color.

"In your dreams!" I shouted, but he was so far behind me that the wind stole the words before he could hear them.

I reached the top of a small hill. On the way down, I stopped pedaling and let the decline take me with it. The trees became an emerald blur. The sunlight blinked on and off through the leaves, leaving shadows like Queen Anne's lace on the path ahead. The wind put its fingers around my lungs and squeezed. I put one hand out to catch the wind. I bet this was what it felt like to drop down a rollercoaster.

"Why'd you stop?" Everett screamed as he came up beside me. He pedaled with the downward momentum until I was the one chasing after his words like catching fireflies for a mason jar. He disappeared when he turned onto a road off the trail.

I kicked back into high gear, my legs ringing in protest. I almost won, but he passed the green Ocean Drive sign seconds before me.

"I win." He skidded his Converses against the concrete.

"Barely." I stuck my tongue out at him and hit the brakes. In the still air, sweat beaded down my back. I hoped I didn't lose my mascara and lip gloss in the wind. "New challenge. Whoever gets to the bike rack slowest wins."

"Did I *tire* you out?" Everett laughed at his own dumb line.

I rolled my eyes. "If that's what you want to believe, then yes."

"It's fine by me. Ocean Drive demands slow biking."

He was right; Ocean Drive boasted million-dollar houses with billion-dollar views, and palm trees were more abundant than mailboxes. Locals rented out these houses to ocean-starved tourists who wanted to wake up with the ocean outside their bedroom window. I understood; I was tourist adjacent, after all.

We biked so slowly it couldn't really be called biking. I pedaled just hard enough to keep from wobbling.

He pointed to a house the blue color of Mason's eyes. Three stories, a blinding white balcony off every door, grass as green as a street sign. "I bet a woman named Matilda Ainsworth lives here. Her husband is on a 'business trip' in Italy. While she waits for him to come back, she eats imported lobsters, fresh crab cakes, and oysters. It's where she gets the pearls for her necklaces."

"You're being ridiculous," I said, but I felt like I could crack my chest open and find a pearl where my heart should be.

"Come on, try it. Tell me who lives here." He pointed to a house the color of dried pink roses. A row of pampas grass sprouted along the driveway paved with individual gray tiles.

"You're such a dork." I nudged his bike tire with mine but decided to play along. "Let's see. His name is William. He made billions playing tennis. He spends his days drinking thousand-year-old wine and eating goat cheese and cucumber slices on his dad's sailboat."

That exact picture was on a billboard on the way to Piper Island. If there ever were a misleading advertisement, it was that one. Piper Island had a lavish side, but it was mostly an island for drinking homemade lemonade on pastel Adirondacks, wearing bikinis for bras or swim trunks for shorts, and spitting watermelon seeds into the grass in hopes that you could grow your own.

"There you go!" He pointed to a navy house. "That's Leonardo DiCaprio's house."

"No way." I pointed to the house next to it, a coral one with windows that reflected the blue sky back to us. "*That's* his house. He would never own a navy house; it's too much like the water the Titanic sank in."

"I think you're right. And obviously *also* a dork. And obviously can't separate actors from their characters."

"It's what I do." I shrugged and let Everett bike ahead of me until he ended up first at the bike rack. "I win."

Everett didn't protest. We steadied our bikes in the bike rack and headed for the shore.

I followed him down the stairs and to the sand. The ocean and the summer breeze roared in unison. My hair joined the rush, but I gave up taming it. Everett hobbled over the mounds to keep his balance. He was so focused that his eyebrows scrunched up. His hair blew in the wind, moving in and out of perfection until he settled on imperfection.

The wind was a sculptor, turning his hair into disheveled-on-purpose art. I wished I were a sculptor, too, but I shoved my hands in my pockets. *That* feeling I could tame.

"Hey, Q, look." Everett pointed to a pile of jagged gray oyster shells. "It's Mrs. Ainsworth's dinner. Her butler just threw them out."

I put my hand over my mouth. "I heard she found a pearl."

"I heard she found *two*," he whispered.

We gasped so loudly Mrs. Ainsworth probably heard from her widow's walk. It spilled into a fit of laughter so loud that I *knew* she heard it. I hoped it helped her miss her husband less.

We stood where the waves stole shells from the shoreline, where the sand looked like coffee grounds. How long would it take the sand to swallow us whole? Probably an hour, maybe thirty minutes. During the rewind of a wave, a litany of coquina clams showed themselves before they shimmied away from the sunlight.

"Is that the shell on your necklace?" Everett asked.

I nodded. "They're called coquinas."

"Where do the holes come from?"

"Moon snails. The clams close up when they get scared, so the moon snail drills a tiny hole in the shell and sucks the clam right out, Matilda Ainsworth style." I touched my necklace, felt its coolness on my fingertips. "Then the shells are left behind, ready to make necklaces with." I'd checked out a few books about shells during trips to the library with Blair and Hadley. I had to know more about the shells I carried like summer around my neck all year round. "So, technically I'm wearing a crime scene around my neck and calling it summer."

He laughed. "The best kind of summer." He picked up one with a hole in it. Coral lines orbited it like Saturn's rings, its underbelly the color of rose quartz. "It's hard to believe something died in this."

"Well, that's life. Sometimes ugly things happen and leave beautiful things behind." I shrugged and studied the shell in his palm. "It's nice."

He looked at me. I couldn't read the expression in his face, but then he shrugged and put the shell in his pocket.

A patch of seagulls flew overhead, then landed halfway between us and the pier. I wanted nothing more than to disturb their peace, run as fast as my feet would let me, watch them fly away.

"Tag, you're it!" I tagged Everett, then took off.

The wind blew through my hair, sending blonde strands down a trackless rollercoaster. I whipped around mid-run, catching a glimpse of Everett taking off for me and the seagulls. The seagulls were farther away than they looked, a mirage against the flat, dark sand. This scene demanded a flowy white dress and long, wispy hair. I didn't have either, but I did have my legs and breathless laughter and my hair clipped at my shoulder blades but still flying. I ran open-armed across the sand where the wind and sun and salt air opened their arms back for me.

For us.

For the sun that pecked at everything. For whatever that feeling in my chest was when I looked at Everett. I screamed and refocused my attention on the path ahead. The seagulls took off like an explosion across the sky, splitting before our very eyes, gone in an instant.

I let him catch up, spinning on sandy heels. He tagged me but miscalculated his force, sending us both tumbling down to the sand, like dandelion puffs in the air after the wind made a wish. We were dizzy and out of breath and smiling at each other on the same patch of cold, itchy sand. It was still early summer, so the heat hadn't yet killed all the things that swayed thin in the air like dandelions.

Did the wind wish for love or joy or stability?

Would I have wished for the same things?

"WHAT'S SOMETHING NOBODY KNOWS ABOUT YOU?" Everett asked.

The bike trail was alive with the magic of a summer night. Insects chirped from the canopied trees. A purple sky peered through the leaves. The air pressed like cool oyster shells against our skin. After golden hour at the beach turned to twilight, it was time to head back home. We grabbed our bikes, but neither of us bothered to hop on. We set off on foot from Ocean Drive to the dark, secretive bike trail.

We weren't likely to beat the streetlights home, but I'd tell Blair we lost track of time.

I didn't feel like talking to the wind this time.

Not with Everett walking beside me.

"Summer is the only time I really feel alive," I said casually, like I wasn't baring my soul.

"I think I already knew that." He laughed. "You're like if summer were a person."

I laughed, embracing the feeling of summer, warm and endless in my wake. Clammy air, purple twilight, insect songs. "Then my plan is working."

He smiled. "I love summer, too."

Then my plan is really *working.* "What else do you like?"

His eyes left mine and focused on the winding trail ahead. This was serious business, talk of grander things than summer itself. "Standing ovations." He snickered like that was supposed to sound silly. "And then when the applause starts to sound like something entirely different."

Today our only applause was the buzz coming from the trees, cheering for two teens about to miss curfew but slowly meandering anyway. "I like when people crack their knuckles before they do something important."

"I like when people are bowling and they do that little lean to try to move the ball."

"I like the crunch of pine cones on the road." I made the noise with the front tire of my bike, hopping over a fallen pine cone.

"I like finding shapes in the clouds. My mom started it once on a long road trip and it kept me busy the whole time."

I thought of the day at the Boardwalk last year, the shapes we made from the clouds, and how they gave me glimpses of him like a Rorschach test. He saw roses instead of thorns, flames as a magical source of warmth, moon jellies instead of sea monsters.

He viewed the world like it hadn't yet betrayed him. Maybe it hadn't.

"I like the word 'quintessential' because it sounds like my name. I always use it during the name game at school," I said.

"Quintessential Quinn," Everett said ceremoniously. Red splotches emerged on his cheeks.

What image would they conjure up if they were Rorschach inkblots? What would I see if I were Everett?

"I like when people talk about the weather when they don't know what else to say."

"I like when it rains at night and the streetlights look all smudged on the windshield," I say.

"I like the voice people use when they talk to dogs."

"Is there anything you *don't* like?"

He looked at me like I'd snuffed out the magic, but he answered anyway. "I don't like when there's cool stuff to look at in the checkout line but the cashier stares at me so I feel like I have to buy something. I bought a turtle figurine with a top hat at the pier once because of that."

I remembered our time at the aquarium a couple days ago. In the gift shop, we'd looked through the mood rings to the dismay of the cashier.

It felt wrong to try them on and not buy them, but I just wanted to see how accurate they were. I hoped mine would turn pink for *romantic*, but both our rings turned dark blue for *calm*. I was anything but, so I chalked it up to the warmth on our fingers.

"I love when the trees sound like summer," I said, snapping back to the present as the symphony around us reached its emotional peak. It sounded like a rain stick, applause, buzzy conversations we couldn't hear the words of.

Everett stared at the darkening sky and laughed, warm like weather we didn't need to talk about. "Would you think I was weird if I told you I know which insect makes each sound?"

If my face were a mood ring, it would have turned whatever color indicated hot skin. I knew there were different species, but they sounded the same to me—a glorious conglomerate of summer night sounds lighting up the bike trail. "I would say, 'Enlighten me, Dr. Bishop.'"

He listened for a moment, mulling over the noises hidden in a clump of trees. "The locust is the easiest to hear. It's the one that starts and stops and starts and stops." He held his hand up and yo-yoed with the air like he was conducting their song. Following his hands, I could hear it for myself, the sound of someone pulling on a lawnmower that wouldn't quite crank. It sounded like if ocean waves could emit radio static.

"The cicada is more constant. Think of it like the background noise. If you're not listening, you'll lose it."

I tuned my ears away from the undulating sound of the locusts. Layered beneath it was a low, twinkling whir. There *was* variation in the sound, but it was small enough to consider it background noise.

"Like a white noise machine," I said.

He nodded. I could barely make out the outline of his cheek from the leaves behind him. Summer nights fought as hard as they could, but when they finally came, they struck like a November sunset—fast and all-consuming.

"What about katydids?"

"It's the third sound. With katydids, you can hear each individual one. They don't drown each other out." He waited for a single katydid to make a comment from the trees. "There. Hear it?"

I did, then the katydid after it. They sounded like squeaky boots conversing about whatever squeaky boots conversed about. The sound wasn't constant like the locusts or cicadas. I couldn't count on the same chorus every time.

Thanks to Everett, the sounds of summer no longer blended together. I could make out the locust from the cicada from the katydid, and I knew I always would. It wasn't something you could forget. Nothing shared on the bike trail could be forgotten. My favorite call was the locust—the most distinct. Most people attributed the summer night sound to cicadas, but if they stopped to listen like Everett, they'd know it was the locusts.

"I didn't know Dr. Bishop was a summer insect specialist," I said.

"I wasn't until last summer. Nights in Chicago don't sound like this, so one night when I couldn't sleep, I listened really closely and finally heard them as different sounds. I knew I wasn't going to be able to sleep if I didn't sort it out. I watched videos of their calls and memorized what made them different."

Everett conjured the vision for me—him lying in bed, plagued with the mystery of night sounds enough to do something about it. The thought was cuter than even his cheeks and his beauty mark and the way he licked his lips when he was in deep thought.

"Summer will never sound the same again." I listened closely to the sweet music in the trees.

In the ending credits of the day, I didn't feel lost in its darkness—not with Everett next to me, not with the distant fireflies lighting our way home. The bugs told each other secrets all night long. They were privy to ours, but they'd never tell.

"Today was mesmerizing." Everett broke the silence. "You're mesmerizing."

My cheeks got hot again, presumably cherry red in the twilight. I'd never heard that word before. Boys at school might have called me pretty or cute every once in a while, but mesmerizing had to mean something else entirely.

I gulped down the urge to ruin the moment.

"Nobody's ever told me that before," I said.

"Well, then nobody's ever paid attention."

"You're...effervescent." I laughed despite the chasm in my chest. "*Effervescent* Everett. Like the name game."

"I haven't heard that one before," he croaked.

I felt like I'd been shaken up in a sand globe, grains of sand swirling around me like summer stars in a time lapse of the night sky, my stomach churning against it. A dark night drowned out by firelight. The sunlight peeking through the perfect curl of a wave. The twinkling sound shells made against themselves.

I was *mesmerizing.*

The thought of being noticed made me want to grow and shrink at the same time. To be noticed was to matter; I didn't usually matter.

But on the bike trail, I did.

Four Summers Ago
Age 14, June 24

IF THERE HAD BEEN A PIT IN MY STOMACH since our day at the aquarium, the entire peach had been there since my second day with Everett.

Hadley's innocence was the only thing that fixed it, the way she spent her days with stuffed animals and library books and animated movies. I used to spend my days like that before I had to grow up.

I was in the kitchen making lunch for us. I slathered peanut butter on bread, washed green grapes, and stirred up some orange Kool-Aid. The mason jars started sweating the second we walked outside for our driveway picnic. Hadley had been really into picnics ever since we read a book about ants raiding a picnic. She took every opportunity to picnic, even when the sun was blistering, inviting the ants to arrive.

We sat in the middle of the driveway, sucking peanut butter off our teeth and washing it down with Kool-Aid. It was refreshing to spend time with someone so unbothered by the grit on the pavement, the heat that sent a waterfall of sweat down my calves.

The smallest part of me thought spending time with someone who saw the world in so much pink would give my perspective some of that whimsy, too.

Unfortunately, there was not much time left for her to color me pink. Blair would be splitting custody with Hadley's dad starting in July, and I wouldn't see Hadley for the rest of the summer. Blair said this would happen more now that Hadley's dad was sober. I was glad he was back on his feet, at least. For Hadley's sake.

I was also glad Haven and Holden were still in Mexico. If not, I didn't know that I would have spent this much time with her this summer. We'd made a summer's worth of memories in nearly two short weeks. We went to the park where I was glad to find my hidden heart untouched. We raided the candy store until we ate ourselves sick. One day at the beach, Hadley was so eager to find a whole sand dollar that I couldn't resist planting a store-bought one for her in the sand.

I still pretended it was real when she showed me each night. I'd probably have to for the rest of my life.

When Hadley went to bed, I would stay up late and work on some poems. I'd been trying to write one about Piper Island each summer, but sometimes they turned into something else entirely. Lately, the pages were as confused as they were romantic. My heart fluttered when I wrote of the aquarium, then it shattered in the same stanza.

Reading was the same. The scandalous teen romance books I used to avoid in the library now sat in neat stacks on my dresser. They spoke of breathless days and heart-pounding nights. Of missed connections and outward forces that wove love together. It was exhilarating and horrifying at once to see me and Everett within them.

This new development even gave me the curiosity and courage to do something more unthinkable than holding Everett's hand. One night, after a poem went sour and morphed into words about my dad,

I texted him. It wasn't sour—though it certainly could have been—but a simple text: *This is Quinn, how have you been?*

What else was there to say given the circumstances?

I hadn't seen or talked to him since he left five years ago. I didn't know if the number Mom had saved in my phone even still worked, but I guessed it was worth the try.

"Will you read the star book again?" Hadley asked when she finished her sandwich, jostling me out of my thoughts. She put her crust down and sipped her Kool-Aid, spilling some into an orange stain on her shorts, but she didn't care about stuff like that.

While we were at the library last week, me getting yet another romance book, Hadley picked out a picture book about constellations. This began a new phase: an obsession with stars. After this, I would have read it to her nine times in four days.

"Go get it," I mumbled between bites of her discarded sandwich crust.

Hadley ran into the house. She almost lost her balance on the front steps, then laughed at herself for it.

Watching Hadley be so unapologetically herself made me want to take lessons about the ways of the world from a six-year-old. Watching her was like opening up a fortune cookie and finding some way to shape its words into my life. My first fortune would be: *Laugh at yourself.* After that would come a million more:

Don't worry about other people.

Find happiness in small things.

Don't be so stupid.

It was simple. So simple, really, that it was all a six-year-old knew. I was just like her when I was six, because there was nothing else to be—no reason not to live by those simple rules. But with growing up came the reality that fortunes weren't all pink. You found it harder to live life so carefree. You got stained by blackened fortunes that dictated the rest of your existence.

You didn't have a dad to spend July and August with.

Your dad was sober—not from alcohol, but from *you*. Only you didn't think fourteen-year-olds could be vices.

You said a stupid, mean thing to your friend at a jellyfish tank. You ruined a beautiful, blue moment when all he was doing was being nice.

Of course he was being nice. It was what he did. According to Haven during off-season phone calls, he couldn't stop talking about you. He was excited to see you again this summer.

According to Haven, he *like*-liked you.

That thought presented itself as some fortune you'd wish you hadn't cracked open, because that meant you had to open up another that said:

You like-*liked your friend back.*

That couldn't happen. Too many fortunes before had made that clear.

Hadley ran across the yard with the book of constellations. I smiled and held my hand out for the book. She was out of breath, sitting next to me with her cheek all sweaty on my arm.

"What's a constellation?" I pointed to the constellation on the cover, quizzing her from last night's bedtime read and all the ones before.

"Star shapes in the sky!"

"That's right. Good job!" I flipped to the first page.

At this point, I could read it with my eyes closed, but I kept them open to watch the glittery stars wink at us in the sun. Hadley traced each one with her finger.

With each passing page, I told the story of Orion, how his hunting ego got him trapped in the galaxy for eternity. The Big Dipper and Little Dipper and their constellations, Ursa Major and Ursa Minor, who lived in the stars as the mistresses of Zeus, cursed into bears.

Hadley's favorite part was next: the zodiac constellations. I read through all twelve, stopping at the Gemini page to remind Hadley that Haven and Holden were Geminis who were real twins, just like the constellation. She always smiled at the coincidence.

I reread her favorite page, the one about Sagittarius's life as a centaur named Chiron. He spent his life teaching archery. One day, he was accidentally shot by a poisonous arrow and chose to trade his immortality with Prometheus, who was doomed to a life of suffering for his own crimes. In return for his generosity, Zeus turned him into the stars we saw today, allowed to spend eternity without suffering.

Hadley looked up at me. "That's my zodiac."

"That *is* your zodiac." I smiled and tapped my finger on her nose, right above her Kool-Aid mustache. "He is a lot like you. Smart and kind."

"This is yours." She paged back to Scorpio which she found only because she memorized the shape of the constellation. "You protected everyone from Orion's meanness."

"You're welcome." I laughed. Was being compared to a murderous scorpion a good thing?

"Thank you!" An idea spread across Hadley's face. "We should draw us on the driveway!"

She ran in again for sidewalk chalk. I flipped back to Sagittarius just as she returned. We covered the driveway with shapes from the sky. They looked good—so good, in fact, that I hoped they looked down happy to see themselves reflected in our jagged driveway.

We ended up drawing every constellation in the book, then I challenged Hadley to a game of tag around the driveway sky. When we ran ourselves tired, we lay in the grass, squinting up at Scorpio and Sagittarius, invisible behind the day sky.

On our way back into the house for an afternoon nap, we picked some weeds from the front yard. But to us, weeds were not weeds, just misunderstood flowers perfect for a windowsill.

WE WERE LYING ON A BLANKET OUTSIDE under a band of stars.

It took some convincing, but we got Blair to agree to let us spend the night out here. She called our bluff, predicting we would sneak in by midnight thanks to the creepy crawlies and incessant insect songs. I heard the differences now, clear as the night sky, thanks to Everett.

I looked back at the kitchen window to see if Blair was checking on us again. The mason jar of weeds made a silhouette in the orange light, already slumped down to say goodnight.

We filled the tent with a couple of sheets and every stuffed animal Hadley owned, including her current favorite, the dolphin from the aquarium. But this was not goodnight.

We peeked our heads out of the tent to find the constellations from the book—for real this time. Even after memorizing the book, the only constellation I could find was the Big Dipper.

I'd been able to spot it for years. Ever since Dad and I had one of our firefly-fluffernutter nights and he pointed it out to me before it was too dark to see his finger against the darkening sky. He told me some story about how the Big Dipper was the dad and the Little Dipper was his favorite daughter. He said they were on a mission to scoop every star in the universe into their dippers as gifts to each other, one for each day they loved each other. I added that part whenever I relived the memory.

Obviously he'd made it up. I figured that one out all on my own.

I couldn't miss the Big Dipper when it was visible. Once you finally saw a shape in the stars, your eyes never forgot where to look. If I didn't know better, I would have thought it shone even brighter for me under a clear night. Especially when I didn't want to see it at all.

I dug my nails into my palm to stop a cry that threatened to explode out of nowhere. That story was not real. It was time to rewrite it for me and my baby cousin who was real and not so much a baby anymore. She used my arm as a pillow, but I didn't mind the pinpricks of it falling asleep.

I tried to show Hadley the dippers, making up a new story about two cousins on a star-scooping mission. After a couple tries explaining left versus right, I gave up and suggested we play a new game.

"Let's play One Sentence Story. We will take turns telling a story one sentence at a time. I'll start: There once was a cat named Mr. Whiskers."

Her head lifted off my arm and planted back down. Her hair tickled. "Mr. Whiskers is the king of space!"

I whispered so I didn't wake the dwindling fireflies. "Mr. Whiskers has a best friend who is a mermaid named Aquamarine."

"One day, *Acca*-marine ran away and it made Mr. Whiskers very sad." Hadley made her voice sound sad.

I looked up and saw a triangulated cluster of stars that looked like a pool of fish, so I added, "Mr. Whiskers asks his fish friends for help."

"They all go looking for him until they run into a snake. The snake's name is Quinn!" Hadley giggled so loudly it certainly woke the fireflies.

"First I'm a scorpion, now I'm a snake?" I acted offended and tickled her side. "This snake is going to get you!"

She giggled again. Maybe I was good at this older cousin thing. I hoped it was moments like these she looked back on fondly to remember me by. When she was old like me, she could have her own nights with friends and call them her firefly-constellation nights. Thinking about them wouldn't make her cry because I'd never leave her.

As if she was reading my mind, Hadley said softly, "I wish I could stay here all summer."

My heart shattered all over again. I needed to stay strong for Hadley, ignore the parts of me that didn't understand why someone wouldn't want to spend the summer with their dad. She didn't know a different world. She was only six. She just loved her older cousin.

I toyed with my sadness of her leaving and my jealousy of her having a dad who fought for her. I mustered up the energy to say, "I know, but you're going to have a great time at your daddy's house. He loves you very much."

"Yeah." She sighed and got more comfortable on the grass. I couldn't feel my arm since Hadley's head had sent it all the way to dreamland.

"Before you know it, we'll see each other again at Thanksgiving and Christmas. We'll tell each other more constellation stories."

Hadley made a noise like she was too tired to form a full sentence. I shifted us both into the tent, surrounded us with stuffed animals, and threw the sheet over her.

"Goodnight, Hadley. I love you."

But she was already asleep and I wouldn't be far behind.

While we were lying under stars, lulled to sleep by our own book of constellations, I couldn't help but hope that tomorrow, my horoscope would be good.

And that we'd make it the whole night out here without being overtaken by ants.

Four Summers Ago

Age 14, June 27

THE TWILIGHT BRUSHED ITS DEEP PURPLE ON THE WORLD.

The palm trees in the Rivera-Sanchezes' front yard were dark against the sky. The violet haze crept to the ground like a fog. It was a scene from a Photoshopped postcard at the pier shop, except this was real. I knew it was the sky's way of welcoming them back to North Carolina.

The summer hadn't felt like Piper Island without Holden and Haven. Now that Hadley was with her dad, I needed them back. I'd survived eighth grade with thoughts of our days traipsing everywhere the light spilled. I missed smelling like sweat and salt water until it was time to smell like shampoo and sleep. I missed my best friends.

Everett and I hadn't had a bad time. I'd argue we had *too* good of a time, but I needed to be careful not to get too close to a jellyfish, lest it stung. Could jellyfish sting themselves?

How else was I supposed to protect myself?

Sitting on my best friends' front porch steps, I watched the sky darken like some unnamed constellation flipping a switch on the sun. With darkness came mosquitoes and cooler air perfect for counting down the seconds. I confused the neighbors' headlights for their van so I closed my eyes until another set of headlights streaked past my eyelids.

I stood up, waving at them through the windows. The car stopped and I ran down their steps. Haven spilled out of the car into my arms.

We exchanged hellos and comments about the small changes to our appearances. She looked so *high school* with her new braces. I had a new freckle on my cheek. She was trying out curtain bangs. I'd finally switched to a middle part. Puberty was almost done chewing, ready to spit us out as two beautiful jellyfish.

Holden was still asleep, drool dribbling down his chin. We tickled his cheek awake. He was the same level of crabby halfway out of dreamland, but he looked the oldest of all of us. The year flattened his cheeks into a real-life jawline. He put the two minutes Haven had on him to shame. Graduating from middle school turned us all into adults.

I hugged him and hoped he lost some crabbiness while in my arms. "You're so tall!"

He was a whole head taller than me now, nearly two heads taller than Haven.

"You sound just like our family." He laughed tiredly and patted the top of my head. "And you are exactly the same height."

"Thanks. I missed you, too."

"Good." He winked and headed inside with his luggage.

I helped Haven with hers, then we went back out to the front porch. A foil pan sat between us on the stairs. Someone inside turned the porch light on for us, purple fog snapping into yellow.

"This is my *abuela's* recipe for *tres leches*." Haven peeled off the top sheet of foil and handed me a fork. "Lemme know what you think."

The *tres leches* was half-eaten, probably wrestled between the twins in the car. It looked like some of my childhood birthday cakes: yellow cake topped with white cream. The only difference here were the cherries lined up in rows and vacant red-stained spaces where cherries used to be. I grabbed a forkful and took a bite. It was nothing like my childhood birthday cakes. It was spongier, and moister. It melted on my tongue like caramels.

"Do you like it?"

"Anything with sugar is a friend of mine." I scooped more on my fork to prove it, and because it was true.

"That's what I told Holden! He swore you wouldn't like it. Clearly, I know you better." She ate her own forkful. "I think he just wanted to eat your share."

"I'm glad he didn't. How was Mexico?"

"It was good, but I can only handle my whole family for so long. Mom kept making us talk to great-great aunts and third cousins I don't ever remember meeting. They made us talk about college and careers like we've got a clue about it. And they kept saying, 'You've gotten so tall!'" She made her voice high-pitched. "'I remember when I could hold you in my arms. I used to change your diapers!'"

"Well, now I feel bad for mentioning it to Holden."

Haven laughed. "He'll survive." She took a huge bite. Her face brightened and she chewed a little more quickly, swallowing to say, "I went shopping for my *quinceañera* dress!"

"Did you find one?"

"Not a good yellow one, but it's not until next May. I wonder how much taller we'll be then." Haven rolled her eyes with a giggle.

She told me about her older cousin, Isabella, who came down from California. Haven wanted to be just like her when she was older. She told me about all the late nights they spent dancing to loud music and driving down desert roads with the windows down. All the love they ate in the form of food. So. Much. Food. When she finished, she nudged me with her elbow. "Now, come on, tell me what you've been up to."

I told her about my school year and the two weeks without her. How nice it was to be back, how Hadley was now with her dad for the summer, and how I'd been spending my time. This included my day at the aquarium with Everett. I told her how stupid his humor was, but not how much it made me laugh. I told her how comfortable it felt, but not the reason why. I told her he was a great guy, but not how much I liked him.

"Do you *like*-like him?"

I nodded so slowly I barely felt it. My face scrunched up like my last bite had been laced with poison.

"Then why do you look like you stepped on a jellyfish?"

Leave it to Haven to read my mind twice.

"Speaking of jellyfish, he was looking at the moon jellies at the aquarium. Then we looked at each other and it was a really nice moment until I ruined it with something stupid. We hung out a couple days later, biked and went to the beach. I didn't do anything stupid then, but I don't know what to do."

I got antsy, squirming under the grasp of what had been holding me down for years.

"Why are you so afraid to live?" Haven whispered. I spotted it as a foggy shadow on the stairs in front of us.

I didn't want to get into it. I'd lived this long without getting into it. It had been long enough that getting into it might feel a whole lot like living it again. Haven had heard snatches of it throughout the years, enough to make a rough sketch of my past, but I'd never filled those blurry shapes with details. But there was something about this summer night, eating *tres leches* with Haven. Her love in the form of food between us. Being with her made the evening smell like summer stars and sweets.

So why not a secret?

"My dad cheated on my mom."

It slipped from my mouth the way the sun sets on a lavender night, slipping completely away before you could even notice it was leaving. Then my past came out all at once, a storm cloud flooding the present. I couldn't look at Haven, so I talked to her shadow instead. To the curve of her nose and all the wispy flyaways and the empty fork in her hand.

"When my mom started to suspect it, she confronted him and he started to make her believe she was crazy for thinking such a thing. Things got bad after that, because Mom knew he didn't love her anymore. She knew this, and he wouldn't admit it."

Haven cleared her throat, then fixed her hair behind her ear and sat up a little taller.

"Fighting became a daily thing. Sometimes they'd fight all through dinner and I ate alone so my food wouldn't get cold. And because I didn't know what else to do. I fell asleep to screaming and crying matches. There's only so much that plugging your ears can do. Dad slept on the couch when they managed to end the fights without one of them storming out. I don't know where my mom would go, but I knew my dad went to his girlfriend's.

"One day, he left while I was at school. Right after he dropped me off. Left all his stuff at home, so I thought he was just running late from work or something. The next day after school, he was still gone."

My eyes started to sting. My words came up thick and full of air.

"The last thing he ever told me was that he would never leave me. Then he just…never came back. He left."

My tears came on fast, like the slippery moon behind a sunset. The first one ran off my cheek faster than I could wipe it.

"That's really confusing when you're nine."

"Quinn, I'm so sorry. I had no idea." She wrapped her arm around me and pulled me to her.

We were an indistinguishable black blob silhouetted against the front porch light. It was warm in her embrace, in the cloak of summer air.

I breathed in and out. Swallowed the thickness from my throat. "I still haven't seen or heard from him since he left five years ago. I tried texting him recently, but nothing. Mom's never been the same. And me, well, you know."

I knew I didn't have to say it. To be me was to be a girl afraid of commitment. A girl disgusted with affection and disgusted with being disgusted. A girl who ruined moon jellies because it was easier than the stings that might come after.

"I know. But you should know that it's not your fault. I know it's hard to believe, but not every relationship is like that." She brushed loose hair out of my face. My hair unstuck from the dried tears on my cheek.

"You are worthy of love. Pinky promise."

She held her curved pinky out to me, glowing yellow under the front porch light.

I finally looked at her, gave her a soft smile and my curved pinky.

I hoped what she said was true. I hoped pinky promises held the same power as cheek eyelashes, flickering birthday candles, dandelion puffs to the wind. Shooting stars. Fountain pennies.

Haven kept her pinky around mine until I let go. Both of us reached for the *tres leches* at the same time. We laughed between bites.

"There's this thing my mom always says: '*Los amigos van y vienen pero la familia siempre se queda.*' Friends come and go, but family always stays. I love it, but I've always had one problem with it. The way I see it, being family has nothing to do with staying. What stays is love."

She put a lone cherry in her mouth, smiling around it like she'd said something so groundbreaking and magical that I could wish on it. Maybe I would.

"Oh yeah?"

Haven sat up again and pulled her hair behind her ear. "For us, it goes a little something like '*La familia va y viene pero las amigas siempre se quedan.*'"

Family comes and goes, but friends always stay.

Now
July 5

I'M GOING TO DIE.

Seconds from taking a breath of salt water. The ocean surrounds me. Waves bob overhead, the moonlight chopped by rippled water. I sense a thousand whales around me. Bigger than airplanes. Hidden in the blackness. Watching me die. My heart leaps for the surface. My eyes sting. I can't break free. Shackled. An anchor. On my ankle. It digs further into my skin when I swim up. The air is right there. My fingers push through. Void of oxygen, light, and warmth, my lungs start to shrivel. I've run out of time.

There's no other choice.

My lungs fill with ocean water.

I WAKE UP PANTING, so rapidly I fear I might run out of air. My hand rests over my bobbing chest. Everything is okay. I'm in a bed. At Everett's house. In Piper Island. Sober.

The room is dark, like the ocean that dream-Quinn died in. Slowly, the blackness fades into a muted blue like the room real-Quinn slept in. The moonlight wedges its way between drawn blinds. Not choppy. Not wave-distorted. The sheer curtains sway from the vent below. My feet disturb the comforter. My ankles are free. I am not drowning in the Atlantic Ocean. I am alive.

I am also wide awake.

I slip out of bed, smooth the covers like I was never there, and pad down the dark hallway. The kitchen clock glows a green 5:19am, an hour before Liezel will start her morning coffee. I need to be anywhere but here.

I open my phone and type a text since I can't just go down the hall and crawl under his covers for comfort: *Thanks for letting me stay. I can't sleep so I'm going to the pier.*

I'm barefoot in Everett's kitchen, leaning against the sparkling kitchen counter, mentally willing Everett to read my text. He's probably sleeping. It's hard for teens to leave their sleep on summer mornings. I'd still be trapped too if it weren't for my nightmare. I don't know why yesterday brought on such a dream. I've been in Piper Island too long, and I've been thinking too much. My thoughts would kill me if they could wield weapons, especially since I forgot to take my antidepressants last night.

I close the front door slowly so the roaring hinges won't wake anyone up. Despite my best efforts, it still hollers at me on the way out.

I bike to the pier under disappearing stars, streetlights guiding me down the empty roads. Goosebumps ignite down to my toes as I pedal the wind harder onto my skin. The strands that fell from my ponytail during the nightmare soar behind me.

As I pass each streetlight, they cast my shadow on the road ahead. The shadow of a girl afraid of everything, even in dreams, which used to be the only place safe from reality.

Main Street is dead this morning, save for locals walking their dogs or heading to work off the island and ambitious tourists swaying to the sand for sunrise. I coast over the white lines in the near-empty pier parking lot. I leave my bike on the rack and hobble up the sandy stairs into the pier shop, the only place open this early.

My phone chimes: *Be there in ten.*

The sound is a jolt to my system. I wasn't prepared for Everett to be awake, and I certainly wasn't prepared to face him so soon after what happened last night.

I kill time walking through the aisles of bright neon fishing lure, shrimp graying over ice, overpriced beach toys. I sift through a basket of cowries. Zodiac constellations are engraved onto the rounded exterior, glossed over to spend eternity there instead of the sky. I find a couple familiar ones. My stomach whines for a breakfast of greasy mozzarella sticks and a slushy from the new machine I'm sure Haven has already tried.

The bell above the door rings when I open it to leave and step into the near morning light. Early risers are already fishing, propped under the lamp poles spread evenly down the pier. Holden and his dad, Santiago, come out this early sometimes for the fish that only bite before the sun rises.

I find a bench a short walk down the pier. It sits above where even the highest of tides can't reach. Here, the sand would catch me before the water had the chance to swallow me whole. I'd take that fate any day, even if it stuck to every bit of me, followed me to the cracks of Blair's hardwoods, survived the shower, and tucked itself into my bed sheets.

Sitting on the pier, I text, then slip my phone into my pocket.

I close my eyes and listen to the push and pull of the waves. The sound of a TV tuned to the wrong station. Haven wrestling wavy hair from her face. Everett's skin glistening. Holden winning at paddleball. Seagulls running from two people chasing them.

I listen to the sound of summer.

I do still love that sound. It's a reminder that the world still works as it should. The moon still has a job. The oceanfront is still a great place to spend too-early summer mornings.

A flock of pelicans fly over the first strip of beach houses, growing bigger as it makes its way over the pier. A seagull down the pier haggles a fisherman who just reeled up a half-eaten shrimp. He waves his hands and yells to scare it away, but it doesn't budge.

"Morning."

Everett stands with his fists stretching his hoodie pockets. His black hair has clearly been defeated by his pillowcase, the sea breeze going for round two. It looks like all he did before leaving was throw his hoodie on. I'm surprised he managed to tie his Converses.

"Good morning," I say. The sight of him nearly kills me, so I stare blankly at the ocean that killed me in dreamland earlier.

He sits on the ocean-most side of the bench. His Quinn-most knee touches mine. "Why couldn't you sleep?"

I suppose I should just tell him. He came all this way.

"I had a nightmare. It was me out there. No matter how hard I tried, I couldn't reach the surface. I was close enough to push my fingers out, but deep enough to drown anyway. I died."

If I look hard enough, maybe I'll see dream-Quinn's fingers poking out from the sea foam. Maybe in my dream, a real version of me watched from the pier, too afraid to do anything. That's why dream-Quinn died: Real-Quinn is a coward who doesn't know how to save herself.

"I'm sorry." Everett turns to me, his elbow on the back rest. His knee leaves mine cold and lonely. "You didn't die. Not for real. You're right here." He touches my shoulder, gives me a supportive shake. "You're with me on the pier. Alive."

"I know, but it felt so real. I'm sorry if I woke you up."

"Some jackass who slammed my front door did." He smirks and nudges me with his elbow.

"They must be the worst." I keep my smile contained until it falls with guilt. "Sorry."

"It's all good. This is much prettier than my ceiling."

"Good." What does his ceiling look like from that angle? Surely just like the guest room ceiling, but not as warm and safe. If it could speak, it would certainly say a lot about what happened last night. *You were in his room all alone. You tried to kiss him. He didn't let you because he wants to kiss you sober.*

Quinn, I dare you to tell me a secret. The strain in his voice will haunt me forever. I can't believe I didn't have a nightmare about *that.*

No matter how good of a distraction this nightmare is, we both know the implications of last night. We both know he tried to pry the truth from me last night. We both know I wouldn't let him.

But I can't dodge the conversation anymore. The collective game of pretend is too much to bear, too awkward not to just jump headfirst into. It's easier than merely dipping my toes in.

"I'm sorry about last night." I finally manage to look at him.

His expression matches the sound of his voice from last night— glass shattered on the floor, void of the sun to mend it with light. This is what he would have looked like in the hammock if I hadn't been close enough to feel him breathe. "You're sorry? About what exactly?"

"For trying to kiss you."

He flits his tongue between his lips, then purses them in a tight line. He nods his head, in deep contemplation over what he's just heard.

"You think the problem with last night was that you tried to kiss me?"

"Well, what is it then?"

He squints his eyes at me like I'm a putrid zombie who washed up on the beach this morning. "That you need to be drunk to want me."

"It's not that, it's—"

"It's what, Quinn?"

The sound of my name. The twitch of his eyebrow. A question I wish were rhetorical. All of this is too much.

I don't know which scenario I'd prefer: drowning with the whales or telling the harmless boy in front of me that I'm scared of *him*. How do you explain that happiness feels like a sign that the ground is about to cave in and swallow you whole? That life is a pile of eggshells one must float across to keep intact? That the only thing alcohol does is take away my fear, not add desire? The desire has always been there...but I *can't*.

I already traded the love of my life for the loss of another one once. Not again.

I swallow a lump in my throat, drowning despite the land. "I can't."

"Then neither can I." Everett's face is bleak in the incandescent dawn. "I have to go." He offers me a thoughtless smile and walks down the fishing pier, his hands in his pockets, his shoulders slumped.

It's the wrong way. You're not supposed to walk away from the sun before it rises.

He's not supposed to let me get away with this.

I'm not supposed to let love slip from my fingertips, watch him disappear inside the pier shop doors and imagine the rest of his day without me.

I look down at the space that used to be filled by him, blink away the tears that have surfaced so I can see what he left behind.

A bag of orange wedge candies.

My thoughts flood with a memory from last summer: me and Everett sneaking store-bought candy into the movie theatre in our hoodies. I finished my orange wedges before the movie started. With my head against his shoulder, my tongue wrestled orange goo from my molars until the credits rolled.

I took too much happiness then, so the universe made its decision.

My tears flow freely now. Everett didn't mean to leave me with a dagger, but there's nothing quite as sharp as the rush of memory, especially when it's a reminder of everything you lost.

I take a bite of an orange wedge to stab myself with the memory. It tastes like melted sun, the pier shop, and the feeling of my temple on Everett's shoulder. I circle orange sugar between two fingers.

The sun rises ambitiously once the first red sliver appears on the horizon, scaring the deep indigo away. I bleed out in front of the waking sun, blinking a steady stream of warm tears down my cheeks.

I wish I could be like the sun, a phoenix rising from the ashes of the ocean. I wish I could be in the presence of the sun dripping in liquid gold but instead choose to look at Everett. What difference is there between the two anyway? I wish I could look at his jaw glowing in the sun, orange light stirred into his brown eyes and tell him, *The sun is just like you, and so is the moon, and so is everything people need to survive but don't appreciate enough.*

But the thought feels like drowning.

I slip the rest of the orange wedges into my hoodie and saunter back into the pier shop. There's no trace of Everett. No animated conversations with the woman behind the counter about the dark reality of human immortality. No strong arms spinning the postcard racks for new releases. No tall, dark-haired figure practicing pinball in the back of the shop.

The pinball machine sleeps alone in the corner. Older than the retro yellowing surfboards hanging from the ceiling—maybe even older than the pier itself—it croaks to life when I pop a quarter in.

I play a round, for old times' sake.

Three Summers Ago
Age 15, June 21

HAVEN WAS DIFFERENT THIS SUMMER. It wasn't just her long hair or her skin's victory over acne or how big her teeth looked since she'd gotten her braces off. No, it wasn't that. She was quieter. She walked carefully against the worn wooden slats of the public beach access, her head down past the sandy bathrooms and volleyball courts.

Where had her confidence gone?

This was the second time we'd hung out in the four days I'd been back. The first was just a quick drive-by before she had to go get ready for her date with her new boyfriend Chance. Not even enough time to catch up on her *quinceañera* or how her and Chance came to be— just a quick hug, a comment about my short curtain bangs, and pinky promises to hang out soon. According to Holden, Chance was now out of town for the weekend, which was long enough to steal Haven away for a day at the beach.

We stumbled in the sand, stepping in Holden's and Everett's existing footprints for balance. We found a mostly clear spot between armies of colorful umbrellas. Holden and Everett stripped their shirts and shoes off before Haven and I finished throwing everything down.

I waited for Haven to say something about them not doing their share, but she just started setting up the chairs like it was all she was programmed to do.

The boys were long gone, already slathered in sunscreen and racing to the water. I spread a towel on each chair and worked on my own sunscreen. Haven and I got each other's backs.

"What are you thinking about?" Haven asked. "You're doing your quiet thing."

I could have said the same about her.

"I'm just sad for Blair." I sat down when she finished my shoulders. I really was upset for Blair. She had already bought three cartons of orange juice and two bags of deflated gas station cotton candy as some way to release her pent-up mom instinct on me.

"Hadley's with her dad?" Haven sat in the chair next to me. She started braiding her hair against the wind's pull.

I nodded. "For the whole summer this time." I looked at Holden and Everett bouncing with the unusually calm waves. My bangs were losing the battle with the wind, but it was worth it since Everett complimented them back in the parking lot. "I'm excited to have fun today."

"I am too." Haven peeled the cap off a Diet Coke, tossed me one too.

"Diet Coke?" I took a sip. Haven hated diet soda. Diet *anything*.

She shrugged. "Chance loves them."

And *there* was the glimmering difference between this summer and last. Last summer, Haven didn't have a boyfriend. While I didn't know much about him besides his name and that they met at school, I could suspect some other things as well. I was good at that, assuming the worst of relationships. If there was anything I knew for sure, it was that sometimes relationships had this tricky way of turning people on their heads.

Haven seemed well on her way to upside down.

I swallowed, attempting to suck my thoughts through my fizzy teeth, only to say them anyway. "Does he know you hate diet soda?"

"It's growing on me." She took a huge swig, her nose folding into itself when she swallowed.

"So, how'd you start dating?"

"Well, we had Biology together last semester and, get this…" She leaned over like it was a secret only the sand between us could hear. "I heard all this crap about him being really entitled, so I was dreading being his lab partner. Then I got to know him and we clicked and one day he asked me out. I said yes and the rest is history."

I nodded. It was a nice story, almost like she was reading it from some romance book tucked away in our bags. Maybe I was being too Quinn about the whole situation, holding on to my benefit of the doubt until it was too heavy to give out.

"What do you guys do together?" I asked, when what I really meant was: *Does he control you?*

"You know, the usual date things." She swallowed what seemed to be the rest of her words.

"I *don't* know, actually." I laughed to keep things lighthearted. We *were* on the beach after all, under a band of blue sky and the soundtrack of whooshing waves and seagulls.

"Oh, right." Haven smiled her brand-new smile at me. "Like…well, I go to his house to watch movies. We go to Hammerhead's sometimes when Holden's not working. We drive around a lot and listen to music in his car."

"Are you happy?"

"Of course I'm happy!" Her eyebrows furrowed.

Did people who claimed to be happy in their relationship usually look so threatened by the thought of the opposite? Could Haven even see it well enough to know better? Was she too close to the situation, too blinded to notice the rest of the world waiting around for her? Or was I too far from the situation, too jaded to notice the rest of the world waiting around for *me*?

I was probably projecting. In disbelief that a relationship could bring joy. Uneducated on how one half of a couple should act without their partner. Bitter, maybe. Jealous, certainly.

"I just want to make sure you're happy, that's all." I finished my soda and tossed the bottle by our feet. The sand stuck to the wet glass.

"You have nothing to worry about. I pinky promise," she said, beaming. Her pinky shone just as bright.

After we linked pinkies, I let the conversation end. There was too much sun and catching up to do.

I told her about my new obsession with daily horoscopes, the new decor I got for my bedroom, and this funny story about our homecoming queen getting dethroned minutes later. Haven shared stories of her *quinceañera* planning, the quest for the perfect dress, and the great uncle who got way too drunk on the night of the party and broke his arm on the dance floor.

We pushed and pulled until the morning sun turned to afternoon.

"Come on, let's go find the boys." Haven wet the sand with the rest of her Diet Coke. "And get the hell in the water before we shrivel up and die."

IN THE OCEAN, IT WAS HARD TO RELAX. Even though I loved everything about the beach, the unknown water still freaked me out. Sharks, stingrays, *real* jellyfish, a riptide. But I wanted to have fun, so I exhaled and tried to ignore the threats that most likely wouldn't happen to me.

"Hey." Haven grabbed my wrist, steadying me from the horizon. "Float on the water like me and Everett."

Everett was outstretched like he was doing snow angels in snow that had melted into an ocean. With his eyes closed, he took light breaths after each wave slid over his face. The waves were calm, so he was too.

Haven threw herself into the only white-capped wave around. She let it catch her and throw her back into a standing position. After the big wave, she did the same thing as Everett.

I wanted to be that calm and careless. I tried to replicate them, but I plunged into the water as soon as I loosened my muscles. Beyond the sudden shock of hot shoulders entering cold water, it was actually refreshing. I steadied myself on the sandy floor and wiped the salt water from my eyes. Haven and Everett watched me, hidden smiles on their faces, visible only in their eyes. Water ran off my eyelashes. My mouth tasted like a salt shaker.

Everett walked toward me with his palms up. "Let us help."

I gulped. This was worse than letting him slather sunscreen on me. Still, I nodded and let them hold me on top of the water.

"I know for a fact you're not relaxed." Haven moved her head to block the sun from my eyes. "You need to relax. Fear makes you heavier."

She was right, but it wasn't my fault; there was a hand on the dimples of my back that might or might not have been Everett's, which made my heart float.

"That's not a thing." I laughed.

"It is to me!"

I tried my best to listen to Haven, to forget Everett was watching the sun illuminate my chest and stomach and thighs. I tried to forget how much twisting and turning romance did to people. Forget the muscles in my neck that whined from how tensely I held them.

A wave drifted over my ears, taking my hearing with me into the muffled underwater world. Finally, I released the last bit of anchors riddling my joints. I couldn't feel my arms. My eyelids played a show for me with the swirly sun rays. I anticipated the ebb and flow of waves like a surfer with a sixth sense.

"There you go." Everett swooned me to unknown territories.

I was floating.

Their hands suddenly disappeared from beneath me. I managed a quick gasp that followed me into the muffled underwater world. Managed a pinch for breath before I was submerged. I kicked off the squishy ocean floor. "Oh my God!"

Haven's hands were over her mouth, probably to hide her laughter. "For the record, that's not what we thought would happen!"

"Sorry, you looked relaxed." Remorse danced on Everett's tongue.

Wiping the salt from my eyes, I sharpened my gaze at them while water made trails down my skin. I couldn't find any anger. I laughed and splashed them as payback. Haven offered me an amused smile. It was nice to see real emotion on her face. Everett shrugged with real regret.

He was cute when he was genuine.

I was stupid when I was dripping in ocean water.

HAVEN AND I FINISHED A SERIOUS GAME of mermaids and made our way back to our chairs. The sand stuck to my wet body like sprinkles to ice cream. I threw myself on my towel between Holden and Everett.

"God, you scared me," Everett mumbled with a gasp, still half-asleep. He was on his stomach, tanning his back. He turned to face me, sun rays leaking into his eyes. A soft smile grazed his face.

I smiled back. I didn't know if it meant anything, what he might take from it, or if he saw me at all in the blinding sun. Maybe he just saw the lingering deep purple and orange sun spots that hadn't yet fizzled out.

When he closed his eyes again, I stole studious glances at him. He had changed a lot since last summer. He looked more like a man than a boy now. His back rose and fell with steady breaths, the sun casting shadows on the ridges from his biceps to back to legs. Did he need more sunscreen? His black hair was trimmed on the sides, but the hair on top of his head was wild and free. I wanted to run my fingers through it, shake some of the sand dried into it, watch him react to my touch. I wanted to trace my warm fingers down his jaw, end up at his lips. I bet they tasted like salt.

What was this, one of Blair's shirtless men books? I planted my hand into the sand and focused on literally anything but the steady thrumming of my heart against the sand. The sun seeped into my pores and thawed the chill from my time in the water. I tuned in to the ocean until it sounded like a nonstop hum, cicadas, TV static, wind when you drove with the windows down.

I opened a book Blair bought me from the bookstore. Words were better on wet and sandy pages. There likely weren't shirtless men in this one, though. Blair had set it on my bed for my arrival this summer, a note scribbled on the title page:

This summer, keep doing that living you do. Maybe fall in love while you're at it? Love, Blair.

Okay, maybe there were shirtless men. I didn't know, but she'd be proud nonetheless. I was lying on a beach surrounded by people I loved and the music and art of everything around us. A boy slept next to me with a permanent smile on his face.

I'd knew I'd be stupid not to throw myself head-first into the real world, make the pages of the book my reality. But it wasn't *stupid* to me—it was *careful, cautious, smart.*

While reading about meet-cutes and summer days and a breathtaking deep blue horizon over an ocean, I dozed off inside my own breathtaking ocean horizon.

During my own summer day.

Next to my own potential meet-cute.

WE WERE BAREFOOT IN THE PIER SHOP, waiting for our order to be called. After my nap on the sand, I woke up with my salty face stuck to a book page and my stomach growling for lunch. Everett insisted on coming to help me carry everything, so we were wrapped up in the smell of greasy food and fish bait and musty air that sent goosebumps rampant beneath our bathing suits.

We killed time weaving through the aisles. I picked through baskets of dusty seashells. The zodiac cowries reminded me of Hadley. The knobbed whelks taunted me for having never found one. The fraudulent bleach-white murexes didn't even wash up this north of the Atlantic. I silently critiqued the designs on the pier tee shirts. If I were a tourist, I'd buy the pastel orange hoodie, but I *wasn't* a tourist.

Everett held up a blue shirt with a photorealistic shark mouth open on the entire front. "I *have* to have this."

We were looking through the pier postcards when I asked Everett what his favorite memory of the pier was.

Everett pointed to a postcard of a stark orange sunrise, the pier a nest of black lines before it. "When we first moved here, back when Mom and Dad still acted like tourists, we came here at least once a week. They'd let me pick out candy while we watched the sunrise. I felt like I'd never seen the sun until I saw it rise off this pier."

"What'd you pick out?"

"Almond Joys. Mounds before I realized it was dark chocolate. I just picked the almonds off for Mom. Or threw them to the seagulls."

"Did you ever get swarmed?" I remembered a day at the beach when a seagull landed on Haven's head after she got too generous with her peanut butter crackers. I hoped that wouldn't happen with our lunch.

"Nope. I think seagulls are scared of me."

"Or maybe they just don't like almonds?"

"Yes, that's definitely it." He laughed, deeper than I remembered it being. "What's your favorite memory of this pier?"

I glanced down the pier through the smudged glass doors, greeted by a blinding orb of sunlight. The sight took me back to a time of laughter whistled through lost baby teeth. I looked back at Everett. "A little after I met you. I was thirteen and Hadley was five. Blair brought us to watch the sunset. She sat in my lap and we shared an orange slushy from the old machine with the clumpy ice. 'Sharing' with Hadley meant she drank most of it. The rest of it ended up on my lap." I tapped the spot on my thigh that once dried sticky from orange syrup.

"You miss her," Everett said matter-of-factly. His face wore an expression that made me lose my filter.

I nodded. "But she's with her dad, so it's for the best."

One side of my bangs fell from behind my ear onto my face. My hair had dried erratically since swimming, a terrible mix of sea salt and breeze. Before I could fix it, Everett swiped it back behind my ear. He didn't give me time to react to *that* either. Instead, he grabbed my elbow and pulled me into the unexplored depths of the pier shop.

The other side of my bangs fell, but I didn't let him see me fix it.

Past some sun-bleached boogie boards and clearance beach chairs, next to the creaky bathroom door, a pinball machine collected dust.

Like a snapshot from an old beach postcard, it pulled us in with a magnetic force emanating from the scratches on the glass and pin-up girls on the scoreboard. It was fittingly beach themed, with palm trees and a beach horizon lining the interior.

"Did you know this was here?" I wiped the glass like I'd discovered an ancient relic in a dusty attic.

"Of course. I'm not a tourist, remember?"

I squinted my eyes at him, my mouth a thin line. His smile almost broke into a laugh, one side curled halfway down his chin. "Yes, thank you for the reminder. But what would a local be doing in the depths of the pier shop in the first place?"

"Fair point." He nodded and fished two quarters from his wallet. "Loser buys the winner candy?"

"Deal." I fed the machine to life with a quarter.

It was a wonder it still worked; half the lightbulbs were out and the other half glowed a dull orange. The bumpers squeaked like windshield wipers on a sunny day.

They worked well enough to land me two bonuses and a handsome 6,530,000 points.

There was something about the rickety button that Everett couldn't figure out. His pinballs went from the launch, straight past the bumpers, and right back into the launchpad. He gave up and pushed the buttons for fun, bouncing back and forth to the creaky tune. Somehow, he managed 2,340,000 points.

While Everett picked up our order, I mulled over my candy options at the front counter. I had my fingers on my chin like the decision between two candies was akin to deciding to restart your life in a beach house.

I decided on a bag of orange wedges.

Walking on dry sand was already hard, but doing it with hands full of greasy pier food was nearly impossible. I couldn't see through my bangs, but Everett's hands were too full to swipe them from my face like he did in the pier. *Why did he do that?* I couldn't do anything but step into his foot prints and hope we were almost there.

We made it back to Holden and Haven who had spread our towels into a makeshift picnic blanket.

We ate hot dogs, onion rings, and hushpuppies, washing them down with sodas. I spat out stubborn grains of sand that made their way into my food. Thankfully no hungry seagulls multiplied in front of us.

When I finished my hot dog, I snapped open my orange wedges.

Haven looked longingly at them. I held the bag out for her, ate a few more, then left Haven with the bag as I headed down the beach, my head glued to the sand. I was looking for a new coquina where the waves came up for their shell exchange.

"What are you doing?" Everett stood behind me, wrestling wind-blown hair off his forehead. I wished I could do the wrestling for him like he had done for me.

"Looking for this year's shell." I held my necklace between my fingers, touching each of the five shells individually.

"Can I help?" His eyes were like sunset.

I nodded and squinted my eyes from two things too bright to look at.

Everett found a couple coquinas, but they didn't have holes so he threw them back. We found plenty of ugly, gray oysters. I kept some red and white calico scallops and a white ark shell safe in my bikini top.

Everett found a perfect shark eye, but a few minutes later, he yelped and threw it back to the ocean. "It pinched me!"

"That explains why it was so pretty," I said with a laugh. Shells didn't decay until their creatures ditched them.

We wandered so far that we couldn't see the towels anymore. With my eyes, I traced our footprints in the sand until they disappeared on the horizon. They told the story of two wandering teens on their quest for shells. Finally, in front of some residential houses, where the sand went mostly untouched, hundreds of coquinas littered the beach. I got on my knees and ignored the grittiness against my skin to pick up as many as my palm could hold. Everett joined me until we found enough to agree on one perfect white coquina with a hole big enough for the chain. I didn't have a pure white one yet.

With the sixth shell safe in my palm and the rest in Everett's pockets, we raced back to the towels. Our feet hit the wet part of the sand and sent water splashing behind us. At base camp, Holden was half-buried in the sand, Haven slapping sand over his legs into the shape of a mermaid tail.

I used Everett's coquinas to decorate his tail with constellations. Scorpio, Libra, and Gemini, for the four of us. I admired my work, smiling so wide I could tell the sun had burnt my cheeks into roses.

ONCE HOLDEN WRESTLED HIMSELF OUT of the mermaid tail, we decided to leave. After a final wash-off in the ocean, we headed back to our bikes. On the way, Haven got a bright idea.

"Us locals don't have the privilege of an oceanfront pool," Haven whispered. She signaled for us to be quiet and stopped us at the gate of a motel, right by a trash can humming with flies.

We lay low until a family passed by and opened the gate. Haven caught up to them before it locked, smiling innocently at the dad. "Sorry, we forgot our pool key." She put her phone to her ear and waved to a random window. "Mom, we're at the pool now. See us?"

We got the hint and smiled and waved at the same nobody.

I looked at the unsuspecting guests and wondered if they even cared about trespassers.

"Great. Promise we'll be safe and head up soon. Love you!"

"You're a genius," Everett whispered.

"I know." Haven shrugged and cranked an outdoor shower on.

I stood under my own cold shower, basking in the swampy smell of island tap water. I watched the sun turn a patch of mist into a rainbow. I watched Everett, too.

He stared face-first at his shower head, eyes closed and his hands wiping sand off the curves on his face.

He was the cutest boy I had ever seen.

Even more so when he turned the water off and shook out his hair in the sunlight. I swore he moved in slow motion. I swore a band played a crescendo somewhere in the distance.

I was being ridiculous, watching him like some creep when I had more important things to worry about.

Hadley being gone this summer.

Haven and all the questions buzzing around her.

Making sure not to let my guard down for Mom.

I turned the water off, standing there soaking wet, practically taking a second shower from the water trapped in my hair. I laughed to myself. How insane was I that after a perfect beach day pulled from the book sleeping in my bag, my thoughts had to ruin it?

I couldn't think about that.

All I could think about was jumping in a pool—safe from a world where I didn't belong.

Three Summers Ago
Age 15, June 21

My BIKINI STRAPS DUG INTO the cherry red skin on my neck. I could tell from the rinse-off in the Rivera-Sanchezes' outdoor shower that today's sunburn would be a doozy. I threw myself on Haven's bed and spread out like a starfish. "God, it feels so good in here."

"I can't believe how long we were outside today."

"I got so burnt." I pressed white handprints into my arm and watched them turn red again. I shouldn't have been surprised. After the pool, we went out for burgers and ate them at a picnic table with a broken umbrella. I didn't think I would be *that* sunburnt while we were out there. But tans never showed up until later; the sun needed time to soak in. I wanted to be tan for the rest of the summer, but I would probably end up peeling burnt skin off my shoulders like fruit stickers from an orange.

"You need this?" Haven held out a bottle of aloe that she and Holden had definitely never used. It was the same one from under their sink last summer, sealed and filled to the brim with bubbly green gel.

I twisted open the bottle. "Thanks."

"No problem." Haven changed into one of Santiago's tee shirts and threw her closet doors open dramatically. Her wavy, black hair had dried double its usual size, cascading down her back. "You need a clean shirt?"

"Am I staying the night?" I rubbed the cold aloe on my red skin.

"Duh." She looked back at me, eyebrows raised. "I can't watch *Blue Crush* and bake a cake at midnight all by myself." She gave a Hammerhead's shirt a questionable-pile-of-laundry smell test before throwing it at me. "That's Holden's. Don't tell him I stole it."

"Pinky promise."

"Wait, you haven't seen my *quince* dress!" Haven pulled a white trash bag from the far corner of her closet. She ripped the bag down the middle. The dress popped out like a pastel yellow firework across the night sky. She held it up so the tulle swished to the floor. The strapless dress glimmered in the sun setting through the window.

"It's beautiful." I touched a few silver rhinestones. "Looks like your invitations."

Haven's *quinceañera* was last month, on her and Holden's fifteenth birthday. I got the yellow glittered invitation during spring break and begged my mom to go as soon as I got back from the mailbox. I cooked her favorite meal that night and pleaded with my hands knitted above overcooked spaghetti. I presented a slideshow the next morning that detailed why I needed to support Haven's new womanhood. I just needed a ride to Piper Island for the weekend. I wouldn't even miss school, but Mom said no each time I asked.

She insisted I'd miss too much studying for finals. She had no time to drive all that way more than twice in one year. She said I could drive down all I wanted once I got my license, but that I wouldn't want to when I was the one behind the wheel.

"Just wait until you're older. You'll understand then," she always said. I kept wondering when was *old enough* to placate adults. Did Haven feel old enough ever since her *quinceañera*? Did it unlock some mysteries of the world? Maybe that was why she and I didn't see eye to eye on Chance. She was a woman now, and I was a measly child, even though I was technically older than her. *Just wait until you're older. You'll understand then.*

Because of that, I missed my best friend's *quinceañera* and filled my absence with a lame hand-sequined card and a twenty-dollar bill. I threw in one for Holden as well, even though the invitation didn't mention him. I earned the money from babysitting our neighbor, so Mom at least kept quiet about that.

"You didn't miss much, besides *tio* Kenny. I didn't have much time for friends. I had to talk to all my family that came from Mexico. Like, *all* of them, some I didn't even see from our visit last summer. My mouth hurt from smiling so much." She flashed me a perfect pageant smile that I'd never seen grace her face.

"I didn't know you had that many teeth."

"Right? My braces were good for something after all. Hey, we can have our own *quince* right here. I'll put on my dress and you can wear my tiara!"

Haven reached for a dainty tiara hanging from a corner of her vanity mirror. "I'm supposed to wear this, but this is our *quince*, so I say the *dama* can wear it today." She nestled the teeth behind my ears with a perfect softness for such a delicate treasure. "Quinn Kessler, princess of the evening!"

I smiled and curtsied for Haven and myself in the mirror. The tiara looked out of place on my chlorinated hair, like a pearl inside a barnacled oyster. A sapphire lost on a littered beach.

Haven stepped into the dress, pulled it over her tee shirt, and bunched her hair in front of her chest so I could zip it up. The dress fit snugly around her torso and flared out at the waist. She bowed in appreciation at the mirror.

Haven played a song I didn't recognize from her phone. She showed me the basic steps to the *baile sorpresa*. As a *dama*, I would have helped orchestrate the dance, if my mom would have let me go. The dance was simple, probably because Holden planned it and couldn't have been bothered to give more than a new tackle box worth of effort. Haven told me on the beach earlier that Saray had to offer him a new one so he'd agree to spend his fifteenth birthday celebrating his sister.

It took me a second to catch on to the dance. I missed a few moves and Haven helped me laugh it off. We mirrored each other under the ceiling fan. The song ended and I finished with a bow, holding the tiara so it wouldn't fall off.

"I would have paired you with Everett for the real dance." Haven grabbed my wrist. "Quinn, you would have *died* at how hot he looked in his tux."

I suddenly felt a different kind of hot, like the sun was setting only on me. Like I was trapped in floodlights on an empty stage. "Why would we be paired up?"

Haven's gaze was pointed, a full house crowd watching me mess up a *baile sorpresa* in a blue Hammerhead's shirt. "Why wouldn't you? Everett likes you. You like him. It's simple mathematics. Well, I guess it's *chemistry*." She looked proud of herself for that one.

I couldn't believe she could manage a joke after such a scary suggestion. But some people were made for relationships. Some people liked attention, even if they knew one day it could get stripped from them all at once.

Some people were Haven.

I gulped and wiped my palms on my shirt. "Because he might hurt me," I whispered into thin air, wishing I could vanish into it. It was the same mantra my mom would repeat if she were in my shoes. It must have been her shoes I was melting in right now.

"Why do you think every guy is going to hurt you? You've always been like this. First Everett, then Chance, now Everett again." Haven rolled her eyes. Her words cut me more than I ever thought they could. Or would.

"Don't act like you don't know what my dad did." The words escaped with a brokenness I hadn't felt since it happened. I raised my voice to take back some control. "You know what I've been through, but you don't know what it *felt* like."

"This is all because your dad left?" Haven's voice competed with mine. "Not every man leaves."

"He never loved my mom and he never loved me!" My own words cut deeper than Haven's, like I was betraying myself by speaking such a brutal truth into reality for the first time. I sucked in through my teeth, trying not to lose my last bit of cool.

Some people didn't know what it was like to be me. Some people fixed their families with ice cream. Some people dated because it was *so* fun. Some people had parents who still loved each other. And them.

Some people were Haven.

"You don't understand," I said.

"I don't need to. It's time to grow up and get over it." Her voice was like flames, spitting onto my already sunburnt face. "You have to stop using your divorced parents as an excuse to be a coward."

Coward. My best friend stabbed the rest of my cool into the thin air. The room almost couldn't hold it all. Her words cut through me and my chest tried to pump them out. Heat peppered on my cheeks. My shoulders bobbed in sync with my quick breaths.

My tears fell from my eyes, straight to my feet.

I caught the first whimper in my hand and ran out onto the balcony of Haven's room. I slammed the door shut behind me so hard that it shook under my bare legs. I knew Haven felt it in the room, and I knew she saw me crying, and I didn't care what she was going to do about it.

The smooth wood pressed into the sunburn on my thighs. I looked toward the ocean's call. The ocean was somewhere beyond here, but it was hiding behind the pine trees. A widow's walk roof peeked through the treetops, looking at the white-capped waves and everything else beyond the horizon.

I pictured a woman from wartime waiting for her husband to come back and wondered if it was easier to lose a man who still loved you or lose one because he didn't love you enough.

I folded my legs into my arms. *I love me enough.* My chest rose and fell faster and faster as I cried into my kneecaps. The tiara slipped from the crown of my head. I forgot I even had it on. *God, I must look so stupid.* I whimpered quietly enough that the frogs couldn't hear me croak. Frogs didn't give kisses to girls who still cried about something that happened six years ago.

Frogs didn't kiss girls who couldn't *get over it*.

I knew I needed to get over it.

I knew it was irrational.

I knew not every man crossed his fingers behind his back during his wedding vows and slept with women that weren't his wife. I'd never forget the sound of my mom crying from her room. Our apartment was small, so no matter how quiet she thought she was being, I heard everything through our shared wall. I heard every "fuck her!" that I thought for years referred to me. I heard every wail she hid behind shaking palms. I heard every half of every argument they had for the four months he was sleeping at his girlfriend's house. I couldn't forget the feeling of being stretched out on the floor in the doorway of my bedroom. How my jaw ached from resting it on my forearms too long. The smell of dust trapped in the floor. The headaches that ripped through my temples from blinking too many silent tears into the carpet.

I'd wake up at 3am with carpet prints on my cheeks, wipe the line of drool from my chin, and sneak into my mom's bed to give her the comfort in sleep that I didn't know how to give her awake. Mom was never in the bed when I woke up. The only thing that stayed was my headache and dried tears.

How could I ever believe that I was good enough, if my own mom wasn't enough? How could I be sure that my boyfriend wouldn't need another woman to make him completely happy?

I was half of a woman who wasn't enough and half of a man who couldn't find enough.

My dad couldn't find a reason to stay loyal to his wife, or a reason to fight for custody of me. If I wasn't good enough for my father, how could I be good enough for anyone else?

I love you, Quinn. I will never leave you.

The seal on the door broke and Haven walked out with two wrapped popsicles. Her dress was still tightened around her frame. She closed the door behind her with her toes. The evening breeze blew baby hairs across her face, hiding a remorseful smile that stayed on her face while she sat down. The wooden slats creaked. Her dress bunched up at her side.

She handed me a popsicle and smoothed out the tulle on her lap.

My popsicle was orange. This gave me a millimeter of a smile, no matter how much I tried to fight it. Maybe that was why it took her so long to come outside—she had to hold the freezer door open and squint her eyes to see the color through the paper wrapper. Maybe she was just doing what she always did when Saray bought a new box of popsicles, or maybe she didn't know how to approach her best friend after making her cry.

Maybe it was both, which was why Haven tapped my toes with hers and tore the wrapper off her own red popsicle. She cleared her throat, cherry juice on her lips. "I'm sorry for what your dad did. I can't pretend to understand what you went through and I shouldn't have acted like I know better. I was an asshole and I shouldn't have said those things. I'm sorry. I don't think you're a coward. You're the bravest person I've ever met."

I watched popsicle juice drip down my stick, not knowing what to say. So Haven took a different approach.

"You deserve a rollercoaster."

I looked at her, swallowed the pain with mucus. "A rollercoaster?"

"Yes, I wish you could see that you deserve a rollercoaster." She looked at me with sunset eyes. They bled the color of steeped black tea. "You deserve someone who shows you the ups and downs of relationships. Yes, there *are* ups and downs, but you need someone to show you that most people stay strapped in with you through the downs."

I thought about that day at the Boardwalk two summers ago. I met Everett that day, but I was too afraid to ride Tsunami. Still, he was excited to ride the carousel with me instead. I knew that wasn't what Haven meant—I knew she was speaking in metaphor—but if I couldn't even find the courage to ride a measly rollercoaster, how would I ever get the courage to ride a relationship?

Did a carousel count?

"I swear on cherry popsicles there's a guy out there who'll wait in line as long as it takes to ride a rollercoaster with you."

I thought about when the carousel stopped. Children filed off their bejeweled porcelain horses, their arms outstretched for their parents. Their eyes glimmered with excitement. If I had been one of those children, my dad wouldn't have been there to greet me and my mom wouldn't have let me ride it in the first place.

I looked at the falling sun. "Every rollercoaster has an end."

"So does everything good in the world. And everything bad too! Our popsicles won't last longer than we or the heat allow." She held one hand upside down. A drop of cherry juice ran off her ring finger and soaked into the thirsty balcony. It barely missed the yellow tulle sprawled out around her. She licked the rest off her hand. "There's always a freezer full of 'em."

I smiled so weakly I wasn't convinced it was visible at all. I looked at my own orange popsicle melting fast in the sunset. The juice caught the sun and glinted when I turned it in circles.

"Every summer you stay here ends, but you always find your way back. Every sun sets, but it finds its way out of the ocean every morning. I won't always be here to eat popsicles with you in my offensively expensive *quinceañera* dress that Mom will most certainly murder me for if I get dirty, but that won't stop me from enjoying this moment. An inevitable end is why I *should* enjoy the present."

She looked at me, part of her lips stained red. The rhinestones on her chest winked in what was left of the sun. "You should enjoy your present, Quinn. Enjoy spending the night with me. Enjoy pretending to like fishing with Holden. Enjoy searching for shells with Everett. Enjoy this sunset that will never look the same again. Hell, enjoy the popsicle juice dripping down your arm."

I allowed myself to enjoy it all: the popsicle girl next to me, the popsicle breeze crinkling the palms, even the popsicle juice making a sticky mess of my arm. I licked the juice off my arm, up the stick, and onto the melting popsicle waiting for me. It tasted like tonight's sunset.

"Enjoy me saying I'm sorry. Quinn, I really am sorry."

I smiled, orange popsicle forgiveness on my lips. "I am enjoying that very much, thank you."

"Good." Haven smiled and put her head on my shoulder.

Cherry popsicle juice dripped onto my shoulder and ran sticky rollercoaster tracks down my sunburnt arm. The juice coasted off my forearm and braked next to the freckle on my thigh.

For once in my life, I didn't mind the mess.

Three Summers Ago

Age 15, July 30

I'D NEVER BEEN TO A HOUSE PARTY BEFORE, but Piper Island had a way of turning nevers into first times. Technically, it was a birthday party for one of Everett's school friends, but I watched Holden shotgun a beer can in front of a beer pong table, so I was calling it a house party.

I leaned against the kitchen sink in the only lit-up spot in the house. What would my mom think if she saw me? Was this the line Blair would draw in the sand if she knew I wasn't actually at Haven's? I felt guilty. Even though I had no plans to drink, it didn't make up for deception.

Holden finished his can, then high-fived Mason who competed with his own can of Sprite. The birthday girl, Kelsie Miller, high-fived both of them. A couple other people joined in the roar until a new song wound them into a dance.

I would have been wise to join them, do a little bit of living while I was here, but I didn't know how to dance and I thought drunk people could tell who among them was not. I settled on watching, at least until Haven got here.

Chance wanted to arrive with Haven separately. It had been an uneventful summer for me, with Haven now spun into Chance. Holden spent a lot of time with Mason, helping him fix up an old speedboat he bought online. He was also trying to catch a glimpse of the great white shark that was spotted at the end of the fishing pier on Memorial Day. Jorge had been training for a skateboarding competition, in an angsty stupor that he swore was just nerves.

Hadley visited for an unexpected two weeks, so I dropped the nothing I'd been doing to build blanket forts and read more advanced constellation books in glowing flashlight bulbs. Hadley had expanded her interests to planets and weather patterns, but I didn't think she'd ever forget the stars. It was hard to forget them when you got a glittery reminder every night.

Everett had been…well, I didn't think Everett had been all that busy, other than with training for a 10K with Liezel. So, *busy*, but not with us.

The summer had run away from us, sent us scrambling to our own corners of the island to do our own things. Still, we'd stitched back together for the night. At least, as much as a house party allowed.

I looked down at my cup of fruit punch, sipped it, and wiped it off my mouth before it stained. It tasted a lot better when I was younger.

"Hey, Quinn, right?" Kelsie stumbled over some red cups littered on the floor and put a purple lei around my neck. "Thanks for coming. I love this whole thing you have going on, very on theme." She pointed to my grass skirt and the coconut bra I tied over a tank top that matched my skin tone. Haven and I picked our outfits from Dollar World when we heard Kelsie's party was luau themed.

I hadn't met many drunk people, but I could tell Kelsie was drunk, giggling between each sentence. I smiled at how carefree she was. Was she this fun sober? Would I have been this fun drunk?

"Of course. Happy birthday."

"You're friends with Everett, aren't you?" She tucked dirty-blonde bangs behind her ear, but they fell just as quickly, curled into the shape of her ears. I knew that feeling well. A streak of gold eyeshadow shimmered in the kitchen sink light. I didn't know that one.

I nodded. "He's in my friend group." I'd never thought of us that way, but as friends who hung out in a group—or *used* to—I guessed that was exactly what we were. It was weird to say out loud, to officially be a part of something other people noticed.

Kelsie put her hand on my shoulder and leaned in to whisper her hot, alcohol-soaked breath into my ear. "Don't tell him, but I've always had a crush on him. He's so cute, don't you think?"

I was too sober for this conversation. If she really wanted to know, then yes, I *did* think. I thought it a lot. I knew I shouldn't tell my secrets to a girl I just met, but this was my first high school party and Kelsie was too drunk to remember.

"*So* cute," I said.

"I know, right?" She doubled over laughing and spilled some beer at our feet. "You're funny, Quinn. I see why Everett talks about you so much. Anyway, it's great to finally meet you!"

She walked away, her words still spinning around my head. It was dizzying. I was drunk on the words that fed me. *I see why Everett talks about you so much.* I couldn't help but smile.

I made my way through the house to see if Haven had arrived. I weaved through air made hot and sticky from open windows and sweaty dancing and drunk breathing. I wedged myself between shoulders and wispy flyaways like slinking through a thick pine forest.

Before I made it to the back door, I spotted her making the living room couch a home. I thought when she got here, she'd come say hey and play Holden at beer pong, but I guessed all she'd done was follow Chance around with a cup in her hand. Maybe she would have gone elsewhere if Chance wasn't holding her waist so tightly.

Chance's hair was too blonde. His eyes were too green. His jawline was too sharp. His features were fine on their own, but together, they made a menacing praying mantis.

Haven was wearing a thick blue sweater—not the coconut bra or grass skirt we bought. My outfit was even more ridiculous without another person. We were supposed to look ridiculous *together*.

"Haven!" I shouted across the living room.

She searched the room, then smiled when she saw me. "Quinn!"

She made her way over. Chance loomed behind her like she was an excited puppy straying too far from her owner.

"You look amazing!" Haven said. "You win best dressed for sure."

"Did you forget about yours?" I asked, raising my voice over the booming music.

"No, but Chance said this sweater is cute on me." She was tipsy, but those words had nothing to do with the alcohol.

"It is." I smiled and bit my tongue from saying what it wanted to say.

Chance stared at me with snakes for eyes. If I told Haven just how not-Haven she was being, he'd turn me into stone too. I understood why Haven was so mind-controlled, so instead of being angry, I grabbed her arm as some lifeline and semblance of normalcy. "Are you coming over later?"

"Maybe. I'll see where the night takes us."

I knew "us" referred to her and Chance, and "maybe" meant only if Chance let her. "Okay. Have fun!"

"I will! Love you!" She smiled before Chance whisked her back into his world.

I stepped out into the backyard where I could finally breathe again. That said a lot since the summer air hung tangibly around everything this time of year. I leaned against the siding. How did Haven go from the carefree girl I'd known all these years to that? I knew it wasn't her fault—people didn't seek out love poisons—but how could we lull her back? Had I been stricken by a different kind of poison? Did I even have the ability to fix someone else?

Did anything even need fixing?

"Is this what I think it is? Dr. Kessler all dressed up at a party? With a beer in her hand? I must be dreaming." Everett wore a Hawaiian-patterned button-up. He must have gotten his green lei from Kelsie. Did her hands linger on his chest when she put it around him? Did they look into each other's eyes? Did Everett like gold eyeshadow?

I saluted him with the cup. "Dr. Bishop. I thought you were observant enough to know that this is fruit punch."

He saluted back. "Same. I remember it tasting a lot better when I was a kid."

I laughed, raising my voice above the pulsing music. "I think it's just too warm."

"Or our taste buds aged with us."

"Like we're *so* old now?"

He shrugged and took a sip. "Older than the last time I had it."

"True." The thought of getting older reminded me of Haven. I hoped so badly that this wasn't what getting older looked like for her.

"We should go somewhere quieter." Everett's words whipped up the hair on my neck.

I nodded and followed him around the pool to a dark corner of the backyard. Two empty swings swayed in the breeze. The chains quivered when we sat down. In our own pocket of night, we sipped our punch and watched the party unfold. A couple held each other in the pool, a pretzel-shaped silhouette against the glowing blue. An intense game of cornhole heated up under the back porch light. A boy wearing at least twenty leis cannonballed into the pool, but the entranced couple were unfazed. The rainbow of leis floated to the top and rode the jets across the surface.

I drew a circle into the sand with my toes, then wiped it level again, finally getting the nerve to say what had been on my mind this summer. "Have you noticed something up with Haven and Chance this summer?"

Everett finished his sip, swallowed, and wiped his lips. "She's different. Holden's pretty pissed off about it. Mason's tried talking to Haven. Jorge wants to kill the guy."

Knowing they all agreed convinced me I wasn't being overly *Quinn* about the whole thing. It was sweet to think of the four of them using the air time of guy's nights talking about Haven, wanting to help her.

"He's controlling her," I said, entranced by the moon in the trees.

"Maybe you can talk some sense into her."

I didn't know if sense was a potion I knew how to brew. "I'll try. When I asked her about it at the beach last month, she insisted she was happy so I've kind of left it. I didn't want to be overbearing. Part of me thought maybe it was normal."

"It's not. I don't know what makes people chase chaos."

Chasing chaos was exhausting, but things were changing as we were getting older. Old enough now to have grown out of flat fruit punch. If I was old enough to be at this party, I should have been old enough to grow out of my own anti-love potion. Forget that we'd elected to sit on the swing set during a house party.

I broke away from my gaze to look at Everett in some silent, grateful way for being so good. So not Chance. So *Everett*. It was crazy how my heart pounded—inappropriate, almost, after talking about something so serious.

Instead of making another moon jelly mistake, I said, "You're nothing like him."

Everett didn't respond, simply sat in the moment before pointing to a cloud. "That cloud looks like a sea turtle giving a thumbs up."

The moonlight was bright enough to illuminate wispy dark gray clouds that struck the otherwise clear night.

"I don't see it," I teased.

The exchange was simple, something we'd done for years, sending each other pictures when we thought we saw something more in a cloud. It was our way to keep in touch when I was back in Raleigh, so I could still see the Piper Island clouds, even when I couldn't share the view with him.

"Then what is it?"

"A baseball glove."

"I don't think so." He gave me a crooked smile. He was bashful, tranced, reeling from my words sweeter than fruit punch. "Can I tell you a secret?"

"What, I'm the best at finding shapes in the clouds?" I asked, stuck in my own trance on the shapes in the sky.

"I still have the bouncy ball I got on the day we met."

His words plucked me from my trance. If I'd been drinking, surely this would have been the moment that I doubled over and vomited everything on the grass. Even without alcohol, I was sick on whatever he was trying to say, sick from how his voice went from silly to serious without a moment's notice.

I looked at him with furrowed brows. "From the Boardwalk arcade?"

He nodded. "I wasn't scared of Tsunami that day."

I thought I already knew that, but why was he telling me now? "Why didn't you ride it with the twins?"

"I wanted to stay with you, see if you really were too good to be true."

I was back in the suffocating pine forest inside. Every branch closed in and stuck to my skin all wrong. I wanted to run away from the forest, live in the landlocked middle of nowhere instead. My head spun. I busied myself with my too-warm fruit punch so I didn't have to come up with a response.

"You're real. I've never been able to get over that."

But I was *too* real. Hadn't that always been the problem? Too real. Too wounded. Too scared.

"Quinn, tell me why I can't get rid of the bouncy ball."

Everett softened his face.

Moved his swing closer to mine.

Stole a glance at my lips.

I pulled back when realization hit me. He was trying to kiss me. I sharpened prickly eyes at him. Pulled my swing from his with my foot. The chains groaned in disapproval.

"I'm sorry." He shook his head as his own realization hit. "I thought—"

He didn't finish the thought.

What did you think? What have you seen in the mysterious clouds of me?

I wanted to accept his apology. I wanted to grab his shoulders and kiss him until we both agreed the fruit punch on our tongues was the sweetest taste in the world. I wanted to collapse with him off the swings and get tangled up in each other until we were itchy from sandy grass.

That's what I *wanted*, but when had that ever matched what I *knew*?

I *knew* Haven was vacant in the arms of another boy.

I *knew* my mom had been vacant since I was nine.

I *knew* I couldn't kiss him, lest I became more vacant myself.

The moon jellies' potion was the strongest of all.

"I can't kiss you," I said, fiery, like he was Chance and I hated his guts. I didn't know whose skin I'd just stepped into, but I hated them, too. My heart thumped in my chest, a sound I couldn't escape even in the farthest, darkest depths of the backyard.

"I'm sorry." He walked away.

His swing threw a temper tantrum in his wake. His silhouette disappeared inside the house and left me trapped inside my own blazing inferno.

I WAS STILL REELING FROM EVERYTHING. I'd lost track of how long it had been, but I was on the front porch listening to the soft hum of music seeping from the cracked windows. The only reason I was still there was so Haven didn't go home with Chance. When I saw her last, she was dancing on the sofa, so I knew she was too drunk for that.

My eyes lulled over to two clouds scraping across the sky. They reached out like two hands for one another. Before they touched, the wind disintegrated the smaller hand into a shape that could only be called a cloud.

A dumb, shapeless cloud.

I didn't know where Everett was, but I was divided between two sides of me that battled like Orion and Scorpio in the night sky. One side of me wanted nothing to do with my feelings for Everett. The other side just wanted to kiss it all better.

One side was stronger than the other—the side I'd grown up learning to live with.

Live with it I did, even if it made me the most unbearable, unfair

person to ever try to kiss in the moonlight. For that reason, I was going
to have to be okay if Everett never wanted to try again.

I would have given up on me, too.

I leaned against the house and considered going back in—force
myself around others to stop the crying coming on—but I deserved
to feel this awful about what I'd done. I slapped mosquitoes off my
ankles and scratched nail marks into them. I deserved to feel awful
about that, too.

I was busy predicting the spots of two firefly flickers when the front
door swung open.

Holden stammered out. Mason was chasing after him like something
happened between them. Holden was on his way down the front steps
when he saw me and changed course.

"Are you insane?" He was wasted, glossed-over eyes giving him away.

Mason stood behind him, conflicted, looking between the two of us.

"What do you mean?" I asked, though I knew exactly what he meant.

"Everett told me what happened. What's wrong with you?" He
looked at Mason, then back at me, his finger in my face. "You're lucky
enough to like someone who likes you back and you don't even do
anything about it."

His words were a bullet to the chest. It hit a nerve and numbed me
to my toes. I was in his line of fire. The floor beneath us pooled with
the blood from my chest. I breathed in and out to calm myself. I'd
never seen him like this, but I had to remind myself that he was drunk.
He was just stressed about his sister's relationship, and he was trying
to be a good friend to Everett.

I swallowed the sadness thickening in my throat. "Holden, I know.
Please, just stop."

He shook his head. "Quit acting like a child."

"Holden, stop!" Mason grabbed at Holden's wrists, unable to win out over his strength.

Holden twisted his hands from Mason's, getting back in my face. "Get over it!"

"Holden, *please*. Calm down. We need to get you home." Mason managed to grab Holden's waist and pull him away from me and this awful party. He looked at me, remorse swimming in his blue eyes. "He doesn't mean it, Quinn. He's really drunk. I'm so sorry."

I couldn't look at anything but Holden, studying his face for any indication that what Mason said was true. It was too late; he was already stumbling to Mason's car.

I heard him sobbing.

It was time to get the hell out of there before I started sobbing, too. I ran into the house, dizzy again from crying and a growing headache and the music still pounding through the air. I was steady enough to find Haven wrapped in Chance on the same couch as earlier.

I grabbed her by the wrists, looked Chance in the face with fire in my eyes, then stomped both of us the hell out of the house.

Three Summers Ago
Age 15, July 31

THE SUN HAD RISEN AGAIN.

My blinds stenciled the sunlight on my seahorse comforter. My head sank heavily into the pillow. I was hungover from crying. I moved my face away from the sun, but by the time I was comfortable, the sun had caught up to me. I groaned and turned around. Haven was fast asleep next to me. Long, sleepy breaths escaped her.

I'd spent the rest of last night walking Haven back to safety at my house, ranting to her drunk ears in the streetlights about all the shit that happened with Everett and Holden. Haven tried her best to act sober when we realized Blair was still up watching TV. She laughed a little too loudly at the local car dealership commercial, so I was sure Blair wasn't convinced. I was expecting a lecture today, maybe a grounding of sorts.

But when I checked my phone, there was only a text from Holden. *I'm sorry. Meet me at Mason's dock?*

I peeled myself from the bed and closed the curtains to save Haven from the rising sun. It had to be even more brutal on hungover eyes. I got half-ready for the day and left Haven an ibuprofen and water on the nightstand.

I texted her that I'd be back with donuts—*yes, the ones covered in Fruity Pebbles*—but I had somewhere to be first.

I BIKED OVER THE CRACKS in the sidewalk and swerved around fallen pine cones. I turned into Mason's driveway, rested my bike on their lawn, and descended toward the dock. In the backyard, two different shades of green cascaded across the yard and contrasted with the dark blue ripples of the sound. The boat Holden and Mason were restoring floated idly on the sound.

Holden sat at the end of the dock, resting against wooden rails with a fishing rod in his hand.

The dock creaked on my first step. I counted each plank as I walked. It took me forty planks to gain the courage to look up at him, another twenty to finally reach the platform at the end.

He didn't hear me, so I moved in for a closer look. "Holden?"

His neck was bent and his eyes were clearly closed behind his sunglasses. His long, sleepy breaths were identical to Haven's. The shark tooth necklace Haven made him for their birthday this year shone around his neck.

Holden was asleep with a fishing pole cast into the water.

I couldn't help my smile. This was so Holden, and I loved Holden, despite the fire he'd breathed in my direction last night.

I tiptoed around his sprawled legs and under the fishing pole. I sat in a clearing between him and the side of the dock, pulling my knees up to my chest to hold them close. The morning breeze danced against my warm skin. Confused goosebumps awoke in the ninety-degree weather.

The water was more green than blue. It would have blurred into the tree line if the sun wasn't sending white glints across the ripples. The sky was the most vibrant of blues, stark against the more subdued trees. I always thought this richness was only possible in the depths of summer when the sun got hot enough to evaporate color from the ocean.

The current from hundreds of miles inland headed for the ocean without a choice in the matter.

If Everett was the ocean, then I was the river's current.

I'd tried to stop myself from feeling things for him, but some things couldn't be stopped, like a rollercoaster on its descent from happiness. The unstoppable force of a riptide.

Wind rustled salt grass in the marsh behind us. A cluster of gnats circled in the distance. My mind got swept away by a single gnat, tracing its path in the sky until it plummeted to the water and I lost track of it. My eyes fluttered closed. I dozed between a dream state and reality.

In the real world, I watched Holden's face long enough to catch it twitch. There was no pain in his face. Not like last night. He looked so untouched by the world, and I hoped he was dreaming of wonderful things, not whatever plagued him last night.

A force from deep within the water jerked at the fishing rod. The rod slid across the grainy wood, propelled by a fish on the line. Holden jumped up, the sleep immediately washing off of him as he jerked the rod to snag the fish.

He didn't notice me behind him while he wound the line up. Anticipation built, then died just as quickly.

He reeled the empty line in, shoulders slumped, then jumped when he saw me. "Shit, Quinn. How long have you been here?"

"Long enough to wonder what you were just dreaming about."

"I dreamt I caught a blue marlin." When he sat down, the distance between us was greater than before. He smiled, but his face fell when reality settled in. "Quinn, I'm so sorry. I was an ass last night. More than an ass. I shouldn't have taken out my frustration on you."

"What's more than an ass?"

His eyebrows raised. "A dick?"

"You were a dick last night," I deadpanned.

He wavered with what I said, then nodded like the taste was fine. "Sure. I'm sorry for being a dick."

I laughed. I'd let it go far enough. "I forgive you. Despite the fact that you were a dick."

"Really?" His smile returned.

"Holden, come on. You think I came all this way to not forgive you?"

"Thank you." He brushed through his hair. It was messy like it was last night. He wouldn't have any more hair to rack if this kept up.

"What happened last night?" I finally asked.

"It's hard to talk about." He chewed on the inside of his cheek, looking at the water. "But you deserve to know at this point. It doesn't excuse my behavior, but..." His hair fell into his face. His jaw clenched. He swallowed. "Last night I saw Mason kiss another guy."

Another? As in, *not Holden.* I nodded, now fully understanding why Holden had been helping him fix up a boat, why they were always together. Why Holden took last night so personally. Mason.

"Do you like him?"

Holden slouched over, shoulders hunched like a cat ready to strike. He stared blankly at the fishing rod between his strewn-out legs. He moved an entire mountain with one small nod.

I put my hand on his shoulder, squeezed for comfort. "Does he know you like him?"

"No. I can barely tell myself."

"Haven?"

He nodded again. "She thinks he likes me back. But she's my sister, she's supposed to tell me that."

"Really? Haven would lie to make *you* feel better? Come on, Holden. Think about it."

He chuckled, warming up beyond the now-broken ice. "I don't know what to do. Last night, I was so drunk when I saw Mason kiss Luke. I didn't react right away because I didn't want him to know I gave a shit. I also didn't want him to think I was mad that he was kissing a boy."

"What does he think you were mad at?"

"You. Because of Everett. When I ran into him and I asked him why he looked so upset, I funneled my anger onto you. Quinn, I've liked Mason since we were thirteen. All I've ever wanted was a chance. To know that you like Everett and he likes you and you didn't kiss him last night, well, I was jealous of you." He shook his head, cleared his throat. "I *am* jealous of you, but I know that everyone's story is different."

Holden was jealous of *me*? I watched the buzzy gnats again, pondering Holden's perspective. His logic was crystal clear, despite the muddy way he went about handling things last night. In his shoes, I'd feel the same way. "I know I can be ridiculous sometimes. I want to fix it. You were right to be upset."

"I wasn't, but I appreciate the lie. Haven might not lie to make me feel better, but you do."

"You should already know I'm not a convincing liar."

Holden didn't prod, which I was glad for, because then I'd have to justify not kissing a boy I liked. I should have done it, then I wouldn't have been on Mason Barclay's dock staring at the water like the ripples could hypnotize me into fixing everything.

"I *do* like him, for the record. It's just hard."

"I know." He smirked, then winked at me. "I'm not going to tell him or anything, but you should."

"Don't even start with me." I stuck my tongue out at him, both of us two sides of the same coin. I took the spotlight off me with my next words. "When you needed Mason, he went with you instead of sticking with Luke. Did you notice that? He took care of you. He chose you."

"He's my *friend*. You would do the same for Haven, I'm sure."

"That's not the same thing."

"Still, I don't want to mess up our friendship. I have to take things slow and read the signs."

"*This* is a sign." I pinched the sleeve of his shirt off his shoulder. "You're wearing his shirt. Like did he dress you and tuck you into his bed or something?"

Holden's face turned pink. "No. He sat with me in the bathroom until I was done puking, then set clothes out for me while I was showering. And he only put me in his bed so he'd know if I threw up again. He was just being a good friend."

Could he really be that clueless? He was speaking like it didn't paint an obvious picture of the *something* between them.

"Those are *signs*," I said. "Where is he now?"

"He went to get more bait."

"Right. Totally something I do in the early morning for my *friend*."

"Speaking of, you should go get Everett some bait," he said facetiously. "Or, like, a new pair of running shoes or something."

I nudged him with my elbow. "I hate you."

"I hate you." It crooned out of his mouth like his favorite song—one he hadn't heard in a long time but he'd never forget the words to.

Three Summers Ago
Age 15, August 2

THREE DAYS HAD PASSED SINCE KELSIE'S PARTY.

After I left Holden at the dock, I brought Blair and Haven donuts. I tried to talk to Haven about Chance, but she only thanked me and assured me she was happy with him, just like our first day at the beach.

She'd been with him the past three days straight.

Not that I knew for sure, since I hadn't seen anyone since the party. Blair finally put her mom pants on and grounded me for going to a house party, though she said she was proud of me for keeping Haven safe and told me she was always a call away if I needed her. This implied she expected there to be a next time, but I left it at that. A girl could only take so many lectures about drunk driving and teen pregnancy before it was more fun to lie in bed, toy with ideas in my journal, and count the popcorn kernels in the ceiling.

She let me use my down time behind the wheel of her car. Getting my driving hours was easier on the sleepy roads of Piper Island. I drove us on errands, ten miles under the speed limit, almost hitting the stop signs from accelerating too fast. The whole time, she made me listen to adult contemporary radio. She rolled the window down every time we passed innocent bystanders, shouting, "Stay off the road, folks, my niece is behind the wheel!" She sang along to said adult contemporary radio, pitchy and shrill and *so embarrassing*.

I took her to the post office for stamps, the tax office for God knows what, the fish shop for fresh crab, the grocery store, the same circle of parking lot until I was dizzy.

Point made, Blair.

On the last night of my prison sentence, I was on the couch watching Blair's favorite terrible reality show, stuffed from crab cakes I'd made with Blair. I didn't tell her that I didn't mind that part of the punishment. It was nice to cook something with such intention, to sing along to Adele who maybe didn't make the *worst* music.

I was almost asleep on the couch when I heard a knock at the door.

Blair and I exchanged a confused look until my phone lit up: *It's me, can you let me in?*

I opened the door so quickly there was a gust of air in its wake.

Haven stood below the yellow porch light. Mascara ran down her cheeks. Her body hid away in one of Holden's Piper Island Fishing Pier hoodies. Her ponytail was clearly disheveled by her pillows.

"What's wrong?" I pulled her away from the moths buzzing around and into the house.

Her brown eyes looked at me like they'd never experienced anything more heartbreaking. "Chance."

It was all she managed before the dam broke and she started crying. It was a loud, slobbery mess that I didn't know how to fix, so I pulled her into a hug to keep her from shattering.

"I'm sorry," I said instead of everything else running through my head.

I told you this would happen.

This is why you shouldn't date bad boys.

I knew he was bad news.

But I really was sorry, so I led her into the kitchen. She leaned against the island, slumped over while I opened the freezer for a fresh carton of cherry vanilla ice cream.

"I once heard that ice cream is the best solution for heartbreak."

Haven managed a small smile. She was done crying, so she wiped the mascara from her cheeks and exhaled into a fresh start. Under the shadow of her hood, her smeared makeup made her look like an assassin.

I sat cross-legged on the floor, wrestling the lid off the ice cream as Haven joined me. We were facing each other, our backs against opposite cabinets.

"Will you do the honors?" I handed her the open carton and a spoon.

She jammed her spoon where there were the most frozen cherries, taking a large scoop that kept her mouth silently working for a while as I grabbed small spoonfuls for myself.

"Do you want to talk about it?" It was the right thing to say after sweetening the moment with ice cream.

Haven pulled her hood down. Her sadness was gone, replaced with a fiery anger and disappointment. "He's a jackass, but you already knew that. How could I have been so stupid? Everyone saw it but me. When I told Holden, he comforted me, of course, but he looked so relieved."

"You're not stupid," I said. "Love just makes us blind sometimes."

"Thanks." She shoved another spoonful in her mouth, then laughed some delirious laugh as if everything dawned on her at once. "I was a freaking puppet, dude. He had me acting like I'm not damn Haven Arda Rivera-Sanchez."

The way she said her name—so wholly, so confidently, so *Haven*—

made my mouth break into an ice cream sweet, moment-brightening laugh. Haven Arda Rivera-Sanchez was a firework who'd been snuffed out a couple months too long. She was back, crackling to colorful, bright life on my kitchen floor.

"Did you break up?" I took another small spoonful.

She leaned in, checking around us for Blair, then whispered, "Yeah, I was done after he accused me of not loving him just because I wouldn't have sex with him." She raised her eyebrows like it was the craziest thing she'd ever said. "I'm just barely fifteen, you know my parents would kill me if I ever did that. They'd kill me if they even knew I was drunk at Kelsie's."

"You don't have to explain yourself. I understand. You shouldn't feel bad for standing your ground."

Dawn rose on her face again. "And then just...*everything* else. He never wanted to hang out with all of us or meet my parents. He'd order salad for me when you know I wanted the grilled cheese. He never wanted me to show too much skin when we were out. Like, *hello*, I'm a person! I can make my own decisions."

With every sentence she added to the list, I felt more and more relief. I was glad Haven finally saw the full portrait of Chance and his need for control, with all its vines and thick fog and rain hung heavily on the canvas.

"Damn right you can."

"I'm better than that. And I deserve better, too." Haven took another, more self-assured bite, her mouth working its way around the frozen cherries. "I'm an independent woman. I always have been." She pointed her spoon at me. Ice cream soup puddled on my thigh. "And you are, too, you know."

I wiped the soup off my thigh and licked it off my finger, laughing at Haven's new outlook, and the fact that we were two independent women entirely dependent on each other and a carton of ice cream.

But that was okay, because life was not meant to weather alone, even if you *could* theoretically survive without a best friend to laugh and cry and eat yourself sick with.

"I'm proud of you." I smiled.

"Pinky promise I'm more proud of you," Haven said, pinky out.

"Pinky promise that doesn't make sense."

"Pinky promise to agree to disagree."

That we could pinky promise to, and we linked pinkies in the warm kitchen light. We squeezed tightly like pinky promises had magical powers. On our canvas, they did.

The night unraveled in mindless conversation and midnight laughter at nothing. We finished half the carton by the time the sugar crash hit. Haven was too tired to make it back home; I was too tired to make it to my bed.

We slunk to the couch, bundled up, and got comfortable in the blue TV light, the terrible reality show welcome company as we fell asleep.

Now

July 5

I'VE ALMOST MADE IT TO DREAMLAND where everybody floats—and hopefully nobody else dies—when a ding from my phone brings me back down to Earth. I've spent the rest of the day after the pier at home, trying and failing to write a poem about sunrise, but I didn't mean to fall asleep. I hate waking from a nap just before twilight. The gauzy indigo window teases that night hasn't yet fallen, but I already missed the good part. I might as well be a recluse for the rest of the night, succumb to my guilt, but the universe has other plans.

I fish my phone from between the couch cushions, illuminated by a candle on the coffee table and a science fiction movie I lost the plot to.

come outside

An ominous text if from anyone other than Haven, but this must be related to our itinerary. Instead of replying, I slide my sandals on to find her in her golf cart idling in my driveway. There's no time to recluse with Haven on my side.

"Pinky promise this will be worth your time." Haven's still in her bikini from a surf lesson earlier, her hair choked into a claw clip four sizes too small. From her earlobes hang small earrings she made last week when she found two fraternal red scallops.

I buckle in. "It better be. I was about to have another one of my shelling dreams."

"What shell?"

"A sand dollar as big as my hand."

After eight whole summers, now on my ninth, I've still never found one. Haven has two on her dresser, which she credits to the freezing winter mornings on the beach she and Jorge brave in the off season.

Haven takes us on the back road that runs parallel to the sound. It's my favorite stretch of the bike route we established as kids. We zoom past lawn ornaments we used to give silly names to, string lights making shapes of people's balconies, and mine and Blair's favorite book mailbox.

Past a small bridge over a patch of marsh, Haven slows as we reach our destination.

The exterior of Sunset Scoop is a bright pink, like someone dropped bubblegum ice cream on the roof to melt in the sweltering heat. I'm half tempted to play the game Blair taught me—get as many free samples as I can before they refuse—but I know what I want today.

Once we both order, we sit at a picnic table in the light of the neon sundae sign. Haven sets down a paper bowl overflowing with ice cream scoops. *Try all the flavors at Sunset Scoop*, one of her itinerary ideas.

"How many flavors have you had so far?"

She conducts roll call with her spoon. "Pistachio, triple fudge brownie, snickerdoodle, and coconut crunch, so this will make 27. I'll have to cut into my college savings soon."

I slide my cotton candy scoop across the table. "Make it 28."

"How'd you know that's why I brought you?"

I stick my tongue out at her.

"Now tell me what's going on with you and Everett."

I shove the spoon into the center of my ice cream scoop to ignore what hearing his name makes my chest do. "You brought me out here to eat my ice cream *and* interrogate me?"

She takes an innocent bite of my cotton candy. "No."

I sharpen my eyes at her.

Finally, she shrugs her shoulders in defeat and rests her chin on inquisitive hands. "Fine. Everett was moody today when he came by to work out with Holden, so I figured something must have happened between you two."

Haven's my best friend, so even though all of me doesn't want to talk about it, I explain everything to her. From my drunken blunder upstairs at Everett's, to the very problem with me considering it a drunken blunder, to my unplanned sleepover, unplanned nightmare, and then Everett coming to and leaving the pier before the sun rose.

"Good for him." She cups her hand over her mouth, eyes widened. "Sorry, but it *is* nice to see him put his foot down."

"No, I know."

"So, what's the problem? Why couldn't you just kiss him while the sun rose? That shit's romantic and you know he wanted to."

"I don't know." I groan with my head in my hands. "Everything was so fresh after my nightmare, and it feels like I'm living the same old story over again."

She throws an assured hand in the space between us, lets it do the talking. "One time, when I was much wiser than I am now, I told you something that I thought would stick. Remember?"

Of course I do. She knows this too, but it's more fun for her to play a part. "I deserve a rollercoaster," I say like a mantra one begrudgingly tells a mirror.

"God, I was so smart, what happened?"

"You are *much* smarter now." I smirk around my spoon to play my own part. I don't have to say his name; she knows what I mean.

"I deserved that one, but my point still stands. Listen, I love you to death, so I feel like it's okay for me to say you messed up. You don't have to kiss him or anything, but you should at least explain yourself."

"Explain why I can't ride rollercoasters?"

She shrugs with her own smirk. "If that's what you want to call it."

"I deserved that one."

AFTER WE FINISH OUR ICE CREAM, Haven guides us to Beachy Keen, the gift shop next to Sunset Scoop. She's on the hunt for a new one-piece for surfing, so I busy myself on a hunt for the most ridiculous item in the store.

It's while walking through the aisles in the gift shop that I get the idea. Not from the shot glasses with boobs, the pool float ash trays, or the beach towels with the marijuana leaves print. No, it's the tray of mood rings that speaks to me. It isn't the silliest item by a mile, but it reminds me of Everett and our day at the aquarium. So, my hunt shifts from the most silly item to the most Everett item, which isn't difficult; tonight, just about everything reminds me of him.

I pick out two mood rings. I have reason to believe they'll change from opalescent green and settle on dark blue—supposedly for *calm*, but actually just average body heat. I fill an entire bag with piña colada taffy and hide one buttered popcorn among it. I finish off my spree with an Almond Joy and a postcard of the Piper Island Fishing Pier.

Haven does a fashion show with the bathing suits she picked out.

After much deliberation, we settle on an ugly tie-dye one guaranteed not to fall off in a nasty wave. My mood ring that started green has slowly eased into deep, ocean blue even though I'm far from calm with all the reminders of Everett in my hoodie pocket.

Haven offers to drop me off at Everett's, but I want to arrive alone—this is my mistake to fix, after all—so I board my bike and plan the conversation in my head. A few times, my throat lets a few words out, but there's only the fleeting wind to hear.

I don't give myself time to think when I get to Everett's. I set my bike down and march to the front door, past the hammock from last night and the recycling bin likely full of beer cans.

The door opens to Liezel, who smiles at me like Everett hasn't yet told her about this morning at the pier. "Quinn, hello! Everett's not here, but I have something of yours. Come in?"

I nod and follow her to the entryway. The house smells like pistachio and vanilla. It looks different with the lights on, different since I have the time to take it in. Hank sits at the kitchen table over a half-assembled jigsaw puzzle. Liezel's empty chair, two glasses of wine, and a steaming tray of purple cookies tell me I'm interrupting something. Hank raises an eyebrow at me, but he smiles and tells me Everett is at the pier with "everyone," then gets back to sifting through the puzzle box.

Liezel comes around the corner with certainly more grace than I did last night. She holds out her palm, where my teardrop earrings gleam in the entryway light. "I found these in the guest room. Yours?"

I grab them like concealing them in my palm will erase her memory of them, but this action is confirmation enough that I slept over without their knowledge, so I nod and thank her for keeping them safe. I can't bring myself to look at them anymore, but I manage brief eye contact and another smile before I turn for the door.

"Quinn, wait." Liezel grabs my arm gingerly, stuns me in place with beckoning brown eyes. She has eyes that make you want to stop and listen, just like Everett's. The wrinkles that hug her eyes feel like home. She walks to the table, wraps a small plate of the purple cookies in plastic, and places it in my arms. "Yam cookies. For you and Blair."

I nod and my heart splits in two. "Thank you."

IT FEELS LIKE AN ETERNITY since I was on the pier this morning. A day of nothing does that to your perception. Shame also mucks it up, but hopefully I can do something about that.

Halfway through my walk down the pier, I find what I'm looking for; all my friends are at the end of it.

Haven sees me first and waves me over, her lips red from a slushy. Holden has a rod cast into the water, absentmindedly reeling in for line tension. Mason slices bait fish with Holden's pocket knife. Jorge bites his tongue against a *fish-have-feelings-too* speech, tapping his foot with his arms crossed.

My knees are almost trembling as I stand on wooden planks over the roaring ocean.

Everett either doesn't see me or is avoiding my gaze, instead watching Mason until a fish starts to bleed, then he looks to the blur of water past the blue orb of the floodlights, the gibbous moon hiding behind stray clouds.

This morning's roles are reversed. With my hands in my hoodie pocket, I walk over to Everett and fish for his attention. "Can we talk? Somewhere private?"

He nods and stands up.

Nobody else notices the tension, or maybe they pretend not to. Haven finally steals a glance my way with a sly but encouraging smile.

Neither of us says anything on our way off the pier, which is the direction we both silently agree to. The pier isn't private enough. Not with families out for late night fishing, people-watchers strolling with their slushies, couples holding hands since their heads are screwed on right. Not in the nosy blue gaze of the lamp poles.

Just before the doors to the pier shop, I turn for the stairs to the sand. It's also crowded down here, but in the shadows, everything feels private. I sit in the dry sand beneath the pier. Everett follows suit, but he leaves a mound of sand between us. Above us, solar-powered string lights hang from the rungs, so artificial stars listen in. I let them.

"I'm sorry." I rest my hand on his arm, a lifeline, proof of my words in my actions. "For making you think I only want you when I'm drunk." It might be the hardest thing I've ever said to his face, but I *mean* it, so my gaze doesn't waver from him. "I do want you. *Especially* when I'm sober."

The creaky pier and staticky waves fill the silence. I think I even hear my heart croak.

Everett's in a trance on a banded tulip shard between us, but he breaks it to look up at me. He chews the inside of his cheek. I try to read his emotions—the bite of apprehension and the taste of acceptance right after. With a curl of his lips, he says, "Pinky promise?"

He laughs, proud of his ice-breaking joke. I know it's a joke, but I still pull his pinky from the sand into mine. My chest springs to life like it's lit up with string lights.

"Of course. I know it doesn't seem like it sometimes, but I think about that night all the time." Talking about it is teleportation. Here, under the pier at eighteen, I'm seventeen again, consumed by karaoke chords, cotton candy cheeks, fumbling nerves inside Ferris wheel lights. All the best parts of seventeen, without the other feelings that usually arise when I think about that night.

"Me too," he says.

We're still holding pinkies, like time elapsing will make the promise stronger. This vulnerability makes it easier to keep my eyes on his, easier to say things I don't really know how to put into words. "I've been feeling guilty about my own happiness," I whisper.

I hear how it sounds coming out, and this is why I've kept it in for so long. Deep down, I know there's no correlation. It's not rational. It's not right. I shake my head, knead my other hand over my face.

"I understand." Everett turns to me, kills the sand mound between us with his knee to wipe the tears from my eyes.

Together, we're a closed circuit. We're linked by more than just our pinkies. Our souls are connected, spindly beings. One of us could get struck by lightning and it'd kill us both.

"You think the universe is transactional." He makes an internal transaction with the information.

Everett's found the words for my sleepless nights, given a face to my night demons. Over the goosebumps on my thighs, I make circles with my thumb like I'm a psychic making sense of a crystal ball. It whispers to me that, *yes, yes*, the universe *is* transactional. The universe has to balance its checkbooks. If you've gone too long without a tragedy, you must be overdue for another.

I nod. "How do I stop my thoughts? How do I stop drowning?"

"I don't know. The world is unfair, but that also means there's no rhyme or reason to what happens."

"I'm trying to believe that. I want to believe that."

"I know. Listen, I don't want you to do anything that doesn't feel right. I shouldn't have left you this morning."

"No, it's okay. I wasn't saying the right things. I do want this." I smile and hand him the Almond Joy. "I'm going to make it up to you."

He rips it open and holds it out to me first. He doesn't have to ask; I bite the almonds off to make a milk chocolate Mounds out of it for him. The chocolate makes the almonds even better.

"For what it's worth, I do," he says between bites. "Like you, I mean. I wouldn't be here otherwise."

"You probably should just run for the dunes. Take off down the sand right now and you'll make it to Sapphire Beach for sunrise."

"Eh, I've heard the sunrise isn't as good there. And I'd miss everyone too much." He gestures to me with the deformed Almond Joy. "You know, the twins and Jorge and Mason."

I throw my head back with laughter that's a little too loud, intruding on the moment. I can't help how it escapes me. "Obviously."

Everett notices something, then taps the teardrop earrings I slipped on before I left his house. "You got your earrings back?"

His touch zaps through me. "I went to your house to find you first. I think I interrupted something."

"Oh, God. They've started making me leave the house on Friday nights. I think they're a little too excited to be empty nesters."

He chuckles and finishes his Almond Joy as I pull out the postcard. If he already has this one in his room, he doesn't say so. Back at Beachy Keen, I scrawled on it with a dying ballpoint pen at the register:

Everett, You are my rollercoaster, and somehow also my moon. Two things that are constant but never stay the same. Two things that glow even when it's dark. One day I'll be a rollercoaster and its moon, too. Quinn.

He reads it in the string lights, then smiles at me.

The mood rings glisten in my palms, waiting for him to finish reading. I have to wear mine on my thumb because they're so big, but he slides his on his ring finger. I start to tell the story of when we studied these at the aquarium, and of course he remembers, filling in the ending—that they always end up the same blue color. We've always shared that theory. They're a sham, but it was never about that.

And maybe it's a trick of the light—or lack thereof—but I think my mood ring finally boasts a new color.

Violet, like my cheeks under the moonlight.

Now

July 17

DAY FALLS INTO NIGHT DURING ITS BALANCING ACT WITH FATE.

Saray Rivera-Sanchez's fiftieth birthday party started hours after the streetlights cut on, the front yard bursting with cars. Their backyard glows from the string lights hanging from a mammoth white tent. Rows of white tables wear plastic tablecloths. Family and friends multiply before my eyes, filling the chairs and talking amongst themselves. There are more people than there is space to move. The music is loud enough for the mainland to hear. The table beside the DJ is covered with tin foil trays of what used to be steaming corn, tamales, and pulled pork.

Everett and I sit at a table near the edge of the tent, sipping the last drops from our sweaty soda cans. Haven brings out a sheet cake decorated with yellow piping and fifty lit candles. The guests sing a birthday song I don't know, but I clap along to the beat, hoping the candles don't erupt.

When the song ends, Saray blows out the candles and some partygoers chant, "*Mordida! Mordida! Mordida!*" before Holden pushes her face into the cake. Though she was expecting it, leaning before the cake with her hands behind her back, Holden timed it in the middle of the word to catch her off guard.

I join in on the booming applause and laughter while Saray licks the frosting from her lips.

Holden cuts the cake and brings us our pieces first. It's their *abuela's tres leches*, cherries and all. While we pick at our slices, I notice a smear of frosting on the corner of Everett's lip. I wipe it off with my thumb. He smiles at me in silent appreciation. If I had told myself about this moment—this soft explosion in my chest—the last time I ate *tres leches*, I would have been sure I was dreaming.

But this is real.

The guests slowly unwind from dinner, dessert, and drinks. They dance the grass into disarray. Santiago is going to throw a fit in the morning, but in the meantime, he and Holden are the number one culprits.

A song comes on that makes a few more stragglers jump up and rush to the makeshift dance floor.

Everett raises his eyebrows with a smirk. "You want to pretend to know this dance?"

I want to tell him that sounds like my worst nightmare, but I don't want my mood ring to change colors. "Maybe later," I say, hoping to buy myself the courage.

Everett doesn't prod and heads for the dance floor.

Holden pulls Everett in with him and Jorge. Jorge pretends he doesn't know the moves, but Everett *really* doesn't know the moves, and Holden laughs as Everett stumbles over his own feet. I bite my smile down and scratch a few lines in the tablecloth to distract myself from him, calm myself down. Everett's just as dorky as he was last year at karaoke, mouthing along to the song even though he didn't know Spanish. My phantom friends from that night tease me from the treetops.

He's always been yours. Why don't you grab him before he slips away? The universe is not transactional.

I've ripped my section of the tablecloth to shreds, my cheeks now a rosy mess, and I decide to divert my attention to the rest of the party.

A little boy sprawls out on a few folding chairs, drooling onto the grass despite the pounding music. A few other kids play tag in the dark pockets of the yard. That used to be us, turning the real world into our own imaginary universe.

The twins' *tio* from the infamous *quinceañera* incident is here from Mexico, and I see Haven hand him more beer before he's done with the last. Their *tio* has a beer in each hand now, doing some hip gyration next to their *abuela*, who already took a few shots with Santiago. Mason brings Santiago and Saray another round of shots. Holden attempts to take one before Saray slips it from his hand and scolds him. Holden laughs and kisses Saray on the cheek as if to say, "I'd never do that." Santiago rolls his eyes and gives his son a noogie.

Haven joins them, an already half-eaten slice of *tres leches* in her hand. Holden tries to steal a bite from her fork, but she swats him on the head. She offers him a stray cherry, pops it into his mouth, and wipes the leftover frosting on his shirt.

The Rivera-Sanchez family slips back into the line dance like they never left.

A heartstring plucks within me. What would it be like to have a family so vast and playful?

Watching the twins and their family sparks something within me. My family may not be vast or playful, but they're mine. And I do love them, even though it's hard to say sometimes. Although it's inching toward midnight—Mom will certainly think I'm wasted and Blair will wake up despite needing the sleep—I grab my phone and send two identical texts, ten letters from the heart.

I almost put my phone away until an idea pops into my head. I'm trying to be more vulnerable in my life, more open. There's still family out there who I can show this part of myself to, even if the feeling isn't mutual.

I type out a third text, same as the other two. This time, to the only number not saved under a name. My thumbs grapple with what my brain wants them to do, but they manage. The cursor leaves and comes back and leaves and comes back. I finally hit send when the cursor comes back. For good luck.

I picture my father getting the ping on his phone. I picture what his new life might look like. Does he still eat fluffernutters? Does he watch the stars at midnight? Does he think of me when fireflies flicker in the darkness?

Am I a name or a number in his phone? Does he have the number memorized like I do?

I picture him reading the three words sitting on his lock screen.

I love you.

It's too late to take it back now. I've sliced open my chest and invited the world in. Suddenly, being exposed on the dance floor is the least of my concerns. Suddenly, it's all I need to steady my mind from the spiral and keep me from crying at a birthday party that isn't mine. I brush my bangs out from behind my ears, smooth the wrinkles in my dress, tack a smile on my face, and walk toward the chaos.

This summer, keep doing that living you do. Maybe fall in love while you're at it?

So what if I'm a few summers late? The universe isn't keeping score.

When Everett notices me walking over under the string lights, happiness strikes across his face.

"Let me show you how it's done," I say with a smirk.

Everett pulls me to the dance floor, our smiles a secret language. Haven squeals and feeds me the final cherry from her *tres leches*. Holden and Jorge show me the moves to the line dance. Mason fixes my dress strap when it falls off my shoulder. We've made this backyard our own imaginary universe, but there's nothing imaginary about it. The world has long been ours, even beyond the days of playground hide and seek, routine bike routes, and picnics by the marsh.

It's never been the warm, sunny ocean that's kept me here summer after summer. It's always been my friends who have churned like the tides into family. It's true what Haven once whispered in the faint porch light: *Family comes and goes, but friends always stay.* They're forever tied with the taste of cherries, forever tied with the vision of falling but the faith that you won't.

The vision of people leaving but the faith that they won't.

The six of us dance like we're wearing headphones and we don't care that the world can't hear the music. But everyone *does* hear it and moves with it beneath the string lights. I turn my smile to the lights, greet them like constellations I simply haven't met yet. I dance next to people I've never met, but they cheer for me in the middle of a dance circle even though all I offer is something like a car dealership inflatable in a windstorm.

I'm a part of the magic and whirlwind of joy. I'm a part of the family, vast and playful.

The desire to check my phone is a distant mirage. When I remember, I stare at my phone on the table and the dark trees behind it with guilt that loves to chew me up. It's an old friend that usually demands too much from me, but finally it gives me a break. Guilt leaves me weightless on the dance floor. Guilt sits in the white chair at the edge of the tent and watches me laugh at myself for skipping a few moves, watches Everett bring me right back like he's a professional now.

Guilt keeps its distance even when the song ends. I'm so high on the moment that I grab Everett's bicep before he leaves for the table. "One more song!" I scream over the music, close enough to his ear that I know he feels my warmth. I wonder if it makes him shiver despite both of us having worked up a sweat.

He nods and moves us near the center of the makeshift dance floor.

As if the DJ were in cahoots with him or me or both of us, a slow song teases from the speakers.

Haven gasps and grabs Jorge for a slow dance. More people join in: Saray and Santiago, Jorge's parents, other couples who I don't know. Holden and Mason sit down a few chairs apart. The empty chairs put a spotlight on them. Holden crosses his arms, a vacant expression on his face, a complete shift from the Holden next to me moments ago. When he locks eyes with me, he raises his eyebrows: proud, knowing, and slightly teasing.

I stick my tongue out at him. His smile almost convinces me that he's okay. Maybe it is real, but he's good at smiling his pain away. He wears a shield of bravado. The real Holden is soft, kind, but still strong. He kisses worms before sending them to their death. He'll squash anyone who crosses his sister. He's the first to cross his *own* sister, but then make up for it with a cold can of soda and a sloppy hug. He'll pick you up off the floor even when he's in pieces himself.

We're the same in that way, linked forever by the swapping of a tequila bottle and sound secrets.

A part of me wants to run down the street into the calm, safe darkness. I want to run away from the slow song and its implications, but I push those feelings away. I deserve to be happy. I deserve to let people in and trust that they won't hurt me. I *need* to slow dance for Holden and Mason, even if it means leaving my body for a song or two.

I grab Everett by the shoulders and guide his arms around my waist. He takes over after that, pulling me closer into the spicy smell of him when he knows it's okay. His hands were made for the crook of my waist. My eyes were made for looking into his. We were made to sway in tune with the cicadas, katydids, and locusts. There doesn't have to be guilt when there's *this*. Hearts thrumming against each other. String lights carving the smiles on our faces. Limbs going where they've never been before.

With my head on his chest, our lungs breathing as one, I feel it. *Safety.* Tethered, but with Everett as my anchor. Heavy, but just because this feels permanent. If I were weightless, floating in the middle of the Atlantic, Everett would be my buoy.

I find a spot for my lips beneath his ear and whisper, "I'm not drunk. Just so you know."

He does the same to my neck. "Wouldn't it be wild if *tres leches* made you drunk?"

In the middle of this dance floor, Everett makes himself a carousel and twirls me. My sky blue babydoll dress goes with me, but Everett brings us back. I careen into his firm chest, erupting into laughter in the arms of Everett Bishop.

It's okay to be happy.

Two Summers Ago
Age 16, June 16

I HADN'T SEEN EVERETT SINCE LAST JULY.

It was two days since sophomore year ended, one since I made the drive down. Being here made his absence tug at me even harder. The last time I talked to him was at Kelsie's last summer.

"I'm sure Everett is coming." Haven stepped in line with me on the road, her wedges clicking along the asphalt. When we got there, her gold eyeshadow caught in the front porch lights.

Of course he was. The bonfire tonight would look a lot like Kelsie's party, with most of the local high school in attendance. It was at a senior's house whose parents were in Spain for two weeks.

I was ready to do everything opposite of last summer, rewrite a new itinerary in the purpling sky.

I'd grown a lot between last summer and now; had a lot of time to think about who I used to be and what Holden said when he was too drunk to stop himself. Tonight, I was wearing a crop top. I curled my hair while Haven straightened hers. My eyelids were golden sparkles.

I looked hot.

Tonight, I was going to erase "almost" from the phrase "almost kiss."

As we got closer to the house on the sound, it got more congested with parked cars and bodies and bikes. I was still an amateur when it came to alcohol, parties, kissing. Love.

In the backyard, teens danced to blaring music, threw cornhole beanbags across the yard, sipped from red cups. Everything glowed yellow from the back porch light and the fairy lights strung about. Beyond the yard, the water neared black in the dying day.

We were in the thick of it, swarming around buff guys in football jerseys, girls wearing sun dresses under the moon, lanky kids in sweaters and flannels as if they forgot it was June. In the growing darkness, I looked around the swimming faces for Everett.

Haven and I walked to the bonfire. It was too hot for the summer, but at least the glow helped me make sense of the faces around us. Still no sign of Everett.

A new song played from the speaker hidden in the darkness.

"I love this song!" Haven grabbed my hand and pulled me toward a clearing in the yard. "Let's dance!"

My nerves elevated in the middle of strangers. Haven moved my arms in sync with the pounding stereo. A breeze from the sound blew hair across my face, swirled adrenaline around me. I threw my arms to the sky, let them glow in the firelight.

This summer, I wanted to complete a new itinerary. Fulfill the prophecy Blair once scribbled in the title page of a summer romance.

I resigned to become part of the music. Songs played that I knew the words to, but I wasn't sure how. I jumped up and down to the thrumming songs, pounding my arms to the beat, going crazy when the chorus hit. I didn't know if it counted as dancing, but it was what everyone else was doing. I lost myself to heavy breathing, the shared belting of nostalgic songs, laughter unheard over blaring music.

I didn't feel like Quinn.

I caught myself smiling under a million stars.

I wanted to be part of this hive mind forever.

"Hey, girls. Beer?" Mason flashed a white-toothed smile and held up three red cups.

Haven thanked Mason with a kiss on the cheek, then brushed her long, no-longer-straight bangs out of her face. She chugged it in about one breath. Lines of beer dribbled down her pink dress.

I grabbed a cup from Mason. The amber drink was a foamy ocean behind a crashing wave, begging me to keep not being me.

Haven wiped her mouth, cupped her hand on my shoulder. "You don't have to drink it."

I knew I didn't have to drink it, but that didn't mean I didn't want to. I wanted to drink this beer. Despite my mom, who'd kill me if she could see these thorns I had for eyes. Despite Blair, who might make me drive her around the island again even though I got my license last October.

For Haven and Mason.

For Quinn, who hadn't truly lived a day in her life.

Before I could decide against it, I inched my head back to chug. It was disgusting. I might as well have licked the floor of a gas station bathroom. My throat clenched in an effort to dam the flooding river, but I didn't stop until there was no more to drink. I swallowed the final trickle, then shivered the taste from my mouth.

I resisted the urge to vomit, drew in a sharp breath, turned the cup upside down, and screamed, "Let's party!"

Haven, Mason, and some other people cheered. We refilled our cups and kept dancing, hands pulsing in the sky to the beat. Mason grinded behind Haven, running a free hand along her waist. Honey-dipped light cast shadows on my best friends' faces. I would forever remember this moment from the smell of pine trees, beer, and marsh. Red plastic cups and plastic faces and plastic music in the air. Warm beer bubbling within me.

A brunette boy staggered by us and cut between Haven and Mason, pulling Mason closer to dance. It looked like they'd danced together before. Mason ran knowing hands under the boy's shirt, planted alcohol kisses on his lips.

He pulled back, shouting over the music, "I'm gonna go with Luke!"

"You boys have fun!" Haven yelled behind her.

Beer unraveled me. I was both living and dying at the same time. Alive from the fire burning in my stomach, dead from the same fire that made me someone I wasn't. I was free. I'd never been afraid of anything in my whole life. I could stand unwavering in a thunderstorm, float on a roaring ocean.

Ride a rollercoaster.

I imagined myself as one of the trees, eavesdropping on the sea of drunk, dancing teenagers. We were happy from up there, happy from down here too, the excitement palpable. Even if summer didn't last forever, this moment spent dancing, with beer glazing over all my problems, would live forever in my head.

I turned around.

Stopped dancing.

The music stopped pounding.

My rollercoaster came to a halt.

Everett.

He sat on a chair by the bonfire, Kelsie Miller across his lap, their lips running wildly over each other's. Kelsie's dirty blonde hair fell into her forehead. It was more blonde than dirty, streaked in natural and maybe not-so-natural golden highlights. Her freckles were pronounced, sunflower seeds on a sunny afternoon. The sun favored her, and so did Everett.

Tonight ran off the rails. The boy I wanted to make things right with had other plans.

Haven turned me around, steadied me. She looked me in the eyes, sorrow drowning her face. "Let's go somewhere else, okay?"

I nodded and let her guide me to a space far away from the fire. We sat side by side on a small stretch of beach. The air felt colder down here. The sand was almost too squishy to sit on. Probably riddled with fiddler crabs. It smelled like dead fish and seagull shit. In the buzzy background, everyone else was still having the time of their lives.

The moon reflected a million tiny, choppy moons on the sound.

"Listen, Everett sucks."

I knew Haven didn't mean it. I knew she didn't believe it. I knew I didn't believe it.

"I'm sure he's still into you...He'll come around...Drunk kisses don't mean anything."

None of Haven's attempts to comfort me worked. My eyes pooled with tears, but I blinked them away before it revealed too much emotion.

"It's okay to cry."

"I'm fine." I shook my head, looked down at the water lapping the shore. I brushed a line into the sand.

I was not going to cry about a boy. He was not that important to me. It wasn't like I'd spent the entire school year thinking about him, imagining his warmth beside me on lonely, sleepless nights. Seeing beautiful shapes in the clouds and wanting to text him all about the stories they told.

This was what having a crush did—it made you feel like crying on the sand, wanting more beer like it hadn't already killed you.

Haven used the glowing orb of the party to pick through the shells around us on the sand. Most were chipped mussels or clams with skin that peeled like dehydrated paint, but a few coquinas lived to tell the tale. She found one with a purple underbelly.

"Look, it's got a hole in it. Wanna make it the seventh shell?"

I shook my head. "I don't want this to be the moment I wear on my neck for the rest of my life." My eyes stung. I wiped them before any tears could form. *Stop being a baby.*

"Fair enough," Haven said. "It's a pretty shell, though."

I grabbed the shells already on my neck, hoping they would teleport me to better days when I wasn't a complete idiot. I wanted to go back to before Everett tried to kiss me at Kelsie's. Before I started my descent for him at the aquarium. Before we met at the Boardwalk. I wanted to relive the moment I got the first shell, tell myself not to be such an asshole.

Then I'd be the one making out with Everett right now.

"Hey Haven, can I steal you from Quinn for a bit?"

I heard him before I saw him, then looked behind me at the silhouette of Chance Walker. Just when things couldn't get worse, he had to encroach with two cups of beer.

Haven's eyes asked what her mouth didn't. *Can I go?*

If she were more sober, maybe she'd remember the taste of cherry vanilla ice cream, how she once talked about him on my kitchen floor. But she was drunk, and Chance had a love potion just for Haven. I could've been less drunk myself, so who was I to judge? I nodded and offered her a fake smile.

They walked away. The look in Haven's face sang louder than the speakers still playing to the stars. It told me she was sorry, that she'd make it up to me.

I lay back on the cold sand. Beer burned inside me and sloshed in my stomach. The stars filling the sky started to dance wherever my eyes looked, doubling up over each other, riding their own rollercoaster until I was too dizzy to watch. Thousands of constellations spread in front of me, but everything blurred together. I couldn't find a single one. Even Scorpio and Sagittarius hid from me.

Hadley would have been so disappointed.

I pulled myself back up, staring forward at nothing. The darkness enveloped me in the unknown. My head spun. I had just flown to the moon and back. I was living in a nightmare that I couldn't wake up from, no matter how many times I opened and closed my eyes.

"Quinn?"

I must have been imagining Holden's voice. Haven said he was staying home for the night since he couldn't handle another day with everyone from school. I thought it might have had something to do with Mason and Luke.

But he was real, standing next to me in the sand, shoulders slumped. His hair was longer than I remembered, messier, but still swept around like it had been at Kelsie's last summer.

"Holden."

He sat next to me, his words slurred. "Are you drunk?"

"A little. Beer. You?"

"Some beer, some of my dad's tequila." He placed a bottle of tequila in the sand. "Let's add it to the list of reasons he'll want to kill me."

I picked up the bottle. A cool breeze hit the glass and lit my fingers up. I flooded my mouth with stale tequila, let it burn a trail down my throat. It tasted like nail polish remover. I almost vomited, but I exhaled steadily to ride out the feeling. I should have taken it as a sign to stop, but I took another large swig, barely leaving time to swallow before more streamed in. It made the pain more bearable, but I didn't know which pain I was trying to mask.

"Save some for me." He took a sip so large I was sure he was going to lose his stomach on the sand. The distant fire lit up his glossed-over eyes and the heartache brewing inside them. "Mason's with Luke again."

I couldn't blame the crack in his voice on the tequila. "I'm sorry."

The air fell silent between two drunk teenagers living inside their own drunk minds. What would Holden have thought if he could read the thoughts plinking in my mind? Everett had moved on from me. He and Kelsie kissed by the fire. He unknowingly broke my heart, and I deserved every bit of it.

Holden looked at me again. "I wish I had a shooting star to wish on."

"What would you wish for?"

"You want the truth or a joke?"

"The truth," I said without thinking.

"Acceptance." It was a whisper drowned out by the crickets and the distant roar of the fire and everyone around it. "You?"

I knew he wanted the truth. My truth wasn't that hard to conjure. I shrugged. "Trust. Let's find us a shooting star."

We didn't find any shooting stars. The stars knew when people wanted them and stayed still in defiance. All the sky sent us were airplane headlights and swirly, twinkling stars. Constellations teased their horoscopes like unattainable prizes, but they didn't give good horoscopes to people that didn't recognize them.

I DIDN'T KNOW HOW MUCH I'D HAD TO DRINK.

Holden left not long after the fruitless shooting star search. I didn't know where he went, but I hoped maybe he didn't need a shooting star after all.

I made my way across the yard. I didn't know where I was going. The world spun around me. It was like I was in the fun house at the Boardwalk. One tiny shift threw the whole reflection off balance. I could fall asleep in the middle of this crowd. Someone would catch me. I could run into the crowd and start a line dance. Someone would follow. I could run through the fire and make it across without catching it. Run across coals and it wouldn't even hurt. Ride Tsunami and feel on top of the world.

I wanted to disappear.

I wanted to shout for everyone to hear.

Partygoers sauntered around me like I was going the wrong way down a one-way street. They danced, tossed their heads back, glowed in the string lights that were now a wet, streaky windshield, blurry across the whole yard.

Haven and Chance were by the fire. At least, I thought it was them. She leaned into him, her neck craned for his sloppy, blurry kisses. Her rollercoaster had rolled backwards. She'd thrown everything away for the boy who stopped her momentum in the first place.

She probably knew more than me about romance, but I knew more than her about how to stay safe on a rollercoaster. I knew more about precaution and security, even if that meant she knew more about happiness. I didn't know which fate was worse. I didn't know if my caution and security had run off anyway, leaving me with nothing.

Everett and Kelsie weren't in the chair by the fire anymore. They were probably long gone now, riding a rollercoaster somewhere far from here.

On the way inside to the bathroom—that *was* where I was going—I ran into a guy. Or he ran into me? I didn't know. I didn't care. He was really hot. Instead of ignoring me, he looked at me and smiled.

"You wanna dance?" he shouted over the music. His hair was the color of coffee beans. His teeth glinted in the firelight. "Name's Charlie."

Sounded fun. I nodded. "Quinn."

I was still nodding when he wrapped his arms around my waist. Slow, sleepy nods. *Stop nodding. Perk up.* Half a second later, maybe even a whole second, his hands made sense of my waist. They inched up above my chest. Tickled at my neck.

His cheeks were red from the heat, from the dancing he'd clearly been doing all night. The alcohol I smelled on his breath. Red was my favorite color. Heat. The color I saw through my eyelids when I sank into the feeling. Golden-red. Flames.

My heart ran a marathon in my chest. Couldn't stop spinning. My head, my heart—spinning. This random guy. What was I doing? He was hot. He didn't matter. He was *really* hot. It was just fun.

I put my palm on his cheek, around his neck, down his back.

Something shifted in his eyes. He kissed my neck, mapping out its pale skin. It felt like fizzy soda popping from a fresh pour. Kissing wasn't something I did—I'd *ever* done—but here I was, turning his face to mine.

Everett's forehead kissed against mine. He started to say something. I cut him off with my lips. Kissed Everett Bishop. Eyes closed. Mouth gaped. I couldn't believe it. We'd found our way to each other, the steel fence I built around my heart be damned. Kelsie be damned.

I grabbed his shoulders. Pulled him closer. My fingers explored the skin under his shirt. Our lips were wet and soft and warm. Red. Fiery. We drowned in each other. I didn't know fire could drown you, but I couldn't breathe.

"Everett," I exhaled, gasping up for air.

"What?"

I opened my eyes. Some guy whose name I didn't remember. He looked like a movie star. I was reeling from a trance. Spinning on the grass. Absolutely *not* Kelsie.

"You good?"

I brushed my hair out of my face. "Yeah."

"You okay with this?"

"Yeah, you?" I said, breath mixing with his.

"Yeah," he whispered.

Then his lips were on mine again. Thank *God*. The kisses were quick. Breathless. Frantic. We were drowning. Had to save each other. I couldn't follow our hands before they were somewhere else. Waist. Back. Shoulder blades. Neck. Face.

Tongues, arguing for control.

We made out under all the confused constellations. Shooting stars be damned.

Two Summers Ago

Age 16, June 17

SLEEP SPAT ME OUT INTO MORNING.

I was in my bedroom but I didn't know how I'd gotten here. My alarm clock read 11:40am. *Oh, God.* I shielded the taunting midmorning sun from my eyes. My head thrummed, pinball clinks inside my skull.

Slices of last night flashed in my mind: beer, burnt orange dancing, Mason. Fire. Everett. Kelsie. The sound. Haven. Chance. A different kind of fire. Tequila. Charlie. A third kind of fire.

What the hell had happened?

A fourth fire showed itself when it dawned on me. Charlie was my first kiss and I didn't even remember the taste. I groaned and covered my hands with my face as embarrassment slithered up my neck. No wonder sleep threw me out of its clutches; I was a mar on the very foundation of humankind, unworthy of dreamlands.

I didn't need Blair; this shame was punishment enough, the splitting pain in my head a final reminder to never touch alcohol again.

I peeled myself from the blanket. It was time to enter today and face the music. My necklace successfully made it off my neck last night, so I put it back on and headed to the bathroom.

In the bathroom mirror, a hungover, heartbroken, and hideous shell of me stared back. The result of a failed effort to remove my makeup last night, mascara still clumped my eyelashes together. Foundation splotched across my cheeks. My eyebrows were vacationing in two different continents. I wiped everything away until the real me returned.

I ignored the sweaty, wind-spun knots in my hair and bunched it into a ponytail. It made my tornado of blonde hair a sunny day instead.

I stumbled to the living room and found lost puzzle pieces there.

Haven flipped pancakes on a steamy griddle. The kitchen island was partially set for breakfast: orange juice, buttered toast, ketchup for some reason.

Holden snored on the couch, using three throw pillows as a blanket, a plastic popcorn bowl on the floor by his face.

If Blair and Hadley weren't out of town this weekend, it would have been my ass frying on that griddle. At least one thing favored me today.

"Good morning." Haven raised her eyebrows. "Or should I say afternoon?"

I slumped onto the bar stool. "What happened?"

"My idiot brother got into our parents' tequila. I decided to save your ass. I also decided maybe my idiot brother deserved saving too." She counted each point on her fingers with self-assurance.

"Thank you."

"That guy you were making out with was *hot*. Charlie, right?"

I nodded slowly enough to keep my brain from falling out of my skull. It clawed at me for a way out. "You saw that?"

Haven popped a chocolate chip in her mouth with a smirk. "The whole island saw it."

"Oh, God. Please kill me."

"My only mission last night was to keep you alive. I'm not going to ruin my hard work now."

"How did you pull it off?"

"Chance 'apologized,' like he'd been doing all year, and said it was summer so we should give us a fresh start. He tried to get me to go home with him. I only had one drink, so I was already sobering up. I left Chance when I saw Holden walking around all mopey about Mason. He can be such a downer." She laughed. "He smelled like tequila, so I stayed with him and we looked for you so we could go home." She raised her eyebrows again. "Imagine my surprise when I saw you by the fire making out with Charlie Lowman."

I groaned again.

"It took some convincing to get you to come with me, then it took an hour to walk back here. Holden vomited in a bush, then you got sick watching him and vomited in the grass. Then you guys ran down the street singing 'Who Let the Dogs Out.' I can't believe nobody called the cops on us. I hope you don't mind I brought us here. Holden's going to be grounded for the rest of his life if dad finds the tequila gone. If I'd taken him home last night, they would have known. I just told them we were up too late watching a movie here."

"You're fine. Blair would do the same if she were here. I'm never drinking again."

"I never pegged you for a tequila girl."

"I'm a nothing girl. Only pancakes and orange juice for me."

"Same. I shouldn't have left you last night, I'm sorry. I'm done with Chance. For real this time."

She held her pinky out for me. I took it.

"It's okay. You saved my life *and* my ass, so I owe you." I mustered the courage to ask the question that I'd been too afraid to ask. "Did Everett see?"

Haven shrugged. "I only saw him one other time after you did."

"Was he with Kelsie?"

She nodded.

"Do you think he likes Kelsie? Like, he wants to be with her?"

"I think he and Kelsie are just like that sometimes. Maybe Everett was just as drunk and stupid as the rest of us."

"Maybe." I shrugged. Alcohol was a master of persuasion. Maybe it persuaded Everett too.

Haven slid me a plate. "So you officially like-*like* Everett now?"

I rolled my eyes, sank my teeth into a plain pancake. Syrup might have killed my stomach. "Let's not pretend I ever didn't."

"You should talk to him. You guys are, like, the worst at talking to each other about what really matters. Maybe you're jumping to a conclusion you shouldn't be jumping to."

I nodded, but the rational part of my brain—the part not taking a crowbar to my temples—knew the truth. People were not seashells to throw into the ocean when another washed up. I couldn't expect Everett to ditch Kelsie for me. I'd already had my chance and blew it. Last summer, he wanted me even though I was broken, but you couldn't take a shell that buried itself in the sand.

Haven drowned her pancakes in syrup. "Besides, I've always thought she was just your stand-in. I mean, she looks just like you."

"No, she doesn't," I said, but I'd made the connection myself last night. She had more freckles than me, but our hair was the same sandy shade. Our eyes both tried to be green in the sunlight. But it wasn't just physical features that made two people similar. Kelsie was her own person, and an arguably better one than me.

"I'll talk to him," I declared before the thought died. Just in case. Just for closure.

"Can one of you please kill me?" Holden murmured from the couch, then he doubled over and vomited the night into morning. Well, *afternoon.*

VENTURING INTO THE SUNLIGHT was the last thing on my list of things to do today. First on the list was throwing up Haven's pancakes. After that, I took some medicine, stomached two slices of bread, then lay on the shower floor until the water washed my headache away. I napped on the couch with my hair still in the towel, then ate almost a whole bag of tortilla chips when my stomach hurt, this time from loneliness. My stomach was over the company now. It was a vicious cycle, I supposed.

Now that the evil sun had set, I made my way over to Everett's. It was cold out tonight, cruel winter in summertime. There was no way that didn't mean something.

When I arrived, the smell of the ocean on my nose, I knocked on the door. The sound echoed to my toes. I shoved my hands in my hoodie pockets, trying to recite in my head the words I'd thought up on the way here. Words I shouldn't say took the spotlight instead:

Just making sure you're not dating a girl who probably makes you happy.

Are you a dumb drunk like me?

You're never allowed to stop liking me!

The door opened before I was ready. Behind it was his dad, Hank—graying hair, but the same wind-spun curls.

He offered me a meek nod before yelling, "Ev! Quinn's here!"

Everett was not far behind. He traded places with Hank and closed the door behind us. He was wearing a blue Chicago crewneck. I thought I might die. He positioned himself in the doorframe like he was scared to come any closer. The moths nearly ate him alive so close to the light. It made a more defined line of his jaw, brought out the secret gold tones in his black hair.

"Hey." Everett cocked his head, furrowed his brows. "What's up?"

The script wiped from my mind.

"Hi. I'm sorry I've been such a bitch," I finally managed to say.

"You're not a bitch," he replied, but it sounded like he agreed a little.

"I've treated you really badly all these years. I'm sorry for that. You deserve to be happy with Kelsie." The words left my mouth laced in syrup—sweet to the taste, difficult to swallow.

His face flipped through a book of emotions. Sadness, guilt, confusion…happiness? I couldn't read it. He looked at the houses across the street, his porch swing creaking in the breeze. He stared at my sandals when the words finally came. "I haven't told anyone yet, but we started dating a few months ago."

It came out like the slow, quiet release of air from a balloon. One word rang in my ears, popped the balloon. *Dating.* I felt hungover all over again. I used all my strength not to cry or indicate just how fiercely my heart pounded in my chest.

We were quiet enough to hear the katydids running amok in the trees. I knew the cicada from the katydid from the locust. The katydid's call was fitting for right now. Messy, loud, curious. Lonely, save for two people on a porch who took turns chirping. I knew that now, thanks to the boy in front of me who I could no longer call mine.

I never *could* call mine.

"Oh. That's good." I packed the words together like building a sandcastle in the rush of a wave. I pretended I wasn't crushed. I was ready at the exact moment Everett wasn't.

"You. Uh—you didn't like me," he said to the dying welcome mat.

I wanted to dig a hole in the sand so big I could get lost in it. That was where seashells hid anyway. I had to leave. Everett had a *girlfriend*. I couldn't be the girl on his porch under the summer stars. I couldn't tell him how much I'd always liked him. Not anymore. "Well, that's all I wanted to say. Have a good night."

His cheeks turned red in the porch glow. "You too."

"Bye." I waved at him and managed a smile. It felt a lot like goodbye for the summer.

I walked away from him, heard the door close behind me. I fought the urge to look back at it. I belonged on this side of the door. I belonged to the sand. My heart caught in my chest for every moment I'd had with Everett, now shattered. Caught at the unraveling of happiness and me.

When I made it onto the cold sand on the beach, my knees buckled. I cried into the crook of my arm, biting my lip so hard it bled. Every silent sob was an oxymoron to the sweet summer song of the cicadas and katydids and locusts.

If a girl cried on the beach and nobody heard her, did she even cry at all? A bloody lip, tears streaming, the coastal air—everything was salty at the beach.

Two Summers Ago

Age 16, June 18

Hey, is this Quinn? It's Charlie from the party the other night. You wanna go out sometime?

I threw my phone at the foot of my bed.

Slunk back into the covers.

The sun rose. Then fell.

Asleep.

Now

August 1

JULY FALLS INTO AUGUST LIKE TIME PUSHED IT OFF A CLIFF.

The car screeches to a halt when we turn onto Adriana's driveway, an hour inland from Piper Island. Adriana is the twins' friend from school who moved away in sixth grade. I'd never met her, but the twins stayed friends with her all these years. She invited the six of us for the night to celebrate the slow unwinding of summer since she heads off to college two weeks before the rest of us.

The house borders a lake, but it's not on stilts like the waterfront houses in Piper Island. It doesn't have to be. There are no storm surges, tides, or rip currents here.

"The drive here was unbearable," Holden says from the front door. "Has this town ever heard of paved roads?" He pulls Adriana into a hug, kisses her cheek, and walks to the kitchen in one motion.

Adriana rolls her eyes, looks at Haven. "How do you live with him?"

Haven shrugs. "Painkillers."

I formally meet Adriana, then we all follow Holden inside. The living room bleeds into the kitchen, both overlooking Lake Lockwood from the sliding glass doors. In the kitchen, the sun glints off the refrigerator. Adriana's dad shucks corn at the sink. Her mom chops raw potatoes. A game show streams from the TV. This snapshot of domestic bliss is too potent.

We set our things down on the hardwoods. I text my mom and Blair that we made it in one piece, then leave my phone zipped in my overnight bag. I help myself to a carrot stick from the veggie platter on the granite island, occupying my hands, still antsy for a text back from my dad.

"You guys need to meet Mia and Tanner!" Adriana leads us to the tiled outdoor patio.

A girl walks barefoot on the patio, hands out to keep her balance, her brunette hair cascading behind her. A boy sips a Coke at the picnic table. His sun-bleached brown hair tells the story of summer days spent at the lake.

We exchange hellos, then shift into the lull of new people in new places—the push and pull of what to do and say next. Holden settles us into the day, heading down the dock with a fishing rod and his tackle box. Mason runs past him to cannonball into the water, Adriana right behind. Jorge challenges Holden to a fishing competition. Mia takes Haven on the jet ski. Tanner catches up to them somewhere on the lake.

That leaves me and Everett on a swinging bench on the dock, taking turns with a bottle of sunscreen.

The lake is sweet tea. The sun's late morning position has driven away the early dawn locusts. Splashy sounds ring out around us: Holden's bobber, Mason and Adriana vying for the same watermelon float, something from behind us plopping in the shallow water. It's comforting to look at a body of water and see the land on the other side. If you didn't know better, you'd think the water was still, a postcard of peace and domestic bliss.

Everett takes it all in with me.

"This reminds me of a lake I used to go to in Illinois. We stayed for one week every summer when Dad finally took off work. We spent all day swimming and grilling at the beach. Dad tried fishing every day. He never caught anything, but he always told us fishing is about the company you keep, not the fish you catch." He makes his voice deep like Hank's, then laughs at himself, Hank's corny adage, or maybe both.

I laugh because he does. "You think that's why he picked Piper?"

"Mom always loved North Carolina's lighthouses, always did puzzles of them and collected souvenirs, so my dad made it happen for her."

I look out at the lake and imagine I'm Everett. I take in how the ripples catch the sun's rays, how small the pine trees look on the horizon, how water dances carelessly on the surface. I feel the memory like it's my own. What's it like to watch your dad suck at fishing but still believe your presence is the reason the moment is perfect?

"I'm glad." I wipe a line of unblended sunscreen into his forehead with my thumb. My mood ring catches in the sun.

"Thanks." He smiles.

I point to the only cloud in the sky. "That cloud looks like an upside-down hot dog."

"It even has mustard on it."

"I hope you mean ketchup." I smirk, searching for a way to disagree, like old times.

The cloud changes with the wind. We race to tell stories about it, read it like a fortune. An octopus riding a bike. Apple pie. An elephant playing tennis. An umbrella pitched on a mountaintop.

Tanner, Mia, and Haven come back into view. They cut the engine in the no-wake zone and bob back to us. Haven jumps into the water.

"Anyone want a ride?" Mia asks.

"I don't really..." I bite my cheek. "Swim."

"This isn't swimming. It's jet-skiing."

"Your life jacket begs to differ."

She makes a face like she can't argue, but she keeps prying. "I swear you'll be okay."

I sit up a little taller, pseudo confidence in my voice. "Pinky promise?"

"Yes," Mia says. "If you want, Adriana can take you."

Adriana nods from a watermelon float in the water. "Pinky promise."

A million thoughts race through my mind, now that the possibility is upon me. *What if something goes wrong? Am I prepared to meet water again? Is the risk worth the potential fun?*

"You can do it, Quinn!" Haven calls out after she settles onto the float with Adriana and Mason, nearly knocking them off in the process.

Mason does something similar, whooping and beginning a chant of my name.

A past version of me would have called this peer pressure—which it is—but my friends have always wanted the best for me, so maybe peer pressure isn't always a bad thing.

I look at Everett, silently seeking his approval. He gives me a droopy smile and shrugs like he wants me to have all the fun in the world but is too afraid to say so. If the idea makes Everett smile, then I don't care that my name is Quinn Kessler. I deserve some fun.

I'm not sure what fully compels me to do something so risky, so outside my comfort zone, but a voice deep within me reaches out and says, "you deserve a rollercoaster."

I pull a green life jacket off a nail in the shelter. It smells of mildew and barely zips over my chest, but it's too late to back down.

The lake roars with applause. I shake my head bashfully. It feels like I'm on stage at Holy Mackerel.

I step down on the footrest and throw my leg across the seat, holding tight to Adriana.

Adriana cranks up the engine while I wave my goodbyes to everyone on the dock. I stick my tongue out at Everett, smiling more than my mouth can contain. Once we're past the no wake zone, she accelerates slowly, then speeds up once I'm more accustomed to the rush.

The water is a sleek glass sheet, the jet ski the blade that slides it clean down the middle. There are no ripples in the water, so we glide across the smooth surface.

I forget to be rational, confident enough to say things I'd normally never even think. "Go faster!"

She obeys, leaving my words hundreds of feet behind us. The lake stretches ahead. The wind rushes straight into my open-mouthed grin. My eyes sting from the bright sun and the water droplets that shoot into my eyes when we bounce over the wake of a speedboat. We're a single unit that lifts off the seat for a second of reckless abandon. So *this* must be what a rollercoaster feels like.

When we land, I feel it all at once.

Freedom hugs me tightly.

Tighter than the anchors that have held me down all these years. They're gone now; I can feel it. They flew clean off my shoulders right around 40 miles per hour.

"Can I do a trick?" Adriana shouts.

"Yes!" Adrenaline screams back.

The rev of the engine responds for her. The wind slaps my face. It's hard to keep my eyes open, but I do anyway and watch Adriana jerk the steering wheel completely around.

I lift from the seat.

Sky and water blur before my eyes.

My body shatters the surface.

The anchors return.

Water hugs me tightest of all.

For the first time since my late-night swim with Everett last year, I'm in the water. I forget how to resurface, but my life jacket does its job, pulls me back into the world Hadley wasn't. I feel like I might die, my breath confused and quick. I wipe my eyes open and try to move forward, but my legs are stuck in Jell-O.

Adriana swims to me, grabs my life jacket. "Quinn, are you okay?"

I nod.

She pulls me back to the jet ski, now idling in the water. "I'm so sorry. I didn't mean to break my promise. I thought you were holding on tight enough and you gave me the okay and I'm just so sorry..."

I listen to her babble the whole way back to the jet ski. I'm not mad at her. I'm not mad at the water. Or the jet ski. I'm mad at myself. How could I ever think I'd be able to walk the Earth not shackled to anchors?

Adriana doesn't exceed 15 miles per hour on the way back. I pant into her back, squeezing my eyes so tightly they wrinkle, trying to ignore the lake water streaking down my legs and how sore my ankle feels when I put pressure on it.

I can't ignore it; it's what I deserve.

When we get back to the dock, Adriana cuts the engine, jumps in, and pulls the jet ski flush with the dock.

Haven jumps up from her towel, helps me onto the dock. "Did you fall in? Are you okay?"

I must look as distraught as I feel. Adriana hands me a towel. I wrap up in it and wring my hair out onto the dock. "It's no big deal." If I keep telling myself that, maybe it will become true.

Adriana mouths another "I'm sorry." I shrug it off like the nothing that falling into a lake should be. She walks back to the backyard where everyone but Haven plays cornhole.

"I promise it was fun," I say to Haven.

"I believe you."

"My ankle is a little sore, but *really*, I'm fine."

"I know." She smiles and lies back down to return to the sun and the book slumped over her towel.

I fan my towel next to hers and lie on my stomach, resting my forehead on my arms.

"Let me read you a story." Haven pages to where she left off.

I don't know what happened earlier in the book, but there's something about the curl in her voice that makes me feel like I've been with it all along. The story is just like Haven: all summer, no worry, the tiniest bit of romance. It's about a girl who works at a sleepaway camp trying to get the super-cute-but-grumpy counselor to fall in love with her. It's obviously something that would only happen in a syrupy beach read, but there's a reason syrup sticks to everything it touches.

I let the words stick to me as the story and the sun lull me into a half sleep that might put me into a permanent one in this midday weather, my body failing as the heat takes me. If I do wake up, I'd have towel prints on my arms, a headache burned into my brain, skin that's only white when you poke it.

So I don't fall asleep. The Mom side of me actually believes I'll die. Instead, I focus on the lake swaying under us. The joy I find in a little thing like that must be the Dad side of me.

Then I realize it's been hours since the last time I thought about checking my phone.

For that, I can at least thank the lake.

LATER, WHILE THE BOYS take to the jet skis, Haven, Adriana, and Mia balance themselves on the watermelon float. I lie on my stomach at the edge of the dock, dangling my hand into the water as a half-assed truce. After a whole plate of seafood boil and a large slice of *tres leches*, all I want to do is laze.

Mia tells us about the night she and Tanner kissed at a gas station and then decided it was just the heat of the moment.

"You know what I think?" Haven stretches a wet hand to the sky and watches the water drip off her fingertips.

"What?" Mia asks.

"I kind of get the impression that he likes you," Haven says. "I bet that gas station kiss meant something more to him."

"Dude, I've been telling her this all summer!" Adriana exclaims.

"Are you kidding me? We both agreed it was awkward. We only kissed because we were drunk on the beauty of graduating high school or some bullshit like that." Mia laughs, splashing one foot in and out of the water like a nervous tic.

"Yeah, in the gas station parking lot." Adriana snickers. "But seriously, that kiss meant something to Tanner."

Haven sprinkles water on her chest. "You could see it on his face when you were talking about it earlier. I see it on Everett's *all* the time. You and Quinn are just alike."

"Okay, we don't have to bring *that* up." I splash Haven who doesn't seem to mind.

"I was going to ask you about that." Mia looks at me. I don't know if she really was going to ask or if she just wants the heat off of her, but she persists. "You like each other, don't you?"

"Everett and I are...complicated. Well, it's more like *I'm* complicated, but that sort of makes us both complicated."

"Yes, they like each other," Haven says, filling in my story gaps like she's reading from her book on the dock. "But Quinn has her reservations and we forgive her for it." She leaves it at that.

"It's hard to be vulnerable." I nervously trace shapes on the surface of the water—a sea turtle riding a bike.

"I get it." Mia looks at me. "Sometimes I feel like I'm floating outside my own body, but it's easier to float than let anyone catch me."

Nobody's ever put it that way, but that's how it feels to be the girl who sees thorns before roses, clouds before a blue sky. The girl whose parents spun pain into her bones.

Sometimes it's easier to float.

As THE SUN SAYS ITS OFFICIAL GOODNIGHT, the warm cloak of summer strips down to an outfit reminiscent of a brisk autumn morning. Cicadas chirp the trees' steady heartbeat. Frogs sing ribbit songs from the marsh.

After an intense dragonfly-catching competition and a tiebreaker round of cornhole, we sit at the edge of the dock for the last snatches of sunset.

I cross my legs over Everett's lap on the swinging bench. Adriana, Haven, and Jorge sit with their toes in the water. Holden and Mason are both cross-legged on a towel. Tanner lies with his head in Mia's lap as she brushes her hands through his brown hair. I raise my eyebrows at her. She does the same to me. *Touché.*

The sky casts a purple haze on Everett's face. Everett strokes his thumb over my ankle and asks me if it hurts. It's still humming from earlier on the jet ski, but I've been using it all day so I tell him it's okay.

His absentminded touch makes me feel like I'm floating.

I study how he watches the lake with such intent. I look at the low-hanging band of indigo clouds on the horizon and try to guess what picture he's imagined from them.

Everett must have read my mind, because he turns to me, smiles softly, then whispers, "They're quill pens."

"They certainly are." I smile, my voice a soft purple dusk.

This is about as close to a perfect moment as I've felt since last summer, one of those moments I have to remind myself to be fully present in. If I don't, it'll pass me by like a dragonfly zipping through dusk before I have the chance to trap it in a mason jar. But I don't need to catch the moment yet, only sit inside it and feel the lull of tired conversations between lake people and beach people.

We take turns swatting mosquitoes off our skin, listening to Adriana strum "Brown Eyed Girl" on her guitar.

Dock lights turn on in the distance like earthly stars, signaling that it's time to go inside, shower, and make our beds in the living room.

When I stand up, pain seethes an angry snarl in my ankle. It's an unbearably loud sensation that forces me to lift off my foot as soon as it strikes. In one motion, I fall on the dock with only my palms to brace my fall.

"Are you okay?" Everett pulls me up.

"I think I sprained my ankle on the jet ski." I lean into Everett as we walk into the house, but *only* because I can't stand on my own.

Pinky promise.

Last Summer

Age 17, June 15

MASON STARTED OUR TOUR of the sound with the inspiration behind his boat's name, *Kingfish*. It was named after his memories with Holden, who not only helped him fix it up, but became his boyfriend shortly after his seventeenth birthday. Jorge's and Haven's secretive nudges had finally paid off and both of them stopped playing games.

I was trying to do something similar this summer.

I thought of one thing only while Mason tried to steer Holden off his tube. One thing while Haven and I danced in the wind. One thing the entire seafood dinner, even as the water outside changed from blue to white to orange with the setting sun.

Everett.

I perched myself on a cushion on the bow, legs folded under me, hyper-aware of how I looked. I imagined myself how Everett would. Was my tank top billowy enough when I was dancing? Did summer bring my light brown freckles back to life? Was my wind-spun ponytail casually cute or just a mess? Did I look mysterious behind my sunglasses?

Everett and Kelsie had broken up last Christmas, so we were back in this game we loved to play.

Haven called me as soon as she found out. It was easy to feel relieved, but even easier to feel guilty for considering someone else's heartbreak a Christmas present. I fought the urge to text him my condolences. I didn't want to open that can of worms so far from summer. I didn't want to be a tease.

I tried not to be a tease now, or a rebound, even if it had been six months. I didn't know why they'd broken up, or who broke up with who, but I couldn't assume it had anything to do with me. Why the hell would it? Still, I couldn't help how my heart hummed. I sat next to him and tried to put my best foot forward, like I was a movie he was about to review.

I swished my pony tail behind my back, pretending it was because I didn't like how it stuck to my warm neck. *Look how carefree I am!*

Boat name backstories were enthralling. The life jacket buckles were mesmerizing. The orange soda was astonishing. *Look how relaxed I am!*

I wore a subtle smile, pretending my resting face actually looked this sweet. *Look how happy I am!*

I loved how the spotlight felt, even if I was only glowing in my head.

Finally, Everett's eyes found mine. I didn't immediately turn my head, but I couldn't help it after a couple more glances at the cotton candy clouds.

I'd never forget his smile, the golden fractals of sunset on his cheeks. I was stuck inside the visions of a sound sunset I never wanted to be rescued from.

Last Summer

Age 17, June 30

"How many more miles?" Haven asked.

"Two." Holden stared straight ahead, holding Mason's hand over the center console.

Mason steered absentmindedly on the highway, headlights the only break in the evening darkness. All I could focus on was Everett's knee bobbing next to mine. Our sides were pressed together. I felt each of his movements like they were my own, but both of us pretended we didn't notice.

The drive from Piper Island to Carolina Beach was a long, eerie shot of darkness that only existed on Ocean Highway, the road that connected every beach on the North Carolina coast. We passed the time with Would You Rather and throwback songs from middle school.

We were only making the trip because Ashe's Donuts just reopened after a string of renovations. It was all Holden had talked about since we first heard whispers of a world-famous donut shop, so Mason booked a motel near the Carolina Beach Boardwalk, home of Ashe's

Donuts. He was the first to take off work, and everyone but Jorge was able to swing it.

Carolina Beach was covered in gift shops with shark mouths for doors, restaurants that were pulled from the sea, mini golf courses that stayed open until the sun came up. We'd driven straight into a trap—the tourist kind—made for families who wouldn't make it out with any money to spare. Everything was lit up for the moon.

Nestled inside temporary carnival rides, gift shops, and smoky bars, Ashe's Donuts was lit up in green neon. The line was about fifty people deep, all rocking on their heels in sugared anticipation. Ashe's was famous—even with locals—because it only opened for tourist season and stayed open late. It was one of those cash-only places with a letter board menu that wasn't needed since there was only one item: a dozen Ashe's Donuts. That was how I knew this trip would be worth it.

While Haven, Holden, and Mason joined the line, Everett and I walked around the Boardwalk. Different from Sapphire Beach Boardwalk, this one ran parallel to the shore and severely lacked actual *boards*. But there was still the cigarette smell, gum-plastered sidewalk, and a kaleidoscope of colored lights.

"Thoughts on the age of this gum?" I asked Everett, pointing to a dried clump that might have actually been tar.

"At least forty years." Everett smiled. His hands were deep in his pockets, but he stood so close to me that our shoulders could kiss.

"I don't feel like disagreeing." I nudged him so our shoulders kissed. *That* was how I knew this trip would be worth it.

I'D HAD THREE DONUTS by the time we checked in to our room at the Salty Seahorse. They were just as soft and sweet as I expected, but the motel sure wasn't.

The whole place looked unswept, if a place could ever be called that. Brown stains lived on the walls as if stunned there with flashing light. The sea glass tile on the bathroom floor was more glass than sea. It boasted what must have been original to the building: marigold upholstery, dusty wall sconces, oak wood paneling. I dropped my duffel bag dramatically on the browning tile floor. It felt fitting.

"I love the smell of mothballs." Holden stretched out on the bedspread, an unfortunate collage of vintage beige seashells.

"Shut up." Mason hit him with a scallop throw pillow.

We made our way to the balcony with the two bags of donuts that survived the drive over. The bag emptied fast, even as it split the spotlight with a family-sized chip bag and juice boxes we picked up from a 24-hour pharmacy up the road.

"If you close your eyes, it almost feels like this is home," Haven said, her eyes closed to imagine Piper Island.

"You don't have to close your eyes, dumbass. It's dark outside," Holden said.

"Yes I do, it's too bright out here to be Piper."

It was true. The light pollution was an orange mirage steaming from the Boardwalk, the hotels, and everything else behind it like a sidewalk in midday heat.

We eased back into conversation, the broken light on the balcony listening to it all. We talked about our upcoming senior year, career goals we were too young to have to decide, where we saw ourselves in five years. Haven wanted to go into nursing. Holden wanted to study marine biology, somehow balance the ethics of fishing and sustainability. Mason wanted to go into some form of business that would take him out of board shorts and into black slacks. Everett wanted to become an astrophysicist.

I was mostly quiet, taking turns with Everett eating the hardened icing from the bottom of the donut bag. I held it out for him to finish off. He wet his thumb and picked up the last icing crumbs. He pulled his thumb out of his mouth with a pop, then poked the freckle on my thigh. "What do you want to do, Quinn?"

"I think I might major in English," I muttered. "But I don't know what I'd do with that after."

"Whatever you decide, I know you'll be perfect," Everett said.

"Thanks." A smile took over my face—a real one. It was an amalgamation of what was happening in my chest. Everett steadied the part of me that felt like it was always churning with cherry syrup in a slushy machine. He was the one whose cup finally caught me, the mouth that drank away my dizziness, even if only for a moment.

DOWN AT THE POOL, Holden cannonballed into the glowing blue water. Mason splashed him with his own cannonball. Haven tossed her towel onto a mildewy lounge chair and dove off the diving board. Her legs were bent enough to make a slightly bigger splash than it should have.

"Last one in is a rotten egg!" she screamed at me and Everett.

We raced to make it into the water first. I was still wrestling my shorts off when Everett pulled his shirt off from his back the way only boys could. He jumped in, so I decided on the slow approach since I was already the rotten egg. I trudged into the water until it became too difficult to take the next step. The water inched up my waist, covered me in goosebumps, hugged me in cold comfort.

"Hurry!" Holden strode toward me.

"No!" I tried to run from him through the water, but it felt like running through Jell-O.

Holden grabbed me and lifted me over his shoulder. I let out small laughs between playful screams, pleading against a fate I knew I couldn't prevent. He flipped me into the five-feet area. The freezing water hit the worst parts of me all at once, but I was already used to it by the time I emerged.

"Still smell rotten eggs?" I smoothed wet hair from my forehead.

"Yes, but it's the ocean this time." Haven laughed from the deep end.

I took a deep breath of the pinch in the air from seashells, salty seahorses, and whatever microorganisms in the water made up the coastal smell. It brought memories of my fingers around handlebars, dancing without a care, crying in a *quinceañera* crown, my thighs clung to polyester seats, Hadley's face changing colors with the fireworks, Sunset Scoop waffle cones I'd only ever let my nose enjoy.

Now midnight spent in a motel pool with my best friends.

And Everett.

"It smells like low tide," Holden said.

I lay back on the surface of the water. Since Haven and Everett taught me two years ago, I had learned to trust the water. It caught me and let me lie on its surface. I let out breaths small enough to stay afloat, spread my arms and legs out to be as free as a moon jelly. The world was muffled under the water. I turned the world off, lost myself to the cool water.

The moon showed half of herself tonight; the other half hid in the shadows. The stars weren't visible from the bright pool deck, but I knew they were with us.

They were one thing I could always count on.

Last Summer

Age 17, July 1

SLEEP CAME QUICKLY after we all showered off the motel chlorine, but waking back up came quicker, especially since the travel show we fell asleep to morphed into an alien conspiracy documentary.

I glanced at the other bed. Mason faced the wall. Holden slept flat on his back, both arms above his head. He looked so much like his younger self, which made me smile. Next to me, Haven was somehow still asleep despite the white UFO lights abducting her face. I giggled. She slept with her mouth wide open like Holden usually did.

The pull-out couch was empty, a wrinkled mound of sheets in Everett's place. The curtain to the balcony was disheveled. My eyes did the math, and then I was upright to finish the equation.

The door whined on my way out. Thankfully, the room stayed sleeping, but the balcony was awake with Everett Bishop.

"Can't sleep?" I sat in the empty lawn chair beside him.

He massaged the back of his neck. "The sofa's like a rock."

"I'm sorry."

"It's all good. It's peaceful out here."

He was wearing the same Chicago crewneck from last summer's goodbye. This moment was different, but hinges of the past squeaked through. A porch, secrets in front of a closed door, the distant roaring ocean, a sky full of stars. Light doing his jaw a favor. My heart knocking on my ribcage.

But Kelsie was a distant memory. I was here, and when I asked Everett if he wanted to go to the beach, he nodded and followed me.

I turned the TV off and slipped the pieces of saltwater taffy I bought earlier into my hoodie pocket. The door shut behind me, but this time Everett was on the other side with me, waiting to walk beside me.

We followed my cell phone light to a spot on the sand. In the pale moonlight, the sand glowed white like freshly laid snow. It felt cold like snow, too, so far removed from sunlight.

He sat down next to me on the sand. I hugged my arms around my knees, faced him. In front of the hazy orange horizon, he was a midnight blue figure of curly hair and hunched shoulders. Blue, but darker than the moon jellies at the aquarium. The universe had given me another chance to toy with blue. I wouldn't dream of calling it ugly this time.

The bridge of his nose careened into his lips. The moon glinted off the waves, but I preferred to watch him, imagine brushing my hand across the sore muscles in his back.

Instead, I pulled a taffy from my pocket and pressed it into his hand. He crinkled it out of the wrapper and took a bite.

His mouth was still working around it when he pressed it back into my hand. "Have the rest. See if we can figure out the flavor."

I didn't think a second about it and popped it into my mouth. I knew the flavor well and smiled knowing the same flavor was on Everett's tongue. We were tethered by the sticky, stringy pull of salt water taffy.

We guessed cotton candy at the same time. I'd know it in every lifetime. We'd do this in every lifetime.

I opened another, took a bite, and gave him the other half.

We debated about the rest. We couldn't agree between pomegranate and cherry. Or root beer and butterscotch. Cinnamon couldn't have been clearer. Buttered popcorn made both of us recoil. Chicken and waffles was a confusing but pleasant surprise. Piña colada made my jaw clench, but it was a welcome feeling.

Soon, my pocket was empty save for wrinkled, sticky wrappers. I didn't know the time, but the moon shone from a different spot in the sky. The breeze was cold and gentle on my hair. If I was more than a blue figure to him now, I'd thank the wind for making me look so effortless.

Everett shifted in the sand. "Can I tell you something?"

"Yeah."

"I broke up with Kelsie."

There was an ocean of things I could have said, but it was time to be diplomatic, not shove myself into his book pages. "I'm sorry. I'm sure breakups are hard."

"No, it's okay. Sorry, I shouldn't have brought it up," he said.

"Why? I thought she was cool."

It was true; I did.

"I know, I just feel like I wasted her time. I feel terrible. I thought I had feelings for her, and we had fun, but..." His abrupt silence illuminated the lull of crashing waves. "It didn't feel like this."

This. Quinn and Everett. Carousel horses. Stories in the clouds. Moon jellies. Warm fountain pennies. Bike rides. Katydids. Ocean water. Pinball. Unbridled laughter. Cicadas. Pinky promises. Porch light. Salt water taffy.

Memories from the summers of us.

"Nothing else does," I croaked. Gulped. Stretched out under the stars to calm the roar within me.

Everett did the same, his blue silhouette plucked from the sky behind him. The magnetism between us felt tangible.

Stars still twinkled despite the town's yellow cast and the bright half-moon. My eyes bounced around the cloak of stars, stringing together new constellations in the sky. I stared until they seemed to move like chess pieces in a game the universe played against itself.

And then it happened.

A star cut through the night sky, leaving a trail of moon dust in its wake. My eyes drew to it like a camera flash in the distance.

I leaned onto my elbows, feverishly tapped Everett's arm. "Did you see that? Did you? A shooting star! Quick, make a wish!"

He chuckled. "I already did."

I lay back down, breathing in and out in clandestine ritual. I almost uttered the same wish I once tossed to the aquarium fountain, but how many cheek eyelash, birthday candle, and dandelion puff wishes had I wasted on something that couldn't change?

Wishing for the past to change was a waste of a wish, so I shut my eyes and whispered something else into the void, something I'd been thinking about a lot lately.

I wish for a rollercoaster.

When I opened them, a still sky rested above. The stars were probably silently deliberating whether my wish should be granted. A celestial jury, astronomical wish granters. Did stars understand metaphors or was I going to wake up tomorrow morning with a wooden track off the motel balcony? Would I ride it if the opportunity presented itself? Did *I* understand metaphors?

Did I even need shooting stars? Maybe it was all up to me.

"What'd you wish for?" Everett asked.

I giggled. "You know I can't tell you."

"Fine, then I won't tell you what I wished for."

"I already know you wished you could beat me at pinball."

"Maybe." Everett laughed.

Last Summer

Age 17, July 18

TONIGHT WANTED SOMETHING MORE FOR ME.

I was restless in bed, my night with Everett at Carolina Beach pinging in my head. "*It didn't feel like this,*" was the bedtime story that wouldn't quite lull me there. Everett was single, and time was ticking for me to do something about it. It had already been a few weeks but I hadn't mustered the courage to make my move yet.

The last time I thought he was single and I was ready, he actually *wasn't* single. He'd moved on to Kelsie, but this summer, I didn't have to let us keep missing each other.

The night was in control. It made me slip out of bed, throw a bikini on, and set off into the night. I hoped I didn't wake Blair or Hadley up when I left, picking my bike off a palm tree and setting off into the night. The air was cold on my bike, but it still felt like freedom.

The feeling fully hit me when I turned onto Main Street, with only a few porch lights and deer awake with me during the witching hour.

I was really doing it.

My therapist would be so proud. I'd tell her about it in our call tomorrow. We'd been talking every other week since last November. Last session, I updated her on Everett—that he was single at the same time I was—and she reminded me of something we'd been working on during the school year: How to happen to your own life before it happened to you. Back home, I'd only gotten as far as captaining the tennis team, but armed with new information about Everett, I could do more. One day, I would ride a real rollercoaster, and then I could probably conquer the world, maybe even escape from the quicksand my dad left me in.

Tonight, it started with Everett. It was time to take a step. If you did that in quicksand, you'd drown in it, but there was no rule about beach sand. Beach sand was just microscopic shells. Shells never drowned anyone.

I texted him before I biked over, but I didn't expect a reply so quickly. There was still no response when I set my bike against his mailbox. Everett's room was off the first-floor balcony, which I knew from the few times we'd come over for beach days, so I had no choice if I wanted to happen to my own life tonight.

I took control back from the night and found myself before his window. *Trespassing*, if Everett didn't notice before the neighbors did. I considered throwing something at the window like in the movies, an oyster shard or something, but I wasn't going to mess with someone else's glass. My therapist would understand.

Instead, I knocked on his window. I didn't breathe in the silence after, like silence meant I wouldn't be caught. I listened for stirring inside, then knocked again. "Everett! It's Quinn!" I scream-whispered so he'd actually brave the noise behind his window.

He drew the curtains back, looked briefly like he thought he was still dreaming, then unlatched his window and swung it open. "What's up?" he croaked.

"Do you want to go swimming?"

WAVES THRASHED THE SHORELINE with a sound like beach thunder ripping down the horizon—layered and prolonged and echoing like a pinball bouncing off thick storm clouds.

The sound was menacing, but I'd made up my mind.

If I'd known years ago that it would one day be Everett with reservations about night swimming, I wouldn't have believed it. There was a lot I wouldn't believe, but somehow this was more shocking than the very idea that Everett and I were walking in our bathing suits down a dark patch of beach. Alone. Together.

"Sharks feed at night," he said.

"Come on, you can't back out now, you already put your trunks on."

"Quinn, are you peer pressuring me?"

"Would it be more apt to say it's *pier* pressure?"

"And you're using *puns*? I must be dreaming."

I pinched him gently on the arm. He was being dramatic, but I needed him to know this wasn't a dream. "You don't have to, but I still am."

"Me too." He pulled his shirt off.

In the faint moonlight, I briefly saw the muscles that made up his torso. If I could see him, that meant he could see me staring, so I watched the sand while I kicked my shorts off. If I looked up, would I see him taking me in? When I eventually did, he wasn't, but maybe he was just good at darting his eyes away at just the right moment. A lot of people were.

"First one in wins!" I shouted, then took to the water as fast as my legs could take me.

I screamed with joy as a wave tore through me and broke my fall in the same moment. I was a pinball bouncing off thick, cold waves, bracing for each one that glowed white and frothy under the moon. It was easier once I got past the insurmountable surf closer to the shoreline. I did a mermaid dive under a calmer wave.

Underwater, I couldn't tell it was the middle of the night, but the reminder came quickly when I resurfaced. It was even darker on Everett's side of the island, where the turtles liked to nest, so any oceanfront lights were a dull red. Still, the moon helped me make sense of where the ocean met the stars. The white-capped waves were their own stars on the inky water, twinkling and ever changing the way stars couldn't.

"Quinn?" Everett exclaimed.

"Over here!" I followed the sound of his voice a few waves away until I saw his head as a silhouette before the moon's glitter. "Did I win?"

"Definitely."

Something grazed my waist but retreated just as fast. "Holy shit!" I recoiled with a yelp, but really there was nowhere to go.

"It's just me," Everett said, then his hands were more intentional under the water. He grabbed my forearm and squeezed it reassuringly, then let it go immediately. It left me cold, but maybe that was just from the sun's absence.

"Holy shit." I exhaled a large breath in relief. I'd thought it was a jellyfish, maybe a stingray, even a curious shark since Everett had put the thought into my head. It was feeding time, even if I wanted to pretend sharks didn't eat.

I was on edge, sure, but to be on edge was to be in it. I'd happened to my own life. I'd thrown myself to the ocean under the moonlight, which was living, even if it felt like dying. And I was okay. Mermaids didn't worry about creatures lurking in the dark water. Mermaids didn't even need to wipe the salt water from their eyes. Their wet hair dried in perfect waves.

A few shaky breaths later, my heartbeat finally slowed. "How do you feel?"

"Scared shitless."

I laughed. "Me too."

We left the water almost as quickly as we got in. But it still counted as living, as it gave my chest the same feeling as everything else had this summer. Including Everett, who was behind me on our way up the ladder of the long-abandoned lifeguard post.

During the day, the lifeguard post housed watchful eyes for lost swimmers, but tonight, all it watched was us. We sat wrapped in our beach towels, our backs against opposite walls, facing each other. Sure, my eyes watched the lights of distant cargo ships and Loggerhead Lighthouse, but with my legs stretched across the lifeguard post, it was easy to think only of him. He was close enough to touch.

"So, really, what's changed with you?" Everett's voice carved him from the darkness.

"What do you mean? I'm always like this."

"Sure."

The truth came out anyway, despite my attempt at humor. It was easier, especially since holding it in felt more like betrayal than protection. "I've been working on happening to my own life. Making a life for myself."

"Life starts with swimming at night?"

I shrugged. "Among other things."

Eventually, I hoped I'd get to the point where I could be in full control. Where life could mean resting my hand on Everett's leg to absentmindedly brush off the sand dried to his skin, just because it hurt too much not to. Just because I could.

Until I was in full control, our conversation was enough. Passing glances were. Nudging legs as silent acknowledgment of their touching.

"I always wanted that as a kid, to be older and make my own rules," Everett said.

"My mom always told me I'd regret wishing my childhood away, but it *is* cool to think about sneaking out for a swim, then actually do it."

All my life, my mom had kept me from it, which was really just to cover the real truth, that it was my dad's absence that held the knife. I was working on forgiving my mom for life happening to her. She lost all her fluffernutter and firefly moments, too, but she stayed. She took care of me all by herself. She knew where I found comfort and allowed me to spend the whole summer here, every year.

She made sure I was safe.

What was the logical next step after doing the most dangerous thing at the beach? I wouldn't tell her about the swimming, but I'd tell her about Everett.

Maybe one day, I'd tell Everett about Everett, too.

Last Summer
Age 17, July 25

EVERETT SAT ACROSS FROM ME at Holy Mackerel, his shoulders sharp and his face in a permanent, albeit subtle, smile.

I knew that smile. I wore the same one. I hoped he liked my new tank top, my wavy hair from last night's braids, the new shade of blush I was trying out on top of the sun's.

He smelled of what I imagined was expensive cologne swiped from Hank's dresser. He'd ironed his tee shirt. Styled his hair to look different than usual—wild and free, like how it looked the day at the beach when I told him where coquinas got their holes. That summer, I felt the first stirrings of this feeling that had yet to let go.

But things were finally different. I'd finally taken control, even if I was murdering my straw wrapper in my fidgety hands.

A few days after Everett and I snuck out for the moonlit ocean, I went to a movie with him. The whole time, I was glowing from the magnetic tension between us. At the dinner table later, Hadley asked if Everett was my boyfriend. I almost choked on my pizza, but managed to tell her I was working on it. There was only so much I could do at once, but I was trying. While Hadley wasn't old enough to understand the hold-up, she understood bravery. She told me so over ice cream dessert, how she'd finally faced her fears and conquered the big slide at Pirate's Bounty earlier that day. It wasn't close to the same thing, but it was enough encouragement to text Everett after she went to bed.

That put us here, eight o' clock at Holy Mackerel on the Sapphire Beach Boardwalk, picking away at the last crunchy French fries. We met here four summers ago, which was not lost on either of us.

The sun was still with us, peeking in from a window out back. Sometimes I thought the sun set so late in the summer because it wanted to stay out past curfew, stay at the beach forever. Maybe it was just like me, and it wanted to sit across from Everett, confused about what to call *him* but almost positive *this* was a date.

My whatever-he-was smiled at me, deaf to the wrestling in my head. A couple on the karaoke stage in the corner finished a duet of "Don't You Want Me" by the Human League. We joined the applause.

Everett looked at me with a playful grin. "Sing with me?"

I considered conquering my fears, but when I looked at the stage, I pictured myself standing there. The microphone shook in my hand, my voice cracked, eyes from the crowd drilled a hole into me and strung me onto a necklace. The thought made my skin crawl, but I didn't want the fun to end. I had to find a middle ground.

"Sing *to* me?" My voice raised with my eyebrows. I hoped Everett wouldn't be able to resist.

He nodded, didn't take even a moment to process, and stood up to stretch. He sipped from his freshly refilled virgin piña colada, cracked his knuckles, dramatically exhaled, and walked to the DJ.

I shook my head at the nobody at the table beside us, rolled my eyes at the nobody in the corner. *I'm with him*, I told the nobody sitting at the bar.

From thirty feet away, I tried to read his face for any indication of what song he would pick. He nodded, whispered something to the DJ, and walked on stage.

"Ladies and gentleman, give it up for Everett," the DJ said.

The crowd roared. It wasn't enough people for Everett to back out, but enough to justify the loud gulp made audible thanks to the microphone. My heart roared for him. I leaned forward, elbows on the table, and held my hands over my mouth in anticipation.

He swallowed what appeared to be the rest of his fear, speaking with the same confidence he gave me. "This is for a special someone in the crowd." He winked at me while the first notes of "Escape (The Piña Colada Song)" filled the room.

"Oh my God!" I mouthed at my own special someone. My lips pressed hard into a smile. I shook my head, a blush working its way to my cheeks. Even if I wanted to hide my face in my hands, I couldn't take my eyes off him.

He rocked back and forth, grabbed the microphone, and began.

He sounded so off key that Rupert Holmes himself would have told him to give up singing forever. He didn't care, so nobody else did either. He wasn't up there to sound good. He was up there for me, his *lady*, who I hoped he wasn't tired of, who I hoped he never had to write the newspapers to escape from.

He was having fun. People like him did.

He delivered the first chorus, singing of piña coladas, getting caught in the rain, and yoga. Singing of infidelity that was okay because it was mutual. *Ironic*, even. A couple who fell back in love. A couple who stoked dead flames with sex in the dunes of a midnight cape.

I felt hot all over, my heart flipping on a hot griddle.

A long pause followed the final word of the first chorus—*escape*. He looked at me with a knowing smile, and just like that, all I wanted to do was escape. I wanted to jump out of my worries, my past, and my fears. I pictured two figures holding hands, running for the horizon like it was something attainable, like they could actually reach the pot of gold at the end of a rainbow.

I wanted to escape real life the way Everett was right now.

For a split second, jealousy consumed me. A thick green toxin slithered through my bloodstream. I wished I could be like Everett, who left his skin at the table and walked on a stage a famous, washed up singer.

I shook the thoughts, watched Everett perform his heart out. I couldn't contain my laughter. He sucked at singing, dancing, and anything else involving a stage, but still, the crowd was enamored.

After the final notes, he thanked the crowd and stepped away from the microphone for a bow. The applause surpassed the sounds of summer. The static was loud enough for people on top of the Ferris wheel to hear.

I was the only one who stood, but he deserved a standing ovation. I clapped until he sat back down and I sat down after him. "I wish I could say I expected anything less from you."

"I'm good, right?" His breath ran ragged, but he was still floating from the applause. He drank the rest of his piña colada.

"Ev, I'm telling you this because I don't lie to my friends. You're probably the worst singer I've ever heard." There was irony in my words. I was lying about not lying. I hoped I wasn't his friend. I hoped he picked up on my flirting.

"The crowd loved it!"

"The crowd's drunk." I raised one eyebrow.

"You're not, and I saw you bobbing your head." He read between the lines, nudged my foot with his under the table.

"It's a catchy song." I sipped from my drink to hide the curl of my lips. My cheeks had been on fire for the last five minutes, but I was confident the lighting was dim enough in there that Everett couldn't tell.

WHEN WE STEPPED OUT ONTO THE BOARDWALK, the summer sun had finally gone back home, trading places with the moon. The moon was bright tonight, a waxing gibbous only a few nights from full.

Hadley once told me that she thought the sun and the moon liked each other, but I swore they were mortal enemies. Why else did they avoid each other like clockwork? Their entire existence revolved around opposing each other.

Although opposites attracted, the sun and the moon didn't count.

But if Everett was the sun, then I was the moon, and that would make us impossible. So I imagined us both as suns, holding still together as the world moved in slow motion around us. Two suns who walked on the Boardwalk, admiring the stars around us, staying out well past curfew, together.

We were even better at breaking curfew than the sun was.

The Boardwalk smelled like freshly buttered popcorn and stamped out cigarette butts. The next time Hadley burned a bag of popcorn before movie night, I could count on it to send me right back to flashy storefronts, greasy food, and the whispers from the butterflies in my stomach: *grab Everett's hand.*

Not yet.

Despite the warm summer night, I felt like I'd jumped into a cold swimming pool, shocked and exhilarated all at the same time. Pure happiness washed across my face like the Ferris wheel protruded into the night sky. It was impossible to feel sad on the Boardwalk. I needed my own personal Boardwalk.

Everett and I walked into the carousel line.

"Do you think the sun has a curfew?" I asked when we reached our spot in line.

"Of course, but it changes every night. The sunset is based on solstices and our location on Earth," Everett said like he had Hadley on the other end of an earpiece, spouting out everything she knew about the Earth's rotation around the sun.

"Nerd." I smirked.

He shook his head, then opened his phone, tapped on his screen a few times, and turned it to me. The weather app was open on his phone. "Today, the sun's curfew was 8:15pm."

"You ever think maybe the sun wants to stay out a little longer?" I leaned against the railing. It was cold on my arm, but it felt good on a hot night like this. I turned so both arms touched it.

Everett faced me, his arms against the railing parallel to mine. The lights from the carousel flashed a whole rainbow of colors onto his face. The entire universe drowned out his eyes. "I think it gets bored of us. Do you miss the sun already or something?"

"I mean, you can't have summer without the sun. The moon doesn't really do much." Summer and sun were so synonymous that even in the dead of winter, when I glanced at a patch of sunny grass the right way, I teleported to summer in Piper Island. The sun was strong enough to fool me sometimes, but the moon didn't have that magic.

"You can always have the sun if you expand your definition of sun." He looked at me again. It felt like I was looking at him through a telescope, close enough to count the stars glimmering in his brown eyes.

I gulped. "What would your definition be?"

"Something that brings light to every day."

"Have you found your sunlight yet?" I asked.

"Yeah."

I tried to read his face. The carousel lights didn't help me detect anything in his expression.

"Have you?" he asked.

I shrugged. There was a lot in my life that I could consider my sunlight, but what if sunlight actually wasn't for me?

Maybe life was easier if Everett and I were moonlight instead—soft, bright, and reliable, like how the moon churned the tides.

Soon, it was our turn to board. The carousel horses we rode last time were occupied, but this was a night for new memories, even if they were cast in the shadows of the past. I pulled myself onto a green and blue horse. Everett was on the yellow and white one next to me. The carousel belonged in the night, its glow a perfect contrast to the indigo sky.

The butterflies in my stomach shouted from somewhere within: *Hold his hand!*

Who was I to clip a butterfly's wings? This was a new night. I was happening to my own life. *I wish for a rollercoaster.* I could do this.

I waited for the carousel to start dancing. The twinkling music sang of days and nights of endless wonder. Music was a form of time travel. The adolescent jingle sent me back to my early adolescence: my temple pressed to the cold bar, thirteen-year-old Quinn making sense of Everett—his hair, his beauty mark, his boyish charm.

Seventeen-year-old Quinn knew the score. Seventeen-year-old Quinn was different.

I did not walk life afraid.

I held my hand out in the space between us. My arm weighed two tons, but my chest was even heavier. Everett looked between my hand

and my face, his eyebrow furrowed, until he finally took my hand in his.

There was everything before this, then everything after. The last and only time we'd held hands was at the aquarium—a guiding hand from the whale—but this was something else entirely. This had weight. This was real, two people holding hands because the space between them was too great. Because people with history like ours should have held hands the first time they rode this carousel. My first tinge of rosy cheeks—my first taste of romance—should have been enough for me, but life was a sticky thing sometimes.

I looked away from him to catch a glimpse of myself in the oval mirror. I couldn't keep my smile from splitting across my face, but why stop it? *I wish for a rollercoaster.* I leaned my head against the bar, looking back at seventeen-year-old Everett Bishop.

Sometimes that was all I knew how to do.

I WAS CARRYING A BAG OF COTTON CANDY so large that it bounced off my kneecaps as I walked. There was no better place to wander aimlessly than here. We walked through the sounds and colors until something spoke to us. This time around, we were headed to a vendor with rows of freshly spun cotton candy. The woman inside must have finished a new batch because the pink vanilla scent pulled us in all the way from the back of the bumper cars.

Everett and I got the thought at the same time, both of us hungry from arcade games and two rounds of bumper cars. We needed something even sweeter than the Boardwalk. He took my hand and dragged us to the opening in a huge glass structure.

"You want some?" I asked Everett, a nod to the day we met.

He looked at the bag with disgust, like he did then. "I'd rather not."

"Are you kidding?" I fit half a clump in my mouth and talked as it dissolved on my tongue. "Fresh cotton candy is one of the greatest pleasures in life. If you've never tasted this, you've never tasted summer."

"I don't know that I want to taste a season."

"It's your loss; summer happens to be the best tasting season."

Everett laughed at me. "But don't coconuts taste like summer?"

I wiped my sticky hands on my shorts. "Not *my* summer."

Life was sticky *and* sweet. There was peace in the balance.

"Not *your* summer?" His eyebrows raised. "That's not how it works."

"Here, please have some summer." I turned to him with pink cotton pinched between two fingers, waving it in front of his face. "Open wide!"

I thought he might object, but he opened his mouth, rewriting the end of the story of us. I wedged it between his lips, watched it melt on his tongue. It was gone in a moment, a smile left in its place.

"You love summer," I whispered and brushed the stray sugar from his cheek with my knuckle. I grabbed another wisp and held it out for him.

"Your tongue is pink." He grabbed my wrist and moved my hand to my own mouth, not breaking eye contact.

"Thank you," I said, stealing the last bit of summer with my tongue.

We walked toward the end of the Boardwalk, caught up in the fantastical version of life that it cast upon us. This soft rainbow fluorescent haze spotlighted the world around us. Everything was beautiful: the rigged clank of metal rings on milk jugs, the adolescent jingle of the carousel, the exhaust smell from the go-karts. An indescribable level of happiness escaped me in breathless giggles and skips in my otherwise steady steps.

Look how carefree I am!

Look how relaxed I am!

Look how happy I am!

This time, I knew he saw me. He was looking when I looked back.

I PROMISED MYSELF IN THE MIRROR EARLIER that I would do it. *I wish for a rollercoaster*, I told myself as I brushed sense into my braided curls. I hadn't planned on grabbing his hand on the carousel, but I knew I would do this. Only one bar protected us from falling into the ocean, but my nerves settled when I inched closer to Everett.

We were one of the first carts to board, so the Ferris wheel moved slowly as the rest of the line boarded. On the slow incline, we nearly mapped out the whole place with I Spy, but on the top, braked in dark solitude, silence was the only thing we spied.

I'd never seen the world from hundreds of feet in the air.

A mosaic of lights stippled the shape of the Boardwalk. On the ground, each light was its own individual being, visible filament threaded through them. Up here, with Everett next to me, I saw how beautifully each bulb worked together to create one solid unit.

Above all the commotion, the moon illuminated the ocean's white-capped waves. The shy stars still showed themselves despite the moon taking center stage. I was beginning to understand the allure of the moon's glow. Moonlight was harmless, comfortable, dark enough for the glowing lights of the Boardwalk but bright enough to see Everett's hands folded together between his knees.

To see the shape of his face against the night sky.

In the silence, Everett's bouncing legs did his bidding. When he thought of me, was there a chapter in his head or just an ellipsis? *Was* he thinking of me? Could there be enough between us for a real story? Were we the forlorn couple who escaped from each other with each other?

"This is beautiful," Everett said, but it wasn't the answer I wanted.

"It is," I said.

"I think you're beautiful, too."

I darted my eyes at him. His words were light striking across the dull sky. My eyes were hungry stargazers. "You are, too. Very nice looking, I mean." *Shit.*

"I'm good with beautiful."

"Good." I took this as permission to grab his hand. That ship had sailed. "What else are you thinking?"

His eyebrows knitted together, then he looked at me with a smirk. "I'm thinking that the invention of the Ferris wheel is kind of wild, if you really think about it. I mean, 1893 in Chicago—"

"No, *really*," I challenged, squeezing his hand in mine. The only way to be more obvious was to just say it, but I wasn't *that* bold. "What are you really thinking?"

We stared at each other in the breeze, toying with each other's hands. He cleared his throat. "I'm thinking I want to kiss you."

My face crackled into a smile. This feeling was its own wild invention. *Thank God.*

Now

August 7

THE SNARL IN MY ANKLE IS IMPOSSIBLE TO IGNORE.

At the house, Adriana's mom takes a closer look and decides I need more than an ice pack. I don't need convincing, and neither does Everett. I tell them to start a movie without us. Holden carries me to the car and Everett drives me to the nearest 24-hour pharmacy for painkillers and a wrap bandage.

He leaves the car on and tells me to stay put. I don't need convincing.

The first beats of an Adele song bleed from the radio. I turn it up and let out a faint chuckle. It was a lifetime ago that Blair grounded me for going to Kelsie's party, but this song sounds like my first taste of the open road, pointless errands, and a magnificent dinner with Blair. For that reason, it also sounds like tears, beer, and Holden's echoey truths.

There are a million ways my life is different now.

I check my phone for a text from my dad, and still, nothing.

Everett walks out of the pharmacy, swinging a yellow bag beside him. He slinks into the driver's side and shuffles through the bag. He pulls out a pint of Gibson's cotton candy ice cream, wearing a smile as big as the ocean.

My face lights up like the fluorescent streetlights outside. "They have Gibson's? It's been years since I last had this!"

I've only had this brand once. I was nine and mom found it at our local grocery store. It was one of the nicer memories with Mom that year, going home and sharing it with her in front of the latest animated movie. After that, Mom and I hunted for it at every grocery store and we never found it again.

Everett and I take a picture with it. I text it to Mom who I know will text me as soon as she wakes up tomorrow. I lock my phone before I impulsively check the unreplied text again.

"They only had the one, so I figured it must be good."

"Better than medicine. Thank you!"

"But you do still need medicine." Everett pulls painkillers from the bag and hands me a water bottle.

"Well, of course." I take two tablets. In the bag, I spot a bottle of aloe and the wrap bandage. Those can wait for after my shower, but my ankle demands medicine now. "Thank you. For everything," I add so he knows "everything" goes as far back as everythings can go.

"No problem." Everett pulls out of the pharmacy into the darkness of the North Carolina countryside.

Everett's headlights illuminate the dark road, robust corn fields on both sides. I roll the window down to hear the tired, steady stream of cicada, katydid, and locust songs. Warm night air spills in. I put one hand out the window and brush through the thick air, distracted until "Escape (The Piña Colada Song)" starts teasing on the radio.

"No way!" I crank up the volume with an ear-splitting laugh.

"Sing with me, Dr. Kessler?"

I respond by singing the first line, using my closed fist as a microphone. It's impossible not to. Everett joins me for a duet. What an oxymoron to belt out such a song on a slow, meandering road. An oxymoron to be this happy after everything I've been through. An oxymoron to sing a song about an affair with a boy I could never imagine falling into a dull routine with, a boy I never want to escape.

A moonlight I never want to shut the blinds to again.

Still, we sing of escapes, piña coladas, and making love in the dunes. It sounds like crunchy French fries, Boardwalk lights, real cotton candy.

It sounds like our first kiss.

There are a million ways my life is different now.

I don't want this moment to end. When we approach the sign for Lake Lockwood, I suggest we stop at the lake access to eat the ice cream. Unfortunately lakes don't have dunes. Unfortunately, I'm still me.

"You know, so everyone doesn't feel left out," I add. "Of the ice cream."

"Yeah, obviously." Everett plays along, parking in the vacant lot. We overlook the black lake now desolate without sun. Not even the moon is out right now; only houses from across the lake break the darkness.

Absent of motion, summer night heat streams in the car. The lake is eerily quiet, but the cicadas, katydids, and locusts have yet to fall asleep. The ache in my ankle has calmed since the medicine, real *and* musical.

Everett opens the ice cream. The lid is already overflowing and soggy from sitting in the car's heat. He puts it on the dashboard and licks the drip from his thumb. I find a plastic spork in his glove box, ripping it out of its wrapper with my teeth.

Orange heat lightning in the distance cracks across the sky, weaving through a thick blanket of clouds.

"You first." He holds the pint out for me.

I thank the warm air for softening the ice cream. Then I thank my sweet tooth for all the joy I find in crunchy pink and blue sugar sprinkles lodged into sugar-flavored ice cream.

"Just like I remember." I smile and pass him the pint and spork.

I take this opportunity to check my phone again. It's second nature now, but I quickly realize my mistake and tuck it between my legs.

He turns his body to me in his seat, his right leg tucked under him and his elbow propped up where his headrest should be. Last week, Holden and Mason buried it in the sand as a prank and forgot to mark the spot, so now it was lost to time.

He takes his own bite, nodding. "It sure is…sweet."

I turn to him, my back to the door, my hair spilling out of the open window. I laugh. "I love how you always use sweet as an insult."

"Isn't it?" He smirks.

I smirk back and take the sweet ice cream from him. Some people just don't understand sugar. We finish the ice cream with large scrapes against the pint, the beginning of a brain freeze riding its tails. Really, I ate most of it and Everett finished the rest before I exploded.

"What's been so important on your phone?" Everett asks.

I want to lie and tell him I'm waiting on a text from Haven or Blair or my mom, but when I notice the streetlights spilling artificial moonlight on my thigh, I remember last summer and what I once thought.

Everett is what I need.

He would never leave me checking my phone for days. He'd be there no matter what, just like the moon even when the clouds hide it away.

"I texted my dad the other day." I feel layers of my skin peel open.

"What'd you say?" His voice is soft, sorry, not at all painful on freshly exposed skin.

"I told him I loved him." Tears threaten to form as a peppery feeling builds in my nose, a thickness in my throat.

"And he hasn't responded?"

"No." I open my phone again to an empty lockscreen, a picture of me and Hadley on the beach. "I haven't texted him in years. I don't know why I even tried. It was stupid."

I shut the phone off. This is the last time I'll hope for nothing.

"It wasn't stupid, Quinn. It was what you felt you needed to do."

"I don't know why I even love him anymore."

The words pop like a balloon too full of air. It jolts me, like my brain didn't even know my mouth could say such a thing.

He's your dad, of course it's okay to still love him, part of my brain thinks, but the other half responds, *He lost the privilege of your love the day he stopped wanting it.*

"He didn't deserve to be your dad anyway."

Everett's truth is so cold it could clip the thick leaves of summer. Even though summer knows it's coming, it still hurts when the first dead leaves hit the ground.

An ocean lies between knowing something and pretending it's not true. But I know those dead leaves. I know the truth. Rock bottom tells me her name, shakes my hand, and pulls me into the depths with her.

Accepting the truth is hard, but hard is the first step toward easy. In order to come back from rock bottom, you have to fall to it first.

I let my pesky brain chew on each of Everett's words like orange wedges that fill your molars for hours.

The more I chew, the more it makes sense.

If a man leaves his wife and nine-year-old daughter to spiral without him, did he ever deserve them?

If not, why do I still love him?

To stop loving my own father would be to stop loving my blonde hair, the joy I find in little things, the sweet tooth I know I got from him.

Hating my dad is to hate half of myself.

Not just the parts of me that I already hate, but the parts of me that make me worth the effort to clean dirty grout, sneak lollipops, find shapes in anything as a distraction, sway in a hammock, trek at 5am to comfort on a pier, slow dance under the stars, drive on a late night pharmacy run.

Hating my dad is to hate the part of me worth falling in love with.

He didn't deserve to be your dad anyway.

"I know." A tear finally falls down my cheek. I let it fall, then wipe the rest away with the back of my hand. I fight the tremble in my chin until my jaw hurts. The pressure finally fades. In the silence after, there is relief in finally having found the words to describe what haunts me.

I feel the weight of Everett's hand on my shoulder.

A raindrop falls on the windshield with a muted thud. We both follow the sound, then look at each other as more raindrops follow. They splatter on the roof like giant needle pricks, *tap tap tapping* on the car. Rain streaks down the windshield, distorting the distant porch lights. I once told Everett how much I liked this sight. That hasn't changed. The rain comes fast. Like me, the sky couldn't hold back its tears anymore either. We rush to roll the windows up before it's too late.

Then an idea strikes like heat lightning across my face, like lyrics of my and Everett's song running across a karaoke machine. "Let's get caught in the rain," I say and push open my door.

Everett circles around to me, pulls me into the rain that feels nothing like needle pricks. I gasp at the rush of cold, look up at the sky. Millions of raindrops fall, visible in the streetlights around the vacant lot. My eyes blink as quickly as my heart pounds.

I buckle from the pain in my ankle, forced to lean on Everett for help. He hoists me up onto the hood of the car. It's sopping wet, but all

I can do is laugh quick, breathless laughs that can't catch themselves in the cold. Everett sits next to me, glowing under the streetlights made brighter as they reflect off the rain-soaked air.

"I like getting caught in the rain," Everett says.

"I was hoping you would." I wipe raindrops off his beauty mark with my thumb. What an oxymoron, to wipe rain off a boy's cheeks when the sky isn't done crying. Happy tears, this time.

He grabs my wrist, smiles at me through the sky's happiness. "Of course I do."

That's what moonlights do.

They illuminate you.

Even the parts of you not worth anything.

What an oxymoron, to live in the same world as Everett Bishop and believe all men are like my dad.

Now

August 10

IT COMES IN THE MIDDLE OF THE NIGHT—a white, alien light that fills my room.

I open my eyes at the same moment, roused by one of my nightly twists and turns. I think I'm being abducted for the first few seconds, but when I type in my password and let the light stun me awake, I know it's worse.

Quick, panicked breaths break the eerie silence, peel me out of dreamland.

I read the text my father sent back.

I'm sorry.

I blink a tear down my nose. Exhale to calm my trembling jaw.

I know, I type even though I don't really know anything at all.

Now

August 10

MY PHONE HAS NO RESPONSE THIS MORNING.

It's the first thing I do: shift in my sunlit covers, unlock my phone, and stare at the conversation still open on the screen. I close my eyes again, rest the phone on my chest.

I picture that conversation if it happened face to face.

We'd be on the public dock on the sound. He'd come to visit and we'd go fishing to rekindle a long-lost father-daughter relationship. I'd tell him about everyone and everything. How the twins and I fished on the same dock and how I thought of him whenever marshmallow creme glued my fingers together. I'd tell him about the days spent smelling of sunscreen, wearing a bikini under my clothes *just in case.* Thoughts of him when fireflies flickered. Laughing over a takeout box of warm hushpuppies. Popsicles. Ashe's doughnuts. My feelings for Everett.

The good life I managed without him.

He'd smile and tell me he's happy for me. He'd wish to be part of the rest, work to earn my forgiveness, tell me it's okay to stop being so guarded due to his mistakes.

We wouldn't catch any fish, but he'd think my company made it worth trying. We'd have one of those moments under the purple sound sky that only happens in movies. Same as the ones we used to have with the fireflies back home. Only now, the fireflies would be frog croaks from the edge of the marsh. We'd try to predict the next time a frog would croak. He'd mimic one at the perfect moment, at almost the exact pitch. I'd laugh like it was the funniest sound I'd ever heard.

Because it would be.

And I'd be happy.

Then I'd say it, more confident than I've ever been: "I love you."

Then he'd apologize.

I can't figure it out after that. My daydream rolls into a credits scene that only happens in movies.

Is there remorse in his eyes? How does the "I'm sorry" leave his mouth? Is it a gentle inland breeze on reddening skin? Is it stormy beach wind that rolls like beach thunder? Is it the most windless day Piper Island has ever seen? I can't decide, but the most telling thing is how void it is of "I love you, too."

He doesn't say it over text, but could he tell his daughter he loves her while he stares at the parts of her that bleed his shade of red?

He can't. He doesn't. He *hasn't*. If he really loved me, he would have said so. He wouldn't have left me waiting so long for a reply. He would be here. He would see the woman his daughter has become. He would be here. He wouldn't have left me a fatherless mess nine years ago.

He would be here.

I know that. I know my dad stopped loving me years ago. I was stupid to think otherwise.

My reply taunts me on the screen: *I know.*

Why did I respond in the middle of the night, the exact minute he sent his? Why did I respond at all? In my sleepy stupor, I was a desperate puppy waiting at the door for my owner to return. Ready to douse him in kisses, already clueless about how long he'd left me alone. *What an idiot.*

I find a different reply from that same night at the Rivera-Sanchezes'. From someone who didn't need time to respond. With my mom, it never takes more than thirty minutes.

I love you, too, baby. Is everything okay?

I reread her excited response to the Gibson's selfie with Everett. My mom, who I've painted as cold and broken since everything happened, sent me a selfie back, smiling beside a glass of mango smoothie. Most of all, she loves me back.

Good morning, I text, and vow to have one myself.

I slink from my bed and ignore the dull whine in my ankle. I wake up in less pain each day, but I've kept it wrapped since Lake Lockwood.

That night on Adriana's couch, my sunburn and sprained ankle took turns keeping me awake. The sunburn lit a fire within me while my ankle throbbed in a rehearsed beat. I felt like I was roasting on a spit. I listened to the ceiling fan squeak, listened to Everett breathe rhythmically on the air mattress next to the couch. Eventually his breathing turned into the silent, awake kind. I whispered for him, and we spent whatever time passed between sleep hypothesizing about what happens in a blackhole. He was close enough to touch, close enough to quell the scary, deep-rooted thoughts that befell a dark, lonely room, close enough to help me defeat my night demons.

On my way to the kitchen, I pass Blair on the couch. Her hair's up in a lazy Sunday morning ponytail and she watches a couple on TV get their beach house remodeled.

I grab a mandarin orange from the fridge and sit next to her. I find an empty space on the coffee table, prop my ankle next to a stack of books and a day-old coffee mug. "Good morning."

"Good morning." Her tone shifts when she sees my face. "What's wrong?" There's no sense in questioning how she just read me like one of her romance books. She is Blair Reinhart, after all.

I look at my orange, shove my thumb into the skin, feel the juice run down my arm and think of Haven and cherry popsicle juice. "Do you think my dad still loves me?"

"Oh, Quinn. What's gotten him on your mind?"

The first thing I notice is the deflection—how she doesn't answer my question but instead makes her voice pillowy and disarming. The second thing I notice is her body shift my way, her fingers pulling at the ends of my hair. *Comfort*, because the outlook is not good. If anyone knows that, it's Blair Reinhart.

"I texted him a few weeks back. Told him I loved him. He responded last night. Didn't say it back."

"What did he say?"

I shrug, peel the fleshy webbing off the orange slice. "He said he was sorry." My nose starts to tickle. I can't afford to keep crying, but my eyes don't keep a tally.

"That's good."

"Is it?" My own voice changes, authoritative and accusatory. "I can't figure out how you can leave for nine years and think that texting a lame apology is good enough. He ruined me, Blair."

My voice changes again, a freefall to rock bottom. I inhale to stop more tears from forming.

"I'm sorry." She laughs. "Shit, sorry. Oh God, I'm really bad at this."

I find a laugh deep within me. She's perfect at this. "You don't have anything to be sorry for. You and Mom, I can always count on you guys. I don't give Mom enough credit."

"She knows," Blair says, serious again. "Listen, if you asked me, I wouldn't call your life ruined. Your life here, from the outside looking in, has been wonderful. Enviable, even. Hadley thought so too. She wanted to be just like you, doing all that living you do."

Finally I look up from the orange to drink up Blair's face. Her lips, the soft smile always on them; her eyes, the sliver of pain always behind them.

"She did?" How on Earth could someone see my life and wish it was theirs? Nobody wishes to be broken…unless they're a little girl who sees nothing but the good in everything, coral pink on a black and white day. Unless they're Hadley.

"She talked about you all the time," Blair says, her voice crumbling.

In the last moment Hadley and I shared together, she asked me about my friends, but I didn't think much about it. I didn't realize how she saw me: a teenager whose fun night always began when her dreams did. I *literally* lived out her dreams.

And I've done even more than that. I had fun without my dad's love. Formed relationships without one of the biggest relationships I wanted in my life. Trusted people despite my dad. Became Quinn Kessler without my dad.

It's here, sitting next to my aunt with an orange slice warming in my hand, that I realize how much I've filled the void my dad left behind.

He's not the one who gave me this piece of Piper Island to cherish forever. He's not the eight coquina clam shells that hug my neck. I can't find him in the sun provoked afternoon naps. He's not swimming in Lake Lockwood's sweet tea water or dewed on the trampoline under blankets of constellations. He's not tucked in the hushpuppy picnics or palm tree shadows. He doesn't clamber up the rungs of a lighthouse or rush across a road from a phantom cop car. He's not in a bed of pine needles or the path of seashells laid to rest like breadcrumbs. He doesn't zap through the neon-tinged world of cotton candy and Ferris wheels.

Only those who matter exist in these smudges of joy.

Like Hadley in every night sky.

"I miss her." I shove the orange wedge in my mouth and chew on its warm silence, let the words linger for a moment, then will them away. I smile an orange smile, the kind that kills hard conversations. "Thank you, Blair. You always know exactly what to stock the fridge with."

"And you make it my pleasure." Blair taps my nose, then peels the wilting skin off its bridge like it's an orange slice. "What fun day of living is this from?"

"Lake Lockwood." I swallow another slice. "I really should reapply my sunscreen."

"I've been telling you that for years, Q." She stands up and kisses my forehead. "I'm getting you some aloe, you lobster."

Then the moment is over, soothed with mandarin orange slices, sunburn, and aloe.

I'm still on the couch when the afternoon rolls around. Blair left to pick up groceries for crab cakes and a vat of SPF 100 sunscreen, "for now and every time you go out in the sun forever!"

The home renovation marathon on TV continues well after my nap. Haven asks me to join her picnic lunch with Holden and Mason on the pier. Holden swears he and Santiago are going to catch a kingfish once and for all. Haven's only keen on watching for an hour or two.

Impossible, I reply. *I'm trying to rest my ankle today. Doctor's orders.*

who's doctor?

Everett.

if he's your doctor, then i'm coming over later to be your nurse

Will you bring me a lollipop?

duh. and a sticker

I almost make it to the end of the current episode when I get an idea. It's less of an idea and more like my mind opened a fortune cookie or read a horoscope written by the stars, telling me what I need to do.

Hadley.

I can do this. I sit up and let my bad ankle get used to bearing weight again. My phone dances between my hands. I debate texting Everett to talk me out of it, but he wouldn't.

I can do this.

I limp to the hallway, stop at the door that I've gone the summer pretending is just a part of the wall. I put my cheek against what is very much a door and feel the cold wood soothe my sunburn. I feel something else, too—my heart thumping a soft knock against the wood, like it's okay to go in now.

I open the door and step inside a snapshot of last August 11.

My bath towel rests on the floor, the strawberry shampoo smell long-since faded from it. Her unmade comforter falls off the bed the way she insisted was just how she liked it. Blair and I both knew it was just her way to get out of making her bed. Her bathing suit drawer hangs open, five bathing suit choices scattered on her floor. I picture her trying on each one but landing on her usual pink gingham.

On her dresser lives a photo of us from a picnic eight summers ago. A year's worth of dust coats the frame. I wipe our faces with my thumb. The humid evening comes back to me. It was so hot even after the sun went down. I remember how many times Hadley said "bumblebee," a word I taught her when one landed on the bouquet of weeds we picked for the windowsill. To us, those weeds were the prettiest things ever plucked from the ground. Worthy of a vase and that special sunlight the sun reserves for a windowsill. When you're a little girl, everything is beautiful and you don't know a weed from a flower.

Hadley's freckled face smiles back at me. Her baby teeth take up her whole smile. Her eyes are sealed shut from the golden hour rays. I smile with my teeth, too, despite the heat and bright sun. Blair tried countless times to get the perfect shot, but nothing beats the candid imperfection of this one.

Hadley fell in love with the stars that night.

Now, she is the stars.

I look at the glow-in-the-dark stars strewn on her ceiling. At the bathing suits on the floor. Her books stacked beside her bed, the original constellation book and a couple newer ones too. On her bedside table, next to the sand dollar I planted for her to find, her blue heart necklace sleeps.

Haven's gift to Hadley once she was old enough to wear it. I'd kept it safe in my dresser until Blair finally let us give it to her. Haven came over with an empty chain and presented it to her. Hadley said it reminded her of a sky full of rainbows. She wore it every day, just like I wore mine. She never wore it to bed, just like I didn't.

I've never taken mine off to swim, so why didn't Hadley wear hers to the beach that day? Why did Hadley even go to the beach that day?

I pick up the glassy pendant, stroke its smooth surface and picture Hadley's hands clipping it on in the mirror every morning. Why did Hadley jump the waves that day? My knuckles bleed white around the cold blue sky. My nails dig into my palm. Why did Hadley die that day?

My knees buckle. Her strawberry bed catches me.

And I cry.

Last Summer
Age 17, August 10

I STEPPED OUT OF THE BATHROOM, my clothes clinging to me from the steamy shower fog. A towel twisted my hair onto the top of my head. My wet feet recovered the sand lost to the hardwoods.

Hadley's bedroom glowed pink from the hallway. I found her in bed, wrapped in a quilt and paging through a book.

I leaned against the doorframe. "Goodnight, Hadley."

"I don't want to go to bed yet," she whined, but her sleepy voice disagreed with her words. "Please don't make me?"

I smiled and held my pinky to the ceiling. "Pinky promise."

"Can you tuck me in?"

Before I left for mini golf with Everett, I needed to paint my nails, blow dry my hair, and tap on sparkly eyeshadow. Ever since we kissed on the Ferris wheel a few nights ago, things were different. The rest of the ride was something like floating, then we landed back on the ground and floated once more. It was a wonder how light the world felt after. We wore the possibilities like tattoos, memories scorned on warm skin.

How high could we float one day?

I was likely to find out tonight, but Hadley wouldn't always be so little and in need of my company.

"Of course." I left my towel in a lump on the floor, squeezed next to her on the twin bed. It was cold on top of the blankets, and my hair made the strawberry pink pillows smell like strawberries.

"How was your day?" I curled up to face her, sharing the space with her dolphin stuffed animal from the aquarium.

"Good. I played at Sophie's. We jumped on the trampoline. I like having a friend with a trampoline. We're going to the beach tomorrow."

I remembered my own excitement about the Rivera-Sanchezes' trampoline. I pictured Hadley and Sophie jumping on it like Haven and I did before the trampoline became just another place to tan. I was glad Hadley had a friend like Haven. Friendship like that was the glue of adolescence.

"I'm glad you have a best friend."

"Me too." She yawned, revealing gaps in her mouth from recently lost teeth. "I hope we'll be best friends forever."

"You will," I said like I was the universe making a pinky promise that would never pull apart. "You'll make so many memories together."

"Like you and me?"

"Just like us."

Her voice was sweet like strawberries. "I like when we make memories together."

My heart swelled. I was warm even on top of the blankets in a tank top and shorts. "Me too."

"Are you going to make memories with your friends tonight?"

"How did you know?" I faked my surprise and tickled her clavicle.

Her face curled up between breathless giggles. "Because you look pretty. And you always have fun past my bedtime."

"I'm going to play mini golf with Everett, then we're going to watch a movie, but I promise I won't have too much fun without you."

"Pinky promise?" She cracked a sly, soft smile that hid her lost teeth.

"Pinky promise." We linked pinkies for real this time. "Let's play One Sentence Story." It was the way stories were always told between us: shared between turns and made perfect together. "There once was a mermaid named…"

She sifted for the perfect name. "Coral!"

I continued, "Coral was the nicest, most beautiful mermaid who…"

"…met a nice merman named Aquamarine…" She giggled. "Pretend that's Everett."

I hadn't expected her to make me the mermaid, or introduce a fictional Everett, but instead of rolling my eyes and pretending it wasn't true, I nodded. I wasn't that girl anymore. I was a girl who flattened a cute outfit on my bed, painted my nails moon jelly blue, brushed mascara on my eyelashes, applied the blush from the Boardwalk on my cheeks.

Thanks to Hadley, I was Coral the mermaid now, lying under glowing ceiling stars before my own starry summer night, so I said, "Together they swam through the stars, in and out of constellations."

"Then one day, Aquamarine gave Coral some stars from the sky."

"One for each day he loved her," I whispered, hoping Hadley didn't hear. I didn't know what prompted it, how our story ended up here, or how many stars Aquamarine gave Coral, but I felt a blend of guilt and softness and anticipation in my chest.

Normal people called that love.

I sifted through my mind for the rest of the story, wondering if Coral was a normal mermaid, but Hadley's breath had become the slow kind that told me she was asleep. I lay there for a few more minutes, breathing in the strawberry smell, counting the stars in the ceiling to determine how many I should give Everett tonight.

I slunk out of bed, careful to keep the mattress still. I unclasped her necklace and rested it on her bedside table. I tucked the comforter over her chest, wrapped her arms around her stuffed dolphin, and whispered a proper goodnight to her sleeping ears. I kissed sweet dreams into her forehead and hoped to hear all about them soon.

Then I stepped out to get ready for my date with Everett.

That was what I called those now.

Last Summer
Age 17, August 11

EVERETT'S GOING TO BE MY BOYFRIEND, I thought as Haven zipped me along Ocean Drive on a golf cart. Well, there was always the chance Everett wouldn't ask, or he'd say no if *I* asked, but I felt more certain than ever that soon we'd be tethered by more than salt water taffy. Certain of his feelings for me, and also of mine for him.

Last night on our mini golf date, we wagered over scores—loser had to buy the winner ice cream. A secret second wager floated in my head—I'd kiss him at the end of the date if I sunk a hole-in-one. I tried my hardest, but only got as close as a lucky, erratic ricochet around giraffe legs. Everett won. He took the scorecard as proof; I took the cute miniature pencil as a keepsake.

At Sunset Scoop, he shared his banana split with me.

"That's why it's called a banana split," he'd said when he grabbed two spoons.

The memory made me smile against the wind from the moving golf cart, cheeks warm despite the breeze in my bikini. I wanted to jump off and run to Everett's house—which was only five streets from here—climb up the rungs to his balcony, and recite the poem I wrote last night with the miniature pencil as a cheesy declaration of love.

I pinky promised myself I would before summer ended, but today, Everett and Jorge were on a day trip to Raleigh to tour prospective colleges. Everett joked he'd send me a photo of a Raleigh cloud, maybe even one floating idly above my house. If he did, I'd have to make a special trip to his house. Only, there weren't any clouds in today's sky. I kept checking my phone, wondering if Raleigh's sky was the same.

When Haven picked me up on the golf cart, she insisted it was her and Holden's turn with me today. "Everett can't just have you all the time. Not so close to your last day."

Back at her house, we bathed in sunscreen and set off for the backyard. Holden was already out back, lying on the trampoline in his swim trunks.

We joined Holden, lying down on either side of him, getting ready to tan in the summer sun.

A hose in Holden's hand spit a rain shower over us whenever we got too hot. It was jarring to go from scorching to freezing in seconds, but it made the drying warmth of the sun afterward that much sweeter. This was a dangerous way to tan, but that was how we'd always done it: gossip under the sun until it made us tired, shower, fall asleep to a movie, then wake up in time for dinner and whatever adventure the evening gifted us.

Today's gossip was all about me and Everett. I told them about what Everett said at Carolina Beach, our night swimming with the potential sharks, us holding hands on the carousel. The cherry was our kiss atop the Ferris wheel.

The twins nearly split a hole in the trampoline, pivoting onto their elbows at the same time to bombard me with questions: *Why didn't you start with that? What do you mean you haven't kissed again? Why are we only just hearing about this? You're* not *dating? What the hell? Quinn, what are you waiting for?*

I'd been asking myself the same thing, but I wasn't going to wait anymore. Not after the twins almost died from shock, finally lying back down when I assured them I would talk to Everett tonight.

I didn't need the evening to gift me anything; I would do it myself. Happen to my own life.

Holden nudged me with his elbow. "Remember when you told me to read the signs about Mason? It's your turn now."

"Yeah, your signs are straight-up billboards," Haven jabbed.

"Hey, you too, *Haven.*" Holden pulled the trigger on the hose. "You and Jorge need to give it up."

Haven gasped and sputtered, and not just because Holden sprayed her in the face.

I laughed, happy to be out of the spotlight.

The afternoon passed with bursts of jumping fits, water hose battles, and teasing. Saray prepared shrimp ceviche for lunch. Jumping, we bounced water from the trampoline and felt it rain down at our feet, collapsing when we got too tired, tangled up in each other again. Holden made us fluffernutters for dessert. We talked about nothing like it was everything. We'd always been good at that. Haven brought out popsicles as a second dessert.

The back door slammed as we were racing the sun to finish our popsicles. Saray rushed down the stairs, calling my name. I peeled myself from the trampoline and met her halfway across the yard.

She held my phone out, a look of panic on her face. "Quinn, your mom's been calling you."

My *mom?* Mom only called on Sunday nights.

I took the phone into my sticky hands.

Nine missed calls.

My heart dropped. My breath hitched. My fingers shook as I fumbled to call her back.

It rang again. Shrill and abrupt, it clipped the sweet air.

I answered it, greeted by my mom's panicked voice before I could get a word in.

What? My palms caught me. Heaviness. Knees cut from the grass. Heart hemorrhaging out. *Why?* Weightless. Floating in Holden's arms. *How?* Crying in Holden's chest. Haven's face when she picked the phone off the ground. My wail that ripped the blue sky open.

My baby cousin was dead.

Last Summer
Age 17, The Rest of August

QUINN WAS NUMB. She'd lost her sun, moon, and stars all at once.

Thoughts of Hadley consumed her, visions of the innocent, freckle-faced girl losing her footing in the Atlantic Ocean, screaming in fear as she lost sight of the shoreline, eventually caving in to her need for air.

Quinn was trapped in a blackhole, falling down a dark pit that felt like it would never end. Hadley used to tell her how a blackhole might feel, but she had never imagined it would feel so infinite.

The only escape from the nonstop horror reel was sleep.

Haven sat next to Quinn at the funeral and held her hand throughout the program. The seats were filled with Quinn's friends and their families, Hadley's school teachers and friends, and Hadley's father. Neither Blair, Josh, nor Quinn's mother had the strength to give a eulogy. That forced Quinn to stay intact long enough to take to the podium with stories of the girl who loved constellations, weeds, and other things only imagination allowed.

"Hadley wanted nothing more than to leave her mark on the

universe, to explore the galaxies, to discover new solar systems. She's dancing with the stars now. I hope the constellations love Hadley the way she loves them. I hope they are everything Hadley dreamed of." Quinn cupped her hand over the microphone to release her sobs. The funeral home filled with the heartbreaking cries of a girl left with nothing.

"She deserved a rollercoaster." It was the last thing Quinn said before she ran out of the room and never came back.

The funeral was cut short. People Quinn didn't know offered their condolences. She wanted nothing to do with them but shook their hands anyway—her hands clammy and her face emotionless. When Everett saw her, he hugged her as if he could squeeze all the sadness straight from her body.

He couldn't.

Nobody could.

Quinn's friends knew it would be a long time before she became herself again. They did everything they could to keep her mind from dozing off the way it always seemed to. Saray filled their kitchen with enough fried rice and tamales to feed a village. Liezel and Everett made sopas and purple yam cookies. When Quinn managed to eat, she couldn't keep anything down and resigned her stomach to the same emptiness as everything else.

Haven, Holden, Mason, and Jorge texted her every day. They sent her stupid jokes, pictures of baby animals, and funny videos. She woke up to dozens of them, only to fall asleep again without replying. The sun was her only indication that it wasn't night time. There was only day and night, but she didn't know how many times they changed shifts.

All she thought about was how happening to your own life didn't stop life from happening to you.

Everything she'd built this summer on was a lie. Happiness was a lie.

Everett drove to her house every afternoon, but he never got the courage to knock on the door. He stayed parked down the street until sundown, long after the cotton candy ice cream he'd bought for her had melted away in the floorboards. Everett would never know how much Quinn needed him, and Quinn would never know how close he had been the entire time.

Those close to the family filled Blair's porch with flowers: roses, daisies, lilies, carnations, anything that would give her some sense of hope. Blair didn't let them in the house, and had no intention of keeping them alive. She wanted the weeds to eat them alive. Weeds were Hadley's favorite, anyway.

Quinn's mother had arrived in time for the funeral and helped Blair with all the logistics of putting your little girl to rest. When summer was coming to a close, she helped Quinn pack her things and drove the two of them back to Raleigh, away from the beach that stole Hadley from them, but never from their pain.

Blair spent the next three months in Hadley's old room.

Quinn vowed never to touch the water again.

Now

August 11

Hadley died a year ago today.

My buzzing phone wakes me up before the sun. Texts from my friends, and one from Mom, light up the morning. They're variations of each other: they love me, they're sorry, they're thinking of me. If I didn't already know today's date like the lines on my palms, I would now.

I copy and paste the same thank you to all of them, then limp to the kitchen. Blair's door is closed, and her car is still in the driveway, so I pry open her door to check on her.

She's wrapped in her comforter, sprawled out on the queen bed, her limbs peeking out in random places. She looks peaceful—untouched by the black cloak of today.

I want some of that peace. I crawl into bed beside her, listen to the soft sound of her sleeping.

I'm not sure I've slept at all until I check my phone; three hours have passed. I want to go back to sleep, but I know it won't find me again. The fan in her room is too loud, my awake thoughts even louder.

There's no going back to dreamland, so I peel myself from her bed and head to the kitchen. I turn the stove on. Four eggs meet the pan and two slices of bread meet the toaster.

There are no flowers in the vase on the island, so I head to the front yard. The flowers on the front porch are still dead, but I don't need flowers. Not today. I pluck weeds from the yard for the vase.

Late-summer-singed dandelions, purple dead-nettles, white clovers. If you're worthy of a windowsill, you're worthy of being called more than just a weed.

The eggs are ready to flip. I break my yolk and leave Blair's untouched. I jelly the toast, flip the eggs onto their plates, and arrange it on the first pan I find under the stove.

Today's breakfast in bed isn't as glamorous as the movies make it seem, but those people didn't lose their only cousin. They didn't wake up to a million reminders of a tragedy. They didn't bear the pain of their heartbroken aunt.

Blair's still sleeping when I open her door.

I set the tray down on her bedside table, pick my plate off to go eat in the living room.

"Quinn?" Her voice stops me before I make it to the door.

I turn around, suddenly aware of how I must look to her. No bra, last night's messy bun spilling down my back, sleep still stuck to my face.

"Good morning." My smile is guilty, but it makes Blair chuckle, so I'll take feeling guilty for the rest of my life.

"Good morning. What are you doing up so early?"

I don't tell her it's almost noon. "I made you breakfast in bed."

She sits up while I set the tray on her lap, sit at the foot of her bed.

"Oh my God, you used a cookie sheet." She laughs, rubbing her eyes and brushing brown hair behind her ears.

"I didn't know what else to use."

"I love it." Her fingers graze the yellow dandelion petals—former white, puffy wishes that made it to adulthood, but never got to be wished on. "I never understood why you two loved weeds so much." She looks at me. "But I get it now."

"Very windowsill-esque." I smile and start in on my egg.

Blair follows suit. We sit in a silence only broken by the clink of metal on glass, the whir of the box fan in the window, some car doors slamming down the street.

"I'm going to see her today," I say, then regret takes over.

Blair looks at me with a stale piece of toast in her hand. She stops chewing. Her face falls and leaves behind a look so grief-stricken that you'd think she'd only just heard the news of her daughter's passing.

"Sorry. I shouldn't have said anything."

"No, you need to." Her smile is so forced, so good at hiding pain that it might as well have been painted on a porcelain doll. A long pause follows, filled with a year of unspoken conversation. Blair finally speaks it. "The first year is the hardest, but we made it."

When I look at her this time, I really *see* her. She survived a year without her daughter. She has a lifetime more to weather, but she's stronger now. She's proven it's possible—that life rolls on after a fall that feels so much like the end.

I've been so focused on all the little things that have changed—the beat-down siding, cluttered living spaces, how little Blair existed this summer—but the same number of things were eerily untouched. We still ignore her room, walk past the dead flowers on the porch, pretend she's not in the stars above us.

But my aunt is still here. She's the same woman I hugged on the porch eight summers ago, who welcomed me into her beach house and has given me the best nine skies of my life. She's the woman I've spent my life aspiring to be, the one I would do anything to see happy again.

"I'm so proud of you."

She cocks her head, wrinkles her eyebrows. A special kind of shock overcomes her, like she can't believe a single soul could be proud of her. She doesn't see what I see, how strong she continues to be in a world that tried its hardest to break her.

I squeeze her hand. "You'll always be her mom."

She squeezes back. "I know."

We look at each other over a forgotten breakfast. The glint in her brown eyes gives me a piece of her strength. Hadley is no longer a physical part of our lives. Since not one horoscope or fortune cookie or wish on a dolphin fin has changed that, I need to accept it as something more than a bad dream, something more than a year-old memory.

I need to stand on the shoreline, face the tsunami while it swallows me whole.

IN THE PIER SHOP, I make a beeline for the baskets of shells that greet my fingertips every time I come. I find the dusty basket on the floor with the large purple cowries. Scorpio rests on top, but I dig to find Sagittarius. I buy both and head into the sunlight.

The drive to the cemetery on the mainland is slow. Scorpio and Sagittarius sit in the passenger seat, reeling over each crack in the road. My hands are firm around the steering wheel. My shoulders roll all the way back. My gulps land heavier past each rung on the causeway. The water glimmers on both sides of me, stretching for miles and stirring with the horizon in a hazy fog. I pretend the water below didn't do this.

I rub Hadley's blue heart pendant around my neck. Causeways and necklaces carry memories no matter how you swing it.

I park under a tree as old as the weathered headstones hiding in its shadows. I sit there for a bit, my forehead against my steering wheel, my thumb still reading Hadley's necklace like a crystal ball. It decides it's too late to back down now.

I need to do this.

I bring Sagittarius with me. My sandals scuff against the asphalt in defiance, but they soldier on, padding against the grass still wet in the shade. I slink around a lawn of phantom memories, almost step over some weeds growing in front of a bright marble headstone. Only touched by a year of beach weather, the engraving reads:

HADLEY REINHART
Touch the stars, baby girl.

I sit in front of Hadley's headstone, hug my knees to my chest, rock against the ground that feels too freshly churned despite the weeds. A mason jar of white clovers rests before the headstone.

I let out a year's worth of tears. The air does nothing to soothe me. It doesn't bring Hadley back. It doesn't make my reality any less real. She shouldn't be down there, left to spend eternity in a dark, silent, dead home. Not while I'm up here. Not while the sun can still warm me and dry tears from my cheeks like just another patch of dew.

She deserved to feel the sun on her forever. She deserved to count the stars glowing for her every night.

She deserved to come back from the beach that day.

Why didn't she come back from the beach that day?

Why did the ocean betray us?

Why couldn't the ocean have taken me instead?

A long, constrained sob drains the rest of me. My eyes tremble close. My heart beats rampantly in my temples. A headache creeps up like a shadow. I close my eyes to let the tears stuck to my eyelashes trickle down and around my nose.

When I open my eyes, my vision is blurry with tears, so I wipe them with the back of my hand, see Sagittarius lying there. I must have dropped her. A purple centaur sits carved in the shell, wielding a bow and arrow.

The archer points its arrow at me. I glide my finger across the glossy top coat, begging it to let go of the arrow and puncture me with it.

It doesn't let go.

She'll never let go.

I scoop Hadley into my palm and place her next to a vase of daisies. I unclasp her necklace from my neck and wrap it around the jar, all of it glistening the same way in the sun.

But I know these things are not Hadley.

It's just a gift shop shell. A jar of clovers. A blue heart necklace.

That's all she is now.

"You deserved a rollercoaster." My voice adjusts to the outside air, throat choking on words not even loud enough for me to hear.

My head pounds. My breathing levels out. The strengthening sun burns into my eyes, and I squint to kill the stinging. My shoulder throbs from the weight of my body. I'm sitting on the grass in front of Hadley's headstone—on top of her patch of six-feet-deep soil, feeling every bit of the pain Hadley no longer can.

The irony finally hits me.

I've spent nine summers avoiding pain that's only felt from the transfer of living nerves, the pain that comes after taking chances some never get the chance to take.

The pain that only comes from living.

Hadley was never afraid of pain and never let the possibility of pain keep her from living her nine years with no reserve. She never let fear get in her way. She chased bumblebees, threw herself down waterslides, lay in the aquarium tank dome, slept under the stars, and dreamt of soaring through outer space. She never took her chance on Earth for granted and never would have thought twice about boarding her rollercoaster.

She was never afraid to live.

But I was.

The ghost that haunts *me* is the past.

I could have been as carefree as the clouds, danced with the soul of a child, let the water hold me, loved with a whole heart, kissed with no scope of the future.

But I didn't, even though no amount of living hurts more than the numbness of death.

Now

August 12

WE'RE ALREADY BAKING IN THE MID-MORNING SUN. Everett leads the way on the sand, both of us trudging forward like we're stranded and hoping to be saved. The wind is so strong I have to fight against it, but it's a relief in the intense gaze of the sun.

It wouldn't be this hard if my ankle wasn't still on the mend. Neither of us anticipated how long a mile feels on the sand. He asked me last night if I was up for an adventure, then told me to be ready to leave by 7am. I didn't think we'd drive so far to the state line, turning just before South Carolina for Sunset Beach.

We've already stopped four times for water, but Everett insists it will be worth it.

I've stripped down to just my shorts and bikini top, beads of sweat accumulating on my forehead.

Everett is just as sweaty. He stuffed his shirt into his bookbag a few sand dollar shards back. "If we make it to the jetty, we've gone too far."

"Where are we going?"

"You'll see. Is your ankle still okay?"

"If I say no, will you carry me?" If I could, I'd rock on my heels to indicate just how much I'm joking. My ankle *does* hurt, but only because the sand is concrete in the middle of the shoreline. But it's nothing I can't handle.

He lets out a chuckle. "If you *really* needed me to. I suppose it'd be my punishment for bringing you here."

It feels like walking in a dream with no end in sight. The dunes have looked the same for the past thirty minutes, tufts of grass and sunken sand where the wind blew too hard. If I didn't know any better, I'd think we haven't made any progress, but when I look back, the Sunset Beach Fishing Pier shrinks into the horizon.

We walk where shells are haphazard raindrops, broken on impact. We're too far from the water to find any newly washed-up ones, but Everett finds a perfect auger for Liezel. Pin shells sparkle like purple fans. Pocket slippers hold water in their palms. Butter clams taunt me with the color and general shape of a perfect sand dollar, so I search with my head held high for any indication of where we're going.

Everett pivots to trudge to the dunes. At the top of the dunes lives a black mailbox secured to a piece of driftwood. Boxy, white stickers spell out "Kindred Spirit" in black lettering.

Everett opens the mailbox. Stacks of wilted notebooks rest inside, a pile of ink pens and pencils beside them. "This is the Kindred Spirit mailbox. For decades, people have come here to write their hopes, dreams, secrets, and letters to loved ones."

So that's why the red flag points up; there's always mail in here. *That's* what infinity looks like. Kindred Spirit has weathered storms, kissed the sun, and braced itself against salt air for so long, but it stands strong to gatekeep the world's wishes.

"I don't know what we're going to find in these letters, but they're written by real people. I've always wanted to see other people's wishes, you know, since you never tell me yours." Everett cracks a smile, then hands me a dark blue notebook. He takes a green one and sits on a wooden bench to read.

I sit in the sand and fight the wind to keep the pages open. The pages crinkle when I slide my fingers across them. They, too, have to be strong for the words of the world. I let the wind take me to random pages, then brace against it to read them:

> *What does someone wish for when they've come all this way? I make a lot of wishes, but this is different. My biggest wish is to see my mom again. I never stopped to think about a simple moment being my last, but I'm glad I smiled at her from the kitchen window that day. I can't smile at her again but at least I can give her this. Mom, I trekked all this way for you. Think of it as me smiling at your ghost.*

> *We never even met, but I feel you next to me in the car,*
> *on the parkway, taking every curve with a laugh,*
> *and listening to songs I never learned were your favorite.*
> *I've thought up the rest of you in my head,*
> *The real-you and my-you ride two parallel lines.*
> *What once existed on the same axis*
> *now move perpendicularly.*
> *So far from each other now,*
> *one sits on a mountaintop*
> *and one sleeps on the beach.*

Last October, I ran a red light. I didn't hit anything, but what if I had? I can't shake the possibilities from my mind. I can't stop dreaming in red and blue lights. Kindred Spirit, please free me from this guilt.

*There are moments when you feel your happiness
as sure as you feel the wind.
Happiness is like breathing,
but right now I exhale it pointedly.
It hits me on the beach too warm for February.
I forced it to happen when I stepped into my shorts and sandals.
"It will be summer today," I told the sky.
It listened.
It sent me weather that made me forget how it felt to be cold.*

Give me a sign. Help me understand if you're still with me. Make the waves wash up a starfish. You always loved saving the ones that were still breathing, even if it meant getting your jeans wet. Peek through the clouds and fix this overcast day. You always thought the day wasn't real without the sun, but I'm not real without you. Send me a messy patch of wind. You always hated how the wind messed up your hair. You tied your bangs up and never cared how silly it made you look, but I never thought you looked silly. Please. Give me something. I need to know you see me. I need to know you're proud of me. I miss you. I love you.

You are crispy leaves and rainy days, which is to say you're sprawling with life even when you think you're dead. Why don't you feel the same way about me?

I close the notebook after nearly reading the whole thing. I look at the ocean. This notebook, this stretch of beach, this warm sand—all of it connects me with the people who wrote these letters. That and the pain, joy, love, and loss of life on planet Earth.

There's no pattern to these strangers' lives. Some are joyous, some are unexpected sunshine on a February morning, some explain the dark circles stained on the page—tears, dried but still crinkling to life.

We're all just people, subjecting ourselves to the world and its woes.

We have family and friends and love and fear.

We fear that the universe will take what's ours; we're grateful the universe gave us ours to begin with. We breathe fear and gratitude in the same breath. In the same life.

You have to have the highs to have the lows.

We all have ups and downs, *rollercoasters*, but we shoulder on.

Everett closes his notebook, then looks at me.

"What do you think?"

"I think I've never felt less alone."

Kindred Spirit is a sacred ground. The ghosts of visitors past cling to the dune grass. The breeze remembers those who have come and gone.

"Me too. I knew there'd be a lot of sad letters, but I didn't expect so many of them to be so happy."

An oxymoron—love letters living in the same notebook as hopeless letters to lost loved ones. A metaphor for life before and after love. Life *because* of love.

Everett pulls something out of his bookbag—a sheet of notebook paper folded and secured with the sticker from an orange. "I'm going to write in the notebook too, but I wrote this for you."

In his tall and thin handwriting, Everett wrote:

I'm not ashamed to say I love math more than the average person. Some people might call me a nerd for that, even though they feel the same way about the stars, which is also math, but I'm not one to judge. If you know where to look, almost everything is math. The shape of a nautilus shell can be measured by the Fibonacci sequence. Tree branches are fractals. The circumference of every circle, from bird baths to buttons, can be calculated with pi. Snowflakes crystallize in symmetrical patterns.

A friend of mine believes that the universe is transactional. Of course, the first thing that comes to mind is what Galileo (not a friend of mine) once said: "Mathematics is the language of the universe." Not to go against Galileo, but I know that the universe isn't always so formulaic. Even though math is the fabric of the universe, the universe is more than just fabric. The universe has organic things like friendship, life, death, and love, which are beautifully random in their occurrences. It makes life scary, but it also makes life fun. In life, you learn that bad things do not follow a pattern. One cannot predict the events of the next day, even if the events of the day before were suspiciously good.

Quinn, your life is not transactional, and that makes it a beautiful thing in itself.

Universally, Dr. Bishop

Freshly fallen tears pool on the letter. The world is a blur beyond my eyes, but these tears are air compared to the ones I've poured out these past few days. I catch the remaining tears on my cheeks before they make a mess of Everett's words. The rest I absorb with my thumb to keep from smudging the black ink.

I smile at him, an oxymoron on my face. "I don't know what to say."

"You don't have to say anything. You don't even have to believe me."

"I believe you."

The universe is not a nautilus shell. Not a tree branch. Not a bird bath or a button. Not even a snowflake. The universe doesn't know math. I am not in debt to something that doesn't even know me by name. The universe is more than fabric, and my life is not transactional. It transcends the beautiful, inarguable equivalence of math.

I look into the fabric of his eyes. "Thank you."

Everett smiles warmly in response, then we dig in to the sandwiches and grapes he packed in his bookbag. While I pluck grapes from their vine, Everett writes his own letter in the green notebook, glancing up at the waves in blips of thought. I write the beginning of my own letter, then get trapped in my own trance. I watch the waves in hopes that they'll write my story for me.

Everett finishes and puts his notebook in the mailbox. He tells me he's going to cool off in the water. I watch him walk the long stretch to the ocean. Finally, the rest of my inspiration strikes. It's impossible for it not to, given the way Everett waves at me from the ocean, smiling at the sun, smiling at me, smiling at *us*.

Quinn and Everett.

My words will live forever in the blue notebook in the Kindred Spirit mailbox:

Eight summers ago, I came here chasing the welcoming nature of the beach. When my father left me for a new life, I felt invisible, but just like my father, I made my own new life. Thanks to Piper Island, I got to be a kid again, form lifelong friendships, and fall in love.

I've never really told anyone that, but you're special, Kindred Spirit. You hold a universe of secrets, wishes, hopes, dreams, and loves. The secret is that I am in love with the boy who brought me here. He's jumping the waves right now. Every couple waves, he looks back at me. I don't think he knows I'm watching, but there's nothing I'd rather watch than him.

Kindred Spirit, I'm not proud to admit it, but I'm scared of a lot of things. This fear has barred me from a lot of joy, but I'm not sure it's kept me from danger. I'm not sure the world is as dangerous as I always thought. I'm not even sure what I'm scared of. I guess it's like swimming in murky water. There's a fear there that you can't quite shake, even when you don't know what you're scared of. The unknown, I suppose, but who knows if there's even a sea monster? How often is there actually a sea monster? The unknown might have a perfect sand dollar or something else equally as incredible.

Another truth is that the ocean has given and taken things from me. That's how waves work.

It's given me Haven, Holden, Mason, and Jorge.

It's taken away my loneliness.

It's given me a lifetime of memories.

It's taken away Hadley.

It's given me my moon, my rollercoaster, my Everett.

I'm still waiting for it to take away my fear.

It owes me that, but I suppose the ocean is not transactional.

The ocean and the universe are similar that way.

I put the pen down, open and close my fist to stretch out the ache from writing on autopilot. I don't know the strangers who will read this letter one day, but I hope it helps them with their own grief, their own tug-of-war with giving and taking. I close the notebook and place it in the mailbox, then comb for shells closer to the waves.

While I'm searching, I see a shell emerge from the falling waves. When I get closer, I spot five flower petals etched on the top. *There's no way.* Five oval-shaped holes emerge from all but the top petal. A bigger oval lives just below the etching. It's more circular than clam shaped. The circumference could almost be calculated by pi. *It can't be.*

Off-white. As big as my palm. Smooth.

An intact sand dollar.

My heart leaps in tune with my ear-splitting gasp. I jump out of my skin to cradle it into my shaking palms. I even let out some expletives, which prompts Everett to run over. I make him pinky promise he didn't plant it here. It's not bleached enough to be store-bought anyway.

How many years have I dreamt of this moment? How many years was I sure I wanted to carry it all the way to my sunny windowsill? How many years would I have needed to convince myself that when I finally found it, I *wouldn't* keep it? The ocean has given, but I don't plan on taking.

Someone else might, but if they do, it's because they've searched their whole life for it. It's because they need it as much as I don't. Not anymore.

Instead, I pen an inky message onto the gritty underbelly, then place it inside Kindred Spirit.

Hadley, you deserved a rollercoaster, and so do I.

Now

August 12

THE SUN SETS PINK on our familiar Sapphire Beach Boardwalk, the final flicker of the day holding out to let us admire the summer silhouette. The line that cuts the ocean from the sky fades into dusk.

Now teeming with neon lights, carnival dings, and a boisterous Ferris wheel blinking in morse code, it's a wonderland of woozy food, woozier rollercoasters, and the wooziest thrum in my chest.

Old gum splatters on the wooden planks. Or brand-new gum, stomped completely black in one day, depending on who you ask. The boy I would ask walks next to me, his hands in his pockets, his face glowing in the lights.

I find freedom in the wind blowing against my skin.

When the photo booth comes into view, spontaneity courses through my veins. It feels like the moment was gifted to me from Hadley somewhere in the stars in response to the sand dollar.

"Let's go to the photo booth!" I grab Everett's hand, pull us in there as quickly as my ankle allows after I finally rested it this afternoon.

For the first time this summer, I am the carefree, silly, happy girl from last summer.

Behind the curtain, Everett and I wedge onto the bench. It's so small that I have to sit sideways. I'm already facing him when the camera starts to count down. I grab the side of his neck, whisper into his ear, "Can I tell you a secret?"

"Hm?" he whispers when the first flash goes off.

I smile, press our foreheads together during the second flash. The universe trapped in his eyes expands. A million galaxies work to steady my heart about to explode.

"I'm not scared anymore." I pull his face to mine.

The universe rips at its soft, fabric seams when I kiss Everett Bishop.

Everett cups my cheek, sinks deeper into the kiss. Our noses jump over each other's. I pull his shirt into my palms and bring him closer to me. I didn't think this space could feel any tighter, didn't think kissing could feel so much like floating in outer space.

He pulls back first, stares at me, his smile curled up on one side. I'm already staring back at him.

We leave the photo booth like nothing happened, but there's no denying it when the photo booth spits the photo strip onto the sandy wooden planks.

Four photos, memorialized in black and white, progressively blurrier smudges of hands and cheeks, two smiles pursed into one another. Sharp jaws, forehead kisses, closed eyes—a rollercoaster of emotions on our faces, all landing softly at the end.

Sometime during the slow unfurling of nerves, the long taffy pull of our kiss, two more photos were taken. The lightbulb burned our second kiss into forever.

I look up at Everett, feeling the blend of guilt and softness and anticipation that normal people call love. "I'm sorry I was scared for so long."

"Quinn." He wraps his hand around my neck, stroking his thumb on the bit of skin in front of my ear. "Nothing matters but right now."

Everett lifts me to the balls of my feet for another kiss.

Beyond the secret cloak of the photo booth, in the bright, beautiful world, Everett and I kiss away six summers of guilt and softness and anticipation.

Just like that, the anti-gravity feeling rushes back—the weightlessness I only feel outside of fear's evil grasp.

In the breathless air after, he takes my hand in his, lets them dangle at our sides. He brushes fallen strands of my hair behind my ear. "I wanted it like this."

New spontaneity takes over this time: the first bite of cotton candy, the stuffed animal in the crane that empties your wallet, the will-they-or-won't-they dance of the carousel horses.

The idea spills out like sunset. I point to Tsunami, lightbulbs tracing its curves against the navy-blue sky. "Let's go ride it."

"Really?"

"*I would love to ride Tsunami with you*," I want to say.

"I would love to ride Tsunami with you," I do say.

We run hand in hand toward the line, kicking dust in the face of old fears, old times. Our arms stretch out to hug new worlds, new opportunities.

Tsunami won't be our first rollercoaster ride.

Nor will it be our last.

Now

August 12

TWO FLASHLIGHTS CUT ACROSS THE PARK. Darkness has long since swept over the island, but there's never truly darkness under the constellations.

Long after our late-night diner banana split turned to soup, I told him I had a surprise for him. I wanted to keep it a secret, but none of the forces of Piper Island could keep it down. It didn't matter that I blindfolded him with two takeout bags tied together. It didn't matter that the car filled with noisy static when he rolled his window down and stuck his hand out to ride the choppy air. It didn't matter that the water was its own dark secret all around, hidden in plain sight inside the distant lights of Piper Island. With our free hands linked over the gear shift, the secret still managed to spill from my lips.

"We're going to the park. There's something I need to show you. Something I want you to do, if you want."

In our flashlight beams, the wooden castle comes into view. Muscle memory takes me to the spot where the walls swap love stories in secret.

When I was eleven, I knew love was something you could play hide and seek with and never win.

At eighteen, in the watchful eye of a summer night Sagittarius, I know love hides in plain sight.

Love lives in black and white kisses.

In Everett's palm, I press a pocket knife I swiped from Holden's tackle box. He nods in silent understanding. The cicadas, katydids, and locusts have rehearsed their whole life to sing the soundtrack of this moment. They nail the bridge, pirouette into an encore.

Everett stands, brushes sand off his knees, kisses love into my temple.

We will move on—this moment a mere sentence in the book of the park—rolling like beach thunder to the next adventure.

We will move on, but somewhere on an island named Piper, at a park with a wooden castle playground, forever lives two names etched into wood:

Quinn + Everett.

Now

August 16

THE HEIST STARTS WHEN Blair leaves for sunrise yoga. I wish I could say that we creep out from the shadows the moment her taillights turn off our street, a SWAT team wielding paint sprayers like weapons, but it happens in waves.

Everett and his parents are first. It *was* Everett's idea, after all, and Hank's construction company. We were wrapped up on his couch talking well after a movie's credits rolled when he suggested it. He knew I'd object, so he told me his dad already cleared his schedule for it. At dinner, Hank did the rest of the convincing, bribery via crab cakes. My only job was to pick a color and get Blair out of the house before the sky blushed.

The Bishop family climb out of the company truck. Liezel lays out tarps on the grass. Everett hooks up power tools and Hank starts sanding the dead blue paint from the siding. I pluck unnamed weeds from the edge of the house and trim the hedges sprouted at the windows.

Haven and Holden come next with donuts.

Mason arrives with popsicles after he overslept his alarm.

Jorge rolls in with takeout boxes of hushpuppies and chicken tenders from last night's rush.

Between snacking and water breaks inside, we take to electric sanders, painter's tape, and paint sprayers. In the oppressive summer heat, we coat the house in fresh paint, all of us singing along to dad rock. Haven and I picked out the color yesterday, both of us swayed by kitschy names until the perfect shade presented itself.

Sweat holds me like a promise. Hair spills from my messy bun. My thighs stick together.

I stop during the rush to change into a tank top and stay inside to clean the inside of the house. Since Everett and I did most of the heavy lifting earlier this summer, this mostly entails surface mess: dusty bookshelves, cluttered counters, piles of laundry. I throw away years-old unread magazines and expired food in the pantry, put away the new groceries piled on the counter. Jorge helps me fold blankets and stage the house into a home. I sweep the hard floors into a pile of stubborn sand and dirt, and Jorge follows with a mop. The smell of bleach and the coconut candle lit on the kitchen island make it smell like my first day here eight summers ago.

How the universe has spun since then.

THE HARDEST THING ABOUT TODAY is the matter on the front porch. I stand there chewing on my thumb nail, staring at the one-year-old roses, daisies, lilies, and carnations rotten in their pots. We can't keep walking past dead flowers, but I can't bring myself to throw them out. It feels too much like forgetting.

"Let me do it," Everett says, reaching for a flowerpot.

"No." I grab his arm, still staring at them. "I have to do it."

We stand there for a bit. He watches me stare at the pot, tears forming in my eyes. I blink and let them fall, then bite my lower lip to keep from crying too much. Everett's still quiet, slinking his arm around me, pulling me into him. Even when he wipes the tears from my chin and rocks me in place, I still can't stop staring. I'm stuck in a trance whisking me back to the day I found out, to the day of the funeral when we loaded the flowers in the car, to the days of staring at them through the window—bright and alive—when I felt anything but.

I need to do it.

I breathe in and out, wipe final tears from my eyes, and grab a pot of carnations. *This is for Blair, this is for Hadley, this is for me*, I repeat on the way to the trash can.

I drop the whole thing in upside down, then let Everett do the rest.

JIMMY BUFFETT AND BRUCE SPRINGSTEEN sing of summers past. Liezel finishes cutting the paint around the eave of the house, which makes the spraying easy. Hair spills from my bun but my hands are too busy with the sprayer to care. I blow it out of my face but it comes right back. I didn't think painting would be such a full body workout, but my muscles light up in protest. I don't object. I just let myself get mesmerized by the steady progress.

This is for Blair, this is for Hadley, this is for me.

AFTER A WATER HOSE BATTLE IN THE BACKYARD, we settle down with fluffernutters. This time, the sticky sandwich takes me back to fishing with Haven and Holden. Old memories died with the flowers. New memories sit across from me on the shady front porch.

I stick my peanut butter and marshmallow tongue out at them. They do it back. Everything about it is perfect.

Twelve hours of dirt, dried paint, and sweat have passed until there's only one blue strip left.

Hank stops his spraying to grant me the honors. My arms shake, both from the finality of the moment and because they aren't used to this. I finish the job in the spotlight of my friends' gaze.

Behind me, the yard erupts in applause. If my cheeks weren't already blazing hot, this moment would do the trick. I wipe sweat off my forehead with the only clean patch of my arm, crack a smile at all of them, and give them a bow fitting of a karaoke stage.

I step back and admire our hard work.

What once was a choked-out, lifeless blue is now alive with the snap of bubblegum pink. Pink cotton candy crystals dissolving on a warm tongue. A strawberry ice cream cone melted in the August heat.

Coral Daydreams—Hadley's favorite color put into words by a paint company.

"It looks amazing." I can't contain myself. I wrap my arms around Hank, who made this all possible. "Thank you."

"Thank *you*." He squeezes his hand on my shoulder, gives me a shake.

I haven't the slightest clue what he could be thanking *me* for, but I don't object.

The jagged edges of the driveway press into my warm skin. The six of us are tattered from the day, covered in an explosion of pink paint, but we can't go celebrate at Sunset Scoop just yet—the best part is yet to come.

My legs fall asleep from Everett's head on my thigh, but I don't care. I brush my hands through his hair, pulling dried paint from individual strands. "Thank you guys. You have no idea how much this means."

"It really was no problem," Holden says.

Haven nudges me. "And you don't know how much you mean to us."

"Yeah, you're the only tourist I can stand," Mason says.

I stick my middle finger up with a smile that means anything but.

Blair's car pulls up to the driveway. Through the windshield, I see her mouth gape open. She looks between us and the house like she can't believe the world she left blue this morning became coral by evening.

I wake up my sleepy legs, running to the driver's side of the car now parked in front of six teenagers and a fresh start.

"Welcome home," I say.

A coral house. Railing as white as a full moon. A house wiped clean from a tragedy and given a second chance.

"This is our house?" Her voice runs rampant. Her hand cups over her mouth. Her eyebrows crease in pleasant disbelief.

"This is our house!" I take her hands and pull her into me, my arms wrapped so tightly around her like I'm trying to squeeze out every last bit of pain. We stand behind an open car door, putting each other back together like we found the last puzzle piece fallen between two cushions.

She pulls back after what feels as long as the tide coming in and going back out.

"I can't believe this." She wipes tears from her cheeks, the first happy tears to grace her face in over a year. "How did this happen?"

"Everett's parents. And us." I point to everyone sitting cross-legged on the concrete. "We've been working since you left this morning."

They all smile and wave back at Blair. Haven jumps up first and hugs her. The rest follow, giving the last bit of their love to a woman who lost her own.

Blair cracks a smile, then looks between all my friends. "Thank you guys so much, for everything. Hadley would have loved this."

The words are full, whole, dancing with the evening breeze.

Hadley's name hits for the first time without sparking remorse, instead filling me with a sense of bittersweet acceptance. I'll feel it every time I see something coral, every time I look to my horoscope for a sense of pseudo direction, every time I find myself too afraid to do something she would have dove head first into. I'll feel it every time I see a shooting star and think it's her in the sky, granting me the life she wants me to live out for her.

I know I will never stop thinking about her.

I know I never want to.

I exhale for the first time in what feels like years, staring in the face of rollercoaster tracks on their way up.

Now

August 17

I WAKE UP IN A PINK HOUSE.

Slip on a pink tank top.

Brush my teeth in a pink mood.

I bounce on pink heels around my almost packed up room, down the hallway, and out the door faster than a pink sunrise can break and spill into blue.

My steps leave emerald footprints in the dew on Haven and Holden's front yard. If grass could talk, it would speak of the summer days spent roaming here. Of secrets told over *tres leches*, water hose battles on the trampoline, the backyard where I got the dreaded phone call.

The front door creaks. Holden's eyes are barely open, his hair freshly peeled from his pillow, but he stomps down the stairs and pulls me into a hug. I'm back in the same embrace I burrowed myself into last summer when I learned the sky lost its stars. The hug feels different today, scabbed over and dwindling. I no longer feel the need to peel the dried maroon off and watch it bleed.

Scars don't hurt when they're healed, but you can't outrun them.

"You're up too early for someone on their last day of summer vacation," I say.

"The sunrise is worth it."

I cross my arms with a smirk. "Sunrise? You only wake up before noon for fish."

He pokes my forehead. "And Quinn Kesslers."

Haven steps down the stairs, a beach bag weighing down her shoulder, pink sunglasses on her nose despite the sky still dark enough for streetlights.

In the prologue to the rising sun, everything is pink. It's impossible not to be, even with the thought of driving away tomorrow.

Today marks a new beginning.

That's why we're awake this early in the first place.

Last night, Everett and I were on the back porch with the cicadas, katydids, and locusts, eating a fresh batch of Liezel's yam cookies when the idea struck. Even as far inland as Blair's house is, the smell of salt hung heavily in the air. A beckoning call. A request for forgiveness. An olive branch.

"I'm tired of hating the ocean," I said from the rocking chair.

Everett looked at me like he couldn't believe the words just left my mouth, but he smiled and promised we'd go to the beach in the morning. There's no better version of the shore than the one that spits out the sun into morning, at least that's what I think.

Our plan to meet up to watch the sunrise turned into an early breakfast on the beach.

The twins and I file out of my car with our things, racing barefoot from the parking lot onto the beach. I stay behind to walk slowly, my ankle still wrecked, and spend more time with the seagrass whispering from the dunes. The sky is so pink I could jump with my mouth open and land with sticky sugar on my tongue. *If* I could jump. *If* clouds really were cotton candy.

Everett, Mason, and Jorge wrestle the wind to lay a blanket on the sand. We sit on the blanket to keep it from flying away. A picnic breakfast awaits: orange juice, cinnamon donuts, blueberry bagels, grapes, and sliced strawberries.

In the distance, a shrimp boat comes in from a scandalous night out with the sea. Small black figures meander toward the horizon: beachcombers, joggers, dogs off their leashes. Surfers won't catch much this morning, but they're front row to the pod of dolphins that swim by for their own breakfast. Patches of sea foam lose the war with the wind and zip like tumbleweeds down the beach. The water waves good morning millions of miles out, a glassy opal sheen the pelicans probably skate on.

We wait for the sun to join us, like watching paint dry on a canvas, but once the first orange slice burns across the sky, the rest rises the way an avalanche falls. The canvas is dry now, its colors a byproduct of light bestowing itself upon the world.

Then everything around us turns from hazy pink to burnt orange. Beachcombers' footprints are small orange mountains on the soft sand. Wind-blown hairs reveal their secret gold undertones. Seashells slip from their camouflage on the dark brown sand. The cream cheese smeared on empty plates glows.

Conversation buzzes between nothing and everything, as it often tends to. Packing woes, college itineraries, the state of Loggerhead Lighthouse after this fall's restoration project ends. There's plenty to silently ponder where the seagulls chirp against the ocean's tune.

"I told my parents last night," Holden says. "About me and Mason.

Well, just about me, but they figured Mason and I were dating."

"How did it go?" Everett asks.

"It was fine." He smiles softly.

"Better than fine." Haven brushes her hands through his wild hair. "They said they want to have Mason over for dinner. *Formally.* And that they love him forever. Just like we all do."

Holden holds his neck behind his hands, but he smiles like he's waited forever for those words. His cheeks blush and he looks like he could cry the happiest tears I've ever seen.

With the sun now part of the day and breakfast done, we disperse.

Haven and I play tic-tac-toe in the sand. I block her row of scallops with a cockle. Mason and Holden stand at the wet sand, so still their feet sink slowly into the world. Jorge picks through a pile of shells on the trash line, looking for shark teeth. Everett lies down next to me, his hands in his hoodie pockets, his head on the sand.

His eyes trace the only cloud in the sky.

"What is it?" I ask, looking between the cloud and his golden face.

"A seagull, but like people draw it," he says without breaking his trance on the sky.

I draw it in the sand with my finger. Context turns the rounded "m" shape into a greedy seagull's wings against an endless sky. My eyes turn it into the cloud soaring above.

THE STICKY SWEET STING of summer's end sweeps me off my feet.

Everett and I walk down the beach, as far as my ankle will take me. The sandpipers run from us, their little legs a blur of reckless abandon. A patch of seagulls finally decide to kick on their wings and flee. A beached cannonball jelly glimmers in the sun.

The water collapses over the sand, disrupting the stillness. Live coquinas shuffle away from the sunlight. Broken, discarded shells make twinkling music against themselves. Soon, they'll whittle into dust, but they'll live forever as bits of sand. The sand soaks up the waves, turning darker where water no longer reflects the brightening sky. In an instant, the waves make it wet and shiny again. A cyclical, infinite film reel.

The waves come and go, even with nobody to watch them.

I'm tired of hating the ocean.

Suddenly, I'm magnetized by the thrumming waves.

A moment passes with a gust of wind before I decide to just do it. I trudge over the increasingly darker sand, walking past freckled olives, nutmegs, baby's ears, jingles, until finally I make it, gasping when water rushes over my toes. The water feels like it always has—jarring and cool and exactly the feeling worth waiting an entire school year to feel again. This time, it's on my terms.

Everett takes each step with me. Beyond the band of jagged seashells, the sand is soft beneath my toes. I stop knee-deep, where the water still hugs my legs but my shorts stay dry. Where I'm not technically *swimming*, but sea foam still fizzes against my skin. Waves still thrum in the same spot they did seconds before. I put my hands in and let the water slip between my fingers.

I close my eyes, breathe in and out with the whir of the ocean.

The ocean is synonymous with summer and sunlight and sunscreen. Ice cream and itineraries and insects. Fireflies and fireworks and fluffernutters. Moon jellies and mini golf and moonlight. Constellations and carousels and cotton candy. *Tres leches* and tanning and taffy.

I never hated you.

I open my eyes to show the ocean I mean it.

When I look at Everett, he wedges a hand in his pocket, then opens it out to me. Resting on his palm is a small pink coquina clamshell from our day on the bike trail. Four summers of us rewind in my mind. They live in rose quartz Saturn rings.

"It's perfect." I string the ninth shell onto the chain, then let Everett clasp it back.

"For your ninth summer at Piper Island." Everett wills the entire summer pink despite everything trying to darken it. Nine summers stick to my skin like salt water.

Everett's touch lingers on my neck, sending shivers down my skin despite everything trying to warm it. He pulls me in for a kiss. After he pulls back, he focuses in on my cheek, eyebrows furrowed as he swipes his thumb across it.

On his thumb rests a stray eyelash plucked from my cheek. "Make a wish," he says.

I close my eyes, ready to continue a years-old tradition, but it doesn't feel right. Just like conch shells don't really tune your ear drums to the sea, cheek eyelashes, birthday candles, dandelion puffs to the wind don't really change your fate.

Shooting stars are just meteors.

Wishes are just acknowledged desires.

Rollercoasters are just wooden structures.

I don't need such illusions. Not anymore.

I open my eyes to the real world before me. The eyelash is already lost to the wind.

"What'd you wish for?" Everett asks.

"Nothing." I smile. I think he believes me this time. "What'd *you* wish for?"

"Same." He grabs my hand, strokes my index finger with his thumb. "There's nothing left to wish for."

The sun has finished painting everything in its path, leaving both of us golden in the morning light. I'll miss this pocket of sand and salt and sunlight, but the sun rises everywhere.

Even in the darkest places.

I'll be back, Piper Island.

Pinky promise.

Acknowledgments

AMY, THIS BOOK WOULDN'T EXIST WITHOUT YOU. My ties to the beach wouldn't exist without you. You're the reason I call shells by their names and know the best spot for every beach vibe imaginable. Thank you for your open doors, open arms, and open mind to my wild itineraries. No amount of ferry trips, ice cream runs, and shelling at dusk with flashlights will be too many.

Mom, I'm sure by now you've mastered the art of drowning me out, but for some reason, you don't. You've listened to my ideas, complaints, and excitement for nine long years. When I begin to doubt myself, you never let me get beyond a few words. You're my biggest cheerleader even when each sentence makes you cry. If you're reading this, congratulations on making it through.

Dad, thank you for your passion about the technical part of writing and formatting. You're the smile across the table on Tuesday nights at the coffee shop. Even though you rolled your eyes, you still slipped me the cash for a latte, despite the fact that I never had the time to help you with your books. Thanks for splitting the best croissant on the menu with me.

Grammy, you gave me a love of reading and a knack for writing that I didn't know back then was from you. I've since read your journal addressed to me, and I know more than ever that words were everything to you. You said it best in your familiar cursive, "I love it when you bring me a book wanting to be read to—Taylor, I hope someday you will love to read as much as I do. Reading is a pleasure."

To my soul sister, Kendall, for listening to nine years of incessant droning and for being the very first Everquinn (Quiverett?) shipper. You understand my characters just as much as I do, and you've talked me out of some wild ideas that have saved the book's ass. Gibson's Ice Cream is all for you.

Holly, you got me into writing in the first place. On the first week of high school, during a chat about Fanfiction, I told you I was looking for a story I couldn't find. You told me to write my own and that simple push brought me into the world of writing, all the way to this point. I'll never forget that.

Milana, I'm honored to share a love of reading, the beach, and reading beach books with you. There's nothing like passionate chats about our latest reads. You've supported my writing for so long, and now it's time for the roles to be reversed.

Taylor, your insight as a licensed Marriage and Family Therapist was invaluable. Thank you for your honesty, interest, and patience as a beta reader. Here's to more beach trips!

Stephanie, for your information on Latin culture and endless support in all my endeavors. I couldn't write this book without including a backyard *fiesta* like yours! Thank you for answering my many questions and for aiding with the translation of the twins' Spanish.

Avery, my not-so-baby cousin, for that day years ago when we sat in the lifeguard post and I told you the whole story while the sun set. One day, you'll ride the rollercoaster you deserve. One day, you'll know how incredible you are. One day, you'll be a firefly flickering outside the jar.

To my first online supporter, Morgan, not only have you supported the book since the original title and TikTok campaign, but you have remained loyal all this time. Thank you for being a beta reader and helping me feel like I'm doing exactly what I should be.

To my author friends: Rachel Bateman, for answering a million writing questions; Charity Alyse, for truly seeing my work and giving me my first (and only) manuscript request; and L. E. Van Veen, from Kenan Hall, to NaNoWriMo, to published, look at us now!

To my students new and old, far and wide, thank you for reading that book your teacher always yapped about. I hope I adequately prepared you for the avalanche of figurative language ("What figurative language is that?"). Please never stop reading and writing, even when other things demand your attention.

Nicole, my incredible editor, you could find a comma on a vast stretch of sandy beach, and you're just about as rare, too. Thank you for being so thorough, kind, and passionate about the music of words.

Rachel, my cover artist, what a talent you are. Thank you for bringing my cover vision to life, even when I was all too particular about it. Your love of the ocean shines on this cover.

Readers, no matter how this book ended up in your metaphorical (or real!) beach bag, thank you for reading it! This dream of mine wouldn't be possible without you! It's surreal to have a slice of my heart in so many hands, but I trust you with it.

Nine Skies:
An Ode to the Carolina Coast

I BEGAN WRITING *THE SUMMERS OF US*, formerly named *Nine Skies*, as a junior in high school. As a freshman, I was exclusively a Fanfiction writer, but I wanted to branch out into my own universe. One day at the public library, I held up *We Were Liars* by E. Lockhart, and said to my dad, "I wish I could write a book like this." I hadn't yet read *We Were Liars*, but I knew I wanted to write a book whose cover could be the ocean and its sky, a book about my lifelong love of the beach.

A week after said library visit, I was struck with an idea. Fueled by years I spent visiting my aunt Amy's various houses along the North Carolina coast, I had the plot of a book.

I spent weeks outlining it in a yellow umbrella notebook, brainstorming plot points, fleshing out characters, and writing random snippets inspired by random beach memories. I dropped a letter grade in precalculus because most of my ideas struck during that class. (Dear students, I brought my grade back up when I realized what was happening, but if you go on to publish a novel because you weren't listening in my class, I suppose I'll forgive you.)

I started writing *Nine Skies* at age 17 (2016) and finished the first draft at age 21 (2020). I went through times where I didn't write at all, to weeks where I couldn't stop. The outline stayed mostly the same, so I could pick a spot to write when inspiration struck. Nothing struck it quite like trips to the North Carolina coast.

After endless attempts to get an agent, writing two more books, and growing into my prefrontal cortex, I realized what needed to be done.

At age 25 (2024), I decided to brush the sand off the *Nine Skies* manuscript and self publish it. I'd happen to my own life. After months of marking up a printed manuscript, rewriting the entire book in a blank document, toiling over a new name, adding brand new chapters, cutting old favorites, murdering darlings, rambling over Post It notes on my bedroom wall, and hiring a professional editor, *The Summers of Us* became something I am honored to put my name on.

The Summers of Us is both completely different and exactly the same.

I cannot properly close this chapter of my life without acknowledging the amalgamation of beaches that inspired the fictional Piper Island. If I want to be known as anything, it's a beachcomber, a footprint in the sand, a beach girl.

I owe it to my aunt Amy, a beach vagabond in her own right, for the access to many vacation spots along the Carolina coast, the first taste of salt, sun, and sand I'll never tire of.

Ocean Isle Beach was my first love, the beach of my childhood, the first beach horizon I ever saw over a causeway. Once, I split my lip on the boardwalk, running to be the first to the waves before tripping on an uneven slat. These years introduced me to Calabash, Southport, and Fort Fisher (home of the real-life "Piper Island Aquarium").

Holden Beach, the namesake of Holden Rivera-Sanchez, was my

home beach during the most transformative summers at my aunt's. Lockwood Folly River feeds into it, which inspired the fictional Lake Waccamaw, "Lake Lockwood." Oak Island was the first time I realized just how big and residential an island could be.

Sunset Beach inspired the Kindred Spirit chapter, where, in real life, I found my first (and second) complete sand dollar after I wrote Quinn's letter in the actual mailbox. I'd been looking for a full sand dollar for my whole life—so much that my dad did to me what Quinn did for Hadley, planted a store-bought sand dollar—and I found *two* of them in the exact manner that Quinn found hers. Kindred Spirit might actually have otherwordly powers.

As a teenager, I took many trips to Emerald Isle which helped me add biking, an ice cream shop, the bookstore, golf carts, sound docks, and a more residential atmosphere to Piper Island. If you were to call Piper Island the fictional version of a North Carolina beach, Emerald Isle is the best match. In fact, the original name for Piper Island was "Sapphire Beach" (inspired by Emerald Isle) which is home of the "Sapphire Beach Boardwalk" (not inspired by Emerald Isle).

Wrightsville Beach was my home beach during my years in college at the University of North Carolina at Wilmington. Each time I went out to write on the sand in my umbrella notebook, I brought one shell back and kept it in an Altoid tin that still rests on my desk today. Carolina Beach was my escape when I wanted to feel like a tourist again. Britt's ("Ashe's") Donuts is just as special as Quinn claims.

Cherry Grove, South Carolina has been my haven during my present years as a teacher. On as many three-day weekends as I can manage, I crash at my aunt's "new" house and explore the bookstore, shell at "The Point," and revisit my childhood haunts in Brunswick County North Carolina.

Other formative coastal locations include Surf City, Kure Beach, Myrtle Beach, Topsail Beach, Cape Lookout, Bald Head Island (the real-life "Loggerhead Island"), Atlantic Beach, Oriental, summer camp counseling in Arapahoe, Beaufort, and a one-weekend stint in the Outer Banks where my family managed all four lighthouses in one day.

Infinitesimal memories will live forever in the pages of this book.

They will always be known to me as the summers of us.

The beach and me.

–Taylor Crooks, 2025

www.ingramcontent.com/pod-product-compliance
Lightning Source LLC
Chambersburg PA
CBHW010529100726
47903CB00011B/2949